A TREACHEROUS PARADISE

Translated from the Swedish by
Laurie Thompson

HENNING MANKELL

ISIS
LARGE PRINT
Oxford

Copyright © Henning Mankell, 2011
English translation copyright © Laurie Thompson, 2013

First published in Great Britain 2013
by
Harvill Secker
one of the publishers in The Random House Group Limited

Published in Large Print 2014 by ISIS Publishing Ltd.,
7 Centremead, Osney Mead, Oxford OX2 0ES
by arrangement with
Harvill Secker
one of the publishers in The Random House Group Limited

CIP data is available for this title from the British Library

ISBN 978–0–7531–9286–3 (hb)
ISBN 978–0–7531–9287–0 (pb)

Printed and bound in Great Britain by
T. J. International Ltd., Padstow, Cornwall

"*There are three kinds of people: those who are dead, those who are alive, and those who sail the seas.*"

PLATO

CONTENTS

PROLOGUE

Africa Hotel, Beira, 2002

One day in the cold month of July, 2002, a man by the name of José Paulo opened up a hole in a rotten floor. He was not trying to make an escape route nor was he looking for a hiding place, but he intended to use the damaged parquet flooring as firewood since the cold of the African winter was harsher than it had been for many years.

José Paulo was unmarried, but he had taken over responsibility for his sister and her five children after his brother-in-law, Emilio, had suddenly disappeared one morning, leaving behind nothing but a pair of worn-out shoes and a number of unpaid bills. His debts were owed almost exclusively to Donna Samima, who ran an unlicensed bar close to the harbour where she served *tontonto* and home-brewed beer with an astonishingly high alcohol content.

Emilio used to spend his time drinking and talking about the time in the distant past when he had worked in the South African gold mines. But many people maintained that he had never set foot in South Africa, and had certainly never held down a steady job in his life.

His disappearance was neither something expected, nor something unexpected. He had simply slunk away during the silent hours just before dawn, when everybody was asleep.

Nobody knew where he had gone to. Nor would anybody miss him all that much, not even his own family. It is doubtful whether Donna Samima missed him, but she did insist that his bills should be paid.

Emilio, the talker and drinker, made virtually no impression on anybody even when he was in the vicinity. The fact that he had now disappeared made no real difference.

José Paulo lived with his sister's family in the Africa Hotel in Beira. There had been a time, which now seemed both distant and incomprehensible, when this establishment had been considered one of the grandest hotels in colonial Africa. It was ranked as comparable with the Victoria Falls Hotel, on the border between Southern Rhodesia and Northern Rhodesia before those countries achieved independence and became known as Zimbabwe and Zambia.

White people came to the Africa Hotel from far and wide in order to get married, celebrate anniversaries, or simply demonstrate the fact that they belonged to an aristocracy that could never imagine that their colonial paradise would one day collapse. The hotel had been the venue for tea dances on Sunday afternoons, swing and tango competitions, and no end of people had been photographed standing outside its imposing entrance.

But the colonial dream of paradise was doomed. One day the Portuguese abandoned their last fortresses. The

2

Africa Hotel started to crumble the moment the former owners had left. The deserted rooms and suites were occupied by poverty-stricken Africans. They deposited their few belongings in the carcasses of what used to be upright pianos and Steinway grands, in dilapidated boudoirs and bathtubs. The beautiful parquet floors were chopped up and used as firewood when winter was at its coldest.

Eventually there were several thousand people living in what had once been the Africa Hotel.

Anyway, one day in July, José Paulo made a hole in the floor and chopped up the parquet. It was freezing cold in the room. The only source of heat was an iron cauldron in which they cooked their food over an open fire. The smoke was channelled out through a smashed and badly repaired windowpane by means of an improvised chimney.

The half-rotten flooring had already begun to smell thanks to its neglect. José thought there must be a dead rat underneath it spreading the stench of decomposition. But when he investigated, all he could find was a little notebook with a calf-leather binding.

He managed to spell out a strange name written on the black cover.

Hanna Lundmark.

Underneath the name was a year: *1905*.

But he was unable to make head or tail of what was written inside it. It was in a language he didn't recognize. He turned to old Afanastasio who lived further down the corridor, in room 212, and was regarded by all those packed inside the hotel as a wise man, because in his youth he had survived a confrontation with two hungry lions on a deserted road outside Chimoio.

But not even Afanastasio could read the text. He approached old Lucinda, who lived in what used to be reception, for assistance, but she didn't know what language it was either.

Afanastasio suggested that José Paulo should throw the book away.

"It's been lying there under the floorboards for ages," said Afanastasio. "Somebody hid it there in the days when the likes of us were only allowed to enter this building in the role of waiters, cleaners or porters. No doubt this forgotten book tells an unpleasant story. Burn it. Use it as fuel when it gets really cold."

José Paulo took the book back to his room. But he didn't burn it, without quite knowing why. Instead he found a new hiding place for it. There was a cavity underneath the window ledge where he used to stash away any money he occasionally managed to earn. Now the few filthy banknotes could share the space with the black notebook.

He never took it out again. But he didn't forget about it.

PART ONE

The Missionaries Leave the Ship

CHAPTER
ONE

It is 1904. June. A scorching hot tropical dawn.

In this far distant here and now, a Swedish steamship lies motionless in the gentle swell. On board are thirty-one crew members, one of them a woman. Her name is Hanna Lundmark, née Renström, and she is working on board as a cook.

In all, thirty-two people were due to make the voyage to Australia with a cargo of Swedish heartwood, and planks for saloon floors and the living rooms of rich sheep farmers.

One of the crew has just died. He was a mate, and married to Hanna.

He was young, and keen to go on living. But despite being warned by Captain Svartman, he went ashore one day while they were topping up their supplies of coal in one of the desert harbours to the south of Suez. He was infected with one of the deadly fevers that are always a threat on the African coast.

When it dawned on him that he was going to die, he started howling in fear.

Neither of the men present at his deathbed — Captain Svartman and Halvorsen, the Ship's Carpenter — could make out any last words that he uttered. He

7

didn't even say anything to Hanna, who was about to be widowed after a marriage lasting only one month. He died screaming and — eventually, just before the end — roaring in terror.

His name was Lars Johan Jakob Antonius Lundmark. Hanna is still mourning his death, having been devastated by what happened.

It is now dawn the day after his death. The ship is not moving. It has heaved to because there will shortly be a burial at sea. Captain Svartman does not want to delay matters. There is no ice on board to keep the corpse cold.

Hanna is standing aft with a slop pail in her hand. She is short in stature, high-breasted, with friendly eyes. Her hair is brown and gathered in a tight bun at the back of her head.

She is not beautiful. But in a strange way she radiates an aura suggesting that she is a totally genuine human being.

The here and now. She is here. On the sea, on board a steamship with two funnels. A cargo of timber, on its way to Australia. Home port: Sundsvall.

The ship is called *Lovisa*. She was built at the Finnboda shipyard in Stockholm. But her home port has always been on the northern Swedish coast.

She was first owned by a shipping company in Gävle, but it went bankrupt after a series of failed speculative deals. And she was then bought by a company based in Sundsvall. In Gävle she was called *Matilda*, after the shipowner's wife, who played Chopin with clumsy fingers. Now she is called *Lovisa*, after the new owner's youngest daughter.

One of the part-owners is called Forsman. He is the one who arranged for Hanna Lundmark to be given a job on board. Although Forsman has a piano in his house, there is nobody who can play it. Nevertheless, when the piano tuner comes on one of his regular visits, Forsman makes a point of being there to listen.

But now the mate Lars Johan Jakob Antonius Lundmark has died, killed by a raging fever.

It is as if the swell of the sea has become paralysed. The ship is lying there motionless, as if it were holding its breath.

That's exactly what I imagine death to be like, Hanna Lundmark thought. A sudden stillness, unexpected, coming from nowhere. Death is like the wind. A sudden shift into the lee.

The lee of death. And then nothing else.

CHAPTER
TWO

At that very moment Hanna is possessed by a memory. It comes from nowhere.

She recalls her father, his voice, which had become no more than a whisper by the end of his life. It was as if he were asking her to preserve and cherish what he said as a valuable secret.

A mucky angel. That's what you are.

He said that to her just before he died. It was as if he were trying to present her with a gift, despite the fact — or maybe because of the fact — that he owned next to nothing.

Hanna Renström, my beloved daughter, you are an angel — a right mucky one, but an angel even so.

What exactly is this memory that she has? What were his exact words? Did he say she was *stony*, or *mucky*? Did he leave it up to her to choose, to decide for herself? Stony broke, or mucky? Now as she recalls that moment, she thinks he called her *a mucky angel*.

It is a distant memory, faded. She is so far distant from her father and his death. From there, and from then: a remote house on a bank of the cold, brown waters of the River Ljungan in the silent forests of northern Sweden. He passed away hunched up and contorted by pain on a sofa bed in a kitchen they had barely been able to keep warm.

He died surrounded by cold, she thinks. It was extremely cold in January, 1899, when he stopped breathing.

That was over five years ago.

The memory of her father and his words about an angel disappear just as quickly as they came. It takes her only a few seconds to return to the present from the past.

She knows that we always make the most remarkable journeys deep down inside ourselves, where there is no time or space.

Perhaps that memory was designed to help her? To throw her the rope she needs in order to climb over the walls confining her within an atmosphere of unremitting sorrow?

But she can't run away. The ship has been transformed into an impregnable fortress.

There is no escape. Her husband really is dead.

Death is a talon that refuses to release its grip.

CHAPTER
THREE

The pressure in the boilers has been reduced. The pistons are motionless, the engines ticking over. Hanna is standing by the rail with her slop pail in her hand. She is going to empty it over the stern. The mess-room boy had wanted to take it from her when she was on her way out of the galley, but she had clung on to it, protected it. Even if this is the day she is going to watch her husband's body being tipped into the depths of the ocean, sewn into a canvas sailcloth, she does not want to neglect her duties.

When she looks up from the pail, which is filled with eggshells, it feels as if the heat is scratching at her face. Somewhere in the mist to starboard is Africa. Although she cannot see the faintest trace of land, she thinks she can smell it.

He who is now dead has told her about it. About the steaming, almost corrosive stench of decay which you find everywhere in the tropics.

He had already made several voyages to various destinations. He had managed to learn a few things. But not the most important thing: how to survive.

He would never complete this voyage. He died at the age of twenty-four.

It's as if he was trying to warn her, Hanna thinks. But she doesn't know what he was warning her about. And now he's dead.

A dead man can never answer questions.

Somebody materializes silently by her side. It's her husband's closest friend on board, the Norwegian carpenter Halvorsen. She doesn't know if he has a first name, despite the fact that they have been together on the same ship for more than two months. He is never called anything but Halvorsen, a serious man who is said to go down on his knees to be readmitted into the Church every time he comes home to Brønnøysund after a few years at sea, and then signs on again when his faith can no longer sustain him.

He has large hands, but his face is kind, almost feminine. His stubble seems to have been painted on and powdered by somebody trying to be cruel to him.

"I gather there's something you need to ask about," he says.

His voice sings. It sounds as if he's humming when he speaks.

"The depth," Hanna says. "Where will Lundmark's grave be?"

Halvorsen shakes his head doubtfully. She suddenly has the impression that he is like a restless bird about to fly away.

He leaves her without a word. But she knows he will find out the answer to her question.

How deep will the grave be? Is there a sea bottom where her husband can rest in peace, in his sewn-up canvas shroud? Or is there no bottom, does the sea continue downwards into infinity?

She empties her pail of eggshells, watches the white seabirds dive down into the water to capture their prey, then wipes the sweat from her brow with the towel she has tied to her apron.

Then she gives way to the inevitable, and screams.

Some of the birds riding the upwinds, waiting for a new slop pail to be emptied, flap their wings and strive to escape from the sorrowful howl that hits them like hailstones.

The mess-room boy Lars peers out in horror from the galley door. He is holding a cracked egg in his hand, observes her furtively. Death embarrasses him.

Needless to say, she knows what he is thinking. She's going to jump now, she's going to leave us because her sorrow is too great to bear.

Her scream has been heard by many on board. Two sweaty deckhands naked from the waist up stand by the side of the galley and gape at her, next to where one of the long hawsers is coiled up like a gigantic snake.

Hanna merely shakes her head, grits her teeth and goes into the galley with her empty pail. No, she is not going to climb over the rail. She has spent the whole of her life keeping a stiff upper lip, and she intends to continue doing so.

The heat of the galley hits her hard. Standing next to the stoves is similar to the life of the stokers down below in the engine room. Women in the vicinity of boilers and lighthouses brings bad luck.

The older generation of seafarers is horrified by the thought of having women on board. Their presence means trouble. And also arguments and jealousy among the men. But when shipowner Forsman announced that he wanted Hanna to join the crew, Captain Svartman agreed. He didn't worry too much about superstition.

Hanna picks up an egg, cracks it, drops the contents into the frying pan and throws the shell into the slop pail. Thirty living sailors must have their breakfast. She tries to think only about the eggs, not about the funeral that is in the offing. She is on board as cook: that situation has not changed as a result of the death of her husband.

That's the way it is. She is alive, but Lundmark is dead.

CHAPTER
FOUR

Shortly afterwards Halvorsen returns and asks her to follow him: Captain Svartman is waiting.

"We're going to sound the depth," says Halvorsen. "If our ropes and lines aren't long enough, the captain will select another place."

She finishes frying the four eggs she has in the pan, then accompanies him as bidden. She suddenly feels dizzy, and stumbles: but she doesn't fall, she manages to keep control of herself.

Captain Svartman comes from a long and unbroken line of seafarers, she is aware of that. He's an old man, turned sixty. The tip of the little finger on his left hand is missing: nobody knows if that is congenital, or the result of an accident.

On two occasions he has been on a sailing ship that sank. On one of those occasions he and all the crew were rescued, on the other only he and the ship's dog survived. And when the dog reached dry land it lay down in the sand and died.

Hanna's dead husband once said that in fact the real Captain Svartman also died, together with the ship's dog. After that catastrophe, the captain stayed on land for many years. Nobody knows what he did. Rumour has it that for part of that time he worked as a navvy and was a member of the vanguard sent out by state-owned Swedish Railways to build the controversial Inlandsbana — a railway line linking the south of Sweden with the north of the country following an inland route rather than the existing coastal railway: the Swedish Parliament was still arguing about it.

Then he suddenly went to sea again, now as the captain of a steamship. He was one of the select few who didn't abandon the seafaring life once sailing ships began to die out, but chose to be part of modern developments.

He has never told anybody about those years he spent away from the sea — what he did, what he thought, not even where he lived.

He seldom says anything beyond the necessary minimum; he has as little faith in people's ability to listen as he has in the reliability of the sea. He has lavender-coloured flowers in pots in his cabin, which only he is allowed to water.

So he has always been an uncommunicative sea captain. And now he has to establish the depth at which one of his dead mates will be buried.

Captain Svartman bows as Hanna approaches him. Despite the heat he is dressed in his full uniform. Buttons fastened, shirt pressed.

Standing next to him is the bosun, Peltonen, a Finn. He is holding a plumb bob, attached to a long, thin line.

Captain Svartman nods, Peltonen throws the bob over the rail and allows it to sink. The line slides between his fingers. Nobody speaks. At one point there is a black thread tied round the line.

"A hundred metres," says Peltonen.

His voice is shrill. His words bounce away over the swell.

After seven black threads, 700 metres, the line comes to an end. The plumb bob is still hanging down there in the water, it hasn't yet reached the bottom. Peltonen ties a knot and attaches the line to a new roll. There too is a black thread marking every hundred metres.

At 1,935 metres, the line goes slack. The bob has reached the sea bottom. Hanna now knows the depth of her husband's grave.

Peltonen starts to haul up the line, winding it round a specially carved wooden board. Captain Svartman takes off his uniform cap and wipes the sweat from his brow. Then he checks his watch. A quarter to seven.

"Nine o'clock," he says to Hanna. "Before the heat becomes too oppressive."

She goes to the cabin she has shared with her husband. His was the upper bunk. They often shared the lower one. Without her knowing about it, somebody has taken away his blanket.

The mattress is lying there uncovered. She sits down on the edge of her own bunk and contemplates the bulkhead on the other side of the cramped cabin. She knows that she must now force herself to think.

How did she come to end up here? On a ship, swaying gently on a distant ocean. After all, she was born in a place about as far away from the sea as it's possible to get. There was a rowing boat on the River

Ljungan, but that was all. She sometimes accompanied her father in it when he went fishing. But when she said she wanted to learn to swim — she was about seven or eight at the time — he told her he couldn't allow it. It would be a waste of time. If she wanted to bathe, she could do that by the bank of the river. If she wanted to get over to the other side, there was a boat and also a bridge.

She lies down on her bunk and closes her eyes. She travels back in her memory as far as she can, back into her childhood where the shadows grow longer and longer.

Maybe that is where she can hide away until the moment comes when her dead husband disappears into the sea for good.

Leaves her. For ever.

CHAPTER
FIVE

Her childhood, deep down there. As if at the bottom of an abyss.

That was Hanna's first memory: the cold, writhing and twisting away inside the cavities in the wooden walls, close to her face as she slept. She would wake up over and over again, and feel how thin the gap was between the newspapers pasted on to the walls — there was no money for wallpaper in the squalid house in which she grew up — and the cold that was constantly trying to gnaw its way through the wood.

Every spring her father worked his way over the house, as if it were a ship on a slipway, patching and mending wherever possible, before the onset of the next winter.

The cold was a sea, the house a ship, and the winter an endless waiting. He would keep on filling the holes and gaps until the frosts arrived in full force. Then it was not possible to do any more, they would have to make the best of it. The house was launched into the winter yet again, and if there were still any leaks allowing the cold to seep through, that was too bad: there was nothing else he could do.

20

Her father was Arthur Olaus Angus Renström, a lumberjack who worked for Iggesund and shared a log hoist with the Salomonsson brothers who lived further down the river. He worked all out in the forest for next to nothing. He was one of the many men of the woods who never knew if the money they earned for their efforts would be sufficient to live on.

Hanna remembered her father as strong, and with a friendly smile. But also at times melancholy, lost in thoughts she knew nothing about. She sometimes had the impression that he had trolls in his head when he sat at the kitchen table, seemingly in a different world, with his hands like lead weights in his lap. He was sitting there in his own house, with the rest of his family, but nevertheless he wasn't there at all. He was in a different world where stones had turned into trolls, reindeer moss had become hair, and the wind whispering through the pines was the chattering of voices of the dead.

He often used to speak about them. All those who had lived in the past. It frightened him to think about how few were living in the here and now, and how many more were already dead.

There was an illness, an epidemic that all women knew the name of: thumping sickness. It broke out when men had been hitting the bottle and thumped everybody within range — mostly their children and the women who tried to protect them. Her father certainly did drink to excess at times, albeit not very often. But he was never violent. And so his wife, Hanna's mother, didn't worry so much about the

21

schnapps as about his melancholy. When he drank he became maudlin and wanted to sing hymns. Despite the fact that at other times he was keen to burn down churches and drive out the priests into the forests.

"*Without shoes,*" Hanna recalled him shouting. "*Chase the priests out into the forests without shoes when the cold is at its worst. That's where they should be banished to, into the forests, barefoot.*"

Hanna's maternal grandmother, who lived in a draughty cottage on the edge of Funäsdalen, scared the living daylights out of her when she talked about her damned son-in-law who would condemn all his offspring to hell as a result of his blasphemous prattle. There they would find in store for them scalding temperatures and sulphurous gases and red-hot coals under the soles of their feet. Her grandmother preached threats and punishments with evil eyes and didn't hesitate to scare her grandchildren so much that they used to burst into tears and were unable to sleep at night. Hanna thought that the worst punishment of all was when her mother forced her to keep on visiting her grandmother.

She remembered how Grandma was always angry. The old woman never stopped complaining about her daughter. She couldn't forgive Hanna's mother for marrying that good-for-nothing Renström, despite her warnings. Why had she fallen head over heels for that man who had nothing to commend himself? He was small, bow-legged and bald even before he celebrated his twenty-fifth birthday. And he had Finnish blood in his veins, and he came from the depths of the forests —

22

from as far away as Värmland, where it was impossible to distinguish between day and night.

Why couldn't she have picked out a man from Hede or Bruksvallarna or somewhere where honest folk lived?

Hanna's mother was called Elin. She submitted to her ancient mother, never contradicted her, accepted everything her mother said without a word of protest. Hanna could understand that it was possible to love somebody who treated you badly, no matter how odd that sounded. That must have been the relationship between Grandma and Elin.

Elin.

Hanna had always thought that it was a name that didn't really suit her mother. Somebody called Elin ought to be slim and delicately formed, with hands like milk and fair hair hanging down over her back. But Elin Wallén, Elin Renström after her marriage, was powerfully built with lank reddish-brown hair, a large nose and teeth that were not quite regular. They gave the impression of wanting to jump out of her mouth and run away. Elin Renström was certainly not a beautiful woman. And she knew it. And perhaps she also regretted it, Hanna sometimes thought when she became old enough to take a critical look at her own face in her father's cracked shaving mirror.

But her mother was by no means subdued as a result of her less than pretty appearance. She had qualities that she made the most of. She made up for her shortcomings by always keeping a strict eye on her family's cleanliness. No matter how draughty and cold her house was, she made sure the floors, ceilings and

23

walls were kept spotlessly clean; and the same applied to her children and her own body. Elin hunted down lice like a battalion of soldiers attacking an enemy. She filled and emptied the tin tub in which they all bathed, carried the water up from the river, heated it over the fire until it became warm, scrubbed everybody down, then carried up more buckets of water with which to wash all the dirty linen that was always piling up.

The four children also watched in admiration as their mother handled their father when he had came home tired and dirty from the forest. She would wash him in a way which suggested she was engaged in an act of eternal love. And he seemed to enjoy the touch of her hands as she scrubbed and dried him, clipped his rough and misshapen nails, and shaved him so closely that his cheeks became as smooth as those of a baby.

But Hanna's first memory was the cold. The cold and the snow, which began to fall around the end of September, and didn't release its grip until early June, when the last white patches finally melted away.

And of course there was also the poverty. That was not a memory as such, but the reality in which she lived while growing up. And it was also the thing that eventually forced her to leave her home by the river.

Hanna was seventeen years old then, her father was already dead, and she spent all her time helping her mother with her brothers and sisters since she was the eldest. They were poor, but they managed to keep the worst of their destitution outside the walls of their house.

Until the year 1903. That summer was afflicted by a long and severe drought, and then an early frost which killed off whatever the drought had failed to burn up.

That was the year when her life changed for ever.

The horizon had previously been a distant phenomenon. Now it came close. Like a threat.

CHAPTER
SIX

Even if she didn't want to remember it, it was a day she could never forget.

The middle of August, low clouds, an early morning. Hanna accompanied her mother to look at the devastation. Everything shrivelled and burnt. The earth was strangely silent. The flour they had left would barely last them until Advent. Nor would they have enough hay to feed their only cow over the winter.

As they walked through the dead field, on a slope down to the river, Elin saw her mother cry for the first time. All those long weeks while her father had been ill in bed and had eventually died, Elin had merely closed her eyes, shut out the inevitable end and the hopeless loneliness that was now in store for her. But she hadn't cried, hadn't screamed. Hanna had often thought about how her mother was directing all her pain inwards, to where she had hidden away somewhere inside her a secret source of strength that overcame all her pains and troubles.

It was then, as they were walking over the dead field and realized that destitution was now on their doorstep, that Elin started talking about how her daughter would have to go away. There was no future for Hanna there by the river. She would have to move to the coast in order to earn her living. When Elin and her husband had come to the bank of the river and taken over the unpromising little smallholding from one of her uncles, they'd had no choice. It was 1883, a mere sixteen years after the last great famine that had devastated Sweden. If famine was now on its way back, Hanna would have to leave while there was still time.

They were standing at the edge of the forest, where the silent field came to an end.

"Are you chasing me away?" Hanna asked.

Elin stroked her nose, as she always did when she was embarrassed.

"I can cope with three children," she said, "but not four. You are grown up now, you can look after yourself, and make things easier both for you and for me. I don't chase my children away. I just want to give you the opportunity of living your life. If you stay here all you can do is hope to survive, nothing more."

"What can I do down by the coast that would be of any use to anybody?"

"The same as you do here. Look after children, work with your hands. There is always a demand for maids in towns."

"Who says so?"

It wasn't her intention to contradict her mother, but Elin took it as impertinence and took tight hold of her arm.

"I say so, and you must believe me when I say that I mean every word that passes my lips. I'm not doing it because it gives me any pleasure, but because I have to."

She let go of Hanna's arm, as if she had been guilty of assault and was now regretting it.

It dawned on Hanna that what her mother was doing was something extremely difficult.

She never forgot that moment. It was right then, and in that very place — at the edge of the grim landscape of famine, standing beside her mother who had just wept for the first time in her presence — that Hanna realized that she was who she was, and nobody else.

She was Hanna, and irreplaceable. Neither her body nor her thoughts could be replaced by anybody else. And it occurred to her that her father, who was now dead, had been just like her: a person who could not be replaced by anybody else.

Is this what it means to be an adult? she thought, her face turned away because she had the feeling that her mother could read her thoughts. Exchanging the insecurity of a child for a different unknown — the knowledge that the only possible answers are the ones you can provide yourself?

They returned to the house, which was hidden away in a copse comprising a few birch trees and a single mountain ash. Her brother and sisters were indoors, despite the fact that this autumn day was not particularly cold. But they played less and tended to be quiet when they were hungry. Their life was a never-ending wait for food, and not much else.

They stopped outside the door, as if Elin had decided never to allow her daughter inside again.

"My uncle Axel lives in Sundsvall," she said. "Axel Andreas Wallén. He works in the docks. He's a nice man, and he and his wife Dora don't have any children. They had two boys, but both of them died, and after that they didn't have any more. Axel and Dora will help you. They won't turn you away."

"I don't want to go to them as a beggar," said Hanna.

The slap came without warning. Afterwards, Hanna thought the blow was reminiscent of the impact from a bird of prey diving down at her cheek.

Elin might possibly have slapped her before, but in that case it would have been triggered mainly by fear. If Hanna had wandered off alone to the river in the spring when it was a raging torrent, and risked falling in and being drowned. But now Elin hit her as a result of irritation. It was the first time.

It was a slap given by a grown-up person to another grown-up. Who would understand why.

"I don't abandon my daughter in order to make her a beggar," said Elin angrily. "I only have your best interests at heart. There's nothing for you here."

Hanna had tears in her eyes. Not because of the pain — she had experienced much worse pain than that in her life.

The slap she had received confirmed what she had just been thinking: now she was alone in the world. She would have to leave and travel eastward, towards the coast, and she would never be able to return. What she left behind would sink deeper into oblivion for every metre a sleigh's runners whisked her away.

It was early autumn, 1903. Hanna Renström was seventeen years old, and would be eighteen on 12 December.

A few months later she would leave her home for ever.

CHAPTER
SEVEN

Hanna thought to herself: the time of sagas and make-believe is over. Now it's time for real-life stories.

She realized that when Elin told her what was in store for her. It sometimes happened that businessmen from the coast who travelled over the mountains in winter to Norway for the Røros market didn't take the usual and shortest route back home, along the River Ljusnan and down to Karböle. Some of them headed northwards after crossing the Sweden — Norway border and then, if the weather permitted it, turned off via Flatruet and along the River Ljungan so that they could do business in the villages on the riverbanks.

There was one businessman in particular, Jonathan Forsman, who usually travelled home via the villages north of Flatruet.

"He has a big sleigh," said Elin. "On the way home it's never as heavily laden as it is when he's on his way to Røros. He's bound to be able to make room for you. And he'll leave you in peace. He won't try to make advances to you."

Hanna looked doubtfully at her. How could Elin be so sure? Hanna was well aware what life had in store for her, she had never been totally devoid of other young girls to talk to. Not least the girls who used to act as maids in the shacks up in the mountains when the farmers' and shepherds' flocks were grazing in their summer pastures: they had all kinds of strange tales to tell with a mixture of giggles and badly concealed discomfort. Hanna knew what it was like to blush, and what could happen inside her body, especially in the evenings, just before she fell asleep.

But that was all. How could Elin know what might or might not happen on a long sleigh-ride to the distant coast?

She asked her straight out.

"He's seen the light," said Elin promptly. "He used to be an awful man, just like most of those old devils with their sleighs. But since he became a Christian he's a sort of good Samaritan. He'll let you travel with him and won't even ask for payment. And he'll lend you one of his fur coats so that you won't freeze."

But Elin couldn't be absolutely sure if he would come, or when. The usual time was shortly before Christmas, but there had been occasions when he didn't turn up until into the New Year. And he had been known not to come at all.

"He might also be dead, of course," said Elin.

When a sleigh set off and was swallowed up by flurries of snow, you never knew whether that might be the last you ever saw of a person, no matter how young or old he was.

Hanna would be ready to travel at any time after her birthday on 12 December. Jonathan Forsman was always in a hurry, never stayed anywhere longer than necessary. Unlike people who always had no end of time to spare, he was an important person and hence was always in a hurry.

"He generally comes in the afternoon," said Elin. "He comes out of the forest to the north, heading southwards along the sleigh-tracks that skirt the edge of the bog and lead down to the river and the valleys."

Every afternoon Hanna would go out and gaze in the direction of the forest as darkness began to fall. She sometimes thought she could hear the bells of a horse-drawn sleigh in the distance, but one never appeared. The forest door remained closed.

She slept badly all the time she was worrying and waiting, kept waking up and had incoherent dreams that frightened her, although she didn't really understand why. But often her dreams were as white as snow: empty and silent.

One of her dreams kept recurring and haunting her; she was lying in the sofa bed with two of her siblings: the youngest of the family's children, Olaus, and the sister closest to her in age, Vera, twelve years old. She could feel the warm bodies of her brother and sister up against her own; but she knew that if she were to open her eyes they would turn out to be different children lying there, unknown to her. And the moment she set eyes on them they would die.

Then she would wake up, and realize to her great relief that it had all been a dream. She would often lie there awake, watching the blue moonlight shining in through the low windows covered in ice crystals. Then stretch out her hand and feel the wooden wall and the newspaper covering it. Right next to her was the cold, writhing and twisting away in the ancient timber.

The cold is like an animal, she thought. An animal tethered in its stall. An animal wanting to break out.

The dream had a meaning that she didn't understand. But it must have something to do with the journey she would have to make. What would be in store for her? What would be demanded of her? She felt awkward in both body and soul when she tried to imagine people living in a town. If only her father had still been alive: he would have been able to explain it to her, and prepare her for it. He had once been to Stockholm, and he'd also been to another big and remarkable town called Arboga. He could have told her that she didn't need to be afraid.

Elin came from remote Funäsdalen and had never been anywhere else, apart from the short journey northwards with the man who became her husband.

Nevertheless, she was the one who had to answer when Hanna asked her questions. There simply wasn't anybody else.

But Elin's answers? Vague, taciturn. She knew so little.

CHAPTER
EIGHT

One day at the beginning of November, when they were at the edge of the forest with an axe and a saw, collecting firewood for the winter, Hanna asked her mother about the sea. What did it look like? Did it run along a sort of giant furrow, like the river? Was it the same colour? Was it always so deep that you couldn't reach the bottom?

Elin paused, held her aching back, and looked at her long and hard before answering.

"I don't know," she said. "The sea is like a big lake, I think. I suppose there are waves. But I just don't know if the sea has currents."

"But surely Renström must have told you? He said he'd been to sea, didn't he?"

"It might not have been completely true. Everything he said might have only happened inside his head. But all he ever said about the sea is that it was big."

Elin bent down to pick up the twigs and branches they had sawed and chopped off. But Hanna didn't want to give up just yet. A child stopped asking questions when it had the feeling that enough was enough: but she was grown up now, she had the right to go on asking.

"I have no idea what is in store for me," she said. "Will I be living in a house with other people? Will I be sharing a bed with somebody else?"

Elin scowled and dropped a bundle of sawn-off branches into their birch-bark basket.

"You are asking too many questions," she said. "I can't tell you what you can expect to find. But there is no future for you here. At least there are people who can help you there."

"I only want to know," said Hanna.

"Stop asking now," said Elin. "I'm getting a headache from all your questions. I don't have any answers."

They returned in silence to the house from whose chimney a thin column of smoke was rising vertically into the pale sky. Olaus and Vera were looking after the fire. But both Elin and Hanna made sure that they were never any further away from the house than would prevent them from climbing up on to a high rock, taking a look at the chimney and establishing that the fire had not gone out. Or that nothing even worse had happened: that it hadn't crept out of the open hearth and begun jumping around the room like a madman.

It was snowing at night now, and there was frost every morning. But the really heavy snowfalls that never lasted for less than three days had still not come creeping over the western mountains. And Hanna knew that if there wasn't sufficient snow, no sleigh would be able to approach through the forests from the main routes further south.

But a few days later the snow finally arrived. As almost always happened, it crept up silently during the night. When Hanna got up to light the fire, Elin was standing by the door which she had opened slightly.

She stood there motionless, staring out. The ground outside was white. There were low drifts against the walls of the house. Hanna could see the tracks of crows in the snow, perhaps also of a mouse and a hare.

It was still snowing.

"This snow's going to lay," said Elin. "It's winter now. There'll be no bare ground again until the spring, at the end of May or the beginning of June."

It continued snowing the whole of the following week. At first the cold wasn't too severe, only a few degrees below zero. But once the snow had stopped falling the sky became clear and the temperature dropped significantly.

They had a thermometer that Renström had bought at some market or other a long time ago. Or perhaps he had won it in an arm-wrestling competition, since he was so strong? The thermometer had an attachment enabling it to be fixed to an outside wall, but it was treated with great care: there was always a risk that somebody might be careless and break the little tube containing the dangerous mercury.

Extremely carefully Elin placed it out in the snow, at the side of the house that was always in shade. Now that the seriously cold weather had arrived, it was more than thirty degrees below zero for three days in succession.

During the coldest days they did nothing but tend the fire, make sure the cow and the two goats had something to chew at, and eat something of the little food they had for themselves. They used up all their strength in efforts to keep the cold at bay. Every extra degree below zero was like yet another enemy army added to those already besieging them.

Hanna could see that Elin was scared. What would happen if something broke? A window, or a wall? They had nowhere to flee to, apart from the little cattle shed where the animals were kept. But they were also freezing cold, and it was not possible to make a fire there.

It was during these bitterly cold days that Hanna felt for the first time that the imminent change in her life might not be so bad after all. An opening in a dark forest where sunlight suddenly shone down into an unexpected glade. A life that might possibly be better than the one she was living now, besieged by the armies of cold and famine? Her fear of the unknown suddenly became a longing for what might be in store for her. Away from the forests, in the fertile plains to the south-east.

But she said nothing about this to Elin. She remained silent about her vague longing.

CHAPTER
NINE

On 17 December, shortly after half past two in the afternoon, they heard the sound of sleigh-bells coming from the forest. It was Vera who heard the horse. She had gone out to see if the hens had laid any eggs, despite the onset of winter. As she returned empty-handed along the narrow passage that had been dug between the metre-high drifts, she heard the bells. Elin and Hanna came running out when she shouted. The worst of the cold had receded, and it had been thawing during the day: but now there was a covering of new powdery snow over the frozen crust after a snowfall during the night.

The sound of the bells came closer, then they caught sight of the black horse looking like a troll or a bear at the edge of the forest. The driver, wrapped in furs, tightened the reins and came to a halt just outside the cottage, which was surrounded by deep snow and misery.

By then Elin had already told Hanna what she had expected to hear.

"It's Jonathan Forsman."

"How can you be sure?"

"Nobody else has a black horse like his. And nobody else wears so many furs."

Hanna could see that was true when the man in the sleigh had stood up and they all entered the cottage. He was wearing furs from both bears and wolves, had been sitting on a reindeer skin in his sleigh, and had a red fox fur wrapped round his neck. When he wormed his way out of all the furs, which were dripping with snow and sweat, it was like watching a man who had been sitting for too long in front of a fire. His face was red and unshaven, his sweaty hair was stuck to his forehead: but Hanna could see that Elin was right — the man who was going to take her away was neither malicious nor threatening. He was friendly, sat down on a stool beside the fire and gave Elin a present: a hymn book he had bought for her in Røros.

"It's in Norwegian," he said. "But the covers are attractive, genuine leather, and the gold embossing sparkles if you keep it clean. Besides, Elin Renström, you can hardly read in any case! Or am I wrong?"

"I can puzzle out the words," said Elin. "If that amounts to reading, then I can."

It was only in the evening, when the younger children were in bed, that Elin broached the subject of Hanna's journey. They were sitting round the fire. Forsman was resting his enormous hands. Before the youngsters had gone to sleep, he had sung a hymn in his deep, resonant voice. Hanna had never heard a man sing like that before. The vicar who conducted services in Ljungdalen had a soft, squeaky voice. When he sung a hymn it sounded as if somebody was pinching him. But here was a man whose singing even silenced the cold that creaked and groaned in the walls.

Elin explained the situation. In just a few words, but nothing more was needed.

"Can you take Hanna with you?" she asked. "She has to go to Sundsvall, to relatives who will take care of her."

Forsman listened thoughtfully.

"Are you sure?" he asked.

"Why shouldn't I be sure? What is there to be doubtful about?"

"That your relatives will look after her? Are they on Renström's side?"

"No, my side. The Walléns. If it had been Renströms I'd never have dreamt of sending her."

Forsman contemplated his hands.

"How long ago was it?" he asked eventually. "That you spoke about it?"

"Four years come this spring."

"A lot could have happened during that time," said Forsman. "But I'll take her with me in any case. So let's just hope there's somebody there who's prepared to accept her."

"Surely they can't all have died over the last four years," said Elin firmly. "Unless there's been some kind of plague we haven't heard about up here in the mountains."

Forsman now took a good look at Hanna for the first time.

"How old are you?" he asked.

"I celebrated my eighteenth birthday the other day."

Forsman nodded. He asked no more questions. The fire continued burning.

That night Forsman slept on the floor in front of the fire. He lay on his various fur coats spread out on the floorboards, covered only by the reindeer skin. His horse had been squeezed into the cowshed with the cow and the goats.

Hanna lay awake for ages. No man had slept in their cottage since her father died. Now there was somebody else snoring and snuffling in his sleep.

Forsman groaned as he breathed in and out, as if he was dragging a heavy burden behind him.

The next day an occasional snowflake came floating down from the heavens. The mercury indicated minus two degrees. Shortly after eight in the morning Hanna sat down in the sleigh with the two bundles of belongings Elin had prepared for her. She had wrapped herself up in all the warm clothes she possessed, and Forsman wrapped a couple more furs around her — she could barely move.

Her brother and sisters wept when she hugged them and said goodbye, first one at a time and then all of them in chorus.

But Elin merely shook her hand. This was the way it had to be. Hanna had decided not to look back once she had sat down in the sleigh. She was weeping deep down inside when Forsman cracked his whip and the black horse started pulling the sleigh. But she didn't show it. Not for anybody.

She thought about her father as they set off. It was as if he were also standing there, next to Elin, watching her leave.

He had returned, just for that moment. He wanted to be present when it happened.

It was 1903, the year when famine once again afflicted the north of Sweden.

CHAPTER
TEN

The journey by sleigh from Ljungdalen to the coast was supposed to take five days. That is what Jonathan Forsman had told Elin, almost as if he were making a promise.

"It won't take any longer than that," he said. "The going is good, just right for the sleigh, and I don't have many business calls to make on the way that could delay us. We'll only stop to eat and sleep. We'll follow the river, then turn off to the north and make our way through the forest to Sundsvall. It'll take five days, no more."

But the journey did take longer. As early as the second day, before they'd even got as far as the forest that marked the border between the provinces of Jämtland and Härjedalen, they were hit by a sudden snowstorm that blew up from the east and that Forsman hadn't anticipated. The sky had been blue, it had been cold and the going was good: but suddenly the clouds had started to pile up. Even the black horse, whose name was Antero, had started to be restless.

They stopped at an inn in Överhogdal. Hanna was given a bed in a room shared by the inn's maidservants: but she ate at the same table as Forsman, and was served the same food as he had. That had never happened before in her life.

"We'll set off again tomorrow," he said after saying grace and checking to make sure that she clasped her hands in prayer properly.

But that night the stormy winds veered to the north and then decided to call a halt. The snowstorm stayed put. They were snowed in and stuck at the dreary inn. Half a metre of snow fell in less than four hours, and the wind resulted in drifts that in places were as high as the building's roof ridge.

It was the afternoon of the fourteenth day of the journey, just as dusk was falling, that they arrived in Sundsvall. Hanna had been counting the days, but hadn't realized that this evening was in fact New Year's Eve. The following day it would be 1904.

Forsman seemed to think that everything associated with the New Year was important. He pushed the horse hard in order to make sure that they reached the centre of town before midnight. New Year's Eve had never been anything special for Hanna. She had usually been fast asleep when the New Year began. She couldn't recall either her father or Elin regarding the dawn of a new year as anything special that deserved to be marked by being awake at midnight, or celebrating in any other way.

The fact that they had spent Christmas Eve and Christmas Day together seemed to mean nothing much, or perhaps nothing at all as far as Forsman was concerned. It was the New Year that was important.

45

The long sleigh journey had taken place in silence when they were travelling through the forests or over the barren plains. Occasionally Forsman had shouted something to the horse, but he had never spoken to Hanna. He sat in front of her in the sleigh like a forbidding wall.

But the last day of their journey was different. He turned round to shout at her, and she shouted back at him as loudly as she could, in order to make herself heard.

Jonathan Forsman regarded the New Year as something holy.

"God has created the turn of the year to make us think about the time that has passed and the time that is to come," he shouted at her in the back of the sleigh.

Before he saw the light, he had always indulged in heathen pastimes on New Year's Eve. He had heated lumps of lead in the open fire and then dipped them into cold water in order to interpret the shapes they made as forecasts of the future. And he had never dared to enter the New Year without being dead drunk.

But now he was enlightened, he shouted at her. He was no longer afraid of anything.

When they reached Sundsvall, the town was enveloped by darkness and cold. Forsman pulled up on the edge of the town, in fact. Hanna was not yet able to check her vision of what Sundsvall would look like with the reality. Most of it was still in store for her as she wriggled her way out of the furs and stepped out of the sleigh.

Forsman's house was built of stone, and comprised two imposingly large storeys. As he pulled up, hordes of people came teeming out of the front gate and the lodge. Antero was led away, and the sleigh was taken care of. All the furs and other contents of the sleigh were carried into the house. Hanna was bewildered by everything that was happening all around her, all these unknown people staring at her, some of them openly, others surreptitiously. She was used to meeting unknown people one at a time. Sometimes it had been vagrants who had wandered up north on the banks of the river, sometimes individual travellers or people carrying axes and saws that her father had brought home with him from the forest. But never anything like this, this teeming crowd of unknown people.

Forsman noticed her discomfort, and bellowed out in a loud voice that the girl accompanying him was Hanna Renström, who would be visiting relations in Sundsvall. But tonight, New Year's Eve, she would be a guest in his home.

By midnight Forsman had gathered together all his family and all his employees, including his grooms and maids. He opened wide a window in the large room that Hanna had gathered was called "the drawing room" and shouted to everybody to be silent. The clock in Sundsvall's church struck twelve. Hanna could see that Forsman was counting the chimes silently as his eyes glazed over.

To her horror she gathered that he was on the point of bursting into tears. Never in her life had she imagined that a grown man could weep. She had a lump in her throat, and realized that something important was in fact happening as the chiming of the clock, carried by the cold air, penetrated the drawing room through the open window. Once the chimes had finished, Forsman started to sing a hymn and all those assembled there joined in — including Hanna, although she did so furtively.

She spent that night in a room shared by three of the maids employed in the house of stone. She shared a bed with a girl called Berta, who was about her own age. Berta smelled less than absolutely clean, and Hanna suspected that she might well smell no better herself. Berta pushed and shoved, claimed most of the bed space, and informed Hanna glumly that she would have to be up by five o'clock, despite the fact that it was New Year's Day and was more or less regarded as a Sunday. But she would have to make the fires and heat up the tiled stoves with the firewood the skivvies brought in.

Berta soon fell asleep. But Hanna lay awake, thinking that there was something missing. It was some time before she realized what it was.

There was no creaking in the stone walls. The cold didn't penetrate the stone walls like it did in the timber-built house she had grown up in.

And it was only then, as she lay in bed inside stone walls, that it finally dawned upon her that she was now living in an unknown world. She could no longer reach out her hand and touch her siblings, or hear Elin's heavy breathing as she slept soundly in her bed.

She was somewhere else now, somewhere that was completely new and unknown to her.

She tentatively placed her hand on Berta's warm body. She missed her brother and sisters who had always been around her. She was on her own now, and she didn't know how she would be able to cope with the void that surrounded her.

CHAPTER
ELEVEN

The following day Forsman sent Jukka, the most trusted of his servants, to help Hanna to locate her relatives. He had been given the address where they were thought to live by Elin, but Sundsvall was not a town where streets and house numbers could always be relied on.

Even worse was the fact that Forsman, who was confident he knew everybody in the town, had never heard of a family called Wallén. But he hadn't told Elin that. He thought that perhaps they lived at one of the sawmills in the vicinity of Sundsvall.

The cold was less severe now. Hanna could feel that it was no longer biting into her skin the way it had done during the long sleigh journey.

Forsman went out into the street with them.

"If you don't find the family, bring her straight back here," he told Jukka, who was standing with his fur hat in his hand.

Hanna thought that Jukka was somewhat cowed and insecure when confronted by his enormous employer in his voluminous fur coat. He was certainly over sixty, but was nevertheless afraid, like a little child worried it might receive a beating.

She couldn't understand why this was.

They set off. As soon as Forsman had gone back inside, Jukka was transformed. He spat and walked with a swagger, elbowing aside anyone who got in their way, and seemed to be in charge of the snow-covered and inadequately cleared street.

Hanna observed the town she had come to in the pale wintry light. For each stone-built house they passed, there seemed to be ten tumbledown little wooden shacks that had grown up out of the ground. Like mushrooms, she thought. If the stone houses were edible, the wooden shacks were the sort of fungi you stamp on and don't put in your basket.

She felt worried all the time. Would she be able to fit in here? Or was she the kind of person who would never feel at home in this town?

And then she came to the sea — but that was nothing like what she had expected either. There was a harbour with lots of big ships, some with masts, others with black funnels. But the water didn't go on for ever, as her father had said it did. She could see land in all directions, and no sign of open water beyond the ice and a network of open channels.

Jukka urged her to keep moving whenever she stopped. He seemed to have just as little time as his employer, and was always in a hurry.

They walked along the icy edge of the harbour. Hanna almost slipped and fell over several times. Her shoes, made by a Lappish cobbler in Fjällnäs, were not suitable for the town's stony and ice-covered pavements.

51

They came to a cluster of wooden houses which seemed to be hugging one another in order to keep warm.

Jukka stopped and asked a man pulling a sledge laden with firewood the way to the address he had been given, to the Walléns. The man, who had a large burn mark on one cheek and a very loud chesty cough, pointed and tried unsuccessfully to explain. Jukka soon lost patience, touched his cap as a gesture of thanks, and they continued walking.

"It's impossible to find anywhere in this damned town," he muttered in his sing-song dialect. "Completely impossible, but I think this is it even so."

He had stopped in front of a two-storey wooden house with a lopsided roof, broken and patched-up windows and a door that threatened to fall out of its frame. Jukka knocked hard on the door. It was opened immediately by an old lady so wrapped up in shawls that the only parts of her that Hanna could see were her eyes and her nose.

"Wallén," said Jukka. "Does the Wallén family live in this house?"

The old woman gave a start as if he had punched her. Then she said something he couldn't understand.

"Take that shawl off, damn you!" he roared. "I'm here on behalf of Jonathan Forsman, the businessman. He wants to know if anybody called Wallén lives here. I can't hear a word of what you are mumbling behind all those rags you're wearing."

The old woman removed the shawl that was covering her face. Hanna could see now that it was gaunt and hollowed, as if she was often left starving.

52

"The Wallén family," said Jukka again, making his impatience obvious.

"They've gone," said the old woman.

"What do you mean, they've gone? Gone to heaven or hell? Give me a proper answer before I lose my temper."

The old woman backed away, but Jukka placed his large boot between the door and the frame.

"There's only one old man left here in the house," she said. "They left him behind. I don't know where they've gone to."

Jukka sucked at his lips and tried to make up his mind what to say to that.

"We'll go in and talk to the old boy," he said eventually. "Show us where he lives!"

The old woman led them up a staircase. Pale-looking children were standing in doorways, staring wide-eyed at the strangers going past. Hanna noticed that there was a stale, acrid smell, as if the house was never aired.

They continued up to the attic floor where the old woman finally stopped outside a door, knocked, then immediately scurried away. When Jukka opened the door, he pushed Hanna inside.

"Go and talk to your relative now," he said. "Either you'll be living here, or you'll have to come back home again with me."

The room contained a bed, a Windsor-style chair and a cracked mirror hanging on one of the walls. Hanna could see a reflection of her face in it — a worried face, somebody she didn't really recognize. Then she looked at the old man lying in the bed who was staring at her as if she had just descended from heaven.

She recalled what her father had said, the last words he had whispered secretly into her ear. About her being a mucky angel. Had he been right?

Was it really an angel the old man seemed to see standing in front of him? Or just a confused serving girl from the distant mountains?

CHAPTER
TWELVE

Jukka was impatient.

"Talk to the old boy now," he growled. "We don't have time to just stand around gaping at him."

He walked over to the window and opened it: it had been closed for so long that it was extremely difficult to move.

"It stinks in here," he said. "A nasty stench of old man. The earth has already started to eat you up, without your noticing. Your body is already full of worms and maggots, chewing away at your flesh."

Jukka glared expectantly at Hanna. She went up to the bed where the old man was lying. He had bits of old food in his beard, his nightshirt was sweaty and dirty. She explained who she was, what she was called, and who her father and mother were. The old man didn't seem to understand, or maybe he hadn't heard. She repeated what she had said, but louder.

In reply he raised a trembling hand. Hanna thought he was trying to greet her — but the hand was pointing to the window.

"I'm cold," said the old man. "Close the window."

Jukka was standing by the window as if on guard. He took a step forward, as if he were about to attack.

"The room stinks," he said. "It needs airing. But do you realize who this is, standing here in front of you? Hanna Wallén. Are you a relative of hers, or not? If you can tell us yes or no, we can leave you in peace."

But the old man didn't understand. He started begging for food — he was hungry, and nobody gave him anything to eat any more.

Hanna tried again. Explained once again who she was, and talked at length about Elin. But it was no use. The old man in the filthy bed was living in a different world, in which the only thing that mattered was his hunger.

"Come on," said Jukka. "Let's go. This is a waste of time. We'll talk to the old woman downstairs. She might know."

If she'd been able to, Hanna would have run out of the house and not stopped until she was back home again with Elin and her brothers and sisters. Nobody wanted to take care of her, the whole journey had been in vain. She didn't belong in this town. She'd been welcomed by a confused, bewildered old man, nobody else.

When Forsman heard about the failed expedition, he tore a strip off the cowering Jukka. Was he incapable of ferreting out where the family had gone to? Would that have been so difficult?

Forsman calmed down eventually, and said to Hanna in his usual friendly voice that he would personally take over responsibility for finding out where the family had gone to. She shouldn't worry. People didn't just disappear into thin air. He would no doubt be able to find the relatives she had come to meet.

"In the meantime you can stay here," he said. "You can make yourself useful about the house. Help the other girls!"

Two days later he had some information to pass on to her. He called her into his office, where he was sitting at a desk, chewing away at a cigar stub.

"That old man you met is just a sort of lodger," he said. "He's not even a relative. He's allowed to lie there in that bed until he dies. Then somebody else will take over the room. A whole family of dockers are lined up to move in. They're no doubt hoping he'll die as soon as possible because at the moment that family is living in a cattle shed. But nobody seems to know where the others have gone to."

He looked hard at her. She was beginning to feel scared, but braced herself.

"I think you should stay here for the time being," said Forsman. "We could do with another maid."

She closed her eyes, and breathed out. She couldn't make up her mind if that was due to relief or to joy. She tried to conjure up the sounds from the house by the river: but everything was silent, her thoughts were interrupted only by the noise of a cart clattering past in the street.

Forsman seemed to gather what she was thinking. He smiled. Hanna curtseyed, and left the room.

She said silently to herself: well, at least I've got something to do here now.

CHAPTER
THIRTEEN

She worked together with Berta from then on. She followed her around, helped her out in her duties, and also allowed her to show her around the town in what little spare time they had. Most of the time was spent washing the clothes of everybody in the very large household, and also the sheets and tablecloths. There was a pump in the inner courtyard, and they fetched water from there to the laundry, which was next to the stables. Hanna couldn't understand how Berta coped with the strenuous work, which kept her occupied for more than twelve hours a day. Berta had started working for Forsman when she was thirteen years old. She told Hanna that her father had died as a result of an accident at the sawmill in Essvik, her mother had died of consumption the following year, and the children had all gone their different ways. Berta kept coming back to her assertion that she had been lucky to get a job in Forsman's household. Although it was hard work and not exactly uplifting, she had a roof over her head, a bed to sleep in and a meal three times a day. What had she to complain about? What right had she to do so?

"If I were to leave, there would be at least ten girls queuing up outside in the street, hoping to take over my job," said Berta early one morning as they were standing by the pump, filling their buckets. "Why shouldn't I cling on to what I have?"

"Will you still be here ten years from now?" asked Hanna.

Berta shook her head and burst out laughing. Although she was still young she had lost several of her upper teeth.

"I can't think that far ahead," she said. "Ten years? I don't even know if I'll still be alive then."

But Hanna persisted. There must be something that Berta dreamt about, surely?

"Children," said Berta hesitantly. "I'd love to have some. But for that to happen I'd have to find a husband. And I haven't. I want somebody who doesn't drink or fight. Where can anybody find a man like that?"

Whenever Hanna asked Berta a question, she answered it inside her own head with regard to herself. What did she want? Would she still be alive ten years from now? Or would she be dead as well? Who was the man she hoped to meet? Did she really hope to meet one? And what about children? Could she really think about having children when she was still a child herself in so many ways?

Towards the end of February an unexpected thaw set in. In the evenings, if they had enough strength left, they would go for a walk through the town. Berta showed her round, did so with pride, with a sort of sense of both owning something and having responsibility. She knew something that Hanna didn't. The town was hers.

Occasionally Berta would ask a few questions about the place where Hanna lived before she had come to Sundsvall with Forsman: but Hanna soon noticed that Berta was not really all that interested in what little she had to tell. Or perhaps it was just that Berta had never seen anything but the town she lived in, and couldn't imagine what it would be like by a river below a high mountain.

Her relationship with Berta was something completely new for Hanna. During the time she lived in Forsman's house she and Berta became close friends who dared to take each other into their confidence. Almost every evening they lay in the bed they shared, whispering. It seemed to Hanna that she had never before had a friend like Berta. The relationship she had had with her siblings and her mother had been quite different.

They dared to talk about the difficult things in life. Love, children, men. Hanna soon realized that Berta had just as little experience as she did when it came to what life had in store for them.

Sometimes in the evenings when they were out walking, always arm in arm, with their shawls wrapped tightly around their hair and chin, boys of about their own age who were loitering around would shout to them: but they never replied, just increased their pace — even if later, when they had gone to bed, they might giggle and talk about what had happened.

60

We're not there yet, Hanna thought; but one of these days we'll stop and start talking to those boys.

Most of the time they spent together, when they were not working, they devoted to helping each other to learn to read. They had realized from the start that their knowledge was more or less equally meagre. Berta had been given a dirty and well-thumbed ABC book by a cook who used to work at Forsman's house. They would pore over it, spelling out words, testing each other, and before long they were secretly borrowing books from Forsman's library, reading aloud to each other with increasing confidence.

Hanna would never forget the moment when the individual letters stopped dancing around in front of her eyes. When they no longer made faces at her but formed words and sentences, and eventually whole stories that she could understand.

It was also during that time that Hanna happened to acquire a Portuguese dictionary. Forsman sometimes sifted through his voluminous library and discarded books and booklets that were surplus to his requirements. One day Hanna had found the dictionary in a waste-paper basket. She thought that anything he'd thrown away she could keep if she fancied it, rather than taking it to the rubbish dump. She showed it to Berta, who was not interested in a foreign language she would never have any use of.

But Hanna kept the dictionary and learnt a few words and phrases that she didn't even know if she was pronouncing correctly.

The late winter continued to be mild in 1904. As early as the middle of March the sailors, who had been spending the winter ashore when the ice prevented them from going to sea, began to gather restlessly in the harbour and on the jetties where sailing boats were beached. Berta explained to Hanna that there were fewer and fewer sailing boats nowadays: more and more owners were buying steamships instead. But there were still sailing ships carrying cargo along the coast, or over to Finland, and perhaps even to the Baltic countries. Quite a few carried timber and fish down to Stockholm, while others headed northwards.

Before long sailing boats would disappear altogether, and be replaced by steamships.

CHAPTER
FOURTEEN

One morning Hanna was summoned unexpectedly to Forsman's office. He didn't often want to talk to her alone. Every time it did happen, she was worried that he might flare up and start complaining about her work or her behaviour.

When she entered the room she found that Forsman was not alone. Sitting on a chair was a man in uniform she had never seen before. She paused in the doorway and curtseyed. Forsman nodded to her and put his glowing cigar into an ashtray.

The man in uniform was older than Forsman. He observed her closely.

"This is Captain Svartman," said Forsman. "He is master of a ship of which I am part-owner. She's called *Lovisa*, and will soon be setting off on a long voyage to Australia with a cargo of Swedish timber, felled in forests owned by me and sawn up in a sawmill owned by me."

Forsman paused abruptly, as he usually did when he wanted to give people time to digest what he had said. Hanna searched her mind for a country called Australia, but failed to find it. However, Forsman had said it would be a long voyage. So Australia couldn't be a neighbouring country.

"I've been thinking about your future," Forsman said suddenly, with such emphasis that Hanna gave a start. "I think you can make more of yourself than just a maid here in my house. I think I can see in you qualities that suggest you could have a bright future. Exactly what will become of you I don't know. It's just that I suspect you have a will of your own. And so I've decided that you will sail to Australia and back with Captain Svartman. You will work on board as a cook. You'll be the only woman on the ship, but everybody will know that you are under my special protection."

Forsman fell silent again and contemplated his cigar, which had gone out. Hanna felt there was something she needed to say immediately.

"I must ask Elin for permission," she said. "I can't go off on a voyage without my family knowing about it."

Forsman nodded thoughtfully and leaned forward over his desk. He picked up a sheet of paper and held it up for Hanna to see.

"Your mother's writing is like a spider crawling over a page," he said. "Her spelling is awful. And she has no idea where to put a full stop or a comma. But she knows what I've proposed to you, and she gives you her permission to go."

Hanna realized now that Forsman was continuing to take responsibility for her, as he had promised. It was clear that the idea of her going on a long voyage on one of his ships had been planned for some considerable time. It took a long time for letters to pass between Sundsvall and the distant mountains.

"In just over a month the ship will have all its cargo on board and be ready to sail," said Forsman. "Between now and then you will go on board every morning. There's an old ship's cook by the name of Mörth who will teach you the ropes. You'll be given some money to pay for the equipment and clothing you'll need, and you'll be paid a good wage during the voyage — more money than you would ever be able to earn as a maid. That'll be all now, but don't hesitate. I know this is something right up your street."

Hanna left the room. She could feel a cold sweat under her blouse.

It was the next day, a Sunday when they had a few hours off work, before Hanna told Berta about what had happened. The sun was shining, and melted snow and ice was dripping from the roofs. They had climbed up a little hill just outside the town where there was a tree trunk that somebody had turned into a bench, using an axe. It was still winter, but the midday sun was quite warm. They spread out their overcoats and sat down. Hanna hadn't prepared anything in advance, but she suddenly had the feeling that now was the time to take Berta into her confidence. She told her everything, and said that she was dreading the task that Forsman had arranged for her. How on earth would she be able to cope with being ship's cook on a voyage to Australia?

"I wish it had been me he'd asked," said Berta. "I wouldn't have hesitated to go."

"But it's so far away," said Hanna, and explained how she had found Australia on the brown globe of the world Forsman had beside his billiard table.

She had been horrified when she discovered that Australia was on the other side of the world.

"I want to stay in Forsman's house," she said. "Who will do all my work while I'm away?"

"Is this drudgery really something to aspire to?" said Berta in surprise. "Besides, it's not really necessary to have an extra maid in this household."

Berta sounded quite definite in her comments. It was as if she understood what was worrying Hanna — but it could also be that Berta was jealous of her. Hanna had the nasty feeling that Berta might prefer not to have her around.

"It's up to you to make the decision," said Berta. "There's nothing I'd like more for you to stay on here. If for no other reason than you lie still at night. I can't put up with sharing a bed with somebody who kicks and tosses and turns all night."

They both burst out laughing, but soon became serious again.

"Talk to Forsman if you are hesitant about it," said Berta. "He's the one who has the final say."

They said no more about the voyage just then. Instead they sat there gazing out over the town and the seemingly endless stretch of white ice beyond the wooded hills. When it became too cold, they stood up and made their way back down the icy path. First Berta slipped, then Hanna. They laughed, then held each other's hands as they continued down the slope. Hanna was thinking about what saddened her most: that she would lose the friend she had made in Berta.

The following day she plucked up courage and knocked on the door of Forsman's office. He shouted "Come in", and raised an eyebrow in surprise when she stepped over the threshold.

"What do you want?"

She remained standing in the doorway. What should she say, in fact?

"Come on in," he said. "Come to my desk! I'm expecting some men from whom I'm going to buy some timber. Tell me what you want. Are you unwell, or what's the matter?"

"I'm fine," said Hanna, curtseying when she spoke to him.

"What is it then? I don't like you standing here curtseying unnecessarily."

"I would like to stay here," she said in a voice so low that Forsman had to lean forward over his desk in order to hear her.

"I don't know what's in store for me on that ship," she said. "But here I think I do a good job."

Forsman leaned back in his desk chair again. His large hands rested heavily on his stomach, where his waistcoat was unbuttoned. He eyed her intently.

"You must go on that voyage. It's best for you. Believe me."

He stood up. The interview was over. Hanna curtseyed and hurried out.

It felt as if she were running.

CHAPTER
FIFTEEN

The hymn book was similar to the one Forsman had given Elin that day in December the previous year, when the sleigh they had been waiting for finally emerged from the edge of the forest. Now it was time for her to board the ship full-time, it was Hanna's turn to get one. She had joined the crew, and had signed a contract and an insurance agreement.

By then she had been taught all the things she needed to know by the old cook Mörth, who couldn't resist groping her but stopped immediately when she thrust his hand away. Then he would wait until the following day before trying again. Even if she disliked the fact that he wouldn't leave her alone, he really did his best to teach her how to prepare good food for the crew. He urged her to keep track of essential stores, and which of the harbours they visited would be most suitable for restocking. He made a map and drew up a list for her, and she realized that without Mörth she would never have been able to prepare herself properly for the voyage.

Forsman took her to one side after he had presented her with the hymn book. He seemed embarrassed, almost emotional, as if he had been drinking. Which she knew he hadn't been.

"I hope all goes well for you," he said. "May God watch over all you do. But I'm also on call if needs be, I promise you that."

Her farewells to the stone-built house and its occupants were short. But Berta and she had made a pact: it was holy, they assured each other, and must not be broken. They had vowed to write to each other until they met again. They had learnt to read and write together, and now it had become clear that there was a purpose behind it all. And if it turned out that Hanna never returned to Sundsvall, at least they would be able to meet in the letters they exchanged.

Forsman accompanied her to the ship. A man in uniform she had never seen before was waiting for them at the top of the gangplank. He was young, barely more than four or five years older than she was. He was wearing a peaked cap and a dark blue tunic, was fair-haired, and stood at ease with a burnt-out pipe in his hand.

Hanna stepped out on to the gangplank. When she arrived on board, the unknown man was waiting for her.

She curtseyed, then regretted it. Why on earth should she curtsey to one of the sailors?

She heard heavy steps behind her. It was Forsman, coming on board with the captain.

"Third Mate Lundmark," said Captain Svartman. "This is our cook, Hanna Renström. If you look after her well, perhaps you will get some decent food on the voyage."

Lundmark nodded. His smile made Hanna feel insecure. Why did he look at her so intently?

But now she knew who he was, at least.

There was a light breeze blowing over Sundsvall's harbour that April day. She closed her eyes and listened to the noise of the wind and the waves. The forest, she thought. The waves sound just like it did up there in the mountains when there was a wind blowing. Irrespective of whether the wind was cold or warm.

She suddenly longed to be with Elin and her brother and sisters. But there was no going back, just now there was only this steamship with its cargo of aromatic, newly sawn planks, about to set off for Australia.

"Lars Johan Jakob Antonius Lundmark," said a voice right next to her. It was the third mate who had stayed behind while the captain and Forsman headed for Svartman's cabin. "Lars after my father," he continued. "Johan after my paternal grandfather, Jakob after my elder brother who died, Antonius after the doctor who once cured my father's blood poisoning. Do you know who I am now?"

"I'm called Hanna," she said. "I only have one name. That has always been enough for me."

She turned on her heel and went to her own cabin. Apart from Captain Svartman, she was the only member of the crew who had a cabin to herself. She sat down on the bunk bed with the hymn book in her hand. When she opened it up, she found two shiny one-krona coins inside.

70

She went back on deck. The mate was no longer there. She stood by the railing until Forsman emerged from the captain's cabin.

"Thank you for the money," she said.

"Money is a good way of helping the word of God to fruition," said Forsman. "A bit of travel money won't do you any harm."

He stroked her awkwardly on the cheek, then left the ship on the gangplank which swayed noticeably under his weight.

The whole ship seemed to lean on one side as it bade farewell to its owner.

CHAPTER
SIXTEEN

Nine hours later, on 23 April 1904, the steamship *Lovisa* weighed anchor and set off for Perth.

The ship sounded a farewell with its foghorn. Hanna stood by the rail aft, not far from her cabin, but had the feeling that she was still standing down there, on the quay.

She had left a part of herself behind. She didn't know who she now was. The future — uncertain, unknown — would reveal that to her.

She stood behind her cabin, under a projecting roof, and looked down at the swirling foam whipped up by the propeller. Drifting snow, she thought. Now I'm on my way to a world where it never snows, where there are deserts, and the dry sand whirls around in temperatures that are beyond my comprehension.

Suddenly the saw that the mate was standing beside her. Looking back, what she first noticed about him were his fingernails. They were clean and neatly cut, and she recalled how Elin used to sit crouched over her father's nails, devoting endless effort and tenderness to her efforts to make them neat and clean.

She wondered who cut the third mate's nails. She understood from something Captain Svartman had said that Lundmark was unmarried. Svartman had also asked her if she had a fiancé waiting for her to return home. When she said she hadn't, he seemed to be pleased. He had muttered something about preferring that not too many of his crew had close family connections.

"In case anything happens," he had added. "All the sea offers us is the unexpected."

Lundmark looked at her with a smile.

"Welcome aboard," he said.

Hanna looked at him in surprise. It was Forsman speaking. Lundmark had imitated his voice with astonishing accuracy.

"You sound like him," she said.

"I can if I want to," said Lundmark. "Even a third mate can have a shipowner's voice hidden away inside him."

A distant call from the bridge cut short their conversation. The black smoke from the funnels was sinking down on to the deck. She had to turn away to prevent it from making her eyes hurt.

Hanna had a fifteen-year-old boy by the name of Lars to help her with the preparation of food. He was also sailing for the first time. He was an orphan, and scared stiff. When he shook hands with her, she could feel how he was ready to snatch his hand away from her if she were to squeeze it too tightly.

Captain Svartman had asked for pork and brown beans this first day of the voyage.

"I'm not superstitious," he'd said, "but my best voyages have always started with my crew being fed with pork and beans. There's no harm in repeating what has already proved itself to be a good thing."

In the evening, when she had made all the necessary preparations for the next morning's breakfast and sent the mess-room boy to bed, she went out on deck. They had now left the archipelago behind them, and were heading southwards. The sun was setting over the forests on the starboard side.

All at once Lundmark appeared by her side again. They stood there together, watching the sun as it slowly vanished.

"Starboard," he said without warning. "There's a reason for everything. It's an odd word, but it means something even so. Star has nothing to do with stars, it comes from 'steer'. In the old days a helmsman would stand with a steering oar in the aft of the ship, and he would have it on his right because then he could use his right arm to move it, and a man's right arm is usually stronger than his left. So the right-hand side was called 'steerboard', and that gradually changed into 'starboard'."

"What about 'port'?" she wondered.

Lundmark shook his head.

"I don't know," he said. "But I'll find out."

It soon became a habit. Every evening Hanna and the third mate would stand there talking to each other. If it was raining or very windy, they would shelter under the projecting roof of her cabin.

But she never had an answer as to why it was called "port".

CHAPTER
SEVENTEEN

This is amazing, she thought. Every morning when I wake up my bed has moved on. I'm in a different place from where I was when I went to sleep.

But something else about her was beginning to change as well. She had started looking forward to her meetings with Lundmark. They talked tentatively about who they were, where they had come from, and she didn't flinch one evening when he suddenly put his arm round her.

They were in the English Channel at the time, edging slowly forward through a bank of fog that loomed up in front of them like a wall. Foghorns were sounding eerily from various directions. They made her think of a flock of animals that had broken up, and was now trying to reassemble. Captain Svartman was always on the bridge whenever they passed through fog, and he had ordered extra lookouts to stand guard. Occasionally black ships with slack sails or ships with smoking funnels would appear out of all the whiteness and glide past, sometimes far too close, making Svartman shake his head in disapproval and give orders to slow down even more. For two days and two nights they were almost motionless. All accessible lamps and lanterns were kept burning on deck, Hanna found it difficult to sleep and frequently left her cabin, but she was always careful not to get in the way.

The next day Captain Svartman asked Hanna to look for the mess-room boy who had disappeared. She found him in the food store, hidden away. He was trembling with fear. She comforted him and took him out on deck, where Svartman pressed a lantern into his hand.

"Work cures everything," he said.

A few days later the fog started to disperse. They increased speed again. Hanna heard talk of something called the Bay of Biscay, through which they would soon be passing.

One evening Lundmark suddenly started talking seriously about himself. He was the only child of a merchant in Timrå who had gone bankrupt and afterwards was scarcely able to keep squalor and famine at bay. His mother was a taciturn woman who could never reconcile herself to the fact that she had only managed to bring one child into the world. She regarded it as both disappointing and shameful.

He had always longed to go to sea. Was always running down to the shore to watch ships coming and going. At the age of thirteen he had signed on as an apprentice on a small cargo boat plying between Sundsvall and Söderhamn. His mother and father had tried to stop him, and even threatened to send the sheriff's officer after him if he went through with it. But when he persisted they seemed to become resigned to the inevitable, and allowed him to do what he had decided was to be his future.

Before falling asleep that night she thought about what the third mate had told her. He had spoken to her in confidence, something that hitherto only Berta had done.

The next day he continued with his story. But he also began asking her about the life she had led before coming to Forsman's house and then to the ship she was now sailing on. She didn't think she had anything much to tell him, but he listened attentively even so and seemed to be genuinely interested.

And so they continued their conversation, every evening if the wind wasn't too strong or Captain Svartman hadn't ordered Lundmark to carry out some extra duty or other outside his normal routine.

Hanna realized that her feelings for Lundmark were different from anything she had previously experienced in her life. They couldn't be compared with those she had shared with Elin and her siblings, nor even the close friendship she had formed with Berta. She spent every moment of the day looking forward to his arrival behind the galley: longing for their meeting.

One evening he presented her with a little wooden sculpture of a mermaid. He had bought it in an Italian port on a previous voyage, and thereafter took it with him on all the ships he signed on to.

"I can't possibly accept it," she said.

"I want you to have it," he said. "I think it looks like you."

"What can I give you in return?" she asked.

"I have everything I need," said Lundmark. "That's the way I feel at the moment."

They stood there in silence for a while. Hanna wished him goodnight and went to her cabin. Later, when she peered through the door she could see him still standing there by the rail. He was gazing out over the sea as darkness fell. He had his legs apart, and his officer's cap in his hand.

The following morning she was sitting in the galley, descaling a freshly caught fish which was to be the sailors' dinner. A shadow fell over her. When she looked up it was Lundmark standing there. He went down on one knee, took her hand which was full of glistening fish scales, and asked her to marry him.

Until that moment they had done nothing but talk to each other; but everybody else on board had regarded them as a pair, she knew that, since none of the other men had approached her at all.

Had she been expecting this to happen? Had she been hoping it would? No doubt she had occasionally had such a thought, the idea that she was sailing together with him, not with a ship laden with timber. Despite the fact that she had only met him when the ship was about to leave Sundsvall.

She said "Yes" without hesitation. She made up her mind in a flash. He kissed her face, then stood up and left to attend the meeting the mates had with the captain every morning.

They stopped in Algiers in order to take on board more coal — Hanna knew by now that this was called "bunkering". The Swedish consul, a Frenchman who had once visited Stockholm in his youth and fallen in love with the city, found an English Methodist minister who was prepared to marry the couple. Captain Svartman produced the necessary documents and was a witness to the marriage together with the consul and his wife, who was so moved by the brief ceremony that she burst into tears. Afterwards the captain took them to a photographer's and paid for a wedding photograph out of his own pocket.

That same evening she moved into Lundberg's cabin. The second mate, whose name was Björnsson, moved into the ship's cramped hospital cabin — Hanna would retain her own cabin, Captain Svartman was reluctant to take it away from her. But if anybody on board fell seriously ill, it would be used to accommodate them.

Captain Svartman was positively inclined towards their marriage. But as they left Algiers that same evening their wedding night was ruined by the fact that the prearranged timetable of duties came into operation, and Lundberg had to take his turn as lookout. There was no question of Captain Svartman giving him the evening off — his benevolence didn't stretch that far. And it would never have occurred to Lundmark to ask for special treatment.

So Hanna had become a wife, Fru Lundmark. Both bride and bridegroom were shy and insecure. The solidly built third mate had been transformed into a little child, scared stiff of causing injury or offence. They embraced cautiously, as they barely knew each other yet. Their lovemaking was low-key, not yet uninhibited passion.

When they passed through the Suez Canal, they both happened to be off duty at the same time — an infrequent occurrence. They stood by the ship's rail, contemplating the beaches, the tall palm trees, the camels slowly waddling along, the naked children diving into the waters of the canal.

What Hanna found hardest to get used to was sleeping with him lying by her side. Sleeping alongside a brother or sister or Berta had been one thing: but now she was sharing a bed with a big, heavy man who often tossed and turned and woke her up.

She felt both secure and restless in the situation she now found herself in, together with him; but at the same time she also felt an intense longing to be back in the life she had led in that remote river valley in the mountains.

At night, after making love, they would talk to each other in the dark, always in whispers as the bulkheads were thin and they were surrounded by other people.

In the darkness and the warmth, he now confided in her that he hoped one day to become the captain of his own ship.

"I'll achieve that if you help me," he said. "Now that I have you by my side, I think it's possible."

She took his hand. Thought about what he had said. And suddenly felt an overwhelming desire to be able to tell Elin about everything that was happening in her life.

When Elin had said that there was no other option, Hanna had to go to the coast, she had been right. But what would she think now about the voyage Hanna was now embarked upon?

I must write to her, Hanna thought. One day Elin will receive a letter. I'll enclose a copy of our wedding photo. She must see the man I've married.

CHAPTER
EIGHTEEN

She was aroused from her memories by the question that still remained unanswered, a bridge between the past and where she found herself now: did she know who she was? Two months after she had left Sundsvall, she became Lundmark's wife, and was now waiting for him to be buried.

She had no answer. Everything was silent around her and inside her. She could not answer the question of who she was or who she had become.

The ship was motionless in the steaming heat. The pressure in the steam boilers was kept low while they waited for the burial at sea to take place. Once that was over, the engine-room telegraph would give the command "Full steam ahead!", and the stokers would once again start shovelling coal into the firebox.

But just now the soot-covered men from the engine room had come up on deck and washed away the worst of the dirt. There was only one man left down below to make sure that nothing caught on fire, or that one of the boilers didn't go out.

Captain Svartman went in person to collect Hanna. He knocked carefully on the door of the cabin she had shared with her dead husband. Now she will have to live there alone, Svartman thought. What shall I do if she is scared of the loneliness? What shall I do with a widow on board?

He opened the door. She was sitting on the edge of the bunk, staring at her hands. In her thoughts she had just been reminding herself of the long journey that had begun in a remote river valley. She had met a man, they had become a couple, but now he was gone.

They had been together for two months. Then the fever that had suddenly struck him down after he had gone ashore in Sudan had killed him. But she was still there. And now he was going to be buried.

When she got up from the bunk she had the feeling that she was on her way to her own funeral. Or perhaps to her execution? Yet again she found herself alone, but now in a much worse situation than ever before. Why should she travel to the other side of the world when the man who had belonged to her no longer existed? Who was she accompanying now? Apart from Captain Svartman, on the way to the starboard side of the ship, the one facing land, the African coast hidden away in the sunny haze and out of sight even with the aid of a telescope?

There was a lookout on the bridge, an able seaman, one of the younger ones. But everyone else had assembled by the side of the soft coffin made out of sailcloth and standing on two trestles next to the rail. The grey cloth was wrapped up in a Swedish flag. It was stained and frayed. Hanna suspected it was the only flag on board. Captain Svartman was not the kind of person who made plans for what to do if one of his crew were to die. Only somebody who behaved rashly and broke his rules could get into trouble. Like the third mate now lying there on the trestles, and soon to be tipped overboard into the sea.

Hanna looked at the men who were standing in a semicircle. None of them could bring themselves to look her in the eye. Death was embarrassing, it made them self-conscious and insecure.

She looked up at the sky, and the sun that was broiling hot even though it was so early in the morning. In her thoughts she suddenly found herself back in the sleigh, behind Forsman's broad back.

Then it was the cold, she thought. Now it's the heat. But in a way they are the same.

And the movement. Then it was a sleigh, now it was a ship slowly, almost imperceptibly, swaying in the swell.

Captain Svartman was dressed in his uniform and with white gloves: in his hand was the book with instructions for how to conduct a burial at sea. He read in a monotonous but loud voice. He had no fears when it came to carrying out his duties as captain.

Hanna suspected that more than anything else Svartman was angry because somebody had ignored his exhortations and gone ashore, even though he must have been aware of the danger he was exposing himself to.

The man who was about to be buried had died completely unnecessarily. A man who had been stupid and not listened to what Captain Svartman had to say to him.

Hanna had the feeling that Svartman was not simply mourning the loss of his third mate. He also felt that he'd been let down.

CHAPTER
NINETEEN

The ceremony was short. Captain Svartman did not deviate from the set text, added nothing personal. He fell silent when he came to the end of the order of service and nodded to his second mate, who had a good singing voice and launched into a hymn. Oddly enough he had chosen a Christmas hymn.

Shine over sea and shore, star in the distance.

The rest of the crew joined in, mumbling, with here and there a jarring false note. Hanna glanced furtively at them. Some were not singing at all.

Which ones were thinking about the man who had died? Some were, no doubt. Others, perhaps most of them, were just grateful that they were still alive.

When the hymn was over Captain Svartman nodded at Hanna, inviting her to step forward. He had explained to her that there were not really any rules or traditions with regard to what a widow in the crew should do as a final farewell to her husband during a burial at sea.

"Place your hand on the sailcloth," he had suggested. "As we don't have any flowers on board, your hand can be the symbol of a final farewell."

He could have sacrificed one of his potted plants, she thought. Broken off one of the flowers and given it to me. But he didn't.

She did as he had suggested, and placed her right hand on the flag. Tried to conjure up Lundmark in her mind's eye. But although he had only been dead for a few days, it seemed that she was already having difficulty in recreating his face.

Death is like a fog, she thought, which slowly envelops the person who is passing away.

She took a pace backwards, Captain Svartman nodded again, four able seamen stepped forward, lifted up the plank and tipped the dead body overboard. Captain Svartman had picked his strongest sailors because the sailcloth contained not only a dead body but also several sinkers weighing many kilos, in order to make sure that the cloth coffin really did sink to the bottom of the sea.

1,935 metres. Her husband was going to have a much deeper grave than the deepest grave on land. It would take almost thirty minutes for the dead body to reach the bottom. Halvorsen had told her that objects sink very slowly at great depths.

The sea burial was over, the crew returned to their work. Only a few minutes later there was a clattering noise in the engine room. The ship was moving again, the interval was over.

Hanna remained standing by the rail. There was no longer anything to be seen in the water. She turned away and went straight to the galley where the mess-room boy had begun preparing lunch. She put on her apron — and then discovered that a deckhand had been sent to help out in the kitchen.

"Even though my husband is dead, I shall do my job," she said.

She didn't wait for a reply but climbed down the ladder to the storeroom to fetch the potatoes that needed to be boiled for the meals that still remained to be served that day.

The potatoes were duly peeled. She emptied the buckets of peel overboard and went back into the galley. Halvorsen was busy repairing a cupboard with racks for saucepans and frying pans. Her husband's best friend on board. He has also lost a companion, she thought. He's also wondering why the third mate took it into his head to go ashore on that unhappy occasion.

She continued her work with the mess-room boy and the deckhand. But when Halvorsen had finished what he was doing he tapped her on the shoulder and beckoned her to follow him out. She asked the mess-room boy to keep an eye on her saucepans, and followed after him.

He was looking down at the deck when he spoke to her, never looked her in the eye.

"What are you going to do now?" he asked.

That was a question she'd had neither the strength nor the courage to ask herself. What *could* she do? What choice did she have?

She was honest with him, and said she didn't know.

"I'll help you," he said. "Just so that you know. If I can."

Halvorsen didn't wait for a response, but turned on his heel and headed towards the bows. She thought about what he had said. And gathered that her husband had asked him to help her in his desperation when he realized how ill he was.

It was Lundmark speaking with Halvorsen's voice. A voice from the deep. A voice that was very good at imitating others.

CHAPTER
TWENTY

They berthed in an African town by the name of Lourenço Marques. The town was small and sparsely populated, reminiscent of Algiers perhaps, with white-fronted houses climbing up a slope. At the top of the hill was a white hotel. The name of the town was impossible to pronounce, so the crew called it Loco — a word she recognized from her Portuguese dictionary, meaning "mad".

Halvorsen had been there before. He urged Hanna not to sleep with the porthole open as there were mosquitoes that carried the dreaded malaria. And she should never wear anything with short sleeves, even though the evenings were warm.

He offered to go ashore with her. They could go for a walk through the town, perhaps stop at one of the countless small restaurants and eat the grilled fish, the prawns deep-fried in oil, or the lobster that was the best in the world.

But she declined. She wasn't yet ready to go anywhere with another man, even if Halvorsen had the best of intentions. She remained on board and thought about the fact that in two days' time they would set sail due east over the big ocean that separated the African continent from Australia.

One night as they were lying in their cramped bunk, whispering, Lundmark had told her that sometimes ships heading for Australia came across icebergs. Although they were sailing on warm seas, some of these icebergs — as big as palaces built of marble — could drift a long way north before they were completely melted by the heat. Captain Svartman had told him that, and everything Captain Svartman said was true.

She stood by the ship's rail, watching African porters dressed in rags carrying provisions on board supervised by Captain Svartman. A white man, bearded and tanned, wearing a khaki suit, was in charge of the porters. It seemed to Hanna that the movements of his hands gave the impression that he was lashing their shoulders with an invisible whip. The porters were thin, frightened. Now and again she would meet their scared, shifty eyes.

Sometimes she thought she could also see something different: fury, perhaps hatred. But she couldn't be sure.

The white man's voice was shrill, as if he hated what he was doing, or just wanted it to come to an end as quickly as possible.

Sometimes when the gangplank was not being used she thought that despite everything she might cross over it, and set foot on the African continent one more time.

But she never did. The rail continued to be her unsurmountable border.

The first night she lay awake in the heat. Halvorsen had said that she could leave the porthole open as long as she covered it carefully with a thin cotton cloth. He had given her a piece of suitable material that he had bought for her while he was ashore.

Now she lay there in the dark, listening to the cicadas, and beyond them occasional drumbeats and something that might have been a song, or perhaps the cry of a nocturnal bird.

The static heat was so stifling that she got dressed and went out on deck. A sailor was guarding the gangplank, which was blocked at night by a thick rope. She went forward to the bows of the ship and sat down on a capstan.

All around her the ship was in darkness, apart from the hurricane lamp by the gangplank. A fire was burning down below on the quay. Men were sitting around it, their faces lit up by the flames. She shuddered. She didn't know why. Perhaps she was afraid, perhaps it was all the unaddressed sorrow that had been accumulating inside her.

She remained sitting on the capstan until she fell asleep. She woke up when she felt a mosquito biting her hand. She brushed it away, and thought that it wouldn't matter anyway if she died.

The following day, the last one they would be spending in Lourenço Marques, she asked Halvorsen what the country they were in was called.

"Portuguese East Africa," he said somewhat doubtfully. "If that can really be the name of an African country."

He shook his head and pulled a face.

"Slavery," he said. "The blacks are slaves. No more than that. I don't think I've ever seen as many brutal people as I've seen here. And they are all white, like you and me."

He shook his head again, and left her.

She had seen his disgust. Just as she had seen in the eyes of some of the black men their fury, and perhaps also a feeling similar to Halvorsen's.

CHAPTER
TWENTY-ONE

It was during that same day that the Swedish missionaries came on board the ship. Captain Svartman met them by the gang-plank shortly before eleven o'clock in the morning. The women in long skirts and white safari helmets, and a small fat man with a club foot came on board. Hanna stopped what she was doing and watched the strangers. Captain Svartman handed them a suitcase full of post, then invited them into his cabin.

Halvorsen had told her that they had a mission station inland at a place called Phalaborwa. It was a long way from the coast. They must have been travelling by ox cart for over a week before arriving in Lourenço Marques.

"Captain Svartman no doubt sent them a telegram when we were docked in Algiers," said Halvorsen. "So they would know roughly when we were due to arrive."

Hanna had been doing some laundry and was about to hang it up to dry on one of the lines the deckhands rigged up for her whenever it was needed, but suddenly she discovered that one of the unknown women was standing in front of her.

The woman was pale, and very thin. She had a little scar along one side of her nose. Her eyes were dull, blue, and her lips narrow. She might have been about forty, perhaps younger.

Hanna thought she looked ill.

The woman said her name was Agnes.

"Captain Svartman has told me," she said. "About your husband who has just died. Would you like us to pray together?"

Hanna was standing with several items of newly washed clothing in her hand. Did the woman mean that they should drop down on to their knees here on deck? She shuddered at the thought.

"I'd be glad to help you," said Agnes.

Her voice was gentle. One of the crewmen spoke the same dialect, a bosun by the name of Brodin who came from the forests of Värmland. Was the woman standing there in front of Hanna really from Värmland?

She glanced at the woman's left hand: no ring. So she was unmarried. And wanted to help. But how would she be able to do that? All Hanna wanted was to get her dead husband back. But he was 1,935 metres down below at the bottom of the sea, and would never return.

"Thank you," she mumbled, "but I don't need any help just now."

Agnes observed her thoughtfully, then simply nodded and took her hand.

"I shall pray for you, and ask for your deep sorrow to be made less painful," she said.

Hanna watched the missionaries leave the ship with the case of mail, and disappear into the town. She kept an eye on them until the last of them, the man with the club foot, was no longer visible.

Then she had a sudden urge to run after them, to go with them as far away from the sea as possible. But there was still something that formed an invisible barrier for her, preventing her from crossing over the gangplank. She was bound to Captain Svartman's ship.

To her dead husband's ship.

CHAPTER
TWENTY-TWO

What happened next, and above all why, was something Hanna would never be able to understand. For the rest of her life the decision she made late that night, after the missionaries had left the ship, was totally incomprehensible. She had undressed and gone to bed. The heat was as oppressive as ever, and no currents of air disturbed the piece of cotton cloth hanging over the open brass-framed porthole. She had already fallen asleep, but suddenly sat up in her bunk wide awake. The thought that Hanna had inside her head was crystal clear, it filled the whole of her consciousness.

Hanna knew that she couldn't stay on board. She couldn't continue the voyage because her dead husband was still on board. She would succumb to her sorrow unless she left the ship.

She curled up on her bunk, sitting with her back against the bulkhead, and held her breath. She had made her decision and now she must leave the ship that very same night, as soon as the sailor guarding the gangplank had fallen asleep.

Hanna tried one last time to convince herself that despite everything she really ought to continue to Australia, but the idea was impossible to countenance.

She would never stand by the rail and watch icebergs, the marble palaces, floating past.

She packed her few belongings in the suitcase that had once been given to her by Forsman. She hesitated for ages, wondering whether to take with her Lundmark's sailor's kitbag. In the end she took only his peaked cap, his discharge book and the wedding photograph taken in the studio in Algiers. The last item she packed away was her Portuguese dictionary.

Hanna left her cabin shortly after four in the morning. The sailor by the gangplank was leaning against the rail, fast asleep, his head resting on his chest.

The cicadas were singing softly as she stepped over the rope and walked along the gangplank, and was then swallowed up by the darkness.

The crew spent all next day looking for her on board, but she had vanished. Captain Svartman sent Halvorsen and two able seamen ashore to search for her. The captain waited for as long as he could. But just before the African dusk fell, he gave the order to cast off.

Hanna Lundmark, the cook, had deserted. Captain Svartman suspected sadly that she had gone mad.

He wrote in the ship's logbook: "The cook Hanna Lundmark has jumped ship. As she was recently widowed, the suspicion is that her sorrow has driven her out of her mind. The search for her was fruitless."

But she was in fact lurking in the shadows of the harbour, unseen by anybody on board. She watched the ship leave port and head off eastwards.

A few days earlier she had been given fifty English pounds by Captain Svartman. This was the amount due to a widow of a crew member who died on board, paid by the shipping company's insurance.

She booked into a cheap hotel in the harbour. She slept uneasily, disturbed frequently by nagging pains in her stomach.

When she woke up it was a warm day in July 1904. At roughly the same time the *Lovisa* came up against its first iceberg.

PART TWO

The Lagoon of Good Death

CHAPTER
TWENTY-THREE

She was woken up by a screech that seemed to come from a human being in dire straits. It was much later that she discovered it was in fact the cry of a lone peacock that used to roam about in the hotel grounds. It was originally one of many based in the gardens surrounding the Portuguese governor's palace, but one day it turned up outside the hotel and had never left. He used to screech every morning, and scared lots of residents with his angst-filled cries.

Peacocks were also associated with a legend, the origins of which were obscure. It had originated in the culture of the blacks, but had then spread to the white residents of the town. Every time a peacock displayed its magnificent tail, a human being somewhere was cured of an intolerable pain.

This peacock didn't have a name. It moved around slowly, cautiously, as if brooding over its solitary fate.

And so Hanna woke up after her first night in Africa. What would she remember afterwards?

Perhaps the night was dream-like, a panoply of visions flitting hastily past? But at the same time there was also something very real: a nagging pain in her stomach. The heat was stifling, the brick walls in the

103

room she had been sleeping in were dripping with damp. Lizards with shiny, almost transparent skin were clinging upside down to the ceiling above her head. There was a crackling sound from the dark floor where insects were lurking in the shadows. A mulatto woman with vigilant eyes had given her an oil lamp with a flickering flame that gave the impression of being the last breaths of a dying man.

And now: dawn. The cry of the peacock was still echoing in her ears. She walked over to the window on unsteady legs and watched the sun rising over the horizon. In her mind's eye she relived the departure of the ship, slowly embarking on its voyage to Australia with a cargo that smelled of forests.

She washed her hands in a washbasin. She hid the pound notes she had received from Captain Svartman among her underclothes in the suitcase that Forsman had presented her with.

A filthy mirror was hanging on one of the brick walls. She recalled her father's shaving mirror, and stood close up to it in order to see the reflection of her face.

She suddenly gave a start and turned round. The door of her room, with the figure 4 untidily written on a scrap of paper pinned to it, had been opened. The mulatto woman who had given her the oil lamp the previous evening was standing looking at her. Then she stepped inside and put a tray with some bread and a cup of tea on the only table there was in the room.

She was barefoot, and moved without a sound. She was wearing a loincloth and had naked, glistening breasts.

Hanna wanted to know immediately what the coloured lady was called. Just now she was living in a world where the only name she knew was her own. But she couldn't bring herself to say anything. The silent woman left, and the door closed behind her.

Hanna drank the tea, which was very sweet. When she put the cup back on its saucer she felt full. She put her hand on her brow. It was hot. Was it the heat of the room? She didn't know.

The stomach pains Hanna had felt during the night returned. She lay down on the bed and closed her eyes. The nagging pain came and went in waves. She dozed off, but woke up with a start. She put her hand on her groin. It was wet. When she looked at her hand it was covered in blood. She screamed and sat up in bed.

Death, Hanna thought, trembling. It was not only Lundmark whose time was up: the same applies to me. She was shivering with fear, but forced herself to stand up and stagger as far as the door. She found herself in a corridor that ran round an inner courtyard. She needed to cling on to the rail so as not to fall down. In the inner courtyard, paved with stone, was a black piano: someone was sitting there, polishing the keys with a linen rag.

She must have made a noise that she wasn't aware of. The man polishing the keys of the piano stopped, turned round and looked at her. She raised her blood-covered hands, as if she were appealing to anybody who was prepared to come and help her.

I'm dying, Hanna thought. Even if he doesn't understand what I say, he must surely recognize a cry for help.

"I'm bleeding," she screamed. "I need help!"

She was on the point of passing out, but managed to stagger back to her room. It felt as if life was draining out of her. She was already on her way down to the same sea bottom as Lundmark.

Somebody touched Hanna's shoulder. It was the same woman who had just served her tea. She carefully lifted up Hanna's nightdress, looked at her lower abdomen, then let it fall again. Her face betrayed nothing of her thoughts.

Hanna longed for the coloured woman to be transformed into Elin. But Elin was not the woman standing in front of her, Elin lived in a different world. As if in a mist, Hanna thought she could see her mother standing outside the grey house, gazing at the mountain on the other side of the river.

The coloured woman turned on her heel and left the room. Hanna could see that she was in a hurry.

I shall find out what her name is, she thought, because I refuse to die.

I'm not going to sink down. Not yet.

CHAPTER
TWENTY-FOUR

Hanna was woken up by the curtain fluttering against the widow as the door opened. It wasn't the mulatto woman returning, but a different woman altogether. She was jet black, with skin that seemed to glisten and her hair in tight plaits apparently stuck to her skull. Her lips were red, heavily made-up. All she was wearing was a thin dressing gown with a pattern of fire-breathing dragons and demons over her silken underclothes.

Her voice was husky, perhaps she was hoarse or had been indulging in too many cigarettes and an excess of alcohol. To Hanna's surprise, as if what was taking place before her very eyes was in fact no more than an extension of her confused dreams, the half-naked woman began talking to her in a language she immediately recognized, even though she had never heard it spoken before. When Hanna arrived at the hotel the woman who gave her the room key had spoken a language she knew was English. She didn't understand it at all, but with the help of her hands and single words she had managed to make it clear that she was looking for a room.

But now this unknown black woman was standing in front of her and bringing to life the dictionary she had once taken out of Forsman's waste-paper basket. So this was how the language she had tried to learn a few words of actually sounded.

Much of what the woman said at first was totally incomprehensible to Hanna, but then she began to recognize an occasional word here and there, and managed to guess rather than understand what was being said.

The woman pointed at Hanna's Swedish discharge book, which was lying on the bedside table. From what she said Hanna gathered that she had once lived with a Swedish sailor called Harry Midgård, who was a terrible man when he was drunk. Hanna suspected that he had worked on a Norwegian whaling ship.

The woman wiped sweat from her neck with the back of her hand.

"Felicia," she said. "I'm Felicia."

Felicia? The name meant nothing to Hanna, but nevertheless she had the feeling that her memory was starting to return.

"How long have I been asleep?" she asked.

"This is the fourth day you've been here."

Felicia had lit a cigarette that she'd been keeping behind her ear. She looked searchingly at Hanna.

It struck Hanna that she had seen a similarly searching look before. It was when Elin had asked Forsman to take her to the coast with him. His expression had been similar as he looked at her, as if he were searching for a truth which was not obvious.

"Do you have the strength to get out of bed?" Felicia asked.

Hanna tried. She was still weak and her legs were shaking when she stood on the floor in a white nightdress which somebody must have put on her while she was asleep. Felicia helped her into a dressing gown which smelled strongly of perfume, and put a pair of slippers on her feet.

They went down the stairs to the inner courtyard which was deserted. Hanna had taken the Portuguese dictionary which she'd brought with her on the voyage. Felicia held her under one arm and led her into a garden surrounded by a stone wall.

It had been raining. The ground was soaking. Hanna thought it smelled like the riverbank after haymaking. The wet soil was bubbling and fermenting.

Felicia helped Hanna to sit down by a jacaranda tree in blossom. She remained standing herself.

"Is it what I think?" Hanna asked.

"How can I know what you think?" said Felicia.

Then she told her in a few words what had happened. Hanna had suspected what the stomach pains had indicated, and now it was confirmed. She had suffered an early miscarriage. Lundmark's child had been rejected. A child without a father that didn't want to be born.

"I know so little," said Felicia.

"It wasn't a child that was rejected, just a lump of bloody goo that didn't have a soul."

Felicia rang the little bell standing on the table. A young waiter in a white jacket appeared and stood beside her chair.

"Tea?" she asked, looking at Hanna, who nodded.

They didn't speak while waiting to be served tea. White butterflies that had been called back to life by the recent rain were hovering around the tree's blue blossoms. The sound of prayers suddenly made itself heard from a minaret somewhere in the vicinity. Hanna was reminded of the call to prayer when she and Lundmark had married in Algiers.

She leaned back so that her face was in the shade of the jacaranda tree. Felicia was standing there, staring at her hands. She had broken a fingernail. That seemed to irritate her.

But she still hadn't sat down, despite the fact that there was plenty of room on the bench. It dawned on Hanna that she didn't know this black woman at all, despite the fact that she had probably saved her life. In fact she was scared of her, just as she had been scared of the black men sitting round the fire on the quay. This fear somehow reminded her of how she had been scared of the dark when she was a little girl.

I can see you, Felicia, she thought. But what do you see? Who am I for you? And why don't you sit down? The bench is big enough for both of us.

The young waiter came with the tea and broke her train of thought. Hanna looked at his hands as he served her.

Only she received a cup. Not Felicia.

"What's his name?" she asked Felicia.

"Estefano."

"How old is he?"

"Fourteen at most. But he hasn't had sex with a woman yet. So he's just a child. His hands are still very soft."

110

Hanna drank her tea in silence. Afterwards, when she had slid the cup to one side, she asked Felicia to tell her about everything that had happened during the days when all she could remember was shadows, loneliness and a pain that kept coming and going in waves.

Felicia was not to leave anything out. She should just say exactly what had happened. And speak slowly, so that Hanna understood.

CHAPTER
TWENTY-FIVE

Felicia said:

"Laurinda, who gave you the lantern when you arrived, told me that there was a white woman staying in room number 4. I didn't know that you had taken up residence in the hotel as I had been visiting my husband and my children in Katembe. I meet them once every month — never at a prearranged time, but when Senhor Vaz thinks it's appropriate. I had just returned and was entertaining my first client when Laurinda came running up. I thought she must have seen a ghost or some kind of phantom, and that she wanted me to kill it. But when I came into your room you immediately became a real, living person. A bleeding woman is more alive than anything else I can think of. The blood running out of our bodies proves that we are alive, but also that we are dying. I understood what had happened even though I didn't know who you were or where you had come from. You should really have danced for me. That's how we get to know strangers in my village and my family. When we see them dance we discover who they are.

"But I got to know you through your blood. I whispered to Laurinda that she should fetch warm

112

water and towels. You seemed to be awake and looking at me, but it was as if you didn't know what had happened even so. One should always talk to frightened people in a low voice, that's something I learnt from my mother. Anyone who shouts in the presence of somebody who is ill can see his or her shout changing into a fatal spear.

"Laurinda came with water and towels, and I took off your blood-soaked clothes. When I rummaged around among your underwear I found some banknotes — a large amount that made me wonder even more who you were. For one English pound you can share my bed for a whole week. You had tens of them. I couldn't understand how a woman could have so much money, even though you are white.

"But I must also admit to thinking that if you died, I would take the money. Assuming there wasn't anybody waiting for you, and that it didn't belong to somebody else. Anyway, I put the notes back among your underclothes — but I knew now where they were. You were bleeding profusely, and your forehead felt hot. There was a moment when I thought it would be impossible to save your life, and that I had been wrong after all. Perhaps it wasn't a miscarriage, but something else that had afflicted you, some illness I knew nothing about.

"Laurinda stayed in the background, but all the time she was on hand to help me. Then I heard Senhor Vaz coming into the room. He spends his life taking people by surprise, catching them doing something they shouldn't. I heard him whispering, asking what had happened: Laurinda didn't know what to say. When I heard him talking about sending a messenger to Dr Garibaldi I got up from the side of the bed where I'd been squatting down and told him that wouldn't be necessary: Dr Garibaldi didn't understand this kind of bleeding. As I did so I thought Senhor Vaz was going to hit me — he never allows one of his whores to express an opinion. But he didn't touch me. I think he could see from my eyes that I knew Dr Garibaldi would only make a bad situation worse. And he didn't want that to happen. That might give his establishment a bad reputation. His clients might choose to go to other whores, even if Senhor Vaz had the reputation of running a brothel that was both spotlessly clean, and had a team of attractive black women. But if a white woman were to bleed to death in one of his rooms, that could be a bad omen. There might be an evil spirit hovering over O Paraiso. Even if all white folk despise what we believe, we have had a certain amount of influence on you. Evil spirits can also injure white people. There was a time when we thought that our African medicine had no effect on people with light-coloured skin. Nowadays we know that isn't true. You are just as scared as we are of the evil spirits that are spread by people that wish us ill. I didn't know who you were, nor where you were going to. But when I saw you lying there with your blood-soaked underwear, I immediately had the impression that somebody wished you ill, that somebody wanted you to die."

Felicia suddenly fell silent, as if she felt she had said too much. There was a clattering sound made by a cart in the street outside.

It seemed to Hanna that there was still so much that she didn't understand. Not only because she could barely grasp what Felicia had said, but because she now realized that the hotel she had checked into the evening she had fled from Captain Svartman's ship was more than it seemed. The hotel was a front for a brothel, something she couldn't have avoided hearing the crew of the ship talking about. And so Felicia, who was standing in front of her next to the beautiful jacaranda tree, was in fact a prostitute.

She thought she ought to stand up, return to her room, get dressed and immediately move into a decent hotel.

But it was Felicia who had saved her, together with the woman she now knew was called Laurinda. Why should she need to flee from them? She had nothing to do with the brothel: all she had done was to take a room that she intended to pay for with her own money.

The money that Felicia hadn't taken, despite the fact that she'd had the opportunity.

Felicia was looking at her, and seemed to read her thoughts.

"A rumour started," she said. "And it spread like wildfire. It was alleged that Senhor Vaz had acquired his first white whore. New clients immediately started queuing up. But they soon realized that you were something as rare as a normal hotel guest. There was no end to their disappointment."

"This Senhor Vaz," said Hanna. "The owner. Who is he?"

"He's a man who can't bear the sight of blood," said Felicia. "When we are bleeding, that's bad for his business — apart from when we entertain those disgusting men who can only bring themselves to have sex with a woman when she's having her period. But he hates everything else to do with blood. As long as you're ill he'll keep out of your way."

"And then what will happen?"

"I assume that as long as you pay for your room, you can stay on."

Hanna suddenly had the feeling that somebody was standing behind her. When she turned round she gave a start and felt scared stiff. At first she didn't grasp what she was looking at. Then it dawned on her that it was a chimpanzee standing there wearing a waiter's white waistcoat, and staring at her.

CHAPTER
TWENTY-SIX

Hanna thought she had gone mad. What she saw couldn't be true. But the ape was standing there on its bow legs. In one hand it was holding a tray with pastries and biscuits. Felicia said something to it. It put the tray down on the table, pulled a few faces, ground its teeth, then went away.

"It's called Carlos," said Felicia. "After some Portuguese king or other. It came here with its owner five years ago, a man who hunted lion trophies on the great inland plains. He brought the chimpanzee with him. In those days it used to wear a topee. But when the owner couldn't pay his bill after over a week with the ladies, Senhor Vaz took the chimp as payment. It sulked for a couple of weeks. But after that it was quite easy to get it used to the white jacket and its name, and for it to realize that it had a better home now than it used to have. It usually sits up on the roof at night and gazes at the forests on the other side of the town. But it never runs away. This is Carlos's home now."

Hanna still couldn't believe it was true, neither what she had seen nor what she had just heard. But Felicia was convincing, she meant what she said.

The sound of music suddenly became audible. Hanna listened and realized that it was coming from the piano, but it wasn't really music, there were no tunes. Single notes were repeated over and over again, as if a child was sitting at the piano, hitting the keys.

Hanna had the feeling that this was something familiar, something she'd heard before. The man she'd seen earlier dusting the keys was now tuning the piano. There had been a piano in Jonathan Forsman's house. Nobody played it, nobody was allowed to touch it. Forsman had the key to the locked lid on his watch chain. But twice a year a blind man came to tune the piano. There had to be silence in the house while that was happening. The piano tuner always came just after Forsman had returned from one of his many business trips with the sleigh or the coach. While the blind man leaned over the keyboard with his tuning key in his hand, Forsman would sit on a chair listening intently to what he heard. For him, perfect harmony was not the music, it was the well-tuned piano.

The piano tuner in the brothel resumed his work. Hanna could hear that he was tuning the keys at the bottom end of the bass register. The fact that he was carrying out the tuning gave her hope, unexpected strength. Nobody tunes a piano when somebody is dying, she thought. In those circumstances either everything is silent, or somebody plays something that soothes or consoles and then moves over into funeral music.

She remembered vaguely something that had happened in Forsman's house when the piano tuner

118

was there and Forsman was sitting back in an armchair enjoying the sound of harmony being restored, and she had suddenly thought: what can he see? What can the blind man see that I can't? She couldn't believe that all he could see before him was blackness.

Hanna could feel that she was tired. Felicia accompanied her back to her room. Somebody had changed the sheets while she'd been away. Her blood-stained underclothes had now been returned, washed clean.

Felicia turned to her in the doorway.

"What shall I tell Senhor Vaz?" she asked.

"That the white woman is still bleeding, not so much now, though. But she needs to be left alone for a few more days."

Felicia nodded.

"I promise not to send Carlos to you with cups of tea. Laurinda will look after you."

When Felicia had left the room, Hanna burst into tears. She did so in silence. Not because she didn't want anybody to hear her, but because she didn't want to scare her body so much that it started bleeding again.

CHAPTER
TWENTY-SEVEN

The whores told lies. Just like all other black people.

When Attimilio Vaz had introduced himself to Hanna, a week after she had taken up residence in his hotel and become sufficiently restored after her miscarriage to be able to leave her room without assistance and walk down to the ground floor for her meals, the first three sentences he spoke to her were:

"Don't believe what they say. It's best to believe nothing at all. The only thing black people here know how to do is to tell lies."

Hanna found this perplexing. Felicia had explained what had happened to her and gone on to look after her — Hanna quite simply couldn't understand the suggestion that she had been lying. To be sure, she had sometimes found it difficult to understand Felicia's peculiar language — but not so much that she could possibly have totally misunderstood or misinterpreted what she'd said and accepted it as the truth when in fact it was all lies.

The day Attimilio Vaz had decided to introduce himself to his hotel guest, he had spoken slowly and been careful not to use any unnecessarily difficult words.

120

Senhor Vaz was born in Portugal, but at some point long ago in his life he had spent time in Sweden, after a short stay in a Danish town that might have been called Odense, he wasn't sure. He had been selling Portuguese anchovies, but she got the impression that it hadn't been quite straightforward. It hadn't been his fault, of course. Attimilio Vaz considered himself to be an honest and upright person who unfortunately was often misunderstood. Even though he had been forced to leave Sweden in great haste after being accused of fraudulent dealing, he had memories of a delightful country and equally delightful people — and he was now pleased to welcome a Swedish guest into his simple but completely clean and above-board establishment.

A few days later, when Hanna felt strong enough to go out for the first time since she had arrived, he invited her to dinner at a restaurant in the same street as O Paraiso.

When she emerged into the street accompanied by her host, she suddenly felt the ground swaying under her feet. It was as if she were standing on the deck of the ship again. She stopped and leaned against the wall. Senhor Vaz was worried and asked if she wanted to go back to her room, but she shook her head. When he took hold of her arm she let him do so. No man had touched her since Lundmark's death. Now she was walking around an African town and a strange man, a Portuguese brothel proprietor, was escorting her to a restaurant.

It wasn't a dream, but she found herself in a world where she didn't belong.

Lundmark had been taller than she was. Senhor Vaz barely came up to her shoulders.

Hanna gathered from a sign on the side of a building that the street they were walking along was called rua Bagamoio. There were bars everywhere, some of them garishly lit up by hissing gas lamps, others dark, with wax candles flickering secretively behind curtains that swayed whenever anybody stepped quickly inside. But it was only this street that was illuminated. The narrow alleys leading off the rua Bagamoio were dark, silent, empty.

It reminded her of the forests that surrounded the river valley back home. There she could stand in a glade, enjoying the light of the sun. But if she took a couple of steps in among the tall tree trunks she entered a different world, deep in the darkness.

Apart from a few black beggars dressed in rags, everybody in the street was white. It was a while before Hanna realized that there were no other women. She was the only one. All around her were white men, some of them sailors, some soldiers, some drunk and noisy, others silent as they slunk furtively close to the walls, as if they didn't really want to be noticed. Inside the bars, however, were a lot of black women sitting on bar stools or sofas, smoking in silence.

She thought that if this was a town, she no longer knew what to call the place where Forsman lived. Did these two places have any similarities at all? The streets

122

where she and Berta had walked around together, and this murky town with its mysterious alleys?

A man was sitting on a street corner in front of a fire, tapping away at a drum that was so small he could hold it in the palm of his hand. His face was dripping with sweat, and in front of him he had laid out a little piece of cloth on which a few metal coins were gleaming. His fingers were pecking away at the drum skin like the beaks of eager birds. Hanna had never heard such a frantic rhythm before. She stopped. Vaz seemed impatient, but dug out a coin that he threw on to the piece of cloth before dragging her along with him again.

"He was barefoot," said Vaz. "If the police appear, they'll whisk him away."

Hanna didn't understand what he meant at first. But she noticed that the man with the little drum hadn't been wearing shoes.

"Why?" she asked.

"No negroes are allowed in the centre of town without shoes," said Vaz. "That's the law. After nine o'clock they have no right to be on our streets at all. Unless they are working, and can produce the appropriate documents. 'No black man or woman has the right of access to the streets of this town unless they are wearing shoes.' That's what the municipal law says. The first sign that a person is civilized is that he or she is wearing shoes."

Once again Hanna was unsure if she had understood properly what he had said. "Our streets?" Whose streets were they not, then?

Senhor Vaz stopped outside a restaurant that seemed to be wallowing in darkness. Hanna thought she could see the word *morte* on the sign board, but that surely couldn't be right. A restaurant in a red-light district could hardly have a name that included the concept of death.

Nevertheless, she was sure. That was the word she had seen, and it meant "dead" — it was one of the very first words she had learnt from Forsman's dictionary.

They ate fish grilled over an open fire. Senhor Vaz offered her wine, but she shook her head and he didn't insist. He was very friendly, only asked her a few questions about how she was feeling, and seemed to be keen to ensure that she was in good shape.

But there was something about his manner that made her cautious, possibly even suspicious. She answered his questions as fully as she could, but nevertheless had the feeling that she had closed all the doors to her innermost rooms, and locked them.

At the end of the meal he informed her that a nurse would be coming to the hotel the following day, and would stay on for as long as Hanna needed her help. Hanna tried to protest. She already had all the help she needed, from Laurinda and Felicia. But Senhor Vaz was very insistent.

"You need a white nurse," he said. "You can't rely on the blacks. Even if they seem to be looking after your best interests, the reality might be that they are poisoning you."

Hanna was struck dumb. Had she heard right? She didn't believe what he had said. But at the same time, she had the feeling that a white woman might be able to give her a different kind of company.

They walked home slowly through the night. Senhor Vaz linked arms with her. She didn't back off.

When they arrived back at the hotel, he bowed to her at the foot of the stairs and withdrew. Although it was late most of the prostitutes were sitting idle on their chairs, smoking or talking to one another in low voices. She gathered that it was not a good evening, and thought with disgust about what usually went on behind the closed doors.

Hanna looked for Felicia, but failed to see her. But when she was halfway up the stairs Felicia emerged from her room together with a white man with a bushy beard and an enormous pot belly. The sight made Hanna's stomach turn. She hurried to her room and closed the door — but just before she closed it her eyes met Felicia's. Very briefly, but despite everything they seemed to be exchanging an important message.

At that same moment she also saw Carlos, the chimpanzee dressed as a waiter, standing next to the piano with a cigar in his hand. He was looking round curiously. At that moment he seemed to be the most alive of all those occupying what was known as a house of pleasure.

CHAPTER
TWENTY-EIGHT

The following day a white woman with a stern-looking face appeared outside Hanna's door. Her name was Ana Dolores, and she spoke only Portuguese plus a few words of the local language Shangana. But as she spoke slowly and clearly, Hanna found it easier to understand her than both Felicia and Senhor Vaz.

After the arrival of Ana Dolores, Hanna was better able to understand what Senhor Vaz had said about black people telling lies. Ana was of the same opinion — indeed, if possible she was even more convinced of it than Senhor Vaz. She became Hanna's guide in a world that seemed to consist exclusively of lies.

Ana had been summoned because Senhor Vaz had been convinced that neither Dr Garibaldi nor the black servant girls would be able to help Hanna to fully recover. The very next day after his conversation with Felicia he had called a rickshaw and made the journey up the hills to the Pombal hospital. He had spoken to Senhor Vasconselous who was in charge of all the extensive hospital administration despite the fact that he was stone deaf and could only see out of his left eye. For many years Vasconselous had been a faithful client at O Paraiso every three weeks. He told his wife about the long and extremely complicated games of chess he played with his old friend Vaz. She didn't need to know that in fact he scarcely knew how to move the various pieces across the board. The only lady he wished to be served by when he visited the establishment was the beautiful Belinda Bonita, who was getting on in years but in view of her maturity attracted certain clients who couldn't stomach the thought of bedding any of the younger women.

Senhor Vaz told Senhor Vasconselous the facts: a white woman had come to stay at O Paraiso out of the blue. To make sure the deaf man on the other side of the desk understood, he wrote down what he was saying in large letters on the notepad with lined yellow paper that always lay in front of the old man.

What he wanted was straightforward. Senhor Vaz needed a trustworthy nurse to work for him in the hotel for as long as the white woman needed medical care. He stressed that it should be a mature woman who always wore her nurse's uniform whenever she visited the hotel. He didn't want to risk any of his clients getting the idea that the first white whore had arrived in Lourenço Marques. A woman who could also assume various playful and erotically arousing identities, such as that of a nurse for instance.

Or to be more accurate, perhaps: the second white prostitute in Lourenço Marques. Nobody, least of all Senhor Vaz, knew if it was a myth or something that had really happened, but it was claimed that there was a white woman who seduced clients into joining her in one of the dark alleys of the illuminated rua Bagamoio.

Nobody knew where she had come from, nobody was really sure if she actually existed. But occasionally half-naked men used to stagger out of the dark alleys with stories to tell about a beautiful white woman who could perform tricks that none of the black women seemed to be capable of.

Senhor Vaz had never believed these stories. He was convinced that in the world that black people lived in, lies carried more weight than the truth. Embedded in falsehoods were also superstition and fear, deceit and obsequiousness. From the very first day he had set foot on the quay in Lourenço Marques he had been convinced that one could never trust black people. Without their white overlords they would still be living the kind of life that Europeans left behind hundreds of years ago.

Senhor Vaz was a firm believer in the civilizing mission of the white race on the African continent. But that did not mean that he treated the women in his brothel badly. It's true that he occasionally smacked the girls if he was annoyed by them, but he never allowed that to develop into serious ill treatment.

Senhor Vasconcelous thought over what his friend had to say, then rang a bell. His secretary, a grossly overweight woman who Senhor Vaz recognized from the cathedral where he always attended Mass every Sunday, came into the room and was instructed to fetch nurse Ana Dolores, who was working on a ward for the mentally ill.

Senhor Vaz was a little worried when he heard this and wondered if his friend Vasconselous had misunderstood

128

him. He didn't need help looking after a white woman who was out of her mind. She had booked into his hotel, paid for several nights in advance, and then suddenly started to bleed. The bleeding had stopped now, but she was still weak and in need of care.

He wrote this latter point down in childishly large capital letters. Senhor Vasconselous read what was written with his short-sighted good eye, then wrote simply *si, entendo*, and lit a stump of a cigar.

Ana Dolores was very thin with a hatchet face characterized by some kind of rancour. Senhor Vaz was doubtful the moment she entered the room and had her task explained to her. As far as he was concerned it was just as important that she didn't scare off his clients as that she took care of the white woman confined to bed in room number 4. But he decided he had to rely on the judgement of his friend.

They agreed on a fee, shook hands, and decided that she should start work that very same evening. Senhor Vaz couldn't tell from the expression on Ana's face whether or not she knew about O Paraiso, but she could hardly have failed to be aware of the fact that rua Bagamoio was the most notorious red-light street in the whole of southern Africa. Vaz had a fair idea of the wages normally paid to an experienced nurse, and had immediately doubled that amount to prevent her from hesitating for financial reasons. He also promised her accommodation in room number 2, which was the biggest one in the hotel — more of a modest suite in fact, a large corner room with a bed recess and a picture window with views over the rooftops down to the harbour and the Katembe peninsular.

And so Hanna got to know Ana Dolores. When she woke up the following morning it was no longer Felicia sitting in the basket chair by the window, nor Laurinda on her silent feet carrying in a tray with a cup of tea and nibbles. Now it was a nurse dressed in white, standing in front of her and staring at her. Without a word she took her hand and measured her pulse. Then, with no indication as to whether she was satisfied or not, she leaned over Hanna's face, pulled her eyelid up and studied her pupils. Hanna noticed that this unknown nurse smelled of some fruit or flower she didn't recognize. Having examined Hanna's eyes, Ana then whipped down the thin duvet and exposed her lower abdomen. It happened so quickly that Hanna didn't have time to hide her modesty. She raised a hand, but Ana brushed it aside, almost as if it had been an insect, and opened her patient's legs wide. Without a word she contemplated Hanna's pudenda, lengthily, thoughtfully. Then she folded back the duvet and left the room.

Laurinda came in with the tea tray. She was wearing a thin white cotton blouse and a colourful *capulana* wrapped around her hips.

Hanna raised her hand and pointed to the door, trying to reproduce an outline of the woman who had just left the room.

Laurinda understood.

"Dona Ana Dolores," she said.

Hanna thought she could detect a trace of fear in Laurinda's voice when she pronounced the nurse's name.

But she couldn't be sure, of course. Not about that or anything else.

CHAPTER
TWENTY-NINE

Hanna was inflicted by some sort of infection that caused her a prolonged fever. She was cared for by Ana Dolores for two months. Her first feelings of being restored to health were followed by a period of extreme exhaustion which almost paralysed her. It was during this time that Ana taught Hanna how to speak Portuguese fluently. Whenever Hanna wasn't feeling too tired, they practised speaking.

But this was also when Hanna learnt how white people ought to treat the black people who worked at the hotel — the hotel which was first and foremost a brothel for white men who happened to be visiting the port. At first Hanna thought it was uncomfortable, having to witness the unconcealed contempt, the harsh condescension that characterized everything Ana did with regard to the black women who entered the sickroom. But as time passed, despite herself Hanna began to react less to what Ana said.

When Hanna had become well enough to leave her sickbed and go for increasingly long walks through town, always accompanied by Ana, she realized that the latter's behaviour was always the same: in the street, in the park, on one of the long beaches or in a shop — not just within the four walls of O Paraiso.

Ana Dolores took it for granted that black people were a lower order of beings. It reminded Hanna of the situation in Forsman's house. Even though he treated his servants better than most — Berta had explained that to her — he also had nothing but contempt for those near the bottom of the social ladder. Not only inside his own house, but in society in general. When Hanna had tried to protest and used herself as an example of Forsman's kindness, Berta had insisted that he didn't treat everyone like that. And Hanna had also noticed occasionally that Forsman could be condescending to the poor people he came across.

Ana explained it to her:

"The blacks are merely shadows of us. They have no colour. God made them black so that we didn't have to see them in the dark. And we should never forget where they came from."

Even though Hanna got used to it, she still regarded Ana's behaviour with unease. When she hit out at black women who didn't move out of her way, or didn't hesitate to smack children who tried to sell her bananas in the streets, Hanna simply wanted to run away. All the time, as if it were an obvious part of the job of caring for Hanna, Ana talked about their inferiority, their deceitfulness, their filthiness in both body and soul. Hanna's resistance decreased. She took on board what she heard, as if it were true after all. She realized that there was a crucial difference compared with the life she had lived in Forsman's house. There she had been one of the poor workers and servants. Here, because of the colour of her skin, she was on a quite different level, superior to the blacks. Here she was the one who made the decisions, who had the right to give orders and punish black people with divine blessing. Here she was the equivalent of Jonathan Forsman. Despite the fact that she was merely a cook who had deserted her ship.

One day, towards the end of the long time Ana was looking after Hanna, they went for a walk in the little botanical gardens a few streets away from the rua Bagamoio, next to the hill where the new, shiny white cathedral was being built. Both of them were carrying open parasols to protect them from the sun. It was very hot, and they sought out the shady areas of the park where it was a bit cooler. Notices on the iron entrance gates to the park informed visitors that benches were for whites only. The text was worded so threateningly that although they had a right to be in the park, blacks preferred not to go walking along the sandy paths. The only ones in the park on this occasion were half-naked gardeners weeding the flowerbeds, constantly on the lookout for poisonous snakes that might emerge from the fallen leaves.

Many of the benches were occupied that afternoon. Relaxing in the park were civil servants from the various colonial offices, mothers with daughters playing hopscotch and sons running after their hoops.

Ana suddenly stopped dead. Sitting fast asleep on a bench in front of her was an elderly black man. Hanna could see the anger in her face even before she hit the man on the shoulder. He woke up slowly, looked enquiringly at the two women, then prepared to go back to sleep.

Once before in her life Hanna had seen an old man open his eyes in that same slow way. It was when she and Jukka had entered the room where the old man who had been a lodger in her relatives' house was lying in his filthy bed. Just like him, this old black man barely knew where he was. He seemed hungry, thin and on the brink of dehydration. His skin was stretched tightly over his cheekbones.

Before Hanna had chance to react Ana had grabbed hold of him, lifted him up like a floppy doll and thumped him so hard that he went flying into a clump of rhododendron bushes. He remained lying there on the ground while Ana wiped the bench with a handkerchief, then beckoned Hanna to sit down.

For a brief moment everything in the park came to a stop. The hoops stopped rolling, the ladies on the benches fell silent, the half-naked gardeners with their sweaty bodies crouching down in the flowerbeds remained stock-still. Afterwards, when normality had been restored, Hanna wondered if the stillness was due to what had already happened, or to what was going to happen.

Would anything at all happen, in fact?

Hanna glanced furtively at Ana, who was holding her parasol in one hand and slowly waving the other one in front of her face. Hanna looked behind her. The old man was still lying among the blossoming bushes. He wasn't moving at all.

I don't understand this, she thought. Lying behind the bench I'm sitting on is an old man who has been beaten and flung on to the ground, and nobody is doing anything to help him. Not even I.

She didn't know how long they remained seated on the bench, but when Ana decided it was time to go back to O Paraiso, the old man had vanished. Perhaps he had crawled deeper into the clump of rhododendron bushes, and hidden himself alongside the poisonous snakes that everybody was scared of.

A few days later something took place that shook her deeply, and made her wonder what was happening to her. Laurinda dropped a dish when she was serving Hanna's morning tea. The dish shattered when it hit the stone floor. Hanna was standing in front of the mirror, combing her hair: she turned round quickly and slapped Laurinda on the side of the head. Then she pointed at the shards and told her to pick them up.

Laurinda crawled around on her hands and knees, picking up the bits of porcelain. Meanwhile Hanna sat on the edge of the bed, waiting for the tea to cool down sufficiently for her to be able to drink it.

Laurinda stood up. That annoyed Hanna.

"Who said you were allowed to stand up?" she asked. "There are still bits of china on the floor."

Laurinda got down on her knees again. Hanna was still annoyed because she could never read Laurinda's thoughts from her facial expression. Was she afraid that Hanna was going to punish her? Or merely indifferent, or even filled with contempt for this white woman whose life she had once helped to save?

Laurinda's eyes were very bright, gleaming with a sort of mysterious inner radiance that Hanna could never recall having seen in the eyes of a white person.

"You can go now," she said. "But I want to know when you are coming and going. I want you always to wear shoes when you wait on me."

Laurinda stood up and disappeared into the darkness. She somehow managed to make her bare heels sound like shoe heels. Hanna assumed she was on her way to the kitchen to partake of some of Mandrillo the chef's stew.

Hanna remained seated in the darkness. Shadows were dancing around the gas lamp. She tried to envisage the house by the river in her mind's eye. Elin, her brother and sisters, the brown and clear water flowing down from the mountains.

But she could see nothing. It was as if everything was hidden behind a film her eyes couldn't penetrate.

She regretted the way she had treated Laurinda. It frightened her — the ease with which she had humiliated this friendly woman. She felt ashamed.

Hanna slept badly that night. The next day the chimpanzee came up to her room. He was carrying a silver tray with a flower from the jacaranda tree, sent to her by Senhor Vaz. There was no message, only his name.

CHAPTER
THIRTY

The blue flower from the jacaranda tree was still alive, floating in a little shallow dish of water, when something happened that changed Hanna's life, yet again.

It was early morning when she went downstairs, feeling fit again at last, even if she was still grieving over the loss of Lundmark.

A white man with his shirt unbuttoned, barefoot, but still with his hat on his head, was lying on a sofa, fast asleep. There was no sign of the women who worked in the brothel: they were still asleep in their rooms — alone or together with clients who had paid for a whole night's indulgence. The only other being awake at this time in the morning was Carlos the chimpanzee. He was curled up on the ceiling light, swinging slowly backwards and forwards as he observed her movements.

There was no sign of Senhor Vaz either. Hanna was enveloped in a musty smell of cigars and strong drink, despite the fact that the venetian blinds were up and the windows open. The black man in charge of the entrance door was asleep in the shadows outside it.

Hanna stood in the open doorway, careful not to wake up the watchman. A group of black men pulling a cart full of buckets of night soil stopped and stared at her. She went back inside. Once the cart had clattered off on its way, she went back to the doorway. Something similar happened again, only this time it was two white men wearing straw hats and carrying leather briefcases who stopped dead and stared at her. Once again she went back inside.

Was there something wrong with her clothes? Hanna stood in front of one of the many mirrors hanging on the walls. She was dressed in white, with a brown shawl over her shoulders, and as usual she had gathered her hair into a bun at the back of her head. She could see that she had lost weight, and was very pale. For the first time in her life her skin was now the same milky white as her mother's. But Hanna's face was her father's. She could see him in the mirror. He seemed to be coming closer to her, and eventually was standing right next to her face.

That thought saddened her. If a door behind her back hadn't opened at precisely the same time, she might well have burst out crying. When she turned round she saw a hunchbacked man, short in stature, almost dwarf-like, enter the room. He limped, and his head jerked every time he took a step. She recognized the piano tuner she had hitherto only seen sitting on the piano stool. He made his way cautiously between all the chairs and sofas. He paused for a moment when he bumped into one of the sleeping man's naked feet, but eventually arrived at the piano.

He sat down, opened the lid, and stroked his hands over the keys as if he were caressing the skin of a woman or a child. Hanna stood there motionless, observing him: she was reminded of Forsman's piano, and the thought struck her that she wanted to go back home as soon as possible. She didn't belong here, and would never do so.

The man at the piano suddenly turned to look at her.

He said something she didn't understand. When she didn't respond, he repeated what he had said.

Then Hanna started speaking Swedish. Silence was not a language. She said who she was, her name, and explained about the ship she had come here on and then abandoned.

She spoke without pausing, as if she were afraid that somebody might interrupt her. The man at the piano didn't move a muscle.

When Hanna finished talking, he nodded slowly. It was as if he had understood what she said.

He turned back to the piano, took a tuning key out of his pocket and started caressing the keys. Hanna had the impression that he was trying to do it as quietly as possible, so as not to disturb those who were still asleep.

The man lying on the sofa sat up drowsily. When he saw Hanna he gave a start and stared at her as if he couldn't believe his eyes. Then he tried to talk to her. She just shook her head and went back up the stairs to her room. She sat down on her bed, took the pound notes from among her underclothes and counted them. It was clear that she definitely had enough to enable her

140

to head back home to Sweden. She might not even need to work her passage, but could perhaps be a paying passenger on a ship sailing to her homeland.

There was a knock on the door. Hanna quickly gathered up the money and hid it under the pillow. When there came a second knock, she stood up and opened the door. She thought it would be Laurinda who was already serving up her breakfast tray, but in fact it was the man who had been sleeping on the sofa. He still had his hat on his head and was barefoot. His shirt was unbuttoned and his pot belly hung down over his waistband. He was holding a bottle of cognac in one hand. He smiled, and spoke in a low voice as if he were encouraging a doubtful dog. She was about to shut the door when he put one of his bare feet in the way. Then he pushed her over so that she fell down on the bed. He closed the door, put the bottle on the table and produced a few notes from his trouser pocket. She was just about to get up off the bed when he gave a roar and pushed her back down again. He put the notes on the table, ripped her blouse open and started pulling up her skirt. When she resisted he slapped her hard. She still didn't understand what he was saying, but she understood what was happening. She managed to wriggle out of his grasp, picked up the bottle he had put on the table and hit him so hard on the arm with it that it broke. At the same time, she shouted for help — as loudly as she could.

The blow and the subsequent shriek made the man hesitate. He let go of Hanna, and stared at her. She heard footsteps and then the door opened.

It was Senhor Vaz standing there, wearing a red silk dressing gown. Carlos was perched on his shoulders, then he launched into an attack on the unknown man. Carlos bit the man's hand so savagely that he submitted.

CHAPTER
THIRTY-ONE

Senhor Vaz was dishevelled. He must have been woken up by Hanna's scream. But even if he was half asleep, he realized immediately what had been happening. The man, a Boer by the name of Fredrik Prinsloo, standing there half naked with uncut toenails like the claws on a cat, had been causing trouble for several years whenever he visited O Paraiso. Now he found himself fighting a desperate but losing battle against the ape that was biting him and ripping off his clothes.

Senhor Vaz shouted out a command. Carlos immediately stopped fighting and jumped up on to Hanna's bed. In one hand he was holding a handkerchief he had managed to snatch from Prinsloo, who was bleeding quite badly.

Fredrik Prinsloo belonged to one of the earliest families to emigrate to Cape Town from Europe. Now he was a major landowner in the province of Transvaal, and had set up a business organizing safaris for rich hunters from America. One of his customers was the then President Theodore Roosevelt, who was a hopeless shot but nevertheless, with the discreet assistance of Prinsloo, succeeded in bagging vast numbers of buffalo, lion, leopard and giraffe.

Senhor Vaz had heard the story about the American president ad nauseam during the many conversations he had been compelled to have with Prinsloo. But despite the Boer's boasts, he had to be handled with respect. Prinsloo was not just a regular customer, but he also recommended Vaz's brothel to his friends whenever they felt the need to engage in erotic antics with black women. As Senhor Vaz had realized that the Boer never failed to start quarrelling with other customers, he introduced a special routine whenever Prinsloo indicated that he was on his way. Vaz dug out a notice that he hung on to the front door announcing that a "private party" was taking place. All this meant in practice was that Senhor Vaz himself kept a close check on the number of clients allowed in that evening.

On these occasions wild rumours circulated around the town of abandoned orgies involving activities that no decent person could possibly imagine even in their wildest dreams. Senhor Vaz was well aware of these rumours, and also knew that they created a sort of magic aura around O Paraiso, which increased its appeal and also his income.

But he had also established that Prinsloo often treated black women extremely brutally. For a man like Prinsloo black skin was merely a shell that concealed stupidity, ignorance and idleness. But to do what Prinsloo did and combine this contempt with what seemed at times to be an irrational hatred was something that Vaz couldn't understand. Why this hatred? Nobody hates animals, apart from snakes, cockroaches and rats. Let's face it, black people don't

144

have poisonous fangs. Extremely cautiously, he had often raised the matter with Prinsloo; but he had beaten a hasty retreat when Prinsloo became hot under the collar and refused to answer.

Prinsloo was also an unpredictable person. He could be generous and friendly, but he sometimes reached a tipping point. When that happened, he would start treating the prostitutes and servants with a degree of cruelty that terrified everybody he came into contact with. Senhor Vaz had instructed his most trusted servants to inform him immediately when Prinsloo had one of his attacks. On several occasions, apparently without provocation, the Boer had suddenly started hitting or whipping the black whore he had been bedding at the time. Senhor Vaz would then intervene with the assistance of the burly security officer who for some reason was called Judas. Their combined efforts would be enough to rescue the naked, bleeding woman from Prinsloo's attacks. The Boer never offered any resistance, but nor did he ever express any regret. What he had done simply didn't seem to bother him. Prinsloo never gave any extra money to the women he had attacked, nor did he hesitate to ask for their services again the next time he visited the brothel.

But Senhor Vaz had drawn a line there. Nobody who had been subjected to Prinsloo's brutality need ever go to bed with him again. He simply explained that she was busy with other clients, and would be otherwise occupied all the time Prinsloo stayed at O Paraiso, which was usually three or four days. He wasn't sure whether or not Prinsloo had seen through him, but the

Boer was allowed to choose from all the other women and precautions were taken to act immediately if ever he started mistreating the woman he had selected to satisfy his desires on any given occasion.

Senhor Vaz worried about the hatred that Prinsloo had manifested. He didn't understand it, and it scared him. It was as if it was warning him about a danger. Something he wasn't aware of himself.

As he stood there in the doorway, half asleep, and observed the semi-naked Prinsloo squaring up to the white woman with her blouse ripped away, he recognized that things had now gone too far. Prinsloo hadn't hesitated to attack one of the hotel residents, and a white woman at that. Senhor Vaz could no longer overlook his behaviour. And he felt he had been insulted personally.

As far as he was concerned, there could be nothing worse. Being insulted meant that death was testing his powers of resistance.

CHAPTER
THIRTY-TWO

Senhor Vaz was short in stature and not especially strong. But his anger was such that he didn't hesitate to grab hold of Prinsloo's shirt collar, drag him out of the room and then push him down the stairs. The scream from the upper floor had woken up the sleeping whores. Many of the women were not particularly fond of some of their colleagues, but they seldom came to blows, although it did happen now and then. But if the danger came from outside their circle, they were all united against it.

Now they were standing by the staircase as Prinsloo came tumbling down. Vaz followed behind him, followed in turn by Judas, and behind him Carlos, who was chewing Prinsloo's white handkerchief.

Senhor Vaz stopped on the bottom step and looked sternly at Prinsloo, who had hit his head and was bleeding from one eyebrow and the hand where Carlos had bitten him.

"Get out of here," he said. "And never come back again."

Prinsloo pressed his hand against his eyebrow and seemed at first not to have understood what Senhor Vaz had said. Then he stood up on unsteady legs, made a threatening gesture at the prostitutes who were standing round him, then took a step forward towards Senhor Vaz.

"You know that I usually bring my friends here with me," he said. "If you throw me out, you throw them all out as well."

"I'll be only too pleased to explain to them why I don't want you here."

Prinsloo didn't reply. He was still bleeding. He suddenly roared loudly and bent over forwards, as if he was in great pain.

"Water," he yelled. "Warm water. I must wipe away the blood."

Senhor Vaz nodded to one of the women, indicating that she should bring some water. He shooed the others away. They returned quietly to their rooms. Prinsloo sat down on the edge of a sofa. When the girl brought him an enamel washbasin he carefully washed away the blood from his forehead and his hand.

"Ice," he said then.

Senhor Vaz himself went out into the kitchen and chopped a couple of large lumps of ice from the blocks in the icebox, then wrapped them up in towels. Prinsloo pressed them against his wounds. When the bleeding had stopped he stood up, buttoned up his shirt, put on his socks and shoes and left through the door.

He left the lumps of ice in the towels lying on the floor next to the sofa. Senhor Vaz carried them into the kitchen, then went back up the stairs and knocked on the door of room number 4. When he heard Hanna's voice he opened the door and entered the room. She was sitting on the edge of the bed, and had replaced the torn blouse with a different one.

Senhor Vaz looked for signs that she had been crying, but found none. He sat down on the only chair in the room.

Not a word was spoken, but Hanna had the feeling nevertheless that he was apologizing for what had happened.

When he eventually stood up, bowed and left the room, she was more convinced than ever that she ought to leave this town as soon as possible.

Africa scared the living daylights out of her. It was full of people she couldn't understand, and who didn't understand her.

She must get away. But even so, she didn't regret having abandoned Captain Svartman's ship. That had been the right thing to do in the circumstances. But what was the right thing to do now?

She didn't know. There was no answer to that question.

She thought: that dark river is still flowing inside me. The ice hasn't formed on it yet.

CHAPTER
THIRTY-THREE

That very same day she went down to the harbour. Senhor Vaz didn't want her to wander around town on her own, and sent Judas as a sort of bodyguard. He walked a few paces behind her. Every time she turned round he stopped and looked down at the ground. He didn't dare to look her in the eye.

How can he possibly protect me? she thought. When he doesn't even dare to look me in the eye.

There were a lot of ships berthed by the various quays. Still more were riding at anchor in the roadstead. It was low tide, and large parts of the lagoon that formed the outer harbour were silted up, with old wrecks sticking out of the black mud. She searched for a ship flying the Swedish flag in the inner harbour, but in vain. Nor could she see a Danish one, the only other flag she had learnt to recognize. The ships in the roadstead were all flying flags she couldn't identify.

It was very busy on the quays, with ships being frantically loaded and unloaded. She watched a net full of elephants' tusks being hoisted up on a crane and lowered into a hold. Gleaming pianos and motor cars were lifted out of another ship, and in one of the nets

150

deposited on the quays were several elegant sofas and armchairs.

The half-naked workers were dripping with sweat as they carried their burdens along swaying gangplanks. And wherever she looked there were white men in topees keeping watch over their slaves like hungry beasts of prey. She soon decided she could no longer bear to watch all these tortured and torturing people. She left the harbour.

Just as she was leaving the waterfront she decided she would take an indirect route back to the hotel. With the sturdily built Judas behind her, she had no need to feel afraid.

He's my fifth attendant, she thought: Elin was first, then Forsman, and then Berta, Lundmark, and now this gigantic black man who doesn't dare to look me in the eye.

She spent a long time wandering around the town that afternoon. For the first time she had the feeling that she was seeing everything clearly. Before, everything seemed to have been shrouded by the strong sunlight. Now at last she was able to become acquainted with this town to which she was originally scheduled to pay merely a fleeting visit in order to take on board fresh water and food supplies before Captain Svartman set off for the long voyage to Australia in his *Lovisa*.

But she had jumped ship here, and was still here. All the darkness she had experienced was now at last beginning to disperse. She was beginning to see properly the foreign world which now surrounded her.

It suddenly dawned on her that it was Sunday. One of the first days in October. But the seasons had changed places. Now it wasn't winter and the cold that was in store. On the contrary, the increasing heat indicated that summer had arrived early this year. She had heard Senhor Vaz discussing this with his brothel clients. The sun can burn you just as the cold can burn you, she thought. But perhaps my skin is hardened to the heat, thanks to the fact that I'm used to the cold?

She had come to the end of a street that opened out on to a hill, on the top of which the town's as yet unfinished cathedral towered up towards the heavens. The bright sunlight was reflected off the white stone walls. She had to screw up her eyes so that what surrounded her was not transformed into a mirage by the heat haze. Wherever she looked, everything seemed to be deserted. There were no other people about. Only the big black man behind her, always motionless whenever she turned round.

She walked up the hill. The cathedral doors were standing open. She stopped in the shadow of the tall tower. It's like a meringue, she thought as she looked at the white stone. Or a cake that I saw in Forsman's house when one of his children was having a birthday party.

She stood in the shadows, wiping her face with a handkerchief. Judas was standing in full sunlight. She tried beckoning to him, indicating that he too should come and stand in the shade. But he stayed where he was, with sweat pouring down his face.

152

She suddenly heard singing coming from the dark interior of the cathedral. Children, she thought — children singing in a choir. The singing was interrupted by an echoing voice, but then it began again, a repetition of the same tune. This was evidently a choir practice. She stepped cautiously into the darkness, unsure as to whether she was allowed to enter this church. Were prayers said to the same God here as in the churches she had previously been to, in the mountains and in Sundsvall? She paused, hesitant, while her eyes slowly got used to the darkness that was in such sharp contrast with the sunlight outside.

Then she saw them. The choir. Children in white robes with a red belt round their waist, boys and girls, all of them black. In front of them a small white man with bushy hair and hands moving like soft wings. Nobody had noticed her yet. She stood there and listened. There were a few more repetitions before the choirmaster was satisfied.

And now the children dressed in white sang a hymn. It was so beautiful that it was almost painful. She stood there listening, with tears in her eyes, thinking that she had never heard anything so indescribably beautiful. The children sang in exquisite harmony, the hymn was powerful and rhythmic. All of them kept their eyes fixed on the little man's gentle hand movements. None of the children seemed to be frightened of him.

It seemed to her that here and now, in the darkness, for the first time, she was seeing people who were not afraid. There was nothing here of what usually scared her to death. Here, inside the dark cathedral, she

153

thought, there was nobody telling lies. There was nothing here apart from the truth in the hymn and the white hands moving like wings full of energy.

Then she suddenly noticed that one of the children, a girl, had seen her and had lost contact with the choirmaster, even though she continued singing in tune.

Hanna thought that she could recognize herself, it was as if she had been transformed into that girl, with her dark skin and big brown eyes.

She and the girl kept on looking at each other until the hymn was finished. Then the choirmaster noticed her. She gave a start and thought once again that she didn't really have the right to be there. But he smiled and nodded, and said something she didn't understand before resuming his choir practice.

Hanna was tempted to join the children. To be a part of the singing. But she stayed where she was in the shadows, transported by the children's voices.

She wished she had dared to join them. But she didn't have the necessary courage.

It was only when the practice was over, the children had left and the choirmaster had packed away his battered old briefcase that she went back out into the bright sunlight.

CHAPTER
THIRTY-FOUR

Judas was still standing on the same spot.

"Why don't you stand in the shade?" she asked, making no attempt to disguise the fact that she was annoyed. His behaviour had spoilt her experience in the cathedral.

He didn't answer as he hadn't understood what she said. He simply wiped the sweat from his brow, then let his arm hang loosely by his side again.

She returned to O Paraiso where Senhor Vaz was pacing up and down in the street outside, looking worried. He was carrying an umbrella as a substitute for a parasol to protect him from the sun. Carlos had climbed up on to the hotel sign and was throwing chips gathered from the stone roof at a dog down below. When Hanna arrived back, Senhor Vaz immediately started berating the black man. She didn't understand what he was saying as he was speaking so quickly, but she gathered he had been worried that something had happened to her.

The black man still said nothing, but she had the impression that he was unmoved by the fit of rage aimed at him. And as she watched Senhor Vaz growing more and more furious, she noticed something that hadn't occurred to her before.

Even if Judas was afraid of his white master, Senhor Vaz was just as afraid. The gigantic black man was not the only one on the defensive. Naturally, he couldn't allow himself to react to the white man standing in front of him and shouting at him. That would be a punishable offence, and could lead to imprisonment or a beating. But now Hanna could see that Senhor Vaz was also afraid — a different sort of fear, but just as strong. And didn't the same apply to Ana Dolores as well? She would boss the black servant girls and prostitutes about, give them orders, and was never satisfied with what they did, nor did she ever thank them. But wasn't she also possessed by a never-ceasing flood of unease and fear?

The outburst came to an end just as quickly as it had begun. Senhor Vaz dismissed Judas with a wave of the hand, and offered Hanna his arm to take her with him into the coolest of the rooms, overlooking the sea. Judas squatted down next to the house.

Senhor Vaz flopped down on to a chair, placed his hands over his heart as if he had just been indulging in something extremely strenuous, and warned her at great length about the dangers of going for long walks in the extreme heat. He told her about friends of his who had suffered from heatstroke, especially after spending time in places where the sun was reflected by white stone, or by the sand on the town's beaches. But above all he warned her against relying too much on the support offered by blacks.

She didn't understand what he was trying to say.

"Is it dangerous for black people to look at you?" she asked.

Senhor Vaz shook his head in annoyance, as if the strain he had just undergone had used up all his patience.

"A white woman shouldn't walk around too much on her own," he said. "That's just the way it is."

"I went to the cathedral and listened to the black children singing."

"They sing very beautifully. They have a remarkable ability to harmonize without needing to practise all that much. But white ladies should only go for short walks. And preferably not at all when it's very hot."

She wanted to ask more about the unlikely danger she had evidently exposed herself to. But Senhor Vaz raised his hand, he didn't have the strength to answer any more questions. He remained seated on the chair, his white hat on his knee, his black walking stick made from a wood known as *pau preto* leaning against one of his legs, and seemed to be lost in thought.

After a while Hanna stood up and left the room. Senhor Vaz had fallen asleep, his mouth half open, his eyebrows twitching, snoring softly.

When she looked out of the front door, she found that Judas was no longer there. She wondered where he lived, if he was married, if he had any children.

But most of all she wondered what he was thinking.

That evening she had dinner in her room once again. One of the black servant girls whose name she didn't know brought her food. She also moved without making a sound, just like Laurinda. She wondered if these silent movements also had to do with fear — the fear she was beginning to see more and more of.

She ate the food: rice, boiled vegetables whose taste she didn't recognize, and a grilled chicken leg. There were many spices, completely new to her. But she ate her fill. She drank tea with her food. What was left over she drank later on when it had grown cold, as a substitute for water in the evening and during the night.

That was one of the last pieces of advice Lundmark had given her before he suddenly fell ill and died. Never drink unboiled water.

She had followed his advice. Now that she wasn't bleeding any more and was no longer carrying what would have been their child, her stomach wasn't causing her any problems.

What she was now carrying was merely emptiness.

CHAPTER
THIRTY-FIVE

She put the tray on the floor outside her room and locked the door. She took off all her clothes and lay naked on her bed. The curtain in front of the window was hanging motionless. There was something sinful about lying naked on a bed, she thought. Sinful because there is no man here who desires me, nobody I would allow to take advantage of me. She reached for the blanket in order to cover up her body, but then changed her mind. There was nobody who could see her hiding away here. If there was a God who was invisible but all-seeing, He would surely allow a person to lie down naked when the heat was so suffocating.

That evening she lay there for a long time, thinking about the fear she thought she had detected in Senhor Vaz's eyes. She had never seen fear like that in her mother or father. There was an upper class in Sweden, of course, but it didn't need to be frightening if you co-operated with it. But here, things were different. Here, everybody was afraid, even if the whites tried to hide their fear behind a front of either calmness and self-control, or well-planned outbursts of rage.

She thought: where is my fear? Am I not afraid because I don't have anybody to be afraid of? Am I completely alone?

The solitary world. She would never be able to cope with that. She had grown up as a human being in the company of others. She would never be able to survive in a world without that communion.

That evening she regretted having jumped ship. If she had continued the voyage to Australia, perhaps the feeling of being unable to cope with the loss of Lundmark would have faded away? Despite everything, there was a feeling of community on board that she was a part of. She felt like an insect, flapping its wings frantically, trapped inside a glass that had been turned upside down.

But that feeling also faded away. She knew she had done what she was forced to do. If she had stayed on board the ship, she might well eventually have jumped overboard. Lundmark's constant shadow-like presence would have driven her mad.

She was about to fall asleep, still naked on top of the bedcover, when she heard the sound of raindrops on the tin roof. The sound gradually grew louder, and before long it was the booming of tropical rain. She got up and pulled the curtain to one side. The mosquitoes had fled the heavy rain, so she could allow the cooling air to flow freely into the room.

It was pitch-dark outside. There were no fires burning. The rain drowned all other noises. There was no sound of voices or the gramophone from the ground floor.

She held out her hand and let the rain patter on to her skin.

I must go home, she thought again. I can't cope with living here, surrounded by all this fear and a loneliness that is threatening to suffocate me.

She remained standing by the window until the heavy but short-lived rain had stopped. She closed the curtain and went back to bed, still without covering herself with the blanket.

The following day, and for many days to come, she went down to the harbour to see if a ship flying the Swedish flag had berthed by a quay or was waiting in the roadstead. Judas always accompanied her, keeping watch in silence a few paces behind her.

It is October, 1904. She is waiting.

CHAPTER
THIRTY-SIX

The piano tuner's name was José, but he was never called anything but Zé, and he was Senhor Vaz's brother. That was a discovery she made after having lived for quite a long time in the brothel. No matter how much she studied the two men, she couldn't see any similarities. But Zé assured her there was no doubt at all that they had the same parents. Even though she soon gathered that Zé was somewhat mentally challenged, she had no reason to doubt him on this point. And why would Senhor Vaz allow him to sit there tuning the piano day after day unless there was some special reason? Senhor Vaz was looking after his brother because their parents had passed away.

In a word, Senhor Vaz loved him. Hanna noted the touching solicitude with which he treated his brother. If any of the clients complained about the constant tuning of the piano, she witnessed with her own eyes how Senhor Vaz would order the man out of the building and would never allow him back in. Zé had permission to tune the piano or polish the keys as often and for as long as he wanted.

But there were exceptions, of course. When the brothel was visited by prominent men from South

Africa, leading figures in the government or the church, Vaz would lead his brother gently to the room behind the kitchen where Zé had his bed. The beautiful Belinda Bonita, who was always well informed about everything that went on in the brothel, told Hanna that there was also an old piano in that room. The keys were still there, but all the instrument's strings had been cut and removed.

So Zé would sit in his room, tuning a silent piano.

Zé lived in a world of his own. He was a few years older than his brother, seldom spoke unless he was spoken to, tuned his strings or merely sat quietly hunched over the piano as if he were waiting for something that was never going to happen. He was like a ticking clock, Hanna thought, with nothing happening to interrupt the regular rhythm.

But that wasn't completely true, she realized one day when she had been living in the brothel for nearly four months. As usual she had strolled down to the harbour together with her gigantic bodyguard, and looked to see if she could find a ship flying the Swedish flag: but there was none to be seen on this occasion either. She had bought a pair of binoculars from an Indian businessman who also sold cameras and spectacles. Thanks to the magnified images she was able to establish that none of the ships waiting in the roadstead was displaying a Swedish flag. Every time she returned to the hotel she did so with mixed feelings of disappointment and relief. Disappointment because she really did want to return home, relief because she dreaded ever having to board a ship again.

The moment she entered O Paraiso she could see that Zé wasn't in his usual place at the piano. But she didn't have time to ask where he was before he made his grand entry. The women who had been lounging around on the sofas or leaning over the billiard table patting balls back and forth with rather silly flourishes of the hand burst out laughing but also applauded him when he appeared. He had changed out of his usual crumpled dark suit into a white one. Instead of the usual dirty beret pulled down over the back of his head, Zé was now wearing a panama hat similar to the one his brother usually wore. In addition he had a white shirt with a high collar and a black cravat, elaborately tied. In one hand he was carrying a bunch of white paper flowers. He stood in front of the woman whose name was Deolinda, but who was never called anything other than A Magrinha, since she was so thin, flat-breasted and totally lacking in the usual female characteristics.

Hanna had sometimes looked at her and wondered how on earth she could attract a man. She preferred not to think that thought through to its logical conclusion, but she couldn't avoid it: Deolinda was ugly. It seemed to Hanna that the whole of her emaciated person radiated sorrow and suffering. But she did have clients, Hanna knew that: she had seen them going with Deolinda. She found it totally repulsive to imagine A Magrinha in bed with one of the white men who patronized the brothel; but she evidently had something that enticed them and aroused their desires.

164

Zé bowed and handed over his paper flowers. Deolinda stood up, took him by the arm and led him to her room in the corridor where clients were entertained. They were sent on their way by merry laughter and renewed applause before the room was once again characterized by apathetic idleness.

There were always a few hours in the late afternoon when nothing really happened in the brothel. Clients rarely if ever appeared. The women dozed off, painted their nails, or possibly exchanged a few whispered confidences.

None of the black women apart from Felicia ever spoke to Hanna unless she asked them a question or requested something. Senhor Vaz had made it clear to her that the women in his establishment were there not only to satisfy their clients, but that they were also supposed to serve the hotel guests. She still didn't know how they regarded her: they greeted her, smiled at her, but never attempted to be friendly with her. And she didn't know what was meant by their being "supposed to serve the hotel guests". After all, she was the only person renting a room.

She sat down at the end of a sofa next to Esmeralda, who was one of the oldest of the women, with a bird-like face and the longest fingers Hanna had ever seen.

Silence descended on the room. Hanna realized that this was the first time she had ever sat down next to one of the black women.

She pointed at the corridor into which Deolinda and Zé had just disappeared.

165

"A pair of lovers?" she asked.

Esmeralda nodded.

"Yes, they are a pair of lovers," she said. "He sometimes gets that feeling. Then he forgets his piano. It happens every other month or so. He changes his clothes, and it is always Deolinda he chooses."

Hanna wanted to ask more questions, not least to make sure that she had understood properly: but Esmeralda stood up in an impressively dignified fashion. As far as she was concerned the conversation was at an end. She glided away to her room, her hips swaying attractively.

Hanna also rose to her feet and went up the stairs. She didn't need to turn round to know that all the nine women left down below were watching her attentively. They look at us when we turn our backs on them, she thought. They are not afraid to look each other in the eye; but they are afraid of our eyes just as we are afraid of theirs.

She closed the door behind her, bolted it, and undressed from the waist up. She washed herself in cold water, using a linen cloth. She licked one of her lower arms and could taste all the salt from the perspiration that had been pouring off her. Then she lay down on the bed and closed her eyes. But she sat up again almost immediately. She had remembered something she hadn't thought about since she left Sweden on the ship which must have long since docked in Australia with its cargo of timber.

She dug out the hymn book with the golden embossing in which she had hidden the gold coins she had once been given by Forsman. Between the pages was also a black and white photograph. It was of Berta and herself, taken in Bernard Dunn's photo-studio in Sundsvall.

CHAPTER
THIRTY-SEVEN

It had been Berta's idea. She was always the one who came out with the boldest and most unexpected suggestions.

"We must have a photograph," she had said. "Before you go away. I'm frightened of forgetting what you look like. Frightened of forgetting what we both look like together."

Hanna started worrying immediately. She had never been to a photographer before, didn't know what to do. But Berta dismissed all her objections. Besides, both she and Hanna had received a little gift from Forsman, like all the others who worked for him. Forsman's business had just celebrated its twenty-fifth birthday, and he wanted to mark the occasion by being generous to his employees. The money would pay for the photograph.

They managed to arrange for a couple of hours off one day in the spring when the days were getting longer. Dunn, the photographer, had a studio on the main square. They had put on their best clothes, polished their shoes, and been placed by a table with a chair. Behind them was a white plaster statue of a dragon-slayer with a raised sword. The photographer,

168

who was Danish and spoke a variation of Swedish that was difficult to understand, instructed Berta to sit down on the chair, with Hanna standing behind her, next to her shoulder. To balance the photograph and give it artistic form, he placed a vase of paper flowers on the table.

It was the flowers in Zé's hand when he bowed in front of Deolinda, so similar to the ones in the photograph, that had jogged Hanna's memory.

She lay on the bed and looked at the picture. They had received two copies, and kept one each. Berta was smiling at the camera, while Hanna looked more serious. She tried to imagine what Berta would have done if she had been the one lying here in bed on the upper floor of an African brothel, disguised as a hotel. But the photograph provided no answer, Berta said nothing.

She laid the photograph on her naked chest, which had started to dry now. I never expected anything like this, she thought. When Elin stood in front of me and said that I must travel to the coast in order to earn a living, I was totally incapable of imagining what would happen. Perhaps what Hanna was thinking now was confirmation of the fact that she had grown up and was an adult now? Perhaps the big secret was the realization that you never knew what was in store for you? If you made the break and left behind everything that was known and familiar?

Elin can't see me now, she thought. Berta can't see me, nor can my brother and sisters. I live in a world that we only share in the sense that it's incomprehensible,

169

not only for them but also for me, and I'm living in the middle of it.

She unbolted the door and fell asleep. Soon Laurinda would come up with her evening meal on a tray — they had agreed that whenever Hanna didn't turn up at the separate table allocated to her by Senhor Vaz, Laurinda would take a tray up to her room. That evening the main course was oily deep-fried fish, something Hanna had somehow managed to get down her on a previous occasion. She tried again, but soon pushed the plate aside and ate the dessert, which was half a coconut with slices of pineapple.

When Laurinda came back to collect the tray, Hanna tried to get her to stay by talking to her. Every time she saw Laurinda she had a bad conscience on account of that slap she had given her some time ago. She thought she could go some way towards making up for that by being friendly and talking to Laurinda. After a lot of patience-testing attempts she had finally managed to make Laurinda reply to her questions with more than monosyllables. Sometimes she could even persuade her to tell brief little tales.

But she had never been able to persuade Laurinda to sit down. She always remained standing, she evidently couldn't even dream of sitting down in the presence of a white woman.

When she first arrived at O Paraiso Hanna had noticed a little tattoo that Laurinda had on her neck, next to her collarbone. A lot of the sailors on the *Lovisa* had tattoos. Her husband, Lundmark, had an anchor with a red rose tattooed on his left upper arm. But

170

Hanna had never seen anybody with a tattoo next to their collarbone before, nor had she ever been able to imagine a woman with tattoos.

She hadn't been able to work out what the tattoo represented. Was it a dog, perhaps?

Now she couldn't wait any longer. She signalled to Laurinda that she should leave the tray on the table and pointed at the tattoo which was visible above her blouse.

"What is it?" she asked.

"It's a suckling hyena," said Laurinda.

When she gathered that Hanna didn't know what kind of an animal a hyena was, and possibly didn't even know it was an animal at all, she walked over to a picture that was hanging on the wall. During the days when Hanna hadn't been able to leave her bed she had lain there and gazed at the painting that depicted in Romantic style a number of different animals that lived in the African savannah.

Laurinda pointed at one of the animals.

"That's a hyena," she said. "It laughed the night I was born. My father heard the hyena out there in the darkness, and afterwards told my mother that it had bidden me welcome and provided me with my first food via its laughter."

Then she recounted in detail what had happened the night she was born, without hesitation and as if she had merely been waiting for the right opportunity. Hanna didn't understand some things, and several times Laurinda had to repeat bits and gesture with her hands or make various noises to make her story clear.

She also imitated the hyena's cry, a laughing sound.

"I was my mother and father's first child," said Laurinda. "But before my uncle died he told me that I was born in the year when there were so many crocodiles in the river that they began to attack and eat one another. It was also the year when the flamingos lost their pink colouring and became pure white. It was a year when lots of strange things happened. My parents lived on the bank of a tributary to the great River Zambezi, in a village where everybody had their own little plantation, their own hut, their own goats, and a smile for everybody they came across during the course of the day. I grew up in a world that I thought could never change. But one day when I was big enough to start helping my mother out in the fields and already had three younger brothers and sisters, a number of white men turned up in the village. They had long beards, their clothes were stained with sweat, they seemed to hate the heat of the sun and they were in a great hurry. They carried guns, and they showed the village chief some papers covered in lots of words. A few weeks later we were driven out of our village by soldiers commanded by the white men. Our little fields were going to be joined together to make a big cotton plantation. Anybody who wanted to stay and work in the cotton fields would be allowed to do so. Everybody else was driven away. My father, whose name was Papadjana, was a man who rarely allowed himself to be bullied and was never downcast when faced with difficulties. These white men with their cotton plantation were a big difficulty, but he had no intention of allowing them to tell him what to do. He spoke to them and said he had no intention of staying and picking cotton, nor of going away. No matter what it said in those papers and irrespective of how many soldiers there were, he was going to stay where he was. He had used a very loud voice when he spoke to the white men, and all the villagers who were standing around began to pluck up courage and give vent to their pent-up feelings when they realized that one of their number wasn't afraid. I don't know what happened next, but some more soldiers arrived and one morning soon after, my mother came with tears rolling down her cheeks and said that my father had been found floating in the river, dead, cut to pieces with knives. It was just as dawn was breaking. She stood there, leaning over me as I lay on the woven mat in the darkness of our hut. She told me I would have to go to the big city. I couldn't stay in the village. She would take the smaller children with her to where her parents lived further inland, but I should make my way to the coast and the big city. I didn't want to, but she forced me to."

Laurinda fell silent, as if the memories were too much for her to bear. Hanna sat quietly, thinking how what Laurinda had recounted was so remarkably similar to her own life. Both of them came from a world in which women were forced out of their homes and had to move to towns and to the coast in order to find work and survive.

"So I came here to this town," said Laurinda eventually. "During all the years that have passed I've

173

always thought that one day I shall go back and look for my mother and my brothers and sisters. Sometimes when I'm sleeping at night I dream that the hyena tattooed in my skin liberates herself and goes for a walk. At dawn she comes back and falls asleep again in my skin. One of these days she will have found my mother and my siblings."

Laurinda picked up the tray and left the room. Hanna lay down on the bed again and thought about what she had heard. What animal had cried in the night when she was born?

There was a light knock on the door. When she opened it, she found Senhor Vaz standing outside. He was dressed up in a tailcoat and carried a top hat under his arm. Next to him was Carlos on his bow legs, also wearing a tailcoat.

Senhor Vaz bowed.

"I've come to propose to you," he said.

At first Hanna didn't understand what he meant. But then she realized that he was actually asking her to marry him.

"Naturally I don't expect you to respond immediately," he said. "But I have made my wish clear."

He bowed again, turned on his heel and walked back towards the stairs. Carlos suddenly started shouting and jumping up and down, then grabbed hold of Senhor Vaz's top hat and climbed up and started swinging from the ceiling light.

Hanna closed the door and heard the chaos that always ensued when Carlos had one of his high-spirited outbursts slowly fading away. His punishment on such

174

occasions was to be locked in a cage for a few days. As he hated the cage more than anything else in the world, he was always compliant after he had been released.

She lay down on the bed and thought about what Senhor Vaz had said.

She felt as if she were being caught in a trap. But she still had the possibility of escaping and leaving the scene.

The following day she decided she would go down to the harbour shortly after dawn in order to see what ships were moored by the quays or waiting in the roadstead. As she came out into the street she noticed that the battered top hat was now on the watchman's head; he was asleep as usual.

Time was short now. She was in a hurry.

CHAPTER
THIRTY-EIGHT

A few days after Senhor Vaz's proposal, a rumour spread across the town that an enormous iceberg had been seen off the coast to the north, and that ocean currents were now driving it southwards. Hanna heard about it from Felicia, who was so excited that she changed out of her skimpy working clothes and put on a respectable dress suitable for walking in town. She had been entertaining a client, an engine driver from distant Salisbury, who visited the brothel twice a year. He had been just as excited as Felicia and all the others by the rumours about the iceberg. Senhor Vaz had already set off for the harbour when Hanna came downstairs, but Judas — who was now wearing the battered top hat — was waiting for her.

The streets were full of people making their way to the shore or climbing up the hills with good vantage points, all of them hoping to see the iceberg before anybody else.

But no iceberg appeared on the horizon. The weather was hot and oppressive. People were standing around under their parasols with sweat running down their expectant faces. Some concluded in disappointment that the iceberg must have already melted in the extreme heat. Older and more cynical observers were in no doubt that it was all a hoax, just as on all similar previous occasions. Nobody had ever seen an iceberg. But every ten years or so a rumour was spread, and the whole town started running to see it.

On the way to the harbour Hanna had noticed something she had never seen before. Blacks and whites were walking side by side on the pavements. Nobody seemed to be worried by that. Now, however, when the possibility of seeing the iceberg was no longer a shared hope, things were back to normal. The whites took control of the pavements, and pushed aside every black man or woman who threatened to come too close.

It was as if, for a few brief moments, Hanna had witnessed the birth of a new social order, as a sort of trial, only to see it disappear again just as quickly.

That same evening, when the mysterious iceberg had become a frustrated memory that would soon fade away, it started raining. It started as drizzle, but became heavier and heavier. At three in the morning Hanna was woken up by the booming sound of rain thudding on to the roof tiles.

She got out of bed and went to look out of the window. The rain seemed to be a grey wall between her and the darkness. But it was just as hot as during the day. When she stretched her hand out of the window and allowed the rain to lash down on to her skin, it felt very warm — as if it had started boiling on its way down to the ground.

She eventually managed to get back to sleep. When she woke up at dawn, the rain was just as heavy. She could see that the street was already flooded.

It continued raining for four days and nights. When it finally stopped, water was trickling in on to the brothel's stone floors, despite the fact that everybody had been required to assist in sewing sacks and filling them with topsoil and gravel in order to keep out the floods surging along the streets. As all links with the interior were broken, the only customers coming to the brothel now were sailors. Senhor Vaz turned them away. There was a state of emergency, the brothel was in distress and was closed. One young man, dripping wet and dressed in a French naval uniform, commented that he was also in distress and his plight was a state of emergency. Senhor Vaz and Esmeralda felt sorry for him and allowed him in.

When the rain had stopped and it was replaced by clouds of steamy damp mist, the air was full of insects fluttering everywhere. All windows and open areas were closed, and gaps and chinks were sealed. When the gatekeeper came in to fetch something, Carlos flung himself at him immediately and started gobbling up the insects that had settled on his body. White insects were sitting round his black head like a wreath of flowers. Carlos ate them all. Hanna could see that they were a great delicacy for the chimpanzee.

Everything gradually returned to normal. People came drowsily in from out of the dampness with steam rising in clouds from their bodies, as if their insides had also been filled with water. During the commotion caused by the alleged iceberg and then the days of heavy rain, Senhor Vaz had not pestered Hanna with questions about her response to his proposal. She had had time to think about it while the rain was pouring down. She had no doubt that Senhor Vaz's intentions were honourable — but who exactly was he, this little man who kept his hair and his moustache and his fingernails impeccably clean, his clothes immaculately creased, and was liable to fly into a fit of fury if he so much as spilled a drop of coffee on to his clothes or his body? He's a friendly man, Hanna thought, at least twice as old as I am. I don't feel anything of the vibrations that existed between me and Lundmark. He makes me feel safe in this world that is so foreign to me, but the thought of loving him, of allowing him to come to bed with me, is impossible.

So she had decided to turn him down when the rain had stopped, the insects had gone away and the brothel had opened again.

Then Carlos vanished. One morning there was no sign of him.

It had happened before that he had run off for a few hours to visit a secret world that nobody knew anything about. There were no other chimpanzees in Lourenço Marques, but sometimes baboons appeared in the town's parks, looking for food. Perhaps Carlos had gone to see them?

But this time the ape didn't return. Carlos was still missing after three days. The women who worked in the brothel went out looking for him. Senhor Vaz sent out everybody he could to search for Carlos. He promised to pay a reward, but nobody had seen the ape, nobody saw it when it disappeared, nobody had seen it since.

Hanna could tell that Senhor Vaz was grieving over the disappearance of Carlos. For the first time his austere mask had slipped, and he was displaying both regret and worry. Hanna was touched by what she saw, and it dawned on her that the man who had proposed to her was also very lonely. Surrounded by girls, but most of all attached to a confused ape that had come into his possession when a client had been unable to pay his bill.

Perhaps that is why Carlos ran away, she thought. So that I would be able to see Senhor Vaz as he really is?

She thought that he reminded her of her father. Elin had always kept him clean, just as Senhor Vaz was careful to look after his body and his appearance. Hanna knew that in one of the rooms at the back of the house where she had never yet ventured, Senhor Vaz had a bathroom: but he never allowed anybody to see him bathing in his enamel tub.

Lundmark had not always been clean. Hanna had sometimes been upset when he came to lie down beside her without having washed himself properly.

During the days when Carlos was missing, Hanna began to see Senhor Vaz in a new light. Perhaps he was not the person she had first thought he was.

One day Carlos came back. Hanna was woken up at dawn by somebody downstairs crying out in joy. When she had dressed rapidly and gone out to investigate, she found Carlos sitting with his arms round Senhor Vaz, who was hugging the ape tightly.

When Carlos came back he had a blue ribbon tied round his neck. Nobody knew where Carlos had got the ribbon from, or who had tied it round his neck.

The chimpanzee's sudden disappearance and equally sudden return remained his secret. But Carlos seemed to be most surprised by all the fuss, and started yelling and hitting out and pulling down curtains when everybody wanted to stroke him or slap him on the back.

Only when nobody bothered about him any more did he finally settle down.

CHAPTER
THIRTY-NINE

Hanna thought: what happens to an ape when it doesn't want to be an ape any longer? Could that also happen to a human being? That he or she no longer wanted to be the person they were?

She wrote down her thoughts in her room on a loose sheet of paper. But of course, she didn't mention anything about it to anybody — not even to Elin, in her thoughts.

After the return of Carlos, Senhor Vaz began courting her again. She had intended to tell him the facts: that she had recently become a widow and that her period of mourning would last for quite a long time to come. But Senhor Vaz didn't make her any new proposals. He simply continued to court her, quietly, sometimes even distantly. One day he took her for a ride in one of the few motor cars in Lourenço Marques, owned by an artillery colonel in the Portuguese regiment stationed in the town. They drove along the narrow road that followed the shoreline. A large-scale promenade was being built alongside the harbour. Hanna saw the black labourers struggling with the heavy blocks of stone in the oppressive heat — but Senhor Vaz, who was sitting beside her, didn't seem to notice them. He was enjoying the sea views, and pointed out a little sailing boat bobbing up and down on the waves.

They turned away from the sea, and the car climbed up the hills to the more elevated part of the town. A number of stone houses were being built along two long, wide esplanades. There were rails for horse-drawn trams.

The car stopped outside a house that seemed to have just been finished. It had a white-plastered facade, and a garden with rhododendrons and acacias. Senhor Vaz opened the car door and helped Hanna out. She looked questioningly at him. Why had they stopped outside this house?

The door was opened by a maid. They went in. There was no furniture in the rooms. Hanna could smell paint that hadn't yet dried, and wooden floors that had only recently been oiled.

"I want to give you this house," said Senhor Vaz without further ado.

His voice was soft, almost husky, as if it were a woman speaking. She had the impression that he was very proud of what he was offering her.

"I want us to live here," he said. "The day you agree to marry me, we shall leave our rooms in the hotel and move here."

Hanna said nothing. She explored the empty house in silence with Senhor Vaz a few cautious paces behind her.

He asked her no questions. He didn't invite the answer he must have been longing to hear.

When they returned to the hotel, Hanna thought yet again that she would never be able to explain to anybody about what had happened to her during the time she had lived in Africa. Least of all how a man who barely reached up to her shoulders and owned a brothel had proposed to her and wanted to present her with a large stone house with a garden and a sea view.

Nobody would believe her. Everybody would take it for granted that it was either a lie, or a wild dream.

Hanna decided to talk to Felicia. Perhaps she would be able to give her some advice.

A few evenings later, when Felicia had said goodbye to one of her regular clients, a banker from Pretoria who always wanted her to be brutal and torture him during their sessions, Hanna went to visit her in her room. Hanna told her the truth — that Senhor Vaz had proposed marriage to her.

"I know," said Felicia. "Everybody knows. I think even Carlos gathers what is going on. He may only be a chimpanzee, but he's clever. He understands more than you would think."

Her reply surprised Hanna. She had thought that Senhor Vaz's proposal had been made most discreetly.

"Has he spoken about it? To whom?"

"He never says anything. But he doesn't need to. We understand even so. But he doesn't realize that, of course."

Hanna suddenly became unsure about what to say next. Their conversation was turning out to be quite different from what she had expected.

184

"Senhor Vaz is a friendly man," said Felicia. "He can be brutal, but he always regrets it afterwards. And he lets us keep nearly half of what we earn. There are brothels in this town where the women hardly get a tenth."

"How come he isn't married?"

"I don't know."

"Has he ever been married?"

"I don't know that either. He came here from Lisbon over twenty years ago, with his brother and his parents. His father was a businessman and worked far too hard in the heat we have here. He died not long after he arrived. His wife went back to Portugal, but the two brothers stayed on. A few years later Senhor Vaz started this brothel, using money he'd got when he sold his father's business. That's all I know."

"So there's never been a woman in his life?"

Felicia smiled.

"Sometimes I simply don't understand the questions white people ask," she said. "Of course there have been women in his life. I don't really know how many, or who they are. But he does the same as other brothel owners do in this town — he never touches his own girls, but goes to his colleagues' establishments."

"Why does he want to marry me?"

"Because you are white. I think he's also impressed by the fact that you can afford to live here and pay for your room. And I suppose he's stricken by the loneliness that affects all white people in this country."

"My money will soon run out."

Felicia looked thoughtfully at her.

"You're not ill any more," she said in the end. "You're strong enough now to continue your journey to wherever you were or are going to. But you choose to stay here. Something is making you stay here. I don't know if it's because you don't have anywhere to go to or to return to, or whether there is some other reason. Anyway, now Senhor Vaz has proposed to you. You could marry a worse man than he is. He'll treat you with respect. He'll give you a large house. That's something my husband would never be able to give me. He's a fisherman, his name's Ateme. We have two children and I'm happy to see him every time we meet."

"Who looks after your children when you're here?"

"Their mother does."

Hanna shook her head. She didn't understand.

"Their mother? I thought you said you were their mother."

"My sister. She's also their mother. Just as I'm her children's mother as well. Or my other sisters' children's mother."

"How many sisters do you have?"

"Four."

Hanna thought that over. There was of course another question she felt bound to ask.

"What does your husband say about you working here?"

"Nothing," said Felicia quite simply. "He knows that I'm faithful to him."

"Faithful? Here?"

"I only go with white men. For money. He doesn't bother about that."

Hanna tried to understand what she'd just heard. All the time the gap seemed to grow wider rather than narrower. She didn't comprehend the world she was living in.

She thought about Carlos again. Perhaps he no longer wanted to be an ape, but he couldn't be a human being.

The lonely chimpanzee had changed into a vacuum inside a white waiter's coat.

What was she turning into?

CHAPTER
FORTY

That evening Hanna decided to accept Senhor Vaz's proposal of marriage. The most important reason for her decision was that she had come to accept that she could no longer cope with living as a widow. And perhaps one day she would be able to feel the same for Vaz as she had done for Lundmark.

The following day she gave him her answer. Senhor Vaz didn't seem to be surprised, but evidently regarded her "yes" as a formality that he had taken for granted.

Three weeks later they were married at a simple ceremony in the Catholic priest's residence next to the cathedral. The marriage witnesses were people Hanna didn't know. Senhor Vaz had also taken Carlos along, dressed in his tailcoat, but the priest had refused to allow the chimpanzee to be present. He was quite shocked, and regarded the proposed presence of Carlos to be blasphemy. Senhor Vaz had no choice but to accept the priest's ban. Carlos waited outside while the ceremony took place, and climbed up into the bell tower. Afterwards they had dinner in the best hotel in town, which was situated on a hill with views over the sea. Carlos was with them, because they had a private room.

188

They spent their wedding night in a suite in the hotel. There was a smell of lavender when Hanna entered the bedroom.

When they had switched the light off she could feel the warm breath of her new husband on her face. For a short, confused moment it was as if Lundmark had come back to her; but then she smelled the pomade in his black hair and knew that this was a different man lying by her side.

She waited for what was going to come next. She spread herself out, prepared herself. But Senhor Vaz — or Attimilio to use his first name — didn't manage to penetrate her. He tried over and over again, but he wasn't up to it: what should have been a lance was a broken twig.

In the end he turned away from her and curled up, as if he were ashamed.

Hanna wondered if she had done something wrong. But the next day, when she plucked up courage and asked Felicia about it, she was told that what had happened was not unusual as far as men were concerned. All in good time Senhor Vaz would no doubt be able to prove that he had the strength on which the whole of his commercial enterprises depended. But the fact was that there was always a threat hanging over a brothel: all men could suddenly become impotent.

Hanna didn't understand everything that Felicia said, but she did realize that what had happened wasn't her fault.

A few days later they moved into the stone house that had by now been filled with furniture. There was a handsome, shiny piano in one room that smelled of mimosa and other plants that Hanna had never come across before.

One evening, a few weeks after her wedding, when Hanna was alone with the maid, she played a note on the piano and made it linger on by treading on one of the pedals.

It was as if the room's shadows were suddenly populated by all those people she had left behind. Jonathan Forsman, Berta, Elin, her siblings and the third mate whose burial at sea she had attended six months earlier.

But her reaction was neither sadness nor regret. A cold wind of dismay blew past her. It came from nowhere as the sound of the piano faded away. What had she done? By attaching herself to a man she barely knew?

She didn't know. But she forced herself to think: there is no turning back. I am where I am.

Nowhere else but just here.

CHAPTER
FORTY-ONE

Every morning she went out on to the balcony that ran along the whole of the house's upper floor. From there she could see the town climbing up and down the slopes beyond the harbour with its many cranes gleaming in the heat haze, and furthest away the sea where ships were waiting for high tide. She had bought a better pair of binoculars than the ones she had before, and Senhor Vaz had paid a black carpenter to make a stand on which the binoculars could rest.

She continued to keep an eye on the ships, but now she no longer hoped to discover one in the roadstead flying a Swedish flag. On the contrary. Every morning she was scared she might see a ship lying there which could take her home. She was afraid that in that case she would begin to think that the ship had come too late.

Attimilio, as she still found it difficult to call him, left the house every morning at eight o'clock. He clambered into one of the horse-drawn coaches that took him down to the harbour district. At about noon he would come back home and they would eat lunch together, after which he took an afternoon nap before going back down to the women again.

Hanna very soon discovered that her new marriage was very different in one particular way from the time she had spent with Lundmark. Now she was almost always alone. Lundmark had always been close at hand when they were aboard Captain Svartman's ship. Her new husband treated her with the greatest respect and was always friendly towards her, but he was rarely at home. He ate and slept, and at night he continued to make his failed attempts to do what Hanna now, to her great surprise, had begun to long for. But apart from that they did next to nothing together. She continued to ask him questions about his earlier life, but he answered evasively or not at all. He didn't lose his temper and didn't seem to be put out by her questions: but he quite simply didn't want to say anything. Hanna thought it seemed as if she had married a man without a past at all.

Looking back, Hanna would regard this time as one of almost total inactivity. There was virtually nothing for her to do, no jobs that needed to be done. The garden was looked after by an old black man who was stone deaf. His name was Rumigo, and he had one of his innumerable sons to help him. Hanna would sometimes stand and watch how gently he handled the flowers, trees and shrubs. Inside the house was Anaka, who had also looked after Attimilio's parents. She was beginning to grow old, but still worked just as hard, and hardly ever seemed to sleep. She lived alone in a little shack behind the house. Hanna sometimes saw her sitting there, smoking her pipe before going to bed.

Anaka would be up again at four o'clock, and served breakfast at six.

Whenever Hanna spoke to Anaka, the maid immediately went down on one knee before her. Attimilio had explained to Hanna that this was not primarily a gesture of submission and subservience, but more of a tradition — a way of showing respect. Hanna found it difficult to cope with these continual genuflections, and tried to persuade Anaka to stop it. But without success. When Attimilio explained that Anaka would do the same to a black man of superior rank, she gave up. The genuflections continued.

There was another woman in the house, a young girl who Attimilio explained was the daughter of his mother's seamstress. She had a Portuguese name, Julietta, and helped Anaka with all the things the latter didn't have the time or strength to do herself. Hanna guessed that Julietta must be fourteen or fifteen years old.

Hanna experienced days in which she felt she was wandering around in an almost trance-like state. The heat was oppressive, occasionally interrupted by short tropical downpours. She spent most of the time sitting fanning herself in one of the rooms in which sea breezes wafted in through the open windows. She had the feeling that she was waiting for something, but didn't know what. She was sometimes afflicted by a nagging annoyance at being superfluous — everything that happened in this large house was done by the black servants. Her own role was simply to do nothing.

Attimilio had explained that she shouldn't hesitate to say if she was dissatisfied with the work carried out by the servants. Now and then she should put on a pair of white gloves and go around the house, running her fingers along picture frames and door frames to make sure that everything had been properly cleaned.

"If you don't keep chasing them up, they'll start skimping," said Attimilio.

"But everything is always beautifully clean."

"That's because you check up on them. The moment you stop they'll cease to be as careful."

Hanna could neither understand nor reconcile herself to Attimilio's constant denigration of black people. She still suspected that she could detect traces of fear behind his harsh words. But her presence in the house did not change his attitudes.

One evening he came home after a shocking incident in the brothel. A customer had fired a revolver and one of the women had received a superficial flesh wound on one arm. He burst out into a vehement tirade attacking the country he lived in.

"This would be a good continent to live in," he roared, "if only there weren't all these black people everywhere."

"But wasn't it a white man who fired the revolver?" asked Hanna tentatively.

Senhor Vaz didn't respond. Instead he made his excuses and retired to his study. She could hear through the closed door that he was playing Portuguese military marches on his primitive gramophone. When she bent down and peered in through the keyhole she could see him marching angrily around the room, swinging his sabre. She started giggling. The man who was now her husband seemed to be more like a tin soldier than anything else. One of the tin soldiers she had seen Jonathan Forsman's sons playing with.

Then she started feeling uneasy again. She had become like other white women in this town: inactive, apathetic and constantly fanning herself.

CHAPTER
FORTY-TWO

After several more weeks during which Attimilio had still failed to make love to his wife night after night, Hanna began to realize that Attimilio was close to unbounded desperation. She turned to Felicia once again, but in secret, one day when Senhor Vaz had gone to Pretoria where he invested quite a lot of the money he earned from the brothel. Once a month a lawyer came to visit him. They would shut themselves away in his study, and nobody else had a clue what they discussed. The lawyer, whose name was Andrade and had a limp, spoke so softly that Hanna could never understand a word of what he said.

Felicia advised Hanna to seek help from a *feticheiro*.

"There are plants you can eat, teas you can drink," said Felicia. "They enable men to do what they want to do more than anything else in the world."

"I don't know a *feticheiro*," said Hanna. "I don't know any medicine men who can give me what I need."

Felicia held out her hand.

"It costs money," she said. "If you give me some, I can get you what you need. Then all you have to do is to mix it into his food or into something he drinks. I don't know all the rules that apply, but I do know that you have to administer it when a west wind is blowing."

Hanna thought that over.

"We hardly ever have a west wind," she said.

Felicia pondered what Hanna had said.

"You're right," she said. "It will be better for you to make use of the full moon. That is also the right time to give him it. I always forget that we never get winds blowing here from the interior of the country — only from the sea or from the ice in the far south. We who live here in the Baia da Boa Morte know nothing about the winds from the vast savannah."

Hanna had never heard the name of the lagoon before. She knew that the town was called Lourenço Marques. One evening Attimilio had explained that it was named after a famous Portuguese general who was a match for Bonaparte when it came to cunning and courage. Hanna had no idea who this Bonaparte was, just as she had no idea that the lagoon had such a remarkable name.

But had she really heard correctly what she had said? "The lagoon of good death?" Could that really be what Felicia had called the bay that sparkled every day in the sunshine?

"Why is the lagoon called that?"

"Maybe because it's such a beautiful name. I always think of the blue water where dolphins swim as a cemetery for people who have a good death. The sort we all hope to have."

"What is a good death?"

Felicia looked at her in astonishment. It seemed to Hanna that Felicia had a special facial expression for occasions when she was having to think about questions that could only possibly have come from a white person.

"Everybody thinks about how they are going to die," said Felicia. "Didn't you tell me about the man you lived with, the man who was a third mate on board a ship and had a name I can't pronounce, who had a grave in the sea?"

"His death was anything but good," said Hanna. "He didn't want to die."

"When my death comes, I don't intend to resist it. Unless somebody is trying to murder me. I want to die peacefully. A good death is never agitated."

Hanna didn't know what to say about Lundmark's death or her own uneasy thoughts about her final moments. She gave Felicia the money she had asked for. A few days later Felicia turned up when Attimilio had left the house in the morning. Wrapped up in a piece of cloth she handled with both respect and perhaps also fear was a green, almost sparkling powder. It smelled strongly of the tar Hanna remembered from the ships in the harbour at Sundsvall.

"You must dissolve the powder into whatever Senhor Vaz drinks in the evening before going to bed."

"He doesn't drink anything in the evenings. He doesn't want to be woken up by his bladder during the night."

"Doesn't he eat anything either?"

"A mango."

"Then you must carefully open the fruit, press the powder into it, and close the skin again."

198

Hanna shouted for Anaka and asked her to bring a mango. They then helped each other to carry out the operation and saw that it was possible to leave no traces of the powder or what they'd done.

"Is that all?" asked Hanna.

"You should put a few drops of lemon into your pussy. Then you'll be ready to receive him."

Hanna's face turned red when Felicia talked about the lemon. Felicia's ability to talk quite normally about something that was still unmentionable as far as Hanna was concerned made her blush.

"That's all there is to it," said Felicia. "The *feticheiro* I spoke to has cured lots of impotent men. Some of them come from a very long way off. Some of them have come from as far away as India in order to become real men again. But he also said that if it doesn't work — which does happen sometimes — he has other, stronger medicines to make your husband's sexual urges start working again."

As the moon was on the wane, Hanna had to wait for quite some time. Meanwhile Attimilio made several more attempts to consummate the marriage, without success. Afterwards, when he had given up and was lying on his side, Hanna gently stroked his black hair, which left a new greasy stain of pomade on the pillowcase every morning. I don't really love him, she thought: but I feel tenderness towards him. He wants to do the best he can for me. He'll never be another Lundmark in bed, but with a bit of help from Felicia perhaps one day he'll be able to become a real man again.

CHAPTER
FORTY-THREE

By full moon Lourenço Marques had been battered by storms for a few days. Carlos had run away again but come back, just as mysteriously as before, this time with a red band round his neck. Senhor Vaz decided he had better keep Carlos chained up, but the women were outraged by the very thought and he let it drop. Carlos resumed his role as a waiter, and would light clients' cigars in exchange for a banana or an apple. Felicia maintained that Carlos had a different glint in his eye now: something was happening to him.

The full moon arrived, the winds had moved on, and Senhor Vaz came home after a long day at the brothel. Hanna had prepared the mango and sat beside him at the dining table as he chewed away at it, deep in thought. She then duly applied the drops of lemon in the bathroom before going to bed and lying down beside her husband. He seemed to be on his way to sleep, so she gently stroked his arm. After a few moments he turned to face her. He went on to make frantic efforts to penetrate her, just as he had done on previous occasions, but still without success — although Hanna could feel that his attempts were more powerful and longer lasting than ever before.

When he gave up they were both sweating. Hanna decided that the very next day she would tell Felicia that stronger medicines were needed to help Attimilio to overcome his difficulties.

She could hear that he had fallen asleep, taking the usual quick, short breaths as if he didn't really have time to sleep.

When she woke up next morning he was dead. He was lying beside her, white and already cold. The moment she opened her eyes, just before Anaka was due to come in with their breakfast tray, she knew that something had happened. He was rarely, if ever, still in bed when she woke up. He would usually be in the bathroom, getting shaved.

He was lying in the same position as he'd been in when he fell asleep. Hanna slid out of bed, her legs shaking. She had become a widow for the second time. When Anaka came in she was sitting in a chair and pointed to the man in the bed.

"*Morto*," was all she said. "*Senhor Vaz e morto*."

Anaka put down the tray, went down on her knees, chanted something that might have been a prayer, then hurried away. It struck Hanna that Attimilio had died in complete silence. He hadn't screamed like Lundmark did.

It was as if he had died in shame, having failed once again, one last time, to make love to his wife.

Two days after the chaotic burial in the town's new cemetery, at which Carlos was also present wearing a dark suit and a new black top hat, Hanna was visited by

Attimilio's solicitor, Senhor Andrade. He bowed, expressed his condolences once again, and sat down opposite her in the group of sofa and armchairs in red plush that Senhor Vaz had had made in distant Cape Town. Unlike on previous occasions, he now spoke loudly and clearly: Hanna was no longer merely an appendage of Senhor Vaz.

Andrade explained the situation:

"There is a will. It's signed, and witnessed by me and my colleague Petrus Sabodini. The will is simple and crystal clear. There isn't the slightest doubt about its intentions."

Hanna listened, but it never occurred to her that what was being said had anything to do with her.

"So, there is a will," said Andrade again. "It makes it clear that all Attimilio's estate and goods and chattels are inherited by you. In addition to the hotel and the other activities associated with it, you now own all his businesses, including a warehouse full of fabrics and nine donkeys grazing in various pastures just outside the town. There are also significant assets in Pretoria and Johannesburg."

Andrade placed a number of documents on the table and stood up. He bowed again.

"It will be a great pleasure to me if in future I can continue to offer you my services as your solicitor, Senhora Vaz."

It was only after he had gone that Hanna grasped what had happened. She sat there motionless, holding her breath. She had become the owner of a brothel. And also of a number of donkeys and a chimpanzee that occasionally ran away when it wasn't lighting cigars for the customers who visited her house of pleasure.

She stood up and went out on to the balcony. Through the binoculars she could see the building where the brothel was situated. She could also make out the contours of the window of the room that had been hers, when she was sick in bed.

A number of ships were bobbing slowly up and down in the roadstead, but she didn't pay any attention to them just now. However, that same day she took Carlos home with her from the brothel, because she didn't want to live alone. She also took the big ceiling light because Carlos always liked to sleep in it.

Carlos would now share the big stone house with Hanna. For as long as she remained in the town spread out there before her, white and steaming in the heat, on the shore of the bay known as the Lagoon of Good Death.

PART THREE

The Tapeworm in the Chimpanzee's Mouth

CHAPTER
FORTY-FOUR

Every morning when Hanna woke up Carlos was sitting in her bed with his hairy back towards her. She didn't like him being there: she was afraid he would introduce stinging and blood-sucking insects into her bed. She chased him away and closed the bedroom door before going back to bed and extinguishing the paraffin lamp. But Carlos always either opened the door, or climbed back in through the window she kept open. He was there every morning. She was the one living in a cage, not Carlos.

In the end Hanna realized that he was longing for company, just as she was. He was missing the companionship characteristic of the life of chimpanzees — allowing another member of the troop to examine his fur and pick it clean. She felt sad once this had become clear to her. She could see her own loneliness mirrored in his, sat down close to him and began searching his skin for dead insects. It was obvious how much he enjoyed that. When Carlos wanted to repay the compliment by searching through her own hair, she allowed him to do so.

She started to see the pair of them as an odd couple, their mutual respect growing all the time even though they didn't really have anything more in common than this morning ritual, which could go on for hours.

In the early days of this new stage in her life as a widow, she kept thinking about how she had changed her name for the second time in her short life. In the course of a brief ceremony in the distant city of Algiers, she had stopped being Renström and become Lundmark. Then that second name had been replaced by Vaz. In all the documents that her solicitor Senhor Andrade brought for her to read and sign, it said that her name was Hanna Vaz, and that her title was now *viuva*, widow.

But the thought of her being suddenly subjected once again to widowhood didn't affect her nearly so much as the realization that she had become a very rich woman. Andrade produced accounts for her to read and sign, and she was astounded when she laboriously worked out the equivalents of English pounds, Portuguese escudos or American dollars into Swedish kronor. She was staggered to think that she now probably had more liquid capital than Jonathan Forsman's total possessions. She sometimes woke up in the middle of the night under the impression that money — shiny new coins and pristine banknotes — was raining down on to her bed. Even after a few months, this wealth seemed totally unreal to her. And money continued to come rolling in. Every morning the short, slim cashier Eber, who was descended from a German family that had emigrated to southern Africa, would come up to her house from the brothel with a leather briefcase crammed full of cash. She would sign

208

for the briefcase, give Eber the empty briefcase from the previous day, and then shut herself up in the study she had taken over from her former husband. In one of the walls was a safe that needed two different keys to open it: she wore them on a ribbon tied round her neck. She would enter the amounts in a cash book, then place the notes and coins inside the safe and lock it again. Not even Carlos was allowed to be in the room when she was counting out the money from the brothel.

Once a month, in accordance with the cashier's instructions, she would prepare the payments that needed to be made. On that day Eber was always accompanied by several Portuguese soldiers who escorted him back to the brothel with the bulging briefcase.

Nobody stayed in the hotel as a paying guest now. Once Hanna had moved out the rooms had either remained empty, or been used by the whores when their own rooms were being repaired after being trashed by some overexuberant client. She even wondered if there had ever been any normal paying guests before her, or whether the hotel business was no more than a front to give the brothel an appearance of decency.

One day when she was putting more money into the safe, she noticed a little notebook lying on the bottom shelf, covered in dust that had somehow, mysteriously, managed to filter in despite the tightly fitting steel door. When she examined it more closely while sitting at the desk, she discovered that it was empty. There wasn't a single word written in it. It was a gift from a Japanese shipping line with Yokohama as its main port. Japanese sailors sometimes visited the brothel. They were clean and polite, but not especially liked by the women because the intensity of their sexual activity could be painfully tiring. Hanna had heard rumours of a Japanese mate who had paid for a whole night, and was alleged to have had nineteen sexual encounters. Whether or not that was true, the Japanese were certainly persistent, and on some occasion or other Senhor Vaz must have received the empty notebook as a present, or perhaps as a souvenir — or possibly even as an apology for an excessively savage erotic outburst.

The leather smelled of calfskin, but it had turned black over the years. The white pages were made of thick paper, but were nevertheless soft and pliable. When Hanna wrote her name on one, she could see how the paper sucked up the dark blue ink. No blotting paper was needed.

She wrote the current date: 26 March, 1905. Carefully, as if every single word could have dangerous consequences, she wrote a sentence: "Dreamt last night about what no longer is."

"Dreamt last night about what no longer is." That was all. But it seemed to her that she had sparked off a new habit that she was determined to stick to. She would no longer simply write down new figures in her account books, but she would also keep a diary that nobody but she would have access to.

From then on she would write down a few sentences after. Eber had been with his bag full of money and she had locked away the previous night's income in the safe. As the days passed she dared to stray from the usual paths where the words she wrote simply referred to something she had dreamt, or what Carlos had done, or what the weather had been like. She started to write about the women who worked for her, both in the brothel and in the house where she was sitting and writing.

After just over a month she made a note about Senhor Vaz and his hopeless attempts to satisfy both her and himself. Her tone became increasingly sharp, the judgements she passed on people increasingly less considerate. No unauthorized readers were going to have access to her diary.

But what she wrote in her diary had no effect on the daily conversations she had with the people she was in charge of. In those situations she was just as friendly and considerate as she had been before. But in her diary she wrote what she really thought. That was where the truth was; but she kept it hidden.

Only one other person knew of the existence of the diary. That was young Julietta, who helped out in the house whenever and wherever necessary. One day she had stood in the half-open doorway and seen Hanna leaning over her diary at her desk. Hanna had called the girl in and shown her what she was writing, well aware that Julietta was illiterate and had no idea about writing nor languages. Julietta had asked what Hanna was writing.

"Words," Hanna had said. "Words about the country I come from."

That was all she had said, despite the fact that Julietta continued to ask questions. Afterwards Hanna had asked herself why she had lied to Julietta. There was nothing in the diary about her life in the mountains and by the cold river. But on the other hand she had often made disparaging comments about Julietta.

Why hadn't she told her the truth? Had she begun to be like all the others in this town, who never seemed to tell the truth? At first she had believed that Senhor Vaz had been right when he claimed that all black people told lies. But then she had discovered that the same applied to all the whites, and to those of Indian or Arabic origins. Everybody lied, even if they did so in different ways. She was living in a country which seemed to be founded on lies and hypocrisy.

She signalled that Julietta should leave the room. Then she wrote down what she had just been thinking: "Black people lie in order to avoid unnecessary suffering. White people lie to preserve the superiority they wish to uphold. And the others, the Arabs and Indians, lie because there is no longer room for the truth in this town we live in."

She also thought, although she didn't write it down, that she regretted having shown Julietta her notebook. Perhaps that was a careless move that would come back to haunt her at some time in the future.

She locked the diary away in the safe and stood by the window looking out over the sea. She took her binoculars and viewed the island called Inhaca which she had once visited, during her "time of inactivity", with Senhor Vas and the solicitor, Senhor Andrade.

She redirected the binoculars at the town, at the harbour district where the brothel was located. If she stood on tiptoe she could see the lookout outside the gate, and possibly also one or two of the girls hanging around in the shadows, waiting for a client.

A thought occurred to her that she had had many times before: I can see them. But the question is, can they see me? And if they can: what do I mean to them?

She replaced the binoculars and stand on the marble shelf in front of the window, and closed her eyes. Despite the heat she could conjure up how she had sat in the sleigh, wrapped up in Jonathan Forsman's furs that smelled of lard and dogs.

When she opened her eyes again, she thought that she really must soon make up her mind. Should she stay where she was, or should she return home?

But on that day of all days, the day when she had shown Julietta her notebook, Hanna was possessed by another emotion.

She was frightened. She had the feeling that danger was approaching. There was something in the vicinity that she hadn't yet discovered.

A growing threat. That she couldn't see. But she knew that it was approaching rapidly, like a sleigh gliding along at speed over tightly packed snow.

CHAPTER
FORTY-FIVE

Not long after she had begun to write about Senhor Vaz in her diary, Hanna called a meeting of the women and everybody else who worked in the brothel. She held it early in the morning when the brothel was nearly always empty. Most of them generally slept when the last of the clients had left. Many of them travelled in horse-drawn carriages, but some in motor cars, all of which were cleaned and polished during the night by the black workers who disobeyed the law that said blacks were not allowed in the town at night. The police turned a blind eye because they always had right of access to the women in the various brothels concentrated along rua Bagamoio provided they left the nocturnal workers in peace.

It seemed to Hanna that the newly polished cars heading for the South African border in the early hours of the morning were a sign that the men who used the services of her brothel wanted to remove all trace of what they had been up to. It was as if the cars and carriages were also soiled by what went on inside the brothel. But now the men were travelling back in their sparklingly clean vehicles to the country where it was morally reprehensible and perilously close to being a jailable offence for white men to associate with black women.

Hanna gathered the women and the security guards around the jacaranda tree in the garden. She had asked Andrade to be present, and had taken Carlos with her, dressed in his white waiter's jacket. She now allowed him to be what he really was — a chimpanzee stolen from his troop somewhere inland. Carlos seemed worried at first about returning to the brothel, but after slapping the lid of the piano hard several times he calmed down and sat on Zé's knee, just as in the old days.

Zé seemed to be barely aware of the fact that his brother had passed away unexpectedly. He had attended the funeral, but had shown no sign of sorrow or pain. He sat at the piano and continued to tune the strings which never seemed to attain the harmony he was striving for.

Hanna started by saying that essentially, nothing would change. Everything would continue more or less as it always had done. As the widow of Senhor Vaz she intended to retain all the rules, duties and benefits that her husband had introduced to give their workplace the best possible reputation that it had always enjoyed. She would continue to be generous with regard to granting time off, and would be no less strict than Senhor Vaz had been when it came to clients who were violent or behaved in any other unacceptable fashion.

But of course, not everything could be the same as before, she said as she approached the end of her little speech that she had learnt off by heart in Portuguese, to ensure that she didn't lose control of her words and thoughts. She was a woman. She didn't have the same bodily strength as her husband had had — she wouldn't be able to intervene if there was some kind of disturbance — and so she was going to appoint a couple more sturdy security guards who would protect the women and guarantee their safety.

But there was another thing which would inevitably be different because she wasn't a man. The women would find it easier to talk to her about some things that would have been difficult to discuss with her husband. She envisaged a situation in which they could all talk more intimately with one another. That had to be an improvement for everybody, she asserted at the end of her brief address.

Afterwards, she was enveloped by a long-drawn-out silence. A single jacaranda flower floated slowly, as light as a feather, down to the ground. She hadn't expected anybody to make any comments, but the silence scared her. It was not the usual silence between whites and blacks: it seemed to have a significance that she was unable to put her finger on.

She flung her hands out wide to indicate that the meeting was over. Nobody needed to stay any longer. The women picked up their chairs and went indoors, and Judas started sweeping the courtyard — but she waved him away as well. Zé returned to the piano with Carlos half asleep on his lap.

It dawned on Hanna what the silence had indicated. Nobody had wanted the closer relationship she had offered them. The silence had been heavy with an invisible reluctance, she realized that now. But she didn't understand it. Couldn't they see that as she was a woman, she really was closer to them? That everything she had said was true, unusually so in this world of hypocrisy and lies?

She had taken her notebook with her, and now she wrote in it — hesitantly, as if she couldn't rely on her ability to interpret her own thoughts: "Anybody who robs somebody of their freedom can never expect to form a close relationship with them."

She read what she had written. She put the notebook back in the woven basket which also contained a shawl and a tin flask that she always carried with her. It contained drinking water that had boiled for many hours before being left to cool down.

The women had returned to their rooms. Nobody was sitting on the sofas yet, ready to receive their clients once again. It was clear to Hanna that they were keeping out of her way so that they didn't need to risk her speaking to them and offering them the closer relationship she had spoken about.

A close relationship, she thought. As far as they are concerned, all that means is a threat to which they don't want to expose themselves.

She stood there with the basket in her hand, unsure about whether the reaction she had been confronted with aroused her anger or disappointment. Or was she in fact grateful and relieved that she didn't need to try to carry out in practice what she had so wrongly envisaged in theory?

Senhor Andrade suddenly materialized by her side. Despite the fact that it was early in the morning, sweat was already pouring down his face. A drop hanging from the tip of his nose filled her with distaste. She had to restrain herself from thwacking him in the face with the handkerchief she had stuffed inside her blouse.

"Is there anything else you require of me this morning?"

"No. Nothing apart from hearing what you thought about it."

Andrade gave a start. New drops of sweat gathered on the tip of his nose. Hanna realized that she had used the familiar form of address, and that he objected to that. She ought to have included the words "Senhor Andrade". He evidently thought that not doing so indicated a lack of respect. But she knew that he was well paid for his services, and she certainly didn't want to exchange him for one of the keen young solicitors from Lisbon who were now converging on Portugal's African possessions in the hope of making their fortunes.

"What I thought about what?"

"My address. The meeting. The silence."

Her distaste was increasing all the time. The beads of sweat on his bloated face made her feel ill.

"It was a good exposition of the facts of the situation," said Andrade thoughtfully.

"You're not in court. Tell me what you really think. About their reaction."

"The whores? What else can you expect from them but silence? They're used to opening other things than their mouths."

Andrade's effrontery almost made Hanna blush. She became the girl by the river again, scarcely daring to look any man she didn't know in the eye. But she also realized that he was right. Why had she thought that she might be able to expect anything other than silence? On several occasions she had been present when Senhor Vaz had assembled the women to address them, but none of them had ever asked a question or requested that anything should be explained more clearly — and most certainly there had never been any question of contradicting him.

Andrade went out into the broiling sunshine and clambered into his car, which was driven by a black chauffeur in uniform. Hanna had arranged for the chauffeur to come and collect her an hour later.

She went up the stairs and opened the door to the room where she had slept those first nights after she had fled from Svartman's ship. She lay down on the bed and closed her eyes. But there was nothing she could return to, not even the memory of those first lonely nights, the bleeding, and Laurinda coming to help her without making a sound.

She left the room without understanding why she had gone up the stairs to the upper floor. She sat down on one of the red plush sofas and waited for the car. Carlos had woken up and climbed into the jacaranda tree. He sat there watching her, as if he expected her to climb up as well and cling on to the branches.

She looked at all the closed doors. She thought about the fact that she knew nothing at all about what really went on inside the women's heads. She would never be able to repeat the conversations she had sometimes had with Felicia. The fact that she was now the owner of the brothel opened up a chasm between her and the women with whom she had previously had a relationship as close as racial differences allowed.

Her unrest made it difficult for her to breathe. She held tightly on to the arms of the sofa so as not to fall. I can't stay here, she thought. I have no business to be here. On a foreign continent where the residents either hate me or are scared of me.

Her thoughts were still unclear, but she had an idea of what she ought to do. The very next day she should summon Andrade and instruct him to find somebody willing to purchase the brothel. There was bound to be any number of willing would-be buyers prepared to pay for the brothel's good name and reputation. Then she would get out of here as quickly as possible. Her future was secure, thanks to the money she already had plus what she would earn from the sale of the brothel. It would be a rich woman leaving Africa behind her. Hers had been a brief visit. Two short-lived marriages, two unexpected deaths, and then nothing else.

I have just one problem, she thought. What will happen to Carlos? I can't take him with me to the cold country where he would freeze to death. But who will be able to look after him, now that he has no desire at all to return to the forests he originally came from? When he doesn't even want to be an ape any longer?

She had no answer to that. When the car arrived and she shouted for Carlos, he immediately climbed down from the tree.

But just as he touched the ground after climbing out of the tree, he had given a start, as if he had burnt himself on the hard, flat soil. He sniffed around, then hurried away.

Hanna stared at him in surprise. Why had he been afraid of the ground underneath the tree? But Carlos gave no indication of why. He simply sat down beside her in the car, grinning as the sea air caressed his face.

CHAPTER
FORTY-SIX

Shortly before his death, totally unexpectedly — as if he had had a premonition of his imminent demise — Senhor Vaz had told Hanna that if she ever needed advice and he was not at hand to give it, she should turn first to Senhor Pedro Pimenta.

"Why him?" she had asked. "I barely know who he is."

"I don't know anybody who is more honest than he is," he said. "He's the only person in this country who I've never caught out telling lies. Talk to Pedro Pimenta if you need advice. And rest assured that you can trust Herr Eber to look after our money — he'd never steal a single escudo of our assets. He believes that God goes out of His way to look after him. You couldn't ask to find a better cashier than Herr Eber. God has erected steel bars between Herr Eber and any thievish inclinations he might have, deep down inside him."

Pedro Pimenta was an immigrant from Coimbra who carved out for himself an astonishing career when he came to the African colony. He had first been an assistant to a tailor who had decided to seek his fortune in the African colonies. Pimenta's real intention had been to emigrate to Angola, and more specifically to the city of Luanda, because rumour had it that the white colonial population was badly in need of tailors. But fate had dictated that the master tailor who paid for Pimenta's ticket had decided to settle in the country that at that time was still called Portuguese East Africa. For the first three months after his arrival, Pimenta, who was only seventeen at the time, had been scared to death by everything the alien continent threw at him. He was terrified of the dark nights, of the whispering voices of the blacks, of the snakes he never saw and the spiders that hid away in the darkness. Even though it was many years since beasts of prey had wandered into the town at night, he was always afraid that a lion would force its way in through his half-open window and rip out his throat. For the first three months Pimenta spent all his time hiding behind barricades. As he was unable to sleep at night, he didn't have the strength to work during the day. The master tailor sacked him, and kicked him out of the little house down by the harbour where he had established his tailoring business.

The fact that Pimenta was out of work did not mean that he was ruined: instead he was forced to overcome his fears and take responsibility for his life. Thanks to a number of forged references, he was given a job by an Indian businessman, learnt the basics of commerce, and before long started up his own business with prices undercutting anything his rivals had to offer. After less than ten years he had become a rich man. He built a house on a hill outside the town, was one of the first people in Lourenço Marques to own a car and a chauffeur, and was considered to be one of the most prominent of the colonial immigrants.

Nobody knew that Pedro Pimenta was illiterate. He managed to keep in his head all the figures he needed to master in his business dealings. When he became more successful he called up a younger brother from Portugal who could both read and write. That brother took care of all the necessary correspondence, and nobody had the slightest idea that all the letters of the alphabet jumped around inside Pimenta's head in total confusion.

Pimenta's big breakthrough came with the dogs. He had the idea one evening when he was visiting the brothel run by his good friend Senhor Vaz. It was shortly after Felicia had started to work there: Pimenta soon became a regular customer of hers, visiting her once every week, always on Tuesday evenings.

On one of his visits there was a man of about his own age sitting waiting for the woman he had just booked, hoping she would soon finish her session with her current client. He and Pimenta started talking. The man, who came from South Africa, ran a business selling guard dogs.

"Fear is an excellent employer," he said. "Especially in South Africa where the whites shut themselves away in compounds surrounded by high fences, and their need for guard dogs is never-ending. They would really prefer to have bloodthirsty, starving wolves, but I provide them with German shepherd dogs trained in Belgium and some kennels in the south of Germany. When they are fully trained to attack black people, they are sent on boats to Durban or Port Elizabeth. My customers queue up and are prepared to pay a small fortune for the strongest and most aggressive dogs."

The man tipped the ash off his cigar and burst out laughing.

"The only drawback with the dogs is that they are not white," he said. "If they were, they would be worth twice as much."

Pimenta didn't understand at first what he meant.

"White sheepdogs?"

"Yes, it would be perfect if one could breed white sheepdogs — albinos, for instance. White dogs, just as white as their owners. They would scare the blacks even more. And hence make their owners feel more secure."

Pimenta nodded and said that was a fascinating idea, of course. But what he didn't say was that he knew a man, a Portuguese veterinary surgeon, who had a few white sheepdogs in his garden.

The following day Pimenta went to see the vet, who was in his sixties and had begun to think about moving back to Portugal before he became too old. He had lived in Africa for over forty years, and on several occasions had suffered serious bouts of malaria that had almost killed him. He was convinced that his inner organs were vulnerable to attacks by bacteria, worms and amoebae. No doctor had been able to solve the problem and they didn't even think it was worth trying to cure him. Pimenta proposed that he should take over the pair of sheepdogs and their recent litter of puppies, all of them as white as snow, in return for a sum of money that would greatly assist the old vet to undertake the journey back home to Portugal. They reached an agreement, and a few months later Pimenta waved goodbye to him from the quay in Lourenço Marques harbour as a regular passenger liner set sail for Durban, Port Elizabeth, Cape Town and Lisbon.

By that time Pimenta had already bought some land outside the town with the utmost secrecy, and he had a large complex of kennels built on it. His brother Louis, the one who could read and write, took over responsibility for it. After two more years, he had a collection of over thirty white sheepdogs. By then Louis had grown tired of the African heat and returned home. And so Pimenta took over control of everything himself. With the help of a retired Portuguese cavalry officer the dogs had been trained to go on the attack the moment a black person approached. Pimenta had paid the commander of the fort to allow his dogs to practise on a group of black miscreants who were being held in the military jail. In order not to appear excessively brutal, Pimenta had supplied the black prisoners with thick fur coats that the sheepdogs were unable to bite through.

Pimenta travelled to Johannesburg and placed an advert in the biggest national newspaper announcing that sensational white sheepdogs, trained as guard dogs, were for sale, albeit only in limited numbers at present.

He had rented a suite in one of Johannesburg's leading hotels. Before long the desperate hotel manager was forced to employ extra staff to cope with the long queue of prospective buyers.

226

Pimenta had taken two of the puppies with him to Johannesburg, a dog and a bitch. They were two of the most intelligent of the dogs he had bred. To demonstrate their aggressiveness he called a black bellboy to his room: the dogs immediately began straining at their leashes, snarling and growling frantically.

He sold the dogs for amounts that made it clear he had the equivalent of top-grade diamonds in his kennels. When he went back home he had with him orders and down payments for over fifty dogs, and had increased his fortune just like a successful gold prospector — without ever having so much as touched a spade or a wash pan.

Pedro Pimenta had become an entrepreneur in fear. He knew how he was going to exploit his knowledge. As far as he was concerned, the fear some people had of others was purely and simply a brilliant business opportunity.

CHAPTER
FORTY-SEVEN

The day after the meeting at the brothel, Hanna paid to borrow Andrade's car and chauffeur in order to visit Pedro Pimenta's estate outside Lourenço Marques.

Pimenta had built an enormous house next to his dog kennels.

He had created a large garden around it, and dug out several ponds in which he fattened up crocodiles before sending their skins to tanneries in Paris where they were made into shoes and handbags. The crocodile eggs were collected from sandbanks further up the River Komati. He had also employed oarsmen to capture newly born crocodiles from the water next to the sandbanks where the mothers were lying on guard. They didn't hesitate to attack if anybody tried to steal their eggs or the youngsters they had carefully carried down to the river in their mouths. On one occasion a large crocodile had succeeded in overturning one of the flimsy rowing boats. Both men had fallen into the water and desperately attempted to swim to the riverbank. One of them had succeeded, but had had been forced to watch as his friend struggled as far as the bank and dug his fingers into the wet sand in order to haul himself up: but as he tried to do so a crocodile seized him by the leg and dragged him down into the water again. His head had appeared once more before the crocodile pulled him back down under the surface for good, and lodged the body in among the tangled roots of the trees near the bank. The body would rot away there until it was ready for eating.

Hanna had heard that story from Felicia, and had no doubt that it was true. She couldn't just dismiss it as yet another of the thousands of yarns told by the men sitting in the brothel, chatting to their whores.

Pedro Pimenta was religious. Felicia had shown her the memorial stone he had erected in the municipal cemetery in memory of the man who had been eaten by the crocodiles. There had been no body to bury. The dead man's clothes had been placed in a beautifully carved wooden coffin. The only word on the memorial stone was the name Walibamgu: Pimenta didn't know the man's surname. He had simply turned up one day at the crocodile pools, looking for work, and Pimenta had recruited him without further ado. As far as Pimenta was concerned it didn't matter that the man had no surname and no past. He was just one of the vagrants from the interior of Africa who only existed for one moment, a Walibamgu with no date of birth — but a date of death.

Pimenta believed in God and attended the cathedral regularly. He donated money for the purchase of new candlesticks, and had also paid for the repair of some pews that had been damaged by termites.

Now he was sitting in the shade on his large veranda with views of the river and beyond that the mountains that seemed to melt away into a permanent mist. Hanna knew that Pimenta very rarely left his home. The only excursions he made were to the brothel and to the cathedral. He turned down all the invitations he received. Not even the Portuguese governor was able to tempt him to attend any of the dinners the rest of the white colonial elite fought among themselves in order to be present at. Pimenta preferred to sit on his veranda, keeping watch on his crocodiles as they grew bigger and fatter in their ponds, and on the white sheepdogs whose aggression was being built up in the extensive kennels. In a pond next to his veranda he kept a few baby crocodiles and fed them himself with small fish and frogs.

Pimenta was wearing a white linen suit and a pith helmet with a protective cloth covering the back of his neck. The shape of his body was peculiar: the whole of his body was thin apart from his stomach, which stuck out like a tumour over his belt. His skin was covered in scars caused by insect bites and pimples, one of his eyelids was sagging as if half of his being was devoted to struggling with overpowering exhaustion. Although he was still young, he had aged prematurely — as was often the case with white people who migrated to the tropics and spent their time there working far too hard.

For several years Pedro Pimenta had been living with a black woman called Isabel, and had two children with her: a son and a daughter. Both of them had been baptized in the cathedral and were called Joanna and Rogerio.

Hardly any of the whites in Lourenço Marques worried about the fact that he had a black lover; but the fact that he lived openly with her, as if they were married, and that he looked after her children as if they were his own — which of course they were — with the help of a private tutor, was condemned by everybody. In some circles he was regarded with contempt, while others looked upon him with a sort of vague worry.

Pimenta shook Hanna's hand when she emerged from the car, and invited her to accompany him to the veranda where there was at least a suggestion of cool breezes from the river valley blowing along the house walls. Isabel came out to greet her. She was dressed just like a white woman and her black hair was gathered in a tight bun at the back of her head. It struck Hanna that this was the first black woman she'd met who had looked her in the eye when they shook hands. The expression in Isabel's eyes gave Hanna the feeling that this was what native Africans had looked like before the whites had arrived in their ships in search of slaves, diamonds and ivory.

Isabel fetched the children so that they could greet her as well. Hanna thought she was looking at two unusually handsome children.

"My children," said Pimenta. "My greatest joy. Often my only joy, come to that."

Hanna wondered why he suddenly sounded so downcast. A cold breeze that didn't come from the river but from inside herself wafted past. She didn't understand how he could talk about joy in a way that actually indicated depression.

Something worried her, although she couldn't put her finger on it.

He took her to the dog kennels.

"Demand is growing all the time," he said. "I thought I would have a monopoly of these white dogs for four years at most, then other breeders would start producing similar dogs to satisfy the market demands: but I now realize that I had underestimated the human need of originals. And these here are the originals, they exist nowhere else."

"How much do the dogs cost?" Hanna asked.

"Anybody who asks about the price can hardly be able to afford one of them."

"I'm not asking because I want one for myself."

"I know. You would be able to afford one."

Hanna gathered that he didn't want to reveal his asking price. Or perhaps he didn't have a set price, but asked individual customers to pay what he thought they would be able to afford.

They continued to the various pools that comprised the crocodile farm. Pedro explained to her that the slowly growing crocodiles needed to be separated from the rest so that they didn't become food for those that had grown somewhat larger.

In a pond with dark green water, all on its own, was an enormous crocodile lying motionless on a flat rock. It was almost five metres long. Nobody knew how old it was. Pimenta wouldn't allow anybody else to feed it. Once a week he would throw food down into the pond. And in fact it was this very day that he was due to feed Noah, as he called it. He asked Hanna if she would like to watch. She really wanted to say no, but nodded her head. He shouted for one of the black workers who looked after the crocodiles. A woolly sheep, a very powerfully built ram, was dragged out of a pen. The black man handed the rope to which the sheep was attached to Pimenta, then hurried off. The ram seemed to suspect what was going to happen — like an animal that can smell the blood of those that have just been slaughtered.

Pimenta hung his jacket on a coat rack next to the pond that was evidently there for this very purpose. He unbuttoned the waistcoat that was stretched over his enormous stomach, folded up his shirt sleeves and untied the rope at the same time as he took a firm grip of the ram's neck. The ram bellowed. The crocodile lay there motionless. Pimenta suddenly grabbed the ram's feet and turned it over on its back, then threw it down into the water where the crocodile was waiting. With a sudden movement that was so quick that Hanna barely saw it, the crocodile left the rock and sank down into the water. It clamped its jaws round the ram, threw it into the air to turn it over, dragged it down under the surface, then reappeared with just the ram's head.

Hanna didn't want to see any more. She turned away and hurried back to the veranda.

"I'll come when the party's over," she heard Pimenta saying behind her.

It's almost as if he were taking part in the feast himself, she thought agitatedly. How is this man going to be able to advise me on what to do with my life?

Her first impulse was to get into the car and drive back to town. But despite everything she stayed on the veranda, and had settled down in a shady corner by the time Pimenta returned from the crocodile's feast. There was not a trace on his face of the scenes that had been enacted in the crocodile pool. He smiled at Hanna, rang a small silver bell, ordered some tea from a servant, and asked why she had come to his house — she had never visited him before.

"I can't sleep at night," she said. "I don't know why I should stay here in Africa, but nor do I know why I should leave. Nor where I should go to."

What she said didn't seem to surprise him. He fanned his face slowly with his pith helmet.

"Those are thoughts that nag away at all of us," he said. "There's no avoiding them. To stay or not to stay. Even if we were born here, we are still on foreign soil. Or perhaps I should say that we are in enemy territory."

"Is that what I'm feeling? All the hatred directed at us because we are white?"

"That's hardly something that we need to worry about. What could the blacks do to us? Nothing."

"There's something they have that we don't have."

For the first time he looked at her in surprise.

"And what could that be?"

"Their numbers."

He seemed disappointed by her answer, as if he had hoped she would astound him, say something he'd never thought of before.

"The idea that they could be a threat to us because there are a lot of them is nothing more than a figment of the imagination for nervous people," he said impatiently. "Nightmares that can never become reality. The more of them there are, the more confused they become."

"I don't regard myself as a nervous type. But I see what I see. And I hear what I hear."

"What do you hear?"

"A silence. Which isn't natural."

Before Pimenta could respond, Isabel came out on to the veranda and sat down on one of the basket chairs. She smiled.

Hanna suspected she had been listening to their conversation. But why had she come out on to the veranda at just that moment? Because she wanted the conversation to come to an end? Or was there some other reason?

In her mind's eye Hanna suddenly saw Pimenta grabbing hold of Isabel's legs and flinging her into the crocodile pit. She gave a start and dropped the cup of tea she was holding in her hand. Having imagined Pimenta hurling his black wife to the crocodile, it was not far to the next image: Pimenta throwing her down as well, despite the fact that she was a white woman.

Pimenta rang the silver bell once more. A servant appeared, picked up the broken pieces of crockery and wiped the floor clean.

She suddenly recalled Berta. Jonathan Forsman had accidentally knocked a coffee cup off a table. She could see the scene in her mind's eye: Berta picking up the bits and then wiping up the coffee. And Forsman didn't even look in her direction.

Which direction am I looking in? Hanna thought. And why do I think what I do about Pedro Pimenta?

The cooling breezes had faded away. The heat on the veranda was motionless. A single peal of laughter rang out somewhere in the distance.

They sat there without speaking. Hanna looked at the others. The beautiful Isabel and the tight-lipped Pedro Pimenta.

I'm not a mirror, she thought. But I know that it's him I'm beginning to look like. And I don't want to.

CHAPTER
FORTY-EIGHT

Shortly afterwards Isabel had left them. Pedro Pimenta no longer had the energy to fan himself with his helmet. He moved over to a garden hammock suspended from springs and iron chains, kicked off his right shoe and inserted his big toe into a loop in a rope attached to a gauze-like fan a metre long, suspended over his head. As he swung back and forth in the hammock, the fan moved up and down. The resulting breeze reached as far as Hanna, who had moved her chair closer to the hammock as requested by Pimenta. Anybody observing the pair of them from a distance would have assumed that their conversation was extremely intimate: but in fact it was only the faint cooling breeze created by the fan that led them to sit so close together that their legs were touching.

"We know nothing about each other," said Pimenta. "We all live here, but none of us knows anything about our respective pasts. I sometimes imagine that one dark night, on board a ship from Lisbon, without anybody seeing us, we all threw our pasts overboard, tightly packed and attached to heavy weights. For instance, I know nothing about you. One day, all of a sudden, you are staying in a room in a brothel that I frequent. A mysterious guest. And then, just as suddenly, you marry Senhor Vaz. When he dies, you become the owner of the most lucrative house of pleasure for gentlemen in this part of Africa. But I still know nothing about you. And you ask me for advice that I can't possibly give you."

"It was my husband who suggested that I should speak to you. If I needed advice. And if he wasn't around."

He screwed up his eyes and looked hard at her.

"That sounds odd."

"That he asked me to talk to you?"

"No. That he thought it would be possible in any circumstances for somebody to give another person advice. He wasn't that sort of man."

"He said exactly what I've just told you he said."

"Obviously, I don't think for a moment that you are telling me an untruth. What good would it do you? I just find it astonishing that he surprises me like this after his death. I don't like it when the dead surprise me."

That was the end of the conversation. Isabel came and squatted down beside her husband. She ran her fingers over his neck and his cheek. Hanna was surprised that he allowed her to display such tenderness so openly in the presence of a stranger.

I have a chimpanzee, she thought, and I pick ticks off his skin. He has a black woman who caresses his cheek. In a way those two activities are remarkably similar.

She wondered what it would be like to have a black man squatting down by her side, running his fingers over her cheek. She shuddered at the thought. Then she remembered Lundmark's rough but well-tended hands, and was overcome by sorrow.

Isabel stood up and left the veranda again. She smiled at Hanna as she left. Pimenta watched her go, his eyes screwed up.

"I can buy the brothel off you," he said suddenly. "If you decide to leave here. I can pay you in Portuguese currency, or in gold, or in jewels. But I'm a businessman. I won't give you a friendship price — I'll try to buy it as cheaply as possible."

The thought of a potential deal had made him so excited that he tugged too hard with his big toe in the rope loop, and the loop broke. He shouted at the top of his voice for a servant by the name of Harri. He came running up and retied the rope. Hanna could see that this wasn't the first time the link had broken when Pimenta had got carried away.

"Why is he called Harri?" she asked when they were alone again. "That's surely not a Portuguese name, is it?"

"He comes from Matabeleland, the English colony. He claims that he once saw Cecil Rhodes in evening dress when he was about to have dinner in the middle of the bush. A large number of pack horses had carried dining tables, silver cutlery and a Persian rug that was laid out in the depths of lion and elephant country. I doubt whether he saw all this with his own eyes, but there is no doubt that Cecil Rhodes treated every campsite as if it were the Savoy hotel in London. That man really was crazy. But I've taken a liking to Harri. He's now more faithful than any of my dogs. And as my dogs play such an important role in my life, blacks who behave like that have all the sympathy I can muster."

"What would happen if I sold the brothel to you?"

"I would maintain its good name and reputation. And take good care of our clients."

"And what about the women?"

He seemed puzzled by her question. The women? His foot started pulling harder at the fan rope.

"You mean the whores?"

"Yes."

"What about them?"

"They grow older. Fall ill. Nobody wants to pay for them any more."

"Then we kick them out, of course."

"Give them some money so that they can buy a stall in the market. Or build them a house if they need one. Those are conditions I shall impose on any buyer. That's what we do for them now, and it must continue that way."

He shook his head almost imperceptibly, and thought carefully before continuing. His foot operating the fan rope was still.

"Naturally I shall continue with the routines that apply now. Why should I want to change them?"

"I'm sure you know that many brothel owners in this town treat their girls very brutally. We have always been an exception."

She realized that the "we" was an exaggeration. It was Senhor Vaz she was speaking about. Her only contribution was not to have changed any of the routines that had always applied before her husband died.

"It will be as I say," he said. "I shan't change anything. Why should I?"

They spoke no more about it. Hanna was invited to a meal consisting of cold soup and a dish of peeled and mashed fruits. She drank two glasses of wine despite the fact that she knew it would give her a headache. Isabel ate as well, but she didn't say anything. Pimenta talked at length, without any attempt to conceal his satisfaction, about the prominent families in South Africa who had bought his white sheepdogs. He recounted with pride how at least two of his white sheepdogs had bitten to death black men who had tried to burgle the palace-like mansions the dogs were guarding. Isabel didn't seem to react when he told this story. She had a frozen smile on her face which never seemed to change at all.

Hanna returned to town later in the afternoon. The sun had disappeared behind thunderclouds that were building up over the mountains near the border with Swaziland.

The conversation with Pedro Pimenta had increased her confusion. She was more unsure than ever about what she ought to do. She couldn't believe that what he had said about not changing anything was true. There was no reason to believe that he would treat the women any differently from the way he treated his white dogs and the crocodiles waiting in his ponds to be killed and skinned. Pimenta was a man who enjoyed throwing living sheep to hungry crocodiles.

She sat in the car with the window open. The wind was pounding the shawl she had over her mouth to avoid having to breathe in the red dust that was swirling around along the road.

For a brief moment she was sorely tempted to instruct the chauffeur to drive her to the South African border: but she didn't, she merely closed her eyes and dreamt about the clear, brown water of the river.

When she got out of the car in front of her house, Julietta immediately opened the front door and took her hat. Hanna realized that her meeting with Pimenta had given her a sort of answer after all. She was responsible for the women her dead husband had bequeathed to her.

She could only live up to that if at the same time she accepted responsibility for herself.

CHAPTER
FORTY-NINE

After a night of heavy rain that once again flooded the streets of Lourenço Marques, a man stood shivering at the front door of the brothel, asking to speak to the woman who owned it. The fact that he knew there was now a woman owner and was evidently not a customer made Hanna uneasy. She was becoming more worried about the unknown, not least people wanting to see her without her knowing why.

That same morning she had sat with her bookkeeper and cashier Herr Eber and discussed the costs of repairs that were necessary after two Finnish sailors had run amok. They had smashed most of the furniture in the sofa room where the whores received their customers. Soldiers summoned from the Portuguese garrison had finally managed to handcuff them. Nobody knew what had triggered their furious outburst, least of all the drunken sailors themselves, who couldn't speak a word of any language other than their odd-sounding Finnish — but on a previous occasion when clients had turned violent, Felicia had said that the cause was almost always the fact that the men had been stricken with impotence and could find no way of expressing their frustration other than trashing the brothel's furniture and fittings, as if that was the cause of their impotence and therefore needed to be punished.

The captain of the Finnish ship had paid for his two crew members to be released, then hastily set sail for Goa, which was his final destination. The money he had paid barely covered the cost of the repairs, and Hanna had decided to draw up a manual listing the precise cost of every kind of damage that might be done to the brothel on some future occasion.

Judas came in, bowed, and mumbled something about a visitor at the front door. Hanna had never heard his name before: Emanuel Roberto. Judas was told to ask the man to wait until Hanna had concluded her session with Herr Eber, who was very precise but slow. There were times when his pedantic, almost somnambulistic writing with his rasping pen drove her to distraction. But she always managed to control herself. She depended on him for information about how all her businesses were going.

When Herr Eber had finally left her room with a deep bow, she summoned Emanuel Roberto. He seemed to stagger rather than walk normally, and his face was distorted by strange tics. Hanna wondered if he was drunk, and her first impulse was to send him packing without even bothering to discover what he wanted. But when he handed over his business card, his hand shaking, and she saw that he was the deputy director of the Portuguese tax authorities in Lourenço Marques, she realized that she had to treat him with respect. She asked him to take a seat, and ordered coffee and a bowl of fruit. His body secreted an odour that suggested his flesh was in a state of fermentation, and Hanna felt obliged to begin breathing discreetly through her mouth.

Roberto made no attempt to pick up his coffee cup, but instead bent forward and drank in a manner reminiscent of an animal at a waterhole.

Unlike his fidgety body, his voice was steady and distinct.

"I had the honour of dealing with Senhor Vaz's tax affairs during all the years he was the owner of this whorehouse," he began.

Hanna objected to his use of the word "whorehouse": it seemed out of place in his mouth.

"According to information I have received from Senhor Andrade," he went on, "Senhora Vaz is now the owner of this house and the activities which take place here. If I have understood the situation correctly, Senhor Andrade will continue to look after all legal aspects, just as he did in the time of the former owner."

He paused and looked at her, as if he was expecting a response. Hanna found it difficult not to burst out laughing. The tics all over his face were much too strong a contrast to his solemn tone of voice. The man standing in front of her seemed quite simply to have been wrongly put together.

When she said nothing he opened his briefcase and took out some elegantly written-out documents on stiff paper, adorned with seals and stamps.

"This is your final tax statement from the last financial year. As your husband was the owner and responsible for all activities for the main part of the financial year, we shall naturally simply present you with our calculations for you to check. But I can tell you that in the current financial year this whorehouse is still the biggest taxpayer in the Portuguese colony. Needless to say it can feel painful for a civil servant to acknowledge that a brothel is the most flourishing and profitable business in the country. Some officials in Lisbon are most upset. Therefore we usually describe your establishment as a hotel. But the outcome is the same, of course: your tax payments exceed those of any other business in the country. All I can say is: congratulations!"

He handed over the documents for her to read. The bureaucratic Portuguese and the ornate handwriting meant that she guessed rather than understood what was written: but the columns of figures were absolutely clear. She reckoned out quickly in her head that she was paying a gigantic sum of Swedish kronor in tax.

The very thought made her feel dizzy. For the first time she understood fully that she had not merely become well off by marrying Senhor Vaz: she was rolling in money. And it was not only in this distant outpost that she was filthy rich: even if she returned to Sweden she would still be extremely wealthy.

Emanuel Roberto stood up and bowed.

"I'll leave my papers here," he said. "If you have any points to raise, please contact me about them within the next fourteen days. But I think I can assure you that everything is in the best of order, correctly calculated and recorded."

He bowed once again, then left the room. Hanna remained seated on her chair for a long time. When she finally stood up she had made up her mind to return to her house on the hill and think seriously about what all this wealth meant for her future.

When she came out into the big sitting room she saw one of the women disappearing into her room with an early customer.

She only saw the man briefly, from behind, as the door closed.

Nevertheless she was certain. It was Captain Svartman who had gone into the room.

CHAPTER
FIFTY

The peacock screeched. It was standing in the middle of the empty street, bathed in sunshine streaming in through the gap between two houses while Indian traders slowly, almost casually opened up their stalls down at street level. All around the peacock was shadow. It seemed to be standing on a stage, illuminated by a single spotlight.

It screeched once again, then started pecking calmly at the invisible seeds that only a peacock's eye could see.

Hanna had stopped dead. The fact that Captain Svartman was in her brothel confused her. She didn't know if what she was feeling was joy at seeing somebody from her earlier existence, or if she was scared of actually meeting him.

But most of all she was astonished. For her, Captain Svartman had never been anything other than the resolute captain whose only passion had been the potted plants in his cabin that nobody except him was allowed to tend. She could never have imagined that he would visit whores in an African port. Perhaps he had come so early in the morning so that there was a minimal risk of his meeting anybody from the ship of which he was in command?

The thought of the ship moved her to act. She left the hotel, took with her one of the black watchmen who had been squatting down asleep in the shade outside the front door, and hurried down to the harbour. The Indian traders who were busy rolling up the blinds in front of their stalls eyed her inquisitively, but were careful not to make it obvious. Hanna had realized a long time ago that many of them knew who she was. She sometimes felt embarrassingly pleased at no longer being a nobody. That was why she was careful to dress smartly for her daily walks between her house and the brothel.

Even during the short time she was married to Senhor Vaz she had had two seamstresses who made her clothes for her. Now she had employed another one who, somewhat mysteriously, had ended up in Africa after a long life in the most renowned circles of Parisian fashion. There were rumours of embezzlement, and perhaps something even worse, but she was still a skilled dressmaker, and Hanna didn't hesitate to pay her whatever she asked for.

Hanna was out of breath by the time she got to the harbour. Berthed at one of the quays furthest out was the ship she knew so well. She stopped in the shadow of one of the enormous cranes that had recently been installed in the harbour. Black labourers in ragged trousers and bare feet were standing in a circle around a white foreman who was assigning work. Hanna had the feeling that he was some kind of priest, preaching the religion of slavery to the black workers.

But her attention was concentrated on the ship. She was filled with contradictory thoughts and feelings. As they were unloading all their cargo of timber in Lourenço Marques, Hanna assumed that must mean the ship was now on its way back to Sweden. She would be able to go back home as a paying passenger, leave everything behind her, sell the brothel that very day. She would obviously lose money on such a deal, but she would still be a very rich woman.

The sight of the ship also put her possible flight in a different perspective. What did she have to return to? Surely her life had turned out to be something she could never have dreamt of?

She returned to the brothel, more unsure than ever about what she wanted. When she entered through the front door she still wasn't sure whether she would reveal her presence to Captain Svartman. She headed for the bench under the jacaranda tree, but before she could get there the door to Felicia's room opened, Captain Svartman came out, and suddenly they were face to face.

At first he didn't seem to recognize her. He paused for a second. Then he knew.

"Are you here?" he said.

"I could say the same about you," she said. "Is Captain Svartman here?"

They looked each other up and down. Hanna felt that she had the upper hand, because he couldn't possibly know what she was doing there in the brothel.

He would probably jump to the obvious conclusion —
that she was there to give pleasure to men in return for
money. But surely he would find that difficult to
believe?

Hanna felt she ought to make it clear that any such
suspicion was unfounded. She shook her head.

"Things are not what you probably think," she said.

She beckoned him to follow her out to the jacaranda
tree and the wooden bench. Zé had materialized from
nowhere and sat down at the piano. He said nothing
but was obviously longing for Carlos, who was probably
his only friend now that Senhor Vaz's heart had stopped
beating. Hanna thought he probably regarded her as an
evil person who had robbed him of his brother and also
the chimpanzee he could always turn to.

Hanna and Captain Svartman drank tea under the
jacaranda tree.

"I wonder who is most surprised," she said. "You at
seeing me, or me at seeing you?"

"I obviously wondered what happened," said
Svartman. "We spent a whole day looking for you. But
then we were forced to continue our voyage."

"I had the constant feeling that Lundmark was still
there on board the ship," she said. "I couldn't cope
with that. There was no other way out for me."

Svartman nodded thoughtfully. Then he started to
smile.

"I'm very pleased, of course. Very glad to see that
you are still alive."

"A friend of mine was married to the owner of this
brothel," she said. "He died. She is very ill. I look after

251

the money that's made here — but I hate the whole business, of course, and only do it for the sake of my friend."

Did he believe her? She couldn't be sure. The ring she had on her left hand could be a leftover from her marriage to Lundmark.

"What exactly happened?" Captain Svartman asked when he had thought about what she said. It still seemed as if he couldn't really grasp the fact that he had met again the third mate's widow, who had jumped ship.

"I booked into a hotel to start with. I had enough money to do that. Then I ended up looking after a house for an elderly man. But all the time I've been looking forward to the moment when I can go back home."

"What prevents you from doing that?"

"My sorrow at having lost Lundmark. And my fear of the sea."

"I think I can understand," said Svartman doubtfully.

As nothing she had said was true, Hanna tried to change the subject. She returned to the moment when she had left the ship under cover of night.

"What did you think had happened?" she asked.

"I thought you might have drowned."

"Drowned by accident, or drowned myself?"

"I suppose I considered both possibilities. But needless to say there were others on board who made wilder guesses. That you had fallen into the hands of white slave traders, for instance. Or been killed by a

252

bite from a poisonous snake that had managed to slither on board, and that you had fallen overboard as the poison began to work."

"But nobody suspected that I had left the ship of my own free will?"

Svartman sounded depressed when he replied.

"I have to admit that not even I could envisage that possibility. And after all, during my many years as captain I've seen lots of sailors disappear in ports all over the world."

She asked about the voyage, and the return route: had they called at Lourenço Marques on the way home as well? Svartman told her they had gone straight to Port Elizabeth to pick up some mixed cargo bound for the French port of Rouen.

She started asking about Halvorsen and the other sailors. And about Forsman and Berta. He answered briefly and suddenly seemed to be in a hurry. Hanna gathered that he didn't want to stay at the brothel any longer than necessary. His visit to Felicia had been a secret, and nobody in the crew must get to know about it.

Hanna was disappointed to discover that Captain Svartman was just like all other men. They concealed the truth about themselves, the things they did in secret, under cover of darkness.

But was she any better herself? Didn't she also go sneaking around? They were simply sitting there under the jacaranda tree exchanging half-truths.

"How long are you staying here?" she asked.

"Until tomorrow."

"I'd like to visit the ship. And naturally, I won't mention the fact that I met you here."

She thought she could detect a doubtful look in his eye as he tried to decide whether or not to believe her. But she looked him straight in the eye. She was his equal now, no longer the scared cook who had curtseyed deeply to him almost a year ago.

She stood up and brought the conversation to a close. She was setting him free.

They said goodbye outside in the street.

"This afternoon will be okay," said Svartman. "I have business to see to this morning, and I must keep an eye on the bunkering."

The peacock was nowhere to be seen. The street was completely deserted in the blazing sunshine. She stretched out her hand.

"I'll come this afternoon, then," she said. "If that's all right with you."

"I'll be there."

He bowed, then seemed to hesitate.

"Peltonen is dead," he said. "He fell overboard one night off the Egyptian coast. Nobody noticed he was missing until the next morning."

"It was Peltonen who measured the depth of Lundmark's grave," said Hanna. "1,935 metres."

Svartman nodded. Then turned and walked away. He turned off into the first side street.

So he's not taking the shortest route to the harbour, she thought. He turned off as soon as possible so that I wouldn't be able to see him.

254

She suddenly wondered if they had seen any icebergs.

Then she was driven back home to her house on the hill, and sat down to write the letters that couldn't wait.

CHAPTER
FIFTY-ONE

It was a shock to her when she read through the letter she had written to Elin. Instead of writing about the voyage, she had written something more like a saga. The only link with reality was her description of how she had met Lundmark, married him, and then been forced to watch as he was buried at sea. But she had left out completely most of what had happened afterwards — her jumping ship and meeting the brothel owner Senhor Vaz. She merely wrote that she was in Africa, in good health, and on her way home. As an explanation of why she hadn't completed the voyage to Australia and hadn't come back to Sweden on the *Lovisa*, she wrote rather vaguely that she had been afflicted with a serious but short-lived illness, and had been perfectly healthy again for ages.

She put the letter down in disgust. It was only now that she realized the full consequences of what Captain Svartman had said. What Forsman had been told when the ship docked in Sundsvall after returning from Australia. And what Elin must eventually have been told in her house in the remote mountains.

Her daughter was dead. For a long time Elin had been forced to live with the sad news that Hanna had died in a foreign country. Nobody knew what had happened to her, or where her grave was. Always assuming that there was a grave.

The thought made Hanna cry. She suddenly realized that Julietta was standing in the half-open doorway, watching her. In a flash of rage Hanna grabbed Senhor Vaz's old bronze paperweight and hurled it at her. Julietta dodged it, and hastily closed the door.

Hanna wanted to cry in peace. But it seemed that there was no time even for that. She tore the letter up and wrote a new one, her hand shaking.

"I'm alive," she wrote. That was the most important thing. "I'm alive." She repeated those words on almost every other line. The whole letter was a sort of long request to be taken at her word. She was alive, she wasn't dead as Captain Svartman had thought. She had gone ashore because she was devastated by grief, and then stayed there when the ship continued its voyage to Australia. But she would soon be coming home. And she was alive. That was the most important thing of all: she was still alive.

That was the letter she wanted to write to Elin. And she repeated the same words, albeit in less emotional style, in the other two letters she wrote that day. One was to Forsman, the other to Berta. She was alive, and she would soon be coming home again.

Eventually the three letters lay on the desk in front of her, meticulously fitted into envelopes that she carefully sealed with the names of the recipients written as neatly as she could possibly manage. She and Berta had taught themselves to read and write — with difficulty, but even so it was an important step away from poverty: she still found it difficult to write, and was unsure about spelling and word order. But she didn't bother about that. The letter to Elin would be the most important message she had ever received in her life. One of her daughters had returned from the dead.

In the afternoon she summoned Andrade's car and was driven to the harbour. She had put on her best clothes, and spent an age in front of the big mirror in the hall next to the front door. On the way to the harbour she suddenly had an idea, and asked the chauffeur to make a detour and stop outside Picard's photographic studio. Picard was a Frenchman who had established himself in Lourenço Marques as early as the beginning of the 1890s. His studio was used by the town's wealthy inhabitants. His face had been disfigured by a shell splinter that had hit him during the Franco-Prussian War in 1870. Although his face was repugnant, his friendliness and his photographic skills endeared him to everybody. But he refused to take pictures of black people, unless they were in the role of servants or bearers, or simply made up the background behind the white people who were being portrayed.

Picard bowed and informed her that he could take her photograph immediately — a couple had just cancelled their slot because their engagement had been broken off. Hanna wanted to be photographed standing up, wearing her big hat, her long gloves, and with her furled parasol by her side.

Picard asked respectfully who the picture was for. He knew exactly who she was, and about her short marriage to Senhor Vaz. Hanna also knew that for some unknown reason Picard had always patronized a rival establishment when he made his regular brothel visits.

"The photograph is for my mother," she said.

"I see," said Picard. "So we want a dignified picture. One showing that all is well on the African continent, and that you are leading a life that has brought you success and riches."

He placed her next to a large mirror and a chair with beautiful arms. He moved a flower arrangement standing on a small table out of the composition after having tried it but found it unsuitable. Then he took the photograph and promised to develop it immediately and make three copies. Hanna paid him twice as much as he asked for. They agreed that the black messenger boy would deliver the photographs to Captain Svartman's ship the moment they were dry.

When she reached the harbour she found Captain Svartman standing on the gangplank, waiting for her. Hanna noted that his uniform had been newly brushed down and his peaked cap polished. She walked up the gangplank, and for a brief, dizzy moment recalled the emotions she had felt when she left the ship. Some crewmen were busy splicing ropes, others were repairing a cargo hatch. She couldn't see anybody she recognized. The captain realized that she was looking for a familiar face.

"The crew is completely new," he said. "After Lundmark's death rumours started to spread suggesting that I was an unlucky captain. Peltonen's disappearance didn't help matters. But my new crew is

259

very competent. As captain I can't go around wishing that earlier crew members were back on board again. I sail with the living, not the dead."

He took her to his cabin. On the way there she saw the new cook coming out of the galley, a young man with blond hair.

"An Estonian," said the captain. "He usually makes pretty good food. He's quiet and clean."

They sat down in the cabin and were served tea by a nervous-seeming boy in a white jacket. Hanna noticed that the potted plants in the brass-framed portholes were well looked after.

"I must know what you said to Jonathan Forsman."

Svartman nodded. He'd been expecting that question.

"All I could tell him were the facts as I knew them. That you had disappeared during our stop at the last port before the final lap to Australia. That we spent a whole day looking for you, but were then forced to continue our voyage. And that I didn't know what had happened to you. Either you were alive, or you were dead: I had no idea which."

"What did Forsman say?"

"He was upset. Shaking. I was afraid he might get into such a state that he had a heart attack. It wasn't me he was directing his anger at, but Fate. The fact that you hadn't come back. I think he felt a heavy responsibility."

"Do you know what he told my mother?"

The captain shook his head.

260

"I assume he tried to give her courage and hope, but I suspect she must have thought that her daughter was dead and buried in a foreign country."

Hanna felt a lump in her throat, and tears gathering behind her eyes. But she didn't want to start crying in front of the captain. She tried to keep a firm grip on herself so as not to break down.

They drank the tea that the boy had poured into their cups, his hand trembling. Hanna recognized the crockery from her time on board.

"This accursed continent!" said the captain out of the blue. "I'm trying to understand how it's been possible for you to live here so long."

"Not everything is bad," she said. "The heat can be difficult, but most of the time it's pleasant. There's no such thing as cold here. I've tried to explain to black people what snow is — like ice, but at the same time as light as a chicken feather falling down from the sky. It's not possible to make them understand."

"But what about the people? The blacks? I shudder when I see how they live."

"I don't know much about that. They live their own lives outside town. In the mornings they come wandering in out of the sun to work as servants or miners. Then they disappear again."

"I hear a lot of talk about violence and robbery. We always post extra guards by the gangplank when we are berthed in African harbours. Other captains have told me about thieves who swim to the ship and climb on board."

261

"I haven't come across anything of that kind all the time I've been living here. The blacks are not like us, but I don't know if they are dangerous. I wouldn't have thought so."

"Can they be trusted?"

"No," said Hanna, mostly because that was obviously what the captain wanted to hear. She suddenly realized that she simply didn't know what she really thought.

The captain studied his hands without speaking.

"It doesn't happen very often," he said eventually. "My visits to those black women."

"Of course not," said Hanna. "I've already forgotten it was there we happened to meet."

The captain seemed relieved. Hanna immediately cashed in on her reward for being so understanding.

"I only went to the brothel to find out why the cashier hadn't been to see me the evening before. I never go there otherwise. I do the work I need to do at a safe distance. I live in a stone-built house that is not much smaller than Jonathan Forsman's."

The captain nodded. Hanna could see that he was impressed by what she had to say, although he wasn't totally convinced that it was true. We don't trust each other, she thought. But we did when we were working together on the boat.

She suddenly had the feeling that she wanted to get away from the ship as quickly as possible. And so she put the three letters on the little table that was screwed down on to the floor.

"Three copies of a photograph are on their way," she said. "A messenger boy will bring them to the ship

262

shortly. I want Forsman and Berta to have a copy, and the third one should be sent to my mother."

She opened her purse and took out several high-value Portuguese banknotes. Svartman declined to accept them. Hanna couldn't help wondering what currency he had used to pay Felicia for her services. She felt uncomfortable when the image of the naked captain lying on top of Felicia's attractive body appeared in her mind's eye.

He accompanied her out on to the deck.

"I'll be going back to Sweden soon," she said. "Other Swedish ships call in here from time to time, but I can't possibly leave just now. I've accepted responsibility for the brothel for as long as the owner is ill, so I can't leave this town until she's fit again."

"Of course not," said the captain.

He doesn't believe me, Hanna thought. Or at least, he doesn't believe what I say. Why should he, after all?

They walked around the ship, and took a good look at the Norwegian forest cat that had come on board in Sundsvall and was now curled up fast asleep down at the bottom of a large coil of hawser.

"How about Berta?" Hanna asked apropos of nothing. "Is she still at Forsman's place?"

"She's had a baby," said the captain. "I don't know who the father is, but Forsman has allowed her to stay on in his house."

Hanna immediately assumed that Forsman himself was the father of the child. Otherwise he would never have allowed Berta to stay.

Berta's loneliness, she thought. And mine. Is there really any difference between them?

A black man came running along the quay. He had a packet in his hand. It contained the photographs from Picard. The captain and Hanna opened the envelope. The black and white picture was a true image of what she looked like, she realized. A woman, still very young, looking frankly and unhesitatingly straight at the camera.

"Both Forsman and your mother will be very pleased," said the captain. "Forsman will probably be extremely relieved to discover that you are alive."

He had one last question for her before they took leave of each other by the gangplank.

"Where shall I tell them you are working?"

"At a hotel," she said. "The Paradise Hotel."

They shook hands. She didn't look back after leaving the ship.

The following day when she returned to the harbour, the ship had left.

CHAPTER
FIFTY-TWO

A few days later. The sea was calm, no cooling breezes were blowing along the dusty streets.

One night Hanna woke up, feeling as if somebody had hit her. Carlos had shouted out from his perch on the ceiling light, then jumped down on to the bed. Hanna knew that monkeys screamed in a special way when they were warning others in the troop about a snake or some other danger they had become aware of. She lit the paraffin lamp next to her bed. When it radiated its flickering light around the room, Carlos seemed to calm down immediately. She thought he must have had a nightmare, something she had suspected on previous occasions when he had started whimpering restlessly in bed, and the following day seemed to be gloomily introspective and preoccupied.

But something was still worrying him. He had climbed up on to the window ledge and was now sitting behind the curtain. When Hanna opened it she found herself looking straight out into the brief tropical dawn — but she could also see smoke and flames rising from a block not far from the brothel. When she opened the window she could also hear shouts and screams in the distance. Carlos climbed out on to the roof, and didn't come back despite her calling for him.

She aimed her binoculars at the centre of the blaze. The dawn light was still only faint, but she could see right away that it was no ordinary fire. Black men were running around with cudgels and bows and arrows in their hands. They were throwing stones and burning bundles of twigs at the soldiers from the Portuguese garrison who had assembled there. Hanna could see bodies lying in the street, but she couldn't make out if they were black or white.

She put down the binoculars and tried to work out what was happening. Then she pulled the bell cord — hard, so that there should be no doubt about her wanting a servant to come to her room without delay, despite the fact that all of them except Anaka were bound to be still asleep.

In fact it was Julietta who came, half-dressed and unkempt, but Hanna could see immediately that she was wide awake. Presumably the others in the house had also realized what was happening down below in the town, and told the youngest of them to answer the bell.

Hanna took Julietta out on to the veranda with her. "What's going on?" she asked.

"People are angry."

"Who's angry?"

"We are angry."

As Julietta said those last words, she also did something out of the ordinary. She looked Hanna in the eye. It was as if she had been stung, Hanna thought. What's going on in the street down below evidently concerns me as well.

"Why are you angry?" Hanna asked. "Please tell me without me having to drag it out of you."

"A white man broke a woman's water pitcher."

Hanna was irritated by the answer, which didn't give her any understandable context. She angrily told Julietta to go and fetch Anaka. When Anaka arrived, she was if anything even more laconic than Julietta.

Hanna got dressed and thought it was lucky that she was expecting a visit from Andrade that morning, with some papers for her to sign. Nobody knew more than he did about what went on in town, whether it happened openly or on the sly. As she was having breakfast, waiting for his arrival, she occasionally went out on to the veranda and took another look through her binoculars. The fire was still burning, and it seemed as if new ones had been started, although they were hidden behind buildings and out of range of the binoculars. She could hear distant shouting and the rattle of gunfire. Carlos was sitting motionless on the roof, following the action.

When Andrade arrived he was red in the face and more agitated than she had ever seen him before. She noted that he had been impolite to her servants, and that he slammed a revolver on to the coffee table before sitting down. Before she had time to ask him any questions, he started to explain what had happened that morning. The sudden uprising had begun a few hours earlier when a group of black men had come marching in from the slums. They had carefully avoided the streets that were usually patrolled by Portuguese soldiers ensuring that the night curfew was observed. Once they had reached the centre of town they had run to a police station and set it on fire by throwing bottles full of paraffin through the windows. The half-asleep soldiers had started shooting the rioters, and then bloody chaos had taken hold.

"So it's an uprising," said Hanna. "There must be a reason for it."

"Must there?" asked Andrade ironically. "These black savages need no reason other than their inherited bloodthirstiness to start a riot that can only lead to their own destruction."

Hanna found it difficult to believe him. It surely couldn't be as simple as he suggested. As early as the day when Captain Svartman's ship had docked in Lourenço Marques, she had thought she could detect hostility and sadness in the eyes of the blacks. She was living in a sad continent where the only ones who laughed — often far too loudly — were the white people. But she was well aware that the laughter was usually no more than a way of disguising apprehension that could easily grow into fear. A fear of darkness, of the people who lived in darkness but couldn't be seen.

Hanna insisted. Something must have triggered the fury of the blacks. Andrade shrugged impatiently.

"No doubt somebody thought he had been treated unfairly and thought it was necessary to die if needs be in order to avenge the perceived injustice. But it will soon pass. If there's one thing I know about these black people, it's that they are cowards. They run away like terrified dogs when things get serious."

He picked up the revolver from the table.

"To be honest I would prefer our meeting to be postponed until tomorrow morning. Calm will have been restored by then, the worst of the troublemakers will be dead and the others will be locked up in the fort. What I feel I must do now is go down to where the fires are burning. I belong to the town's civil militia who have been trained to stand shoulder to shoulder with the soldiers whenever there is a threat to our safety. I can certainly be of some use with the aid of this revolver."

There was something jubilant in Andrade's voice that scared Hanna. But at the same time she wanted to find out what was actually happening close to her brothel.

"I'll come with you," she said, standing up. "This is naturally more important than the papers I'm supposed to sign."

"From the point of view of safety it might be better for you to stay here," said Andrade. "Niggers running amok are dangerous."

"I have the brothel to look after," said Hanna. "I'm responsible for my employees."

She wrapped a shawl around her shoulders, put on the hat with the peacock feather and picked up her umbrella. Andrade could see that there was no chance of her changing her mind.

They drove through the town, which was unusually quiet. The few blacks in the streets were walking as closely as possible to the house walls. Soldiers from the town's garrison were everywhere. Even the town's firemen were carrying weapons, as were many civilians who had formed small groups to protect their neighbourhood if the riot were to spread. During the whole of the drive down to the fires and the centre of the revolt, Andrade talked about what he was going to do. Hanna was disgusted by the way in which he seemed to be looking forward to the opportunity to fire his gun at some of the black rioters.

But nothing turned out as Andrade had hoped. When they came down to the town and the chauffeur turned into a side street leading to the brothel, they found themselves in the midst of a violent confrontation between soldiers and a raging mass of black men. It was bayonets and rifles against cudgels and billhooks, fear versus limitless fury. The car was surrounded by furious Africans who started rocking it from side to side in an attempt to overturn it. There was a smell of burning paraffin everywhere. Hanna was horrified by the thought of being trapped inside a burning car. She tried in vain to force the passenger door open. The sound of rifle shots suddenly rang out. A black face that shortly before had been pressed up against the glass was suddenly transformed into a mess of blood and shattered splinters of bone. Hanna shouted to Andrade to use his revolver, but when she turned to look at him she saw that he was white with terror, and a pool of urine was expanding over his white linen trousers. The chauffeur managed to open the driver's door, get out of the car, and was then immediately swallowed up by the crowd of people. Hanna was now so scared, she was afraid of losing consciousness. But the fear of being burnt to death was even stronger. She forced herself to clamber over into the front seat and get out of the car just as the chauffeur had done.

She was surrounded by black people, their faces, eyes, smells, cudgels and knives. Hanna remembered something Senhor Vaz had told her. If you were confronted by a lion, the worst thing you could do was to run away. That would only result in the lion taking up the hunt and felling the fugitive with a bite at the back of his head.

Hanna also knew that she shouldn't look the lion in the eye. So she lowered her gaze and forced herself to begin making her way through the crowd of people. At any moment she expected to be stabbed, or to be hit on the head by a cudgel. But a path opened up for her. She suppressed the urge to start running, and continued walking slowly, her heart pounding inside her blouse. There was still a clatter of rifle shots on all sides. She gave a start after each one. She stumbled over a man lying dead on the street with his chest torn apart, and paused. But then she forced herself to continue.

Suddenly a troop of cavalrymen on agitated, sweaty horses came galloping up. In just a few seconds the mass of people that had been crowding around her melted away. The street looked like a battlefield, filled with burnt rags and broken cudgels, and among them the gleaming cases of the soldiers' cartridges. The street and pavements were covered in a large number of distorted black bodies, some of them almost naked. A man was howling in pain or in rage, she couldn't make up her mind which. The white soldiers in their dark blue uniforms were standing with their rifles at the ready, as if they were afraid that the dead would rise again and attack them. White people were now beginning to assemble at a safe distance. They were making a sort of growling noise, as if the hatred they felt could not be satisfied by the sight of the dead, but needed to continue punishing them.

The howling man suddenly fell silent. Hanna began walking slowly back to Andrade's car. The chauffeur had already returned, and was sitting with his hands round the steering wheel, staring straight ahead, right through her.

Andrade was sitting hunched up in the back seat. The urine stain on his white trousers had begun to dry. He was holding his revolver in his hands as if it were a crucifix.

Hanna looked at him, and thought that she hated him for his cowardice. But at the same time she couldn't help but be pleased that he had survived and was uninjured. Everything is full of contradictions, she thought. Nothing is as straightforward as I wish it were.

She was surprised to find that she felt nothing at all for the dead black corpses all around her.

Swarms of flies had already begun to gather around the dead bodies. Horses and carts that had been requisitioned by the soldiers stood in the shade. Soldiers with white handkerchiefs over their faces began to gather up the corpses.

Like dead animals, Hanna thought. Just slaughtered, but not yet skinned.

She hurried away. Andrade shouted something after her but she didn't gather what it was he wanted.

272

She didn't stop until she was inside the brothel.

The black women were sitting on the sofas, looking at her. She thought she ought to say something.

But she had no idea what.

CHAPTER
FIFTY-THREE

Their silence unnerved her, as did the fact that they were looking her in the eye. All she had experienced that morning was so frightening and so overwhelming that she was now the one who averted her eyes. She went back out into the street where an officer she recognized was handing out ammunition to the soldiers standing guard on the street corner. He visited the brothel regularly and promised to drive her back home in his army car as soon as he had finished. She sat down in his car and waited. As there was no roof, she raised her parasol to protect herself from the scorching sun. Swarms of flies were buzzing excitedly around her head as if she were dead as well. She flapped her hand at them, and had the feeling that everything that was happening was a dream she had not yet managed to wake up from.

The young officer sat down at the wheel himself. Next to him was a soldier with a gun at the ready. When they pulled up outside the stone house the officer asked if she would like to have an armed guard outside her front door, but she felt safe in her own home. In addition, she knew full well that the officer was trying to do a deal — he would provide a guard if she allowed

274

him access to one of the women for free. That annoyed her.

And so she declined his offer and went in through the door that Julietta was holding open for her. She took her mistress's hat, gloves and parasol.

Hanna asked her to come upstairs to the veranda. The smell from the fires in the town below was still noticeable. Anaka brought her a carafe of water. Julietta was waiting a few metres away from the sofa where Hanna was sitting. Hanna pointed to a chair, and Julietta sat down very gingerly, on the extreme edge of the seat.

"What happened?" Hanna asked. "Don't make anything up. Just tell me what you know for sure."

Julietta spoke slowly as she knew Hanna found it difficult to understand what she was saying. Hanna frequently had to ask her to repeat a sentence or two, but out there on the veranda that morning, Julietta spoke more clearly than she had ever done before. Perhaps that was because she knew that what she had to say was very important for her.

A young woman by the name of Nausica had gone to fetch water from a well on the outskirts of Xhipamanhine, one of the town's biggest settlements for blacks. Like all other women, she was balancing the water pitcher on her head. The pitcher was large, it contained twenty litres: but Nausica was proceeding gracefully along the path as she had done so many times before. Then according to Julietta, something happened just as the woman was coming back to the settlement. Nausica had been confronted by three white men, all of them young, carrying shotguns to shoot the seagulls that were gathered at the site of the large rubbish dumps by the shore. It was a swampy area where nobody and nothing lived, apart from the malaria-carrying mosquitoes that had one of their biggest incubation sites just there. Nausica tried to make way for the three men without losing control of the heavy water pitcher. But just as they were passing one of the young men hit the pitcher with the butt of his shotgun and smashed it, so that the water poured down over Nausica. She sank down in a heap on to the ground, hugging her knees hard. Behind her she could hear the men laughing. Some women working on their tiny *machambor* had seen what happened. Only when the three men had disappeared along the path did they dare to venture forward to see if Nausica was badly injured.

But there was somebody else who had seen what had happened. It was Nausica's father, Akatapande, who now came running along the path. He was an engine driver on trains travelling between Lourenço Marques and the South African border at Ressano Garcia. This incident happened to coincide with the two days off he had every month. Having established that Nausica was not seriously injured, his first instinct was to chase after the three men who had attacked her. Nausica and the other women tried to restrain him — he was risking being beaten to death or shot by the white men who were hardly likely to worry about a father who was protesting about his daughter having been humiliated. But they couldn't hold Akatapande back. He raced along the path until he caught up with the three men who were still laughing about the woman who had been soaked through.

Akatapande started by cursing the three men. At first they seemed to pay no attention to him at all, but continued walking down to the beach. However, Akatapande stood in their way and started punching one of the men on the chest. One of the others clubbed him down with the butt of his shotgun. When Akatapande managed to get to his feet, he was immediately clubbed down again. Then the first man aimed his gun at Akatapande's head and shot him. Then they had continued on their way, quite calmly, as if nothing had happened.

News of Akatapande's death spread with the speed that only extremely brutal attacks could bring about. When an officer summoned from the fort decided not to instigate an investigation because one of the men concerned was the son of one of the governor's closest associates, the subdued muttering in Xhipamanhine began to grow into a furious outcry, and by the early morning had developed into the riot.

Hanna had no doubt that what Julietta had told her was the truth.

And she had become aware of something else: what upset the blacks most of all was that the young men hadn't reacted at all to what they had done.

A dead black man — nothing to bother about.

Julietta stood up, but remained on the veranda. Hanna asked her if there was anything else she wanted to say.

"I want to work at the hotel," said Julietta.

"Don't you like it here?"

No answer.

"We don't need any staff in the hotel. Nobody books in there any longer."

"That's not what I mean."

It dawned on Hanna, to her surprise, that Julietta wanted to start working as a prostitute. She wanted to sit alongside the other black women on the sofas, waiting for customers. Hanna was upset. Julietta was still a child. She was younger than Hanna had been when she had snuggled down among Forsman's greasy furs in the sleigh that had transported her through the frozen countryside to the coast.

"Have you ever been with a man?" Hanna asked angrily.

"Yes."

"Who? When?"

No answer. Hanna knew that she was not going to get one. But she had no real reason to doubt that Julietta was telling the truth about her experience.

I know nothing about these black people, she thought. Their life is a mystery about which I can't even begin to conjure up some kind of explanation. It's just as unknown as the whole of this part of the world I find myself living in.

"That's out of the question," she said. "You're too young."

"Felicia was sixteen when she started."

"How do you know?"

"She told me."

"I didn't know you talked to the women who live down there."

"I talk to everybody. And everybody talks to me."

Hanna thought the conversation was starting to go in circles.

"Anyway, I'm the one who decides. And I say once and for all that you are too young."

"But Esmeralda is old and fat. Nobody wants to go with her any more. I want to start in her place."

"How do you know that nobody is interested in her any longer?"

"She's told me that."

"Has Esmarelda said that?"

"Yes."

Hanna no longer knew if Julietta was telling the truth or not. But unfortunately Julietta was quite right about Esmeralda. The old prostitute had recently gone even further downhill. She drank in secret, always seemed to be eating chicken coated with thick layers of fat, and she had completely lost control of her weight. At one of their morning meetings Herr Eber had told Hanna sorrowfully that nowadays Esmeralda was earning virtually no money at all. She spent most of her time sitting on sofas, with nothing else to do. Only an occasional drunken sailor would turn up late at night, collapse into her arms, then fall asleep and remain in her bed until he was lifted up by one of the guards and thrown out — naturally having first paid for the intercourse he thought he had had, but most often couldn't remember.

Esmeralda's situation was not something Hanna wanted to discuss with Julietta. She was still upset by the girl's request to start working in the brothel. She dismissed her from the veranda without saying anything more.

That same afternoon Hanna sent a messenger to Felicia with a brief message she had placed inside an envelope and sealed it. Hanna didn't want the letter to come into the wrong hands. "I need to talk to you about Esmeralda."

Felicia came up the hill to the stone house that evening. There was still a smell of smoke on the veranda and outside the windows. Felicia was able to tell Hanna that all the dead bodies had now been removed from the street. The riot had fizzled out. Soldiers with guns at the ready were still patrolling the most important thoroughfares, but nobody expected anything drastic to happen. On the other hand, the brothel was almost empty.

Felicia sat down on the chair in Hanna's study. Hanna gave her an envelope, this one sealed as well.

"I'd like you to give this to the girl Nausica, please," she said.

"Nausica is a sixteen-year-old girl who can't read."

"The envelope doesn't contain anything written. I'm giving her money. For her father's burial and a new water pitcher."

Felicia hesitated before accepting the envelope and putting it inside her blouse. Hanna wondered if Felicia might be considering if her honesty was being tested.

But she said nothing about that, and started talking about Esmeralda instead. Esmeralda was about twenty when she came to the brothel — Felicia didn't know where Senhor Vaz had found her. In the early days Esmeralda had been one of the favourites, for several years the most sought after of the women.

Hanna wanted to know about Esmeralda's life outside the brothel.

"She's married and has five children. Another two have died. Of those still alive four are girls and the other a boy. He is the youngest, and is called Ultimo. Her husband is called Pecado, and he makes a living by selling birds he has caught with nets."

"Where do they live?"

"In a house in Jardin."

"Where the riot began?"

"Where all riots begin. There or in Xhipamanhine."

"What is their house like?"

"Like all the other houses."

"What does that mean?"

"Leaky, patched up, built of whatever Pecado has managed to get hold of."

"Have you been there?"

"Never. But I know even so."

Hanna thought over what Felicia had said. Everything seemed to be beyond her comprehension.

"What do you advise me to do?" she asked in the end.

Felicia was evidently prepared for that question. She took some small clear glass jars from out of one of the

281

side pockets in her skirt. They were filled with water, and white worms were swimming around inside.

"I think Esmeralda deserves a chance to get rid of all the fat she is carrying and become in demand again. She'll be able to do it. She knows already that she's no longer justifying her place on one of the sofas."

Felicia leaned over towards Hanna and gave her the glass jars. At that very moment Carlos sneaked silently into the room. He climbed up on to the wardrobe in which Senhor Vaz used to keep his suits and shorts and ties. Carlos sat there motionless, eyeing the two women and the glass jars.

"They are tapeworms," said Felicia. "I got them from a *feticheira* who knows more than anybody else in these parts about how to help people to lose weight. All Esmeralda needs to do is to put one of these tapeworms into a glass of milk and then drink it. It will start growing inside her body, and could eventually become as much as five metres long. It will gobble up most of the food that Esmeralda eats. She will quite soon be thin again. Most tapeworms need many years to grow, but not this particular type."

Hanna observed the white worms and felt quite sick. But she knew that what Felicia had described would come to pass. Her main concern was not Esmeralda, but that Julietta shouldn't end up with the white men who regarded the women in the brothel with superior contempt.

The following day, when the final remnants of the uprising had been cleared away, the streets cleaned up and the cartridge cases removed, Hanna had a meeting with Herr Eber. She also exchanged a few words with Felicia, who reported that Esmeralda had drunk the milk containing the tapeworm late the previous evening.

As Hanna was on her way to the outside gate, she happened to glance into the interior courtyard where the jacaranda tree was. She noticed that Esmeralda was kneeling beside the tree.

It seemed to Hanna that something was happening around that tree that she didn't understand. But there was nobody she could ask about it. The white people she knew would understand no more than she did, and the blacks would give her evasive answers.

There was no end of possible answers. But none would be able to clarify the situation for her.

CHAPTER
FIFTY-FOUR

At first Hanna couldn't believe her eyes. Nevertheless the fact was that Esmeralda really did start to grow thinner.

Every time Hanna looked at her, she'd changed. Herr Eber also kept presenting Hanna with a constantly increasing number of bills from seamstresses who had been taking in Esmeralda's clothes. Hanna still felt uncomfortable whenever she thought about that white worm in the little glass jar, but it was quite obviously now growing apace in Esmeralda's stomach, eating all the food that previously produced bigger and bigger layers of fat around her body.

Hanna had put the rest of the glass jars in the wardrobe where Senhor Vaz's suits and shirts were hanging. Despite her uneasiness, there were evenings when Hanna simply couldn't resist taking out one of the jars and studying the white worm wriggling away inside it. How this tiny animal could grow and become as big as five metres long in a human being's stomach and gut was beyond her comprehension. She would put the jar back in the wardrobe with a shudder.

Carlos sat on top of the high wardrobe, watching her.
"What can you see?" she would ask.

Carlos would reply with his usual jabbering, then just yawn and scratch away absent-mindedly at his stomach.

Two days later Esmeralda disappeared. She had gone away during the night. Late in the evening Felicia had seen her going into her room to sleep. None of the guards had seen her leaving the brothel. Hanna asked Felicia directly if there was any cause for concern: Felicia shook her head, but Hanna thought she could detect a hint of doubt, although she couldn't be sure.

But it soon became clear that she hadn't gone to see her family. That made everybody start worrying.

Contrary to her usual practice, Hanna stayed in the brothel during the day. She sat by herself on one of the red sofas. The only customers were some Russian sailors. A train was expected later in the day from Johannesburg, carrying some Englishmen and Boers whose only reason for the trip was to have sessions with Hanna's black women.

Shortly after three in the afternoon there was a buzz of excited voices in the street outside. Hanna had fallen asleep in the corner of her sofa. An unknown man was talking to one of the guards in a language Hanna didn't understand, or even recognize. Felicia came out of her room, wearing a flimsy dressing gown, and joined in the conversation.

Suddenly silence fell. Felicia came in from the street, and announced in an unsteady voice that Esmeralda was dead. Her body had been floating in the dock. The town's *bombeiros* had been called to retrieve the dead woman. Together with one of the guards and Felicia,

285

who was still wearing her pink dressing gown, Hanna went down to the harbour. As they approached they could see a small crowd gathered at the far end of the quay. When they got there the corpse was just being lifted out of the water. Esmeralda was completely naked. Despite the fact that she had lost a lot of weight during the time she had the tapeworm inside her, her body was still swollen and enveloped by large rolls of fat. Hanna felt that it was shamefully cruel for the body to be pulled up out of the water with no clothes on.

It was a sort of burial in reverse, she thought. I watched Lundmark being tipped into the sea. Now Esmeralda is being lifted out of the selfsame water.

The governor had decreed that every dead body found in Lourenço Marques that might possibly have been the result of an assault should undergo a post-mortem. Felicia and Hanna accompanied the firemen to the mortuary that was situated behind the hospital. There was an overpowering stench when the doors were opened. The doctor who was due to carry out the post-mortem was standing outside in the courtyard, smoking. Hanna noted his dirty hands and frayed shirt collar. He introduced himself as Dr Meandros, and spoke Portuguese with a strong foreign accent. He came originally from Greece. Nobody knew for certain how he had ended up in Lourenço Marques, but some suggested that he had been on a ship that ran aground off Durban. He was a skilful pathologist. It was very rare for him not to be able to establish the cause of death, and hence conclude whether or not it was self-inflicted.

Dr Meandros rolled up his shirtsleeves, threw away the butt of his cigarette and stood on it, then went back into the stinking building. Hanna and Felicia went back to the brothel in a rickshaw powered by a man with enormous ears.

"Why was she naked?" Hanna asked.

"I think she wanted to show everybody who she was," said Felicia.

Hanna tried in vain to work out what she meant by that.

"I don't understand your answer. Explain for me why she decided to take her own life in that filthy dock, and why she undressed before doing so."

"Nobody has found her clothes."

"How am I supposed to interpret that? That they have just vanished into thin air? Or that somebody has stolen them?"

"All I know is that they weren't there on the quay. Nobody saw her coming there with no clothes on. Nobody saw her jump into the water. Perhaps she was carrying large stones in each hand, to make sure that she sank."

"But why should she do that with no clothes on?"

"Perhaps she did have clothes on when she jumped into the water. And then took them off before she died."

"Why?"

"Perhaps she wanted to die in the same way as she had lived."

Although she still didn't really know what Felicia meant, Hanna suspected that she was trying to make a comment about Esmeralda's death. Dying the way she had lived. With no clothes on, naked to the world.

Hanna asked no more questions. When Felicia had got off at the front gate of the brothel, which was being guarded by Judas, she asked the man pulling the rickshaw to go back up the steep hills to her house. He was dripping with sweat when they got there. She paid him twice as much as he had asked for, but even so it was only a few escudos, worth next to nothing.

Julietta was standing in the entrance, looking at her. Hanna could see the curiosity in her eyes, but didn't want to talk to her. She simply gave the maid her hat and parasol and told her that Dr Meandros should be allowed in the moment he arrived. She took it for granted that Julietta and the rest of the staff in the house already knew that Esmeralda was dead. Invisible or silent messages were passed with astonishing speed among the blacks of Lourenço Marques.

Carlos was sitting on her desk chair chewing at a carrot when she entered her study. She let him stay there, sat down on the visitor's chair and closed her eyes.

When she woke up she realized she had been asleep for four hours, a deep and long sleep that felt as if it lasted a whole night. There was no sign of Carlos. She went over to the desk chair and sat down. She had been dreaming. Unclear fragments slowly rose up into her mind. Lundmark had been in it. He had been sitting at the brothel piano, hesitantly fingering the keys. The jacaranda tree had been cut down. Senhor Vaz had been wandering around in a dinner jacket, smoking a cigar

288

that smelled like the fires caused by the rioters. But she couldn't see herself in the dream. She hadn't taken part in it, was simply an observer on the outside, looking in.

She summoned Julietta, ordered tea, then sent her brusquely on her way — as if to remind her that she still hadn't forgotten Julietta's outrageous request to be transferred to the brothel.

She had just finished drinking her tea when Dr Meandros arrived at the front door. When he came up to her study she could see that his hands were still dirty. There were what could well have been dried bloodstains on his scruffy jacket.

He sat down and asked for a glass of wine. When Julietta brought a glass on a tray, he emptied it as if he had been dying of thirst. But he declined firmly the offer of a second glass.

"There's no doubt that the woman committed suicide," he said. "Her lungs were full of dirty water from the dock. It would be sufficient, of course, to give the cause of death as drowning, but I made a more comprehensive examination of her body. Visiting and travelling through a person's intestines can be an adventurous journey. I was able to ascertain that she had probably given birth to a lot of children. Her obesity had resulted in deposits in her blood vessels and brain. Her body was old for a woman who was as young as I take it she was."

Hanna interpreted that last remark as a question.

"She was about thirty-eight. Nobody knows her exact age."

"That can probably be an advantage for black people," said Meandros thoughtfully. "For those of us who know the date and perhaps even the time of day or night when we were born, it can be a confounded nuisance being constantly reminded of the exact moment. A rather more vague time is preferable in many ways."

Meandros seemed to be lost in his own thoughts for a while. Then he continued.

"The most interesting and surprising thing, however, was that she had a very big and particularly flourishing tapeworm inside her stomach and intestines. I wound it around one of my walking sticks and measured it with a tape measure: it was four metres and sixty-five centimetres long."

Hanna pulled a disgusted face. Meandros noticed her reaction and raised his hands in apology.

"I don't need to go into any more details," he said. "The body can be released for burial. I have signed the death certificate and given the cause of death as a clear case of suicide."

"I shall pay for the burial."

Meandros stood up, swayed suddenly as if he had suffered an attack of dizziness, then held out his hand for Hanna to shake. She accompanied him down to the front door.

"What do they usually die of?" she asked.

"The Africans, you mean? Diabetes is rare. Heart attacks and strokes are also quite unusual. The commonest causes are infections cause by malaria-carrying mosquitoes, dirty water, too little food, too little dietary variation, too heavy work. There is a vast chasm between our ways of living and our ways of dying. But tapeworms can affect white people as well."

"How do we get a tapeworm inside our bodies?"

"We eat them."

"Eat them?"

"By accident, of course. But once they get into your body, they stay there. Until they eventually decide it's time to leave. They say it has happened that tapeworms have left bodies through the corner of an eye — but the usual route is of course the natural way."

Hanna didn't want to hear any more. She also doubted if what he said about the corner of an eye was true. She opened her purse to pay the doctor for his visit, but he refused point-blank to accept any payment. He raised his hat and set off on the walk down the hills to the hospital where he had as much responsibility for the dead as he had for the living.

The next day Felicia went to visit Esmeralda's family. Hanna had decided to close down the brothel during the afternoon when the burial was to take place. This had never happened before, despite the fact that several of the women had died during Senhor Vaz's time. Hanna also made sure that all of the women had decent black clothes. When they eventually gathered as a group, all dressed in black with dark hats and veils, it seemed to her that it was a ghostly collection she had standing there before her. They all seemed to be dead already.

A funeral procession of the dead. Dead people mourning a dead person. And in parallel with all this, the thought of the almost-five-metre-long tapeworm. Her desire to throw up came and went in waves.

Hanna had hired a horse-drawn hearse with benches at the sides. Felicia was waiting in the cemetery, with Esmeralda's husband and children. Felicia whispered to Hanna that Esmeralda's ancient father was also present. They gathered around the open grave where the coffin was resting on two rough wooden trestles.

The cemetery was split in exactly the same way as the town: on the right, just after the entrance, were the resting places for the whites — marble sarcophagi or impressive mausoleums. Then an area of less imposing graves, and beyond that the field where the blacks were buried. Their graves were marked by rickety wooden crosses, or nothing at all. Hanna decided on the spot that Esmeralda would have a decent gravestone with her name on.

The black priest, dressed in a white cowl, spoke one of the languages Hanna didn't understand. She occasionally registered the name Esmeralda, but understood nothing else of what he said. She thought that was quite appropriate: she had no idea about Esmeralda's life, and so it was right that she should continue to be unknown to Hanna in death.

We are the ones who have brought about this situation, Hanna thought, somewhat remorseful. We have turned their lives into something that suits us, rather than them.

Hanna stood there watching Esmeralda's children, and her husband, who was staring at the priest with his teeth clenched. When it was all over, she summoned

Felicia and asked her to tell Esmeralda's husband that the family would receive a regular payment. The man came over to thank Hanna. His hand was wet with sweat, his grip slack like that of a man scared to grasp the hand of another person too firmly.

Hanna returned home. Herr Eber, who had attended the funeral, was instructed to make sure that the brothel was opened for business again, and that the black mourning clothes were taken care of.

As she left the cemetery she noticed that Julietta was communicating in whispers with Felicia next to a mausoleum for an old Portuguese ship's captain. Her first instinct was to box Julietta on the ear, but she resisted the temptation, turned away and left the grave — which was already being filled in.

When she got home she went to lie down on her bed. She slept like a log for several hours. Afterwards she ate some of the food she had been served, but the thought of the tapeworm came back to haunt her, and she slid the plate to one side.

With the paraffin lantern in her hand, she went into her study to write about Esmeralda's death and burial in her diary. But when she entered the room and the lamp banished the shadows, she saw that Carlos was sitting on her desk chair. He was holding in his hand one of the glass jars he had taken from the big wardrobe, and had unscrewed the lid. Only now did Hanna realize that the jar was empty. Then she saw the tapeworm wriggling away in the side of Carlos's mouth. She screamed and tried to take hold of the worm, but Carlos swallowed it. Her first impulse was to hit him, but instead she prised apart his jaws and thrust her fingers down into his throat to make him sick. Carlos screamed and resisted. He was strong, and she couldn't hold on to him. Anaka and Julietta heard the noise and came running to assist. Hanna couldn't manage to explain what Carlos had swallowed, just that it was important that he should vomit it up. They grabbed hold of Carlos and this time it was Anaka who managed to force her hand so far down into his throat that he started to vomit. Yellow carrot juice spurted out all over the desk.

Hanna didn't know the Portuguese word for tapeworm. She fetched one of the glass jars that were left in the wardrobe, showed them the tapeworm, and then the jar on the desk that was empty. They all poked around in the contents of Carlos's stomach, but didn't find it. Hanna was furious, sent Julietta to fetch more lamps, and told Anaka to thrust her fingers down into Carlos's throat once again. But all that came up was nasty-smelling stomach juices.

They never succeeded in finding the tapeworm.

Carlos jumped up on to the ceiling light and refused to come down even when Hanna tried to console him and offered him the drink he liked more than anything else: milk. But he didn't come down. Carlos was a wounded animal that hid himself away in his impregnable fortress — a lampshade.

Julietta and Anaka cleaned up the desk. Hanna went out on to the veranda. The town down below was shrouded in darkness. One or two fires in the far distance. Perhaps also the sound of drums.

294

From somewhere came the sound of laughter. It reminded her of the night when she had made up her mind to leave Captain Svartman's ship.

Perhaps it's the same man laughing, she thought. But I am quite a different person now: how can I be sure that I've heard his laughter before? And besides, on that occasion I didn't need to worry about a chimpanzee that has eaten a tapeworm.

It was dawn before she went to bed.

By then Carlos had also gone to sleep, curled up like a frightened child in the ceiling light.

CHAPTER
FIFTY-FIVE

Hanna turned to Felicia once again. She told her about the tapeworm that Carlos had swallowed, but the only advice Felicia had to offer was to wait until it left the chimpanzee's body of its own accord. Hanna asked whether there was a cure, anything the woman with the knowledge of medicine could give Carlos to kill the worm while it was still inside him, but Felicia said that the mysterious female magician who had sold her the tapeworms refused to have anything to do with apes or any other animal. She refused to treat elephants or mice, her knowledge was restricted to human suffering and the remedies she could offer them.

Hanna became so desperate that she borrowed Andrade's car and was driven to the cathedral to talk to one of the Catholic priests. She assumed that the priests there could give advice on everything to do with human life. Even if it was the health of a chimpanzee that she was worried about, it was her own worries that she wanted to be free of.

The heat was like a solid wall in front of her as she travelled to the cathedral. Even though it was early in the morning the heat was so intense that her eyes ached as she hurried towards the darkness behind the open doors. Once inside, Hanna stood still for a while and allowed her eyes to become used to the darkness. The cathedral was empty, apart from a few nuns dressed in white, kneeling before a picture of the Madonna, and a solitary man in a white suit sitting in a pew with his eyes closed, as if he were asleep. There was a smell from the newly painted doors. Some black women in bare feet were gliding over the stone floor, carrying dusters and long poles with feathers on the end, with which they carefully caressed the highest-hanging pictures of the saints.

A priest dressed in black came out of a room in the chancel. He paused in front of the high altar and polished his spectacles. Hanna stood up and walked towards him. He put his glasses back on and eyed her up and down. He was young, barely more than thirty. That made her feel hesitant — a priest ought to be an old man.

"The senhora looks as if she wants to confess," he said in a friendly tone.

"What do people look like then?" she responded. "Guilty? Full of sin?"

The claim that she looked as if she wanted to make a confession touched a sore point in her. She could not deny that she was the owner of the town's biggest brothel, and earned money from the organized sin that was for sale there. But the priest didn't seem to react against her negative tone of voice.

"Most of all people who want to confess express a longing. They want to liberate themselves."

"I don't want to confess. I've come here to ask for advice."

The young priest pulled up two chairs and placed them facing each other. The cleaners had vanished, but the sleeping man was still there in a pew not far away.

"I'm Father Leopoldo," said the young priest. "I've recently come here from Portugal."

"My name's Hanna. My Portuguese is not good. I need to speak slowly in order to find the words I need, and I often place them in the wrong order."

Father Leopoldo smiled. Hanna thought that his face was handsome even if he was very pale and almost gave the impression of being undernourished. Perhaps the priest also had a hungry worm in his intestines?

"Where do you come from, Senhora Hanna?"

She recounted her background in brief, but chose not to mention the brothel: she merely said that she had married a Portuguese man called Senhor Vaz, who had died suddenly shortly after the marriage.

"You said you needed some advice," said Father Leopoldo, who had listened intently to her story. "But you still haven't asked me a question that I can react to."

I can't possibly start talking about a chimpanzee that has swallowed a tapeworm, she thought dejectedly. The priest will either think I'm crazy, or that I've come here to the cathedral to poke fun at him and all that's holy.

Nevertheless, she explained the situation. She told him about the chimpanzee that meant so much to her, about the contents of the glass jar and the tapeworm that was now living inside its body. The priest was not at all annoyed by what she said: he believed both what had happened and her worries about Carlos's fate.

"I don't think you have told me everything," he said when she had finished, still just as patient and friendly as before. "It's difficult to give advice to somebody who doesn't tell the whole story."

Hanna realized that he had seen through her. Even if Vaz was not an unusual name in Lourenço Marques, Father Leopoldo evidently knew about the Senhor Vaz who had run the biggest brothel in town. Perhaps he had even heard about his marriage to the Swedish woman, and his death that had taken place so soon afterwards?

There was no longer any reason to hold anything back. She told him about Esmeralda, and that she herself was now the owner and proprietor of the brothel.

"I'm afraid for my chimpanzee's life," she said in the end. "And I simply don't know what I'm going to do with what I now own and am responsible for."

Father Leopoldo observed her from behind his rimless spectacles. She didn't find his look censorious. She thought it likely that even a young priest was used to hearing the oddest of tales, whether or not they were told to him during confession.

"There is a veterinary surgeon here in Lourenço Marques called Paulo Miranda," said Father Leopoldo. "His clinic is right next to the big market. Perhaps he can give you some advice on how to cure your ape?"

"What can he do that the local women who know about medicines can't do?"

"I don't know. You asked me for advice. Besides, I think that traditional native medicine is based mainly on magic and should be opposed."

Hanna would have liked him to see those white tapeworms, and to explain to him how much weight Esmeralda had lost by showing him the clothes she had worn when she was at her fattest. But she said nothing.

The priest continued to look at her, and pushed his chair closer to her.

"In everything you say I detect a searching for something else," he said. "Something different from the ape and your worries about what it has in its stomach. As I understand it, the advice you are seeking has more to do with your own life. As the owner and hostess of the biggest brothel in Lourenço Marques, I don't need to tell you what the Church thinks about the type of life of sin that takes place in that establishment. All I know about your homeland of Sweden is that it can be very cold there, and that large numbers of poor people have left it and travelled over the sea in search of a better life in America. But not even there would the life you are now leading be regarded as decent or honourable."

His words affected her deeply.

"What should I do?" she asked. "I was left the brothel in my husband's will."

"Close it," said Father Leopoldo. "Or sell it to somebody who can transform it into a respectable hotel or restaurant. Give the women money so that they can begin to lead respectable lives. Leave this country and go back to where you come from. You are still young.

The ape can return to the bush, It will no doubt soon find a troop it can join."

Hanna said nothing about the fact that Carlos had lost his identity as an ape a long time ago, and now lived in a twilight world in which he was neither an animal nor a human being. His home was a ceiling light rather than a forest.

"You are running away from something," said Father Leopoldo. "That flight will never come to an end if you don't return to your homeland. And leave all this messy business behind you."

"I don't know if I have anything to return to."

"Surely you have a family, Senhora? In which case you have your roots there, and not in this town."

Hanna noticed that Father Leopoldo was staring at something behind her head. When she turned round to find out what it was, she saw one of the Portuguese garrison's highest-ranking officers. He was wearing his uniform, with a sabre hanging from his belt and his officer's cap under his arm. Father Leopoldo stood up.

"I'm sorry I can't continue this conversation, but do come back some other time."

He gave Hanna an encouraging smile, then accompanied the soldier into one of the confessionals. The curtains were drawn on each side of the centre wall. Hanna thought that the high-ranking officer probably had a large number of sins to confess. She had recognized him immediately. He was a regular customer at the brothel, and sometimes had strange requirements of the women who served him. Some of his perversities were such that the women refused. Hanna had blushed

301

the first time she'd had explained to her what the officer wanted. He asked for two women at the same time, and that they should pretend to be mother and daughter. Her first reaction was to ban him, but he was a good customer. Felicia had also told her that much worse requests sometimes came from some of the South African customers who were more deserving of a ban.

They had been sitting under the jacaranda tree, talking. Felicia had explained all the peculiar perversions men sometimes had when it came to their association with women. She had been astonished, and blushed. She had never experienced anything remotely like that in her short erotic life with Lundmark and Vaz. She realized that there was a lot she knew nothing about. Things that the proprietor of a brothel certainly ought to know.

She stood up to leave the cathedral, still unsure about what she ought to do.

The man who seemed to have been asleep was suddenly standing in front of her. He was holding his white hat in his hand, and there was a friendly smile on his face.

"I couldn't help hearing what Father Leopoldo said. Sometimes things can be heard very clearly in this enormous cathedral. It's only in the confessional that nobody can hear what's being said. But I want to stress that I'm not normally an eavesdropper. My name is José Antonio Nunez. I've spent many years in this country, doing business. But I've put all that behind me now, and nowadays I devote myself to quite different things. Things that are important in this life. I wonder if I might steal a few minutes of Senhora Vaz's time?"

302

"I don't know you. But you know my name?"

"This is not a big town. Or at least, the white population is not so great that one can remain anonymous for very long. Let me just say that I knew your husband, and ask you to accept my condolences. I really did wish Senhor Vaz a happy and successful life."

Hanna reckoned that the man standing in front of her was in his forties. His friendliness seemed convincing. It seemed somehow that he didn't really belong to this town — in the same way that she was also a foreigner.

They sat down. He was confident and determined, she less so.

"I'll keep it short," said Nunez. "I'm prepared to relieve you of the establishment of which you are the proprietor. I would pay off the women, just as Father Leopoldo recommended. What is of value to me is the actual building. After all my years as a businessman, I'm trying to pay back something of all the benefits I have accrued. If you sell the building to me, I shall turn it into a children's home."

"For black children?"

"Yes."

"In the middle of the white men's red-light district?"

"That is precisely my intention. To create something that reminds people of all the parentless black children drifting around like leaves in the wind."

"The governor would never allow it."

"He's a friend of mine. He knows that he's dependent on me to keep his job. A lot of white people in this town accept my advice."

Hanna shook her head. She didn't know what to believe. Who was this man who had been sitting there with his eyes closed, and now suddenly wanted to buy the brothel?

"I don't know if I'm going to sell," she said. "Nothing has been decided."

"My offer still applies tomorrow, and perhaps some time into the future. I know you use the solicitor Andrade. Ask him to contact me."

"I don't even know where you live."

"He does," said Nunez with a smile.

"I need some time to think this over. We can meet here a week from now. At the same time."

He bowed deeply.

"I'll be here. But a week is too long. Let us say three days from now."

"I don't know who you are," she said again.

"I'm sure you can easily find out."

Hanna left the cathedral. Once again she needed some advice, and she knew there was a person she could turn to. Not only to ask about Nunez, but also about what Father Leopoldo had said.

That same afternoon she was driven out to Pedro Pimenta's farm, where dogs were barking and crocodiles thrashing their tails before vanishing into the murky waters of their pools.

When she got out of the car and the engine had been switched off, she heard the sound of glass shattering inside the house. The veranda was deserted.

Hanna looked around. Everything seemed strangely empty. Then a white woman came racing out of the door, her hands covering her face. She was followed by a girl, screaming and trying to catch up with the fleeing woman.

They disappeared down the hill leading to the crocodile pools. Then silence once again.

A boy a few years older than the girl came out of the door. Hanna had never seen him, the girl or the sobbing woman before.

The boy, who might have been sixteen or thereabouts, paused in the doorway. He seemed to be holding his breath.

He's like me, Hanna thought. I can recognize myself in him — there in the doorway stands a boy who doesn't understand a thing about what is happening all around him.

CHAPTER
FIFTY-SIX

The scene Hanna was observing was transformed into an oil painting with the frame formed by sunbeams. The boy's face seemed to melt as he stood there in the doorway. The dogs in their cages had fallen silent: they just stood there, tongues hanging out and panting heavily.

Quietness at last! Hanna thought. In this peculiar town it is never normally silent. There's always somebody speaking, shouting, screeching or laughing. Not even at night does the town seem to rest.

But just now: silence.

The boy stood there motionless, tied down in the middle of the painting. Hanna was just going to walk over to the steps leading up to the veranda when Pedro Pimenta came out through the door. He stopped next to the boy, who stared at him. Pimenta was holding a blood-soaked handkerchief. He had a wound in his forehead that hadn't quite stopped bleeding. He can't have been shot, Hanna thought. A shot in the forehead would have killed him. Then she remembered the sound of shattering glass, and assumed that the sobbing woman must have thrown something at him.

Pimenta looked down at the blood-soaked handkerchief, then caught sight of Hanna standing under her parasol. He seemed tired, lacking the usual energy and friendliness he normally displayed when he had visitors. Instead of inviting her up to the veranda, he went down the steps to her. The wound in his forehead was a deep scratch just above his left eye and running up to his greying hair.

"Did you see where they went to?" he asked.

"If you mean the woman and the girl, they headed for the crocodile pools."

He pulled a worried face, then shook his head.

"I must find them," he said. "Go and sit down on the veranda and wait until I get back. Everything can be explained."

"Where's your wife? Who's the boy?"

Pimenta didn't answer. He threw the handkerchief on to the ground and hurried off down the slope towards the pools.

Hanna sat down on the veranda. The boy was still in the doorway. She nodded at him, but he didn't react. It was still silent on all sides. She stood up and went into the house. There were glass splinters all over the floor, which was covered by lion hides and zebra skins. Hanging on one of the walls was the mounted head of a kudu, with its long spiral-shaped horns. Hanna tried to imagine what had happened. Not knowing who the woman and the boy were, she couldn't imagine the sequence of events. The glass shards glittered like pearls scattered over the animal skins.

She found all the domestic staff collected in the kitchen. They were scared, crowded together, protecting one another. Hanna was going to ask them what had happened, but changed her mind. Pimenta's wife and the children must be somewhere in the house. She searched the ground floor, then went up the stairs. In the biggest bedroom, where Pimenta slept with Isabel, Hanna found her and the two children. They were sitting on the bed, huddled up next to each other.

"I don't want to disturb you," said Hanna, "but I was worried when I heard the sound of breaking glass and saw Pedro with a bleeding forehead."

Isabel looked at her without answering. Unlike the servants, she was not afraid, Hanna could see that straight away.

Isabel was furious, full of simmering anger of a kind that Hanna had never seen in this woman before.

"What's happened?" she asked.

"It's best if you leave," said Isabel. "I don't want you to be here when what has to happen actually happens."

"What's that?"

"That I kill him."

The children didn't seem at all surprised. Hanna thought that could only mean one thing: that they'd heard her say it before.

Hanna sat down gingerly beside Isabel and took hold of her hand.

"I don't understand what's going on. How can you say to me, in the presence of your children, that you're going to kill your husband?"

"Because I am."

"But why?"

Isabel turned to look at her. Hanna could see that Isabel found it impossible to grasp that Hanna didn't get it. What is it that I can't see? she asked herself. I'm caught up in a drama that I don't understand.

Isabel suddenly stood up and smoothed down her skirt, as if running her hands over her body in that way would give her strength. The two children looked at her. Isabel bent down in front of them.

"Stay here," she said. "I'll be back shortly. Nothing will happen to you."

Then she took Hanna by the arm and escorted her out of the room.

"What's going to happen now?" Hanna asked.

"You've already asked me that question. I don't know what's going to happen. You can leave if you want to. Or you can stay. Do whichever you like."

They had come down the stairs by now. The boy was still standing in the doorway. Isabel swept past him without even looking at him. She doesn't like him, Hanna thought. A grown woman distancing herself from a young boy. A suspicion, vague as yet but perhaps the beginnings of an explanation, began to grow in her mind.

Isabel flopped down on the sofa on the veranda. Hanna moved a basket chair closer to the wall and sat down carefully. Still the boy didn't move. It seemed to Hanna that she was now entering the oil painting she had imagined earlier. She was no longer just an observer.

Pedro Pimenta appeared on the slope. Walking just behind him was the white woman, who was no longer crying. She was holding the girl's hand tightly. The girl was silent. Hanna couldn't hear what the woman was saying to Pimenta. He suddenly stopped, and started gesticulating with his hands. It looked as if he wanted the woman to take the girl with her and go away. He continued towards the veranda, started running, with the woman after him. When they came up on to the veranda, she exploded: "I believed you," she screamed. "I've kept all the letters you wrote, all the protestations of the enormous love you had for me. I kept asking to come and visit you with the children. I simply couldn't bear to keep on waiting in Coimbra any longer. But all the time you kept on telling me that Lourenço Marques was too dangerous. The same thing in letter after letter."

She took a crumpled sheet of letter paper out of her pocket and started reading in a shrill voice.

" 'In Lourenço Marques the streets are full of cunning leopards and prides of lion prowling around at night. Every morning the remains are found of some white person or other, often a woman or a child, that has been eaten. Poisonous snakes find their way into the houses. It's still too dangerous for you to come here.' Did you write that, or didn't you?"

"I wrote the truth."

"But there are no wild animals in the streets here. You lied."

"They were here in the streets some years ago."

"Nobody I've spoken to has seen a single lion in this town for the last thirty years. You lied to me in your letters because you didn't want us to come here. The love that you described doesn't exist."

The furious woman had forced Pimenta up against the wall of the veranda. The girl had joined her brother in the doorway. Isabel was sitting tensely on the sofa, watching what was happening. Hanna thought that perhaps she ought to leave: but something that wasn't merely curiosity held her back.

The woman suddenly turned to look at the far side of the long veranda. Joanna and Rogerio were standing there. They had appeared without a sound, like their mother.

"Who are they?" yelled the woman from Coimbra.

"Can't we sit down and try to talk our way through this calmly and peacefully?" said Pimenta.

But the woman continued to force him up against the wall.

"They are my children," said Isabel, standing up. "They are the children I have with Pedro. And now I'd like to know who you are, and why you are behaving like this towards my husband."

"My husband? My husband? But I'm the one who's married to him! Am I not married to you, Pedro? For nearly twenty years? Who's she? A black whore you've picked up?"

Isabel thumped the woman, and promptly received a thump in return. Pimenta separated them and urged both women to calm down. Isabel sat down, but the other woman started hitting Pedro instead.

"Can't you tell me the truth for a change? What's she doing here? Who are those children?"

"Teresa! Let's calm down a bit to start with. Then we can talk. Everything can be explained."

"I am calm. I'm just fed up of all the letters in which you've lied to me and urged me to stay in Coimbra."

"All the time I was scared stiff that something might happen to you."

"And who's she?"

Pimenta tried to lead her away to one side, perhaps so that he could talk to her without Isabel understanding what was said. But Isabel stood up again. She fetched her children and pushed them forward to Teresa and Pedro.

"These are Pedro's and my children," she said.

Teresa stared at them.

"Good God!" she said. "Don't tell me their names!"

"Why not?"

"Is the boy called José? And the girl Anabel?"

"They're called Rogerio and Joanna."

"Well, at least he hasn't given them the same names as the children he abandoned. At least that was a step too far."

Hanna tried to understand. So Pimenta had a family in Portugal and another family here in Lourenço Marques.

Teresa had stopped shouting now. She was speaking in a low but firm voice, as if she had drawn a horrific conclusion which nevertheless gave her the calm that truth endows.

"So that's why we weren't allowed to come here," she said. "So that's why you wrote all those damned letters about the dangers of this place. You'd got yourself a new family here in Africa. When I was finally unable to wait any longer, I thought you would be pleased. Instead, I came here and found you out. How could you treat us like that?"

Pimenta stood leaning against the wall. He was very pale. Hanna had the impression that standing in front of her was a man who had been caught after committing a very serious crime.

Teresa suddenly turned to look at her.

"Who are you?" she asked. "Does he have children with you as well? Where are they? Perhaps you are also married to him? Are your children called José or Anabel?"

Hanna stood up.

"He's only my friend."

"How can you have a man like that as your friend?"

Teresa suddenly seemed totally abandoned. She looked from one of them to the other. But it was Isabel who progressed from words to action. Lying on the table was a knife that Pimenta used to carve small wooden sculptures, which he burnt when they were finished. She grabbed the knife and thrust it deep into Pimenta's chest, pulled it out, then stabbed him again. Hanna thought she could count up to at least ten deep wounds before Pimenta's body slowly slithered down on to the floor of the veranda. Isabel took her children and disappeared into the house. Teresa collapsed. For the first time the boy left the doorway. He squatted down beside his mother and put his arms round her. The girl started crying again, but quietly this time, almost silently.

Many hours later, when Pimenta's dead body had been sent to the mortuary and Isabel had been led away wearing handcuffs and with a chain round her right foot, Hanna went back home. She had also met once again Ana Dolores, the nurse who had helped her to become fit again, and tried to explain to her the difference between black and white people. Ana had taken care of Teresa and her children, but handed over Isabel's children to the servants with instructions to take them to their mother's sister. She lived in a slum whose name Hanna had failed to grasp. She was distressed to think that they would be taken away from the well-organized white world where they had grown up, and instead plunged into the chaos that reigned in the inaccessible black settlements.

On the way back to town Hanna asked the chauffeur to stop the car by the side of the road. They were on the bank of the river, just before the old bridge that was so narrow, it could only cope with one-way traffic. An old African stood on duty there with a red and a green flag, directing the few cars that used it. The shock of what had happened was only now beginning to register with her.

"What will happen to Isabel?" she asked.

"She'll be locked up in the fort," said the chauffeur. There was no trace of doubt in his voice.

"Who will pass judgement on her?"

"She's already condemned."

"But surely the fact that Pedro double-crossed her and let her down must be taken into account? Just as he let Teresa down."

"If Teresa had killed him, she would just have been sent back to Portugal with the children. But Isabel is a black woman. She has killed a white man. She will be punished for that. Besides, who would get upset over the fact that a white man had let down a black woman?"

They spoke no more about the matter. Hanna noticed that the chauffeur didn't want to reveal what he really thought.

They continued their journey back to town when the man at the bridge raised his green flag. Hanna felt a surge of anger when she noticed that the flag was broken and frayed.

She asked to be taken to the promenade to the north of the town. She took off her shoes and walked over the soft sand. It was low tide. Small single-masted fishing boats were bobbing up and down in the distance. Black children were playing on the part of the beach that wasn't reserved for whites only.

Saving Isabel will be identical with saving myself, she thought. I can't leave here until I've made sure that she gets a fair trial. Only then will I be able to make up my mind what I'm going to do.

She walked along the beach, watching the tide come slowly in. Just now Isabel was the most important person in her life. What happened to Isabel was inseparably linked with herself. She was surprised at how natural and convincing that feeling was. For once in her life, she had no doubts whatsoever.

She was driven back home and paid the chauffeur. That evening she sat at her desk and counted up all the cash she had collected since Senhor Vaz's death. She would now use some of the money to pay for a lawyer.

Carlos was sitting on top of the wardrobe, observing what she was doing. He suddenly jumped down and sat beside her at the table. He picked up a bundle of notes and began counting them with his long, black fingers, bundle after bundle. Seriously, as if he actually understood what he was doing.

PART FOUR

*The Butterfly's Behaviour When
Faced With a Superior Power*

CHAPTER
FIFTY-SEVEN

There was still a long way to go before dawn when the woman called Ana and usually referred to as Ana Branca was woken up by a man's hand touching one of her breasts. For a moment she thought it was Lundmark who had returned from the dead, but when she switched on the light she saw that it was just Carlos who had touched her in his sleep, as if he were feeling for something he'd lost in his dreams. He was woken up by her violent movement. She didn't know if it was disappointment or merely a feeling of shame at being touched up by an ape, but she pushed Carlos out of bed. He gathered that she was angry and jumped up on to the ceiling light. He sat there, looking at her — she could never decide if those eyes of his were sad or amused.

"You confounded ape," she yelled. "Don't ever touch me again!"

Then she switched the light off. She could hear that Carlos's concern was gradually fading away, and he was able to relax on the lamp as it swayed back and forth over the bed. She immediately regretted what she had said and done. After all, Carlos was very close to her —

like a dog, but cleverer, and just as affectionate. He wasn't messing her about.

She also thought it was remarkable that the tapeworm Carlos had swallowed didn't seem to have harmed him at all. Perhaps the stomach juices of an ape are so acidic that a worm able to survive inside a human being can't live inside an ape's gut? She had promised Rumigo, who looked after her garden, some extra payment if he would examine Carlos's excrement to see if there was any sign of a tapeworm. He hadn't found anything yet, but she was sure he would continue to look — he didn't dare not to.

Ana used to be called Hanna. She had also lost her previous second name, Vaz. She lost it the same day as the peacock disappeared.

Despite its clipped wings, Judas swore that he had seen it flying away over the rooftops. Hanna refused to believe him, and in a fit of rage threatened to have him beaten if he didn't tell her the truth. Had he killed the bird and eaten it? Had he plucked off its feathers and sold them as adornments for women's hats? But Judas was adamant: the bird really had flown away.

It was only when one of the harbour guards on his way home from work swore that he had seen the peacock flying out over the sea that Hanna was forced to accept that it really was the truth. She was living in a part of the world where birds whose wings had been clipped could suddenly recover their ability to fly. It was no more peculiar than the claims about ghostly dogs with no legs or paws roaming the streets at night. Or that tapeworms inside a human being's stomach could grow to be five metres long.

Hanna thought that it was a premonition. If she wanted to achieve the impossible, she must do the impossible. She must become somebody else.

And so she was now called Ana Branca, nothing else. Ana Branca is a lonely person, she thought. She was losing the respect that Hanna Vaz had enjoyed. Her decision to try to get Isabel absolved from the murder of her husband Pedro had aroused widespread indignation on the grounds that she had failed in her foremost duty — upholding the solidarity of the white race. Defending the status of her own race at all costs.

Ana was unable to go back to sleep. When the first light of dawn illuminated her window, she got out of bed. This was the morning when she was due to meet Senhor Andrade and talk to him about what was likely to happen to Isabel.

Her first thought that morning was the same as the last one she had the day before. It was the image of Isabel in her underground cell in the fort, where a tiny window at ground level was the only way in for the same light of day that Ana could see was now lighting up the sea and the town, the palm trees along the promenade, and the hills marking the border with the African interior. Isabel slept on a bunk with a single blanket and a mattress stuffed with grass. The cell was either freezing cold or so hot that the damp dripped down from the ceiling. During her first weeks in the cell she had a shackle round one of her ankles, but Ana had succeeded in persuading Lima, the commanding officer of the military prison, to have it removed.

Ana intended to visit Isabel later that day. Every time she had to humiliate herself by asking permission from Lima, who usually kept her waiting inordinately long before making a decision. Sometimes he wasn't even there — or pretended not to be there. Ana always took some food with her, the only thing she was permitted to give Isabel. Only twice had she been allowed to take her clothes. Isabel had been in jail now for two months. She smelled of sweat and dirt every time Ana met her, but Isabel couldn't use the small amount of water she was given in order to wash herself: she had to drink it. Ana knew that two white men who were imprisoned after beating up and killing a third were treated quite differently. But when she complained to Lima about this, it was as if he didn't hear what she said. He would look past her, or through her, while absent-mindedly polishing the stripes on his uniform.

Ana Branca is a lonely person, she thought as she stood by the window. She had rebelled against her own race by standing up for Isabel, who was wasting away in the bowels of the fort.

It was nine o'clock when Andrade arrived and handed his white hat and walking stick to Julietta, who made a fuss of him and bowed after escorting him to Ana's study. Ana and Andrade no longer shook hands: that gesture, which had never been a mark of friendship but had signified respect, was a thing of the past. He sat down opposite her at her desk.

What she wanted to know first of all was if there was a risk that Isabel might be decapitated or hanged. She had asked her solicitor that question several times, but never received a satisfactory answer.

"The death penalty was abolished in Portugal in 1867," said Andrade. "In other words, I can't see any risk of her being executed. I've tried to explain that before."

Ana felt relieved. But could she be absolutely sure?

"I've consulted all the law books," said Andrade, "and the fact is that nobody is condemned to death any more apart from those found guilty of treason. I've also written a letter to the Ministry of Justice in Lisbon, but I haven't had a reply yet. But I don't hesitate to say that there are a lot of us who think that the death penalty ought to be reinstated, especially in the Portuguese colonies in Africa. That would force the blacks to refrain from even thinking about committing crimes against white people."

"Who will pass judgement on her?" she asked.

Andrade was surprised by the question, possibly even annoyed.

"Pass judgement on her? Surely she has already condemned herself."

"Where will the trial take place? Who will be the judges? Who will defend her?"

"This isn't Europe. We don't need a judge in order to lock up a black woman who has committed murder."

"So there won't be a trial?"

"No."

"How long will she be locked up in the fort?"

"Until she dies."

"But won't she be given a chance to defend herself?"

Andrade shook his head in irritation. Her questions were annoying him.

"Portugal's relationship with this black country is still not legally regulated. We are here because we want to be here. We send our own criminals back to Lisbon or Oporto. We don't bother about blacks who commit crimes involving other blacks. They have their own laws and traditions, and we don't poke our noses into that. But in this unique case, we lock her up in the fort. End of story."

"But surely she has the right to a lawyer? Somebody who can argue her case?"

Andrade leaned forward.

"Isn't there somebody who is now known as Ana Branca who is looking after that side of things?"

"I'm not a lawyer. I need advice. There's nobody here in Lourenço Marques who is willing to help me."

"It might be possible to find an Indian lawyer in Johannesburg or Pretoria who would be prepared to take on the case."

Andrade took a gold pen from his breast pocket and wrote a name and address on the back of a business card.

"I've heard about somebody who might do it," he said as he put the business card on the table. "He's called Pandre and comes from Bengal. For some strange reason I don't understand he has learnt Shangana, which is no doubt the language Isabel speaks

324

when she's not babbling on in Portuguese. He might be able to help you."

Andrade stood up and bowed. When Ana offered to pay him, he shook his head in disdain.

"I don't accept payment for when I'm not working," he said. "I'll find my own way out."

He paused in the doorway.

"If you decide to leave our town, I'm prepared to offer you a good price for this house. Can we say that I'm first in the queue if that's the way things go? As a reward for the bit of help I've given you this morning?"

He didn't wait for a reply, but left the building. She could hear his car starting in the street outside.

Carlos had crept into the room unnoticed, and was now sitting in his usual spot on top of the dark brown wardrobe that still contained Senhor Vaz's clothes.

What exactly does he understand? Ana thought. Nothing? Or everything?

CHAPTER
FIFTY-EIGHT

Ana took a horse-drawn cab down to the brothel. There she picked up Judas who accompanied her to the fort when the worst of the midday heat was over. She was always a little worried when she walked past the armed guards: perhaps the doors to the fort would close behind her? Judas was carrying the basket containing the food for Isabel. Judas suddenly began talking — a very rare occurrence.

"I don't understand," he said. "Why is Senhora Ana helping this woman who stabbed her husband?"

"Because I know I might well have done the same thing myself."

"He should never have got involved with a black woman."

"Isn't that what white men do every evening in my establishment?"

"Not in the way that Senhor Pimenta did. He sired children with her, and recognized them as his own. That could only end in one way."

They walked in the shadow to the low building where Indian vendors sat at their stalls smelling of foreign spices.

Ana paused and looked at Judas.

"I'm going to keep on fighting until I've got Isabel out of prison," she said. "You can tell that to everybody you talk to."

Commanding Officer Lima was standing on the steps to the building where the fort's weapons were stored. He seemed to be bored stiff, and was rocking back and forth on his heels. On this occasion he simply waved her through without a word. Judas handed her the basket, then stood there motionless at the spot where she had left him. As usual, he waited for her in the scorching hot sunshine. Ana could hear that Lima was talking to one of the soldiers. About me, she thought. No doubt scornful comments about me.

Isabel was sitting on her rickety bunk. She said nothing, didn't even look at Ana when she stepped into the murky cell. Despite the fact that Isabel smelled awful, Ana sat down beside her and took hold of her hand, which was very thin and cold.

Not a word was said. After a long silence, Ana took the empty basket from the previous day, and left the cell. As long as Isabel kept eating, there was still hope.

Two days later Ana took the train to Johannesburg. It was a journey she had never made before, and she would have liked to have a companion: but there was nobody she could trust among the whites she knew — at least, not in connection with the matter she hoped to resolve.

A horse-drawn cab took her to the house in the centre of town where the lawyer Pandre had his office. When she arrived, she was surprised to find that he was in — something she had hardly felt able to hope for. He even had time to speak to her, albeit for quite a short time before he had to attend a court proceeding.

Pandre was a middle-aged man, wearing Western clothes but with a turban lying on his desk. He was addressed as *munshi* by his male secretary, who was also Indian. He invited her to sit down, and Ana could see that he was curious to find out why a white woman would want to come and consult him, so far away from Lourenço Marques. His Portuguese was not fluent, but significantly better than Ana's. When she asked if he spoke Shangana, he nodded — but gave no explanation of why he had bothered to learn one of the languages spoken by the blacks.

He listened intently while she told him about Isabel, and how she had killed Pedro Pimenta.

"I need advice," she said in the end. "I need somebody to tell me how I can convince the Portuguese that she should be set free."

Padre looked at her and nodded slowly.

"Why?" he asked. "Why should a white woman want to help a black woman who has landed in the worst possible of situations?"

"Because I have to."

"You speak broken Portuguese. May I ask where you come from?"

"Sweden."

Pandre thought over her response for a while, then left the room and returned with a dented and stained globe in his hand.

"The world's a big place," he said. "Where is the country that you come from?"

"There."

"I've heard about something called the Northern Lights," he said thoughtfully. "And that the sun never sets during the summer months."

"That's true."

"We all come from somewhere," said Pandre. "I'm not going to ask you why you have come to Africa, but please tell me what you are doing in Lourenço Marques."

During the long train journey she had made up her mind to tell the truth, no matter what questions were asked.

"I run a brothel," she said. "It's very successful. I inherited it from my husband. A lot of my customers come from Johannesburg. Just now there are thirteen women of various ages and various degrees of beauty in my brothel, so I can afford to pay for your services."

"What do you want me to do?"

"Go to visit her. Get her to talk. And advise me what to do in order to have her set free."

Pandre sat there in silence, slowly rotating the globe and pondering what she had said.

"I shall charge you one hundred English pounds for my visit," he said eventually. "And I also have an extra request, bearing in mind the business you conduct."

Ana understood without his needing to say anything more.

"Of course," she said. "You will have access to the brothel whenever you feel like it. Gratis, naturally."

Pandre stood up and looked at a clock hanging on the wall.

"I'm sorry, but I have to go now," he said. "One of my clients, who I unfortunately failed to defend successfully, is due to be hanged in the municipal prison. He has requested that I should be present. It's not something I'm going to enjoy doing, of course; but on the other hand, it doesn't upset me all that much. Anyway, I take it that we have reached an agreement. I can pay a visit to your black woman next week."

It required quite an effort on Ana's part not to storm out of the room when the lawyer displayed such total indifference to the plight of a client who was about to be hanged. Just how would this man be able to help Isabel?

"Is it a man who's going to be hanged?" she asked.

"Of course it's a man."

"Black?"

"White. A poor man who could only afford an Indian lawyer to defend him."

"What had he done?"

"He cut the throat of two women, a mother and daughter, in an attack of jealousy. Very brutal. It was obviously impossible to avoid the death penalty. Some accused can be saved, others can't. And some don't deserve to be saved. Unless we are intent on transforming human beings into beasts of prey."

Pandre bowed, rang a bell and left the room. The obsequious secretary came in, and noted down her address in Lourenço Marques.

"What does *munshi* mean?" she asked.

330

"The word means 'a man who is a teacher' in Hindi. It is usually an honorary title. Herr Pandre is a wise man."

"But nevertheless his clients are hanged?"

The secretary flung out his arms as if he were regretting what he'd said.

"That very rarely happens. Herr Pandre has a good reputation."

"Does he have any black clients?"

"He never has had so far."

"Why not?"

"The courts decide which lawyers will represent blacks. All blacks have to be defended by whites."

"Why?"

"To avoid any suggestion of bias."

"I don't understand that."

"Laws and jurisprudence are matters for specialists. Herr Pandre understands. As I said, he is a wise man."

The following day she travelled back to Lourenço Marques. She had not forgotten the secretary's words.

When she returned to the brothel Felicia informed her that somebody had placed a headless chicken on the steps outside the prison governor's residence. An amateurish drawing of Isabel on a piece of brown wrapping paper from one of the Indian stalls had been attached to one of the chicken's legs. It could only mean that a lynching might take place at any time.

The threat had become more menacing, more imminent. Things are closing in on me, Ana thought. Everywhere, everything.

CHAPTER
FIFTY-NINE

After her trip to Johannesburg Ana began spending more of her time in the brothel. Felicia, who was by now her only confidante, had told her that certain clients had suddenly begun to mistreat the women. Ana therefore wanted to be present among them as the men were hardly likely to try anything on in her presence. She could see immediately that the women were both surprised and grateful. On the other hand, if any of them treated a customer off-handedly or merely did the minimum necessary to satisfy his desires, Ana would immediately give the person concerned a telling-off. They were not allowed to use their treatment of clients as a way of taking revenge on those who wanted to harm Isabel.

One morning Ana gathered all the women together, along with Zé and Judas, and told them about her visit to Johannesburg and the meeting with Pandre. She didn't say anything about the promise she had given him for the time being, but she could tell by the reaction she received that even if there was an element of surprise and astonishment, they were delighted to discover that Ana had not abandoned Isabel. While the whites in Lourenço Marques regarded her as a disgraceful criminal who had killed an innocent man, for the blacks she was not exactly a heroine — she had after all killed the father of her children — but a woman who had made a valiant attempt to rise out of her misery and offer some resistance.

Ana thought that was an appropriate description of Isabel's fate: that she had risen up and offered some resistance. Even if she was now locked up in a cramped prison cell, guarded by menacing and often drunken soldiers, it was as if she had walked away from her plight and left behind all the white people who despised her.

That same day, a white man she had never seen before came to the brothel and asked for a job. It did happen from time to time that white men, often in a bad way thanks to a fever or alcohol, came to her asking for work. She had hitherto always sent them packing as they had nothing to offer her that could be of use.

But the man standing before her now made a different impression. He wasn't dressed in shabby clothes, nor was he unwashed with a straggly beard. He introduced himself as O'Neill, and explained that he had worked as a bouncer in bars and brothels all over the world. He also produced a well-thumbed bundle of references from previous employers.

Ana had often wished she had a white bouncer in the brothel. Even if Judas and the other security guards did what they were supposed to do, she was never absolutely sure that they would react as she wanted them to.

She decided to employ O'Neill on trial for a few months. He seemed to be strong and radiated determination. She thought it would soon become clear if he was a person she could employ permanently.

Later on Ana had a conversation with Felicia under the jacaranda tree. It was evening by now. Felicia was waiting for one of her regular customers from Pretoria, a religious gentleman farmer who was always talking about his eleven children, and that the only reason he visited the brothel was that he no longer wanted to have sex with his wife because she was worn out after giving birth to all those children.

Ana asked her about Isabel's family. There was so much she still didn't know. It also surprised her that none of Isabel's relations had been to see her in the fort. Ana was the only person who visited her, apart from Father Leopoldo who always did the rounds of those imprisoned there. Ana had been to the cathedral again to see him, and he told her that Isabel never spoke to him either. She kept it to herself, but that knowledge gave her a feeling of relief. She knew that she could well have become jealous if Isabel had chosen a priest to talk to.

Felicia was dressed in white, just as the gentleman farmer always wanted her to be.

"I don't know much," said Felicia. "Isabel's sisters are looking after the children. She also has an elder brother called Moses. He works in the mines in Rand. He'll no doubt come here as soon as he can. If he can."

"Are her parents still alive?"

"They live in Beira. But the sisters have decided not to tell them anything about what has happened."

"Why not?"

Felicia shook her head.

"Perhaps because they are afraid that the news would cause their parents such great grief that it kills them. They are old. Or maybe they don't want them to be afraid that the whip would start lashing their shoulders as well. Everybody seems to be waiting for the brother who works in the mines."

"When will he come?"

"Nobody knows. Neither when nor if he can come."

Ana began talking about the headless bird that had been lying on the prison governor's steps.

"Who could have done that?"

Felicia drew back, as if Ana were accusing her of doing it.

"I don't mean that you did it, of course. But who would want to kill her? No white man would put a dead bird on a step as a warning. Surely it must have been somebody black?"

"Or somebody who wanted to make it look that way."

Ana realized that Felicia was right.

"So you think it was a white man?"

"Only a white person would want her to die."

"Why do you think she refuses to speak?"

"Because she's grieving.

"Grieving?"

"Grieving for the husband she was forced to kill."

"Because he had deceived her?"

"She knows that all whites do that."

"Are you saying that all white people tell lies?"

"Not to other whites. But to us."

"Do I tell lies?"

Felicia didn't answer. She continued looking at Ana, didn't turn her eyes away, but remained silent. So I shall have to answer the question myself, she thought. She's making me decide. It's my decision and nobody else's.

"I still don't understand what you mean when you say that Isabel is grieving. She misses her children, of course. But that's not grief."

"She's grieving for the children she never had. As she was forced to kill her husband."

Ana had the impression that their conversation was going round in circles and getting nowhere. She sensed rather than understood the logic in Felicia's words.

"Who would want to kill her?" she asked again.

"I don't know, but essentially I believe that every single one of all the thousands of white people living in this town would be prepared to hold the knife that stabs right into her heart."

"Who has anything to gain from her death? It wouldn't bring Pedro back to life."

"I don't know," said Felicia. "I can't understand the way you think."

Ana got no further. Felicia stroked her hand over her newly washed white dress, carefully smoothing away the wrinkles. She wanted to leave.

"Who am I to you?" Ana suddenly asked.

"You are Ana Branca," said Felicia in surprise.

336

"Nothing more?"

"You own this tree, the ground it's growing in and the building around us."

"Nothing more?"

"Isn't that enough?"

"Yes," said Ana. "That's more than enough. It's so much that I can barely manage to cope with it."

A gigantic man with a large beard and a weatherbeaten face appeared in the open door leading into the garden. It was Felicia's client. Ana watched them walking towards Felicia's room. She looked very small by his side.

Just like I must have done, Ana thought. When I walked beside Lundmark to the consul in Algiers, to get married.

She remained sitting under the tree. It had been raining earlier in the evening. Steam was rising from the soil, and there was a sweet smell coming from the tree's roots. There was also another smell, but she couldn't make out where it was coming from. The underworld was intruding. Ana thought of herself as Hanna again, and remembered all the smells that rose up from the marshes and heather-clad moors where she grew up.

For a short while the feeling of homesickness was overpowering. No memories could awaken this longing as strongly as smells and fragrances, reminding her of something that she had lost and would always miss.

There under the tree she decided to stay in Africa until the lawyer Pandre had been to visit Isabel and given her advice. If the bottom line was that there was no way in which she could help the imprisoned woman, there was no reason for her to stay here any longer. She wouldn't give up, but neither would she surrender to illusions.

Her thoughts were interrupted by a voice she thought she recognized. Emerging from one of the rooms, together with Belinda Bonita, was a man who, she could see that from the way he walked, seemed to be not completely sober. His back was turned towards her. At first she couldn't understand what he was saying. Then she realized it was a language she understood when the person talking it wasn't slurring his speech.

She knew now who it was with his back turned towards her. Halvorsen. The man who had been Lundmark's best friend. The one who had promised her his support if she needed it after Lundmark's death and burial.

CHAPTER
SIXTY

For the second time, somebody from the original crew of the *Lovisa* had come to her brothel. But she had to ask herself if she might be mistaken after all. Halvorsen had been a serious man, deeply religious, and not a heavy drinker like most others of the crew. Svartman, Lundmark and Halvorsen had been among the sober ones, she thought. But he was having difficulty in keeping his balance, and his Norwegian was slurred. She had the feeling that he was irritated because Belinda Bonita hadn't understood what he said. On board the ship Halvorsen had always spoken in a low voice, not much more than a whisper. Now he was shouting, as if giving orders.

When he finally turned round and flopped down on to one of the sofas — with a bundle of banknotes in his hands, which Belinda quickly took from him — Ana saw that she had not been mistaken. It was Halvorsen all right, his hair plastered down, wearing his best clothes: she had last seen him dressed like that when he stood on deck at Lundmark's burial, watching the corpse, weighed down with an iron sinker, disappear down into the depths.

She could still remember the magic number of metres: 1,935.

When Belinda had left Halvorsen, who was now sitting mumbling to himself, Ana stood up. O'Neill was standing behind him, wondering whether to help him out, but Ana waved him aside and sat down carefully beside Halvorsen. He turned his head slowly to look at her with bloodshot eyes. He had hardly changed since she saw him last, a few hours before she had slipped across the gangplank and jumped ship. Perhaps his hair had become slightly thinner, his cheeks hollower. But his enormous hands were exactly the same.

She smiled at him, but could see immediately that he didn't know who she was. There was nothing in his eyes to suggest that he recognized her. As far as he was concerned she was an unknown woman, a white woman in a black brothel where he had just availed himself of the services of the beautiful but cool Belinda Bonita, who had stuffed his banknotes inside her blouse and gone back to her room to get washed and perhaps also change the sheets.

Halvorsen screwed up his eyes and tried to look at her with just one eye. He still seemed not to know who she was.

"It's me," she said. "Hanna Lundmark. Do you remember me?"

Halvorsen gave a start. He shook his head, couldn't believe his ears.

"I'm not a ghost," she said, trying to speak as clearly as possible. "It really is me."

Now he knew. He stared at her incredulously.

"You disappeared," he said. "We never found you."

"I went ashore. There was no way I could continue the voyage. It was as if Lundmark was still on board."

"1,935 metres," said Halvorsen. "I still remember that."

He sat up, straightened his back, tried to force himself to become sober.

"I didn't believe I would ever see our cook alive again," he said. "Least of all here. What happened?"

"I went ashore. I got married again, and became a widow once more."

Halvorsen pondered upon her words, then asked her to repeat them, but more slowly this time. She did as he asked.

"We thought you were dead," he said. "Nobody could believe that you would leave the ship voluntarily in an African port."

"I'd like to hear about the voyage," she said. "Did you see any icebergs?"

"We saw one iceberg, as tall as a church. It was just after we left this port. The nights were always a worrying time — nobody ever discovers an iceberg until it's too late. But we got to Australia and came back again."

"I kept going down to the harbour, but I never saw you berthed there."

"We bunkered further north, in Dar es Salaam. Or was it further south, in Durban? I can't remember."

Ana realized that Halvorsen must have remained on board all the way back to Sundsvall. That meant that he must have met Svartman, who always gathered together and greeted his crew when they returned to their home port.

"I assume you stayed with the ship all the way back home?"

"I stayed on board all the way to Sundsvall. But then I travelled to Norway and signed on to a different ship."

"I'm not worried about that. I'd just like to know what Forsman said."

Halvorsen frowned.

"Forsman? Who's he?"

"The ship's owner!"

The penny dropped.

"He came rolling up to the quay in a sort of wheelchair."

"Had he injured himself?"

"He'd had an accident and had to have a leg amputated. But he was determined to go up on deck. He hopped around like a lame bird."

"Was he alone?"

"I think he was accompanied by a Finn, but I can't remember his name."

Ana continued questioning him, but he didn't know anything about Berta or any children. Although it was obviously pointless, Ana couldn't help asking him about her mother. Had anybody mentioned Elin? The woman who had a daughter who never came back to Sweden?

Halvorsen knew nothing about anybody called Elin.

"I never spoke to Forsman," he said. "It was Svartman who did that. I know nothing about what they said about you and Lundmark, his death and your disappearance. I travelled to Spitzbergen and spent the winter there in the belief that I'd be able to hunt down so many furs, I'd be able to afford to buy a little farm somewhere in Trøndelag. All that happened was that I nearly froze to death, was driven mad by the darkness, and completely lost all faith in the God I used to turn to in times of trouble. He doesn't exist for me any longer. But I think I've collected in advance enough forgiveness for all the sins I haven't yet committed."

Halvorsen couldn't help laughing somewhat plaintively. Then he suddenly leaned towards her, so close that the stench of strong drink hit her full in the face.

"As you are here, I take it you are also for sale. That negress certainly knew what she was doing. But it can never be the same as it is with a white woman. Do you cost as much as she does? Or maybe you charge even more?"

Halvorsen placed a hand on her breast and gave it a squeeze. She was reminded of Carlos's hairy fingers, and pushed him away. Halvorsen thought it was the start of a game, and felt her again. This time she slapped him hard and shouted for O'Neill.

"Throw this man out," she said. "And make sure he's never allowed back in. Never ever."

Halvorsen didn't even have time to protest before O'Neill had pulled him up off the sofa and dragged him out into the street.

The door closed behind him.

Ana thought that the difference between Captain Svartman and Crewman Halvorsen had been ironed out the moment they entered the establishment where women were for sale. But she couldn't get over the fact that Halvorsen had thought she was a whore. At that moment something ended irrevocably.

CHAPTER
SIXTY-ONE

After Halvorsen's unexpected visit, Ana began noting things down in her diary more often. What had previously been an occasional activity now became more and more important for her. She wrote down in minute detail absolutely everything about Halvorsen's visit, and his churlish behaviour.

The day after his visit she went with O'Neill down to the harbour. There were two English ships and one Portuguese berthed at the quay. She had no way of knowing which of the ships Halvorsen was a crew member of. Nor could she work out afterwards why she had made that visit to the quay. Perhaps it was nothing more than curiosity that she had no control over?

During the night a swarm of grasshoppers had descended on Lourenço Marques. Nobody knew where they had come from, nor why they had chosen Lourenço Marques to fall down and die in. There were dead or dying grasshoppers lying all over the place — in the streets, on steps and on roofs. When she walked from the brothel to the harbour, she had the impression that this was what a battlefield looked like: every grasshopper was a wounded or dead soldier.

The only one who seemed to appreciate all these grasshoppers was Carlos, who sat on the roof of Ana's house feasting on the insects.

That afternoon, when she made her usual visit to Isabel in the fort, she was confronted by an officer she had never seen before. That day she had chosen to take O'Neill with her rather than Judas. Commanding Officer Lima had succumbed to some illness that was probably malaria, and had been taken to hospital. His military adviser had taken over Lima's place. He introduced himself as Lemuel Gulliver Sullivan. Despite his English name, he spoke fluent Portuguese. He was a young man, and could barely have celebrated his thirtieth birthday. Ana hoped that his youth would contribute to more tolerance and consideration for Isabel than Lima had displayed.

But the moment he started speaking, she realized that what she had hoped for would not, in fact, take place.

"As long as I am in charge here, stricter rules will be applied," he began. "Those who are imprisoned in this fort are criminals. Their punishment must be felt. At this very moment I am discussing with my fellow officers about the possibility of reintroducing whipping. Giving miscreants a good walloping has always produced good results."

Ana thought at first that she had misheard what he said. Was Isabel's life in her wretched cell going to become even worse than it was already? She said as much, without attempting to conceal her concern.

"Her crime must be treated extremely strictly," said the new commanding officer. "The only thing that matters in this case is that she killed a white man. If we don't clamp down strictly on that, it could be interpreted as a sign that the respect we demand is not total and unconditional."

Ana could see that it was pointless to try to argue with Sullivan.

"Are there other regulations that will come into force from now on?" she asked instead.

"We shall not permit more than an extremely limited number of visitors."

"Who, to be precise?"

"You, of course. And that priest who keeps turning up and trying to accumulate lost souls. Plus a doctor, should that become necessary. But nobody else."

"What about if she should acquire a legal adviser?"

Sullivan burst out laughing and advertised the fact that he was short of quite a large number of teeth, despite his age.

"Who on earth would want to advise her? And about what?"

Ana asked no more questions. She went down the stairs into the darkness where Isabel was sitting motionless on her bunk bed, looking as if she hadn't moved since Ana's visit the previous day. But the basket was empty: Isabel was still alive. She was eating.

"Somebody will come to visit you," said Ana. "I think and hope he's a clever man who might be able to help me to have you set free. He'll pretend to be a doctor when he enters the fort. As he speaks the same language as you, nobody will be able to understand what the pair of you are saying, not even me."

Isabel didn't respond, but Ana had the impression that she was listening.

"The next time I come I'll bring you some clean clothes," she said. "By then it will be three months since you were locked up here. I'll ask once again for them to give you sufficient water for you to get washed."

Ana only stayed for a few minutes. The important thing now was not her visits, but whether or not Pandre would be able to change her situation.

On the way back she made a detour via the harbour. When O'Neill wondered why, she snapped at him. She didn't like him asking questions all the time. She had begun to discover sides of O'Neill she didn't like. She was annoyed by the way he eavesdropped on her, and, moreover, she had heard that he'd been seen in the company of the owner of another of the town's brothels. Perhaps she had made a mistake in employing him?

"What does she do all day?" he asked. "Does she regret her sins? Does she hammer on the cell walls as if they were tom-tom drums? Does she turn up the whites of her eyes?"

Ana stopped dead.

"One more word from you and you can go away and never come back."

"But I'm only asking a few questions."

"Not a word. Not a single word. From now on part of your duties is to remain silent."

O'Neill shrugged, but Ana could see that he had understood the risk he was running.

When they came to the harbour Ana noticed that one of the English ships had left. She suspected that must be the ship that Halvorsen had signed on to as a carpenter.

She had also noted that O'Neill was staring hard at her. When she left the harbour she told him to stay where he was until she had disappeared round the first corner.

A few days later Pandre sent a telegram to say that he was on his way. Ana met him at the newly built railway station. Although Pandre had said in his telegram that he only intended to stay for two days, he had a large number of suitcases, bags and hat boxes with him. Four porters and two trolleys were needed to transport the luggage to the car that she had once again borrowed from Andrade. A horse-drawn carriage was filled with all the luggage for which there was no room in the boot of the car.

They drove to the hotel where, in accordance with the instructions in Pandre's telegram, Ana had rented the largest suite they had. Ana had been a little worried when she went to the hotel: would they accept Pandre, who was coloured, as a guest? But the hotel manager had assured her that a lawyer of Indian origin would be most welcome. Ana was committed to paying all expenses for Pandre's visit, and handed over a sum of money to pay for his stay. She began to wonder if Pandre was intentionally doing all he could to squeeze out of her as much money as possible; or was this the way he always lived whenever he left Johannesburg on business?

After Pandre had taken a bath, changed into a newly ironed white linen suit and then spent some time admiring the view, they sat down to eat in the empty dining room.

Dark clouds were gathering over the inland mountains, presaging a storm that would arrive in Lourenço Marques by the evening. Ana told Pandre about her conversation with the new prison governor, and explained that Pandre would only be allowed in if he played the role of a doctor.

"I don't have a white coat with me in my luggage, I'm afraid," he said. "Being a lawyer doesn't normally mean that one needs to adopt a disguise."

"I don't think that will be necessary, either."

"Tell me more about this man. Officers in the military are often suspicious by their very nature. Will he be able to see through a false doctor?"

"I don't know. He introduced himself as Lemuel Gulliver Sullivan. But he spoke fluent Portuguese so I suspect he's only an Englishman by name."

Pandre burst out laughing as he rolled a gleaming serviette ring between his fingers.

"Is that really his name? Lemuel Gulliver Sullivan?"

"I wrote the name down the moment I got back home."

"Was he surrounded by horses?"

"The soldiers' horses are stabled in the outskirts of the town. There are only a few goats inside the fort."

350

"I mean his soldiers. Did they look like horses?"

Ana didn't understand his question. She was immediately on her guard.

"Why should he be surrounded by horses?"

"Yes, that's a good question. Perhaps he was surrounded by unusually small people instead? People who would be able to stand inside this serviette ring as if it were a wine barrel. Or are his soldiers giants?"

He could see that she didn't understand his references.

"Lemuel Gulliver is a character in a novel," he said with a smile. "I've never heard of anybody cheeky or conceited enough to call their son after that remarkable fictional character. I take it you don't know about the books featuring that man?"

"I run a brothel," said Ana. "I'm trying to help a woman to get out of prison. I don't read books."

"That sounds reasonable enough," said Pandre. "I don't suppose that young commanding officer reads all that many books either. If any at all. But in any case, his father must have read *Gulliver's Travels*."

They ate in silence. Pandre occasionally asked her a question, mainly as a polite indication that he hadn't retired entirely into his own private thoughts. He asked about the climate, the rainy season, animal life and various tropical illnesses. She answered as best she could, and wondered if he intended to visit her brothel that same evening, to take advantage of the special offer he had asked for and received.

But that wasn't his plan. After the meal he stood up, bowed and asked to be collected at ten o'clock the following morning. Then he bowed again and left the dining room. Ana paid the bill, and was driven home.

Carlos had come down from the ceiling, replete with all the grasshoppers he had been gobbling. He was lying on her bed, belching contentedly. Ana sat down at her desk, opened her diary, but left it untouched to start with. She thought about the impression that Pandre had made, now that she had spent some time with him, and only then wrote down everything that had happened since he arrived.

One of these days she hoped to be able to read aloud for Isabel everything she had written. The story of the long journey she had undertaken in order to secure Isabel's liberty.

She knew now how she would conclude her diary: she would note down the date and time when Isabel had been set free.

And she would also write the answer to the question she spent most of her time thinking about: was everything that had happened since the death of Lundmark merely a temporary parenthesis in her life?

The last thing she would write would be about Isabel's and her own freedom.

She closed the diary, extinguished the paraffin lamp and remained sitting there in the dark. She thought: Isabel is locked up in her disgusting dump. And I'm confined in a different sort of prison.

CHAPTER
SIXTY-TWO

The following day: intense heat.

Pearls of sweat were glinting on Pandre's brow when he came out of his hotel and stepped into the car. He was carrying a leather briefcase. It occurred to Ana that it could very well have contained a stethoscope and other instruments that a doctor would need.

Lemuel Gulliver Sullivan was waiting for them on the steps, just as his sick predecessor had always done. Ana thought he looked like a little boy in a uniform that was too big for him and boots that were far too shiny.

She introduced Pandre.

"Here is the doctor I spoke about with your predecessor — I assume he told you Herr Pandre would be coming?

The commanding officer nodded, but he regarded Pandre with undisguised antipathy.

"I thought I had better come with you," he said, "and listen to the doctor's conversation with his imprisoned patient."

"The conversation will take place in the patient's own language," said Pandre in a friendly tone of voice. "That is purely in order that she can describe her aches and pains properly, so that I can ask the right questions and give answers that are clear to her."

"I'll come with you in any case," said the governor. "I'm interested to see if you can persuade her to talk at all. So far she hasn't uttered a word. Perhaps she was born without any vocal cords? I don't even know if her voice is low or high-pitched."

"It's low," said Ana. "I shall understand what they say to each other in her native tongue. I can translate for you."

Pandre looked fleetingly at her. He understood what she was intending to do, and regarded her for the first time with genuine approval.

They walked down the stone steps to the fort's basement. A half-asleep soldier quickly straightened his back, saluted and began to raise the grating in front of the iron door. The commanding officer turned to Pandre.

"I assume that you don't have a gun in your briefcase," he said. "Whether it's to shoot the prisoner dead or to set her free."

Pandre opened the briefcase and took out the stethoscope Ana had imagined might be inside it. How on earth had he managed to get hold of that? He's prepared himself well, she thought. Perhaps he's the right man to help Isabel after all.

They stepped into the dark basement where the musty air was motionless. An unshaven, half-naked white man was shaking in his cell as they passed by.

"He's going to be moved to a lunatic asylum," said the commanding officer. "He is convinced he has a large insect in his stomach that is eating him up from the inside. He beat a man to death because he refused to listen to him going on about the insect's insatiable hunger."

Pandre listened attentively and politely to what the officer had to say. He doesn't seem to be affected by the musty air, Ana thought. Perhaps there are similar prisons in the town and the country where he comes from.

They passed by another cell where a man was lying asleep, stretched out on the floor, gasping for air.

"He's a Spaniard by the name of Mendoza," said the commanding officer as he continued to guide them through the darkness. "He killed his brother on a coaster, and now he's trying to punish himself by refusing to eat. He ought to go to the asylum as well, but they refuse to accept him. I expect him to die within the next few days. Some of my soldiers are placing bets on how long he will live. I don't like that, but there's not much I can do about it."

They entered Isabel's cell. Ana noted that the basket was empty. Isabel was sitting motionless on her bunk.

"You have a visitor," roared the commanding officer.

Isabel didn't react. Pandre nudged the officer's arm to indicate that he shouldn't yell at her again, then went up to Isabel and sat down beside her. Ana stood by the side of the bunk, while the officer remained in the half-open doorway. Ana had no idea of what Pandre was saying to Isabel, but Isabel bucked up the moment the lawyer started speaking to her, and answered his questions in her own language.

The commanding officer rattled his sabre impatiently. Ana took a step closer to him and began to tell him the story she was making up as she spoke.

"They're talking about her children," she said. "They are discussing her great sorrow at having been deceived by her husband, and her regret for what she has done. She's telling him how much she wants to leave this dump of a prison and start work in one of the white missionary stations, spreading the true faith among the black population."

Ana tried her hardest to imbue the story she was making up with as much conviction as she could possibly muster. The commanding officer listened in stony silence. He's not really interested, she thought. Isabel means nothing to him. It doesn't matter to him if she lives or dies. He only came along with us because he was bored stiff.

She continued to elaborate on her story while Pandre and Isabel spoke quietly to each other. When the conversation was over — and it stopped suddenly, as if absolutely everything had now been said — Ana rounded off her account by repeating what she had said about Isabel's longing to devote her life to a Christian missionary station.

When they returned to the hotel they sat down in the shade of some frangipani trees and gazed out over the sea. Pandre had said nothing in the car after saying a polite goodbye to the commanding officer. Now he swayed slowly back and forth in the garden hammock, a glass of iced water in his hand.

"Isabel is ready to die if she has to," he said. "She will die rather than admit to any guilt. Her silence is due to her dignity. Her soul. She kept repeating that word over and over again. 'It's all about my soul.'"

"Doesn't she want to live for the sake of her children?"

"Of course she wants to live. Perhaps she might be able to escape. But if her only way out is to admit to being guilty, she would rather die."

Pandre continued rocking back and forth, gazing out to sea. He stretched out the hand in which he held the glass of water and pointed at the horizon.

"That's India over there," he said. "Thirty years ago my parents came to Africa from there. Perhaps I or my children will go back one of these days."

"Why did your parents come to Africa?"

"My father sold pigeons," Pandre said. "He heard that there were a lot of white people in southern Africa who were prepared to pay large sums of money for beautiful pigeons. My father had learnt how to glue extra tail feathers on to his pigeons so as to get a higher price for them."

He looked at Ana with a smile.

"My father was a confidence trickster," he said. "That's probably why I have become his opposite."

He put down the glass of water.

"I can't really give you any advice," he said. "The only thing that can save her is if she can escape. Perhaps the commanding officer can be bribed? Perhaps one of the soldiers can be persuaded to leave her cell door open one evening? I'm afraid I can't suggest anything else. But as you have plenty of money, you have access to the one thing that might be able to get her free. I simply don't know how best you can use your money in this particular case."

"I'll do anything to get her out of that prison."

"I suppose that's what I'm suggesting. That you do anything at all you can."

Pandre took an envelope out of his inside pocket and gave it to Ana.

"Here is my bill," he said. "I'm intending to visit your women tonight. I'd like to be picked up from here at nine o'clock. I'll have dinner alone in my room."

He stood up, bowed and walked over to the white hotel building. Ana stayed where she was, thinking over what Pandre had said. She knew that he was right. Isabel was trying to choose between dying and saving her soul.

Is that what I'm doing as well? she asked herself. Or has the possibility of choosing already passed?

She remained sitting there until the sun set. Then she went home, changed her clothes and went to pick up Pandre at nine o'clock. He was now wearing a dark suit with a high stiff collar, and smelled of a perfume Ana had never before come across on a man.

"That stethoscope," she said when they were sitting in the car. "Where did you get it from?"

"I made my preparations," said Pandre. "Before I was picked up I paid a short visit to the hospital. A friendly doctor let me have an old stethoscope very cheaply."

They sat in silence for the rest of the journey.

When they arrived at O Paraiso, Pandre sat down on one of the red sofas, was served a glass of sherry, and then started to assess the women carefully, one by one.

Ana sat down on a chair in a corner of the room, and watched him from a distance. She still hadn't opened the bill he'd given her. They had agreed earlier on £100, but she suspected Pandre would have added considerable extra costs that she would have to pay him.

She observed Pandre and his critical eyes.

Isabel's dump of a prison seemed very close by. A chain round Isabel's leg chafed and rattled quietly somewhere deep down inside Ana.

CHAPTER
SIXTY-THREE

When Pandre eventually chose the woman he wanted to be with, and pointed at her as if he were selecting an animal for slaughter, all present were surprised to find that his finger was aimed at the pale and almost repulsive A Magrinha. Ana thought at first that it was Felicia he had selected, as she was standing next to A Magrinha. But when she saw Pandre stand up and bow in front of the extremely thin woman that hardly any of the customers ever chose, there was no doubt about it. She was astonished; but if there was one thing she had learnt during the time she spent in the brothel, it was that the desires of men and their views on what was tempting were impossible to predict. It also occurred to her, not without a degree of satisfaction, that Pandre's selection of A Magrinha meant that the cost of his visit had decreased because A Magrinha was a net loss to the brothel rather than making any money for it. Perhaps the time had now come to have one final talk with her, ask Herr Eber to pay her enough money for a vegetable stall in one of the town's markets for the blacks, and then to send her packing once and for all.

But she got no further in her thoughts before something unexpected happened and distracted her.

There were rather a lot of clients in the brothel that evening, crowded round the little bar in one corner of the room with their glasses and cigars, and as Pandre was on his way with A Magrinha to her room a tall, well-built man suddenly stepped in front of them and blocked the way. O'Neill, who could always sense when danger was in the air, got up from his seat next to the door. Ana did the same. The man standing in front of Pandre was called Rocha, a person with an Italian father and a Portuguese mother. He worked in the colonial administration, in charge of the maintenance of roads and sewers, and visited the brothel every week. He was usually well behaved, but he occasionally lost his temper when he had been drinking too much. When that happened he would be escorted off the premises before he could cause any damage.

Ana suspected instinctively that something very serious was about to happen. Rocha pushed A Magrinha to one side and began speaking to Pandre in broken English.

"I have choosed her to spend the evening with me," said Rocha.

"I find that very hard to believe," said Pandre, without losing his friendly smile.

"To say as it is, all the women have already clients for the evening. You come too late."

Ana had approached close enough to hear the brief conversation, and knew immediately what it meant. She had noticed how many of the white customers had reacted when a coloured man entered the brothel. It had never happened before during her time in charge, although Senhor Vaz had told her how he very occasionally made an exception for influential Indians from Durban or Johannesburg. As nobody had protested openly, she thought that the complaints would come directly to her later, after Pandre had left the brothel. That somebody might ask her what she meant by allowing such a person in when all the other customers were white, and that she would reply that she was the one who decided whether anybody should be turned away or not. She knew that they wouldn't like it, no matter how much she stressed that it was an exception.

All conversation had ceased, everybody was looking at the two men and the girl, who hardly knew what was happening around her.

"Is there a problem?" Ana asked.

"Not really," said Pandre. "It's just that this man is standing in our way. We were just about to withdraw."

"He has stolen the woman I have picked for this evening," said Rocha.

He spoke Portuguese to Ana. When he started to translate, Pandre raised his hand to stop him. He had understood everything that was said.

Rocha pulled A Magrinha roughly to his side, as if to underline what he had said. In a flash Pandre took her back again — but before either Rocha or Ana had time to react, A Magrinha had snapped out of her trance-like state. She pushed Pandre to one side and stood next to Rocha.

"He is going to be with me tonight," she said. "Not that brown man."

Pandre's smile vanished. It was as if a flame had been blown out. He turned to Ana. She could see that he was furious.

"I insist that I have made my choice," he almost snarled.

"That's my impression too," said Ana, turning to A Magrinha and gesturing that she should go back to Pandre.

"I don't want to," she said. "He's brown."

"And you are black," said Ana. "I'm white. And I'm the one who decides what you're going to do."

"No," said A Magrinha. "I'm not going to get undressed for him."

Rocha smiled. O'Neill had moved closer as it looked as if blows were about to be exchanged. But Pandre gave up. Ana knew that he was not accepting defeat, he was still furious: but he could see that things could become very nasty, and he wanted to avoid that.

"I'm going back to my hotel," he said. "I assume that the payment for my services will have arrived before I leave Lourenço Marques around noon tomorrow."

He bowed, then hastily left the establishment, followed by O'Neill. The men clustered round the bar applauded approvingly. Rocha pushed A Magrinha away contemptuously, and she flopped down on to a sofa. Ana could see that right now she hated the place she found herself in — more than ever before.

When Ana heard the car's engine start, she went out into the street. O'Neill was standing there, smoking.

"That man should never have come here," he said. "It's none of my business, of course. But if you let the likes of him come in, you'll soon find that all the other customers disappear."

Ana didn't respond. She knew that she ought to go in and order Rocha to leave the premises, but instead she crossed over the street and went into a little bar run by two Portuguese brothers. One was small and fat, the other a hunchback. The bar was cramped. It contained a wooden counter, a few tables in the dark corners, and a number of street walkers who divided their time between parading up and down outside and having drinks bought for them in the dark interior of the bar. Ana asked the hunchbacked brother for a glass of cognac, emptied it rapidly and ordered another. She recognized one of the women lurking in the shadows. She had frequently asked to joined Ana's brothel, but been rejected by the other women because she had a reputation for stealing. She was also in the habit of punishing customers who didn't treat her well by poisoning them with magic potions. The poison didn't kill them, but rendered the men impotent for a considerable length of time.

When Ana saw that the woman was coming towards her, she gestured with her hand that she should keep her distance, put money on the counter to pay for her drinks, and went back out into the street.

The night sky was clear. She thought about her father and the evenings when he used to show her the constellations he was so familiar with. She waited there in the street until the car returned from Pandre's hotel, and just before clambering in she turned to O'Neill.

"Tell the women I want to see them all at seven o'clock tomorrow morning."

"They'll be asleep then."

"No, they won't," said Ana. "They will be awake, washed and dressed. At seven o'clock tomorrow morning I want to see them gathered around the jacaranda tree."

"I shall be there."

"I want to talk to the women, not to you. You will not be there."

She closed the car door. She could see through the rear window that O'Neill was standing with an unlit cigarette in his hand, watching the car leave.

Carlos spent that night lying asleep, looking like a hairy ball, in the bed beside Ana. He touched her arms now and then in his sleep, as if he were climbing. As he didn't whimper at all she assumed that meant he wasn't having nightmares. If indeed apes had dreams like humans did. She wasn't sure, but perhaps by now Carlos had moved sufficiently far away from his life as an ape. She had the impression that more and more often he was having dreams that scared him. Ana herself lay awake, dozing off briefly now and again, but most of the time rehearsing for the meeting tomorrow morning. She needed to prepare them for the difficulties which were going to get worse for as long as she continued trying to secure the release of Isabel. She would tell them that she had no intention of giving up, no matter what problems that might cause. But at the same time she wanted to know what they thought

365

about it all. Did they understand Isabel's situation? Was there any desire to help her?

During the night Ana got out of bed now and then — quietly in order not to wake Carlos up, even if she was never sure if he was only pretending to be asleep. She leafed through her well-thumbed and shabby Portuguese dictionary in an attempt to find the right words to express what she wanted to say the next morning. She went out on to the veranda in the warm night air. The guards were asleep beside their fires, a solitary dog trotted past without a sound in the street below. From the sea she could see the twinkling lights of ships waiting for high tide so that at dawn they could progress into the harbour and berth.

One of these days I'll go down to the quayside as well, she thought. With a life newly shattered, in an attempt to mend it. That's what brought me here. Soon it must also lead me on to the next stage, even if I don't yet know where my destination will be.

CHAPTER
SIXTY-FOUR

Everybody was already there when Ana arrived at the brothel the next morning. On the way, she had stopped at Pandre's hotel and handed over an envelope sealed with sealing wax to the half-awake manager. It contained the money Pandre had asked for. As she left the hotel, she wondered if she would ever see him again. She didn't really know anything about him, apart from the fact that his father was a confidence trickster who used to glue false tail feathers on to pigeons.

There was no sign of O'Neill when Ana entered the brothel for the early-morning meeting. A chair had been placed under the jacaranda tree for her. To her surprise it was Felicia who started talking the moment she sat down. It became obvious to Ana that the women had prepared for the meeting in advance, perhaps just as thoroughly as she had.

Felicia spoke on behalf of them all.

"We know that Senhora Ana is trying to help Isabel. That is something that surprises us, and we respect you for it. No white man would do that. Probably no other white woman either. But we are also aware that your doing so is causing difficulties for us. We are getting fewer customers, and the ones that do come are not as generous as they were before. We've also noticed that they sometimes treat us more roughly than they used to. The word in town is that men are choosing to go to different establishments with different women, as a protest against what you are doing to help Isabel. That means that we are earning less — if it goes on like this we shall soon have no customers at all. In other words, this place would lose altogether the good reputation it used to have."

Felicia had spoken as if she were reading from a script. Ana knew she was right. The number of customers had indeed gone down — at first only slightly, but lately much more noticeably. Herr Eber was worried and had shown her a graph illustrating how income was falling — not exactly over a precipice, but down a hill that was growing steeper and steeper.

Nevertheless, Ana was both annoyed and disappointed by what Felicia had said. She had hoped for approval and support for her efforts to get Isabel released. She found herself feeling contempt for these black women who sold their bodies without a second thought. All that mattered to them was their income.

She realized immediately that the thought was unfair. She was the one who earned more than anybody else from the activities of the brothel. She was the one who could afford to spend time and money on attempts to help Isabel. She was the one who had the means to bring Pandre to Lourenço Marques from abroad, and she was the one who might eventually be able to bribe somebody to allow Isabel to escape.

But what Felicia had said continued to annoy her. Even during the time when Senhor Vaz was alive, the women in his establishment had earned much more than those in any of the town's other brothels.

"The difference in earnings can't be all that great," said Ana. "Is there really anybody among you who has cause for complaint?"

Ana noticed that her voice was tense. She wanted them to be aware of her anger.

None of the women spoke. They all stared into space. Nobody reacted even when two orange-sellers in the street outside started quarrelling. The women were normally more interested in fights or noisy quarrels outside the brothel than almost anything else.

"I want to know," said Ana. "Is there anybody who has noticed a significant fall in earnings?"

Still nobody spoke — but then, as if in response to an invisible sign, all of them raised their hands.

Ana stood up. She felt she couldn't bear this any longer.

"I shall personally pay each of you however much you think you have lost as a result of my helping Isabel," she shouted. "Come to me every month with bills for what you would have earned from customers who haven't shown up. I shall pay them. I shall become your new customer!"

Ana stormed out of the brothel without looking back, and was driven straight back to her house. She sat for ages in front of her open diary without actually writing anything. She didn't yet know how to deal with her big disappointment.

After a while, she went over to a window and looked out over the sea. Small fishing boats with triangular sails were scudding along over the waves, making the most of a fresh following wind. Carlos had climbed up on to the roof and was sitting on the edge of the chimney with an orange in his hands.

Ana was just about to leave the window when she noticed a black man standing in the street down below, looking up at her. She had never seen him before. He was strongly built, and wearing what looked like overalls. When he noticed that she had seen him, he turned round and walked away. She shouted for Julietta.

"Have you seen a black man standing in the street, looking up at my house?"

"No," said Julietta.

"I've just seen one down below, looking up."

"I don't know who it could have been. But I can ask."

By the time Ana got into the car that afternoon to be driven down to the fort, Julietta had still not managed to find out the identity of the man in the street. Nobody seemed to have seen him. Ana began to wonder if she'd imagined it.

Sullivan was standing on the steps waiting for her when she arrived.

"The prisoner was injured last night," he said, off-handedly as if it didn't concern him.

At first Ana didn't understand what he meant.

370

"The woman for whom you bring food was injured during the night."

"What happened?"

"Somebody tried to kill her. But failed. It's also possible that it was only somebody trying to disfigure her, to make a mess of her face."

"How could that happen?"

"We are investigating the circumstances."

Ana didn't wait to hear what else Sullivan had to say. She ran across the open courtyard with the grassy patch where goats were grazing. A soldier had already raised the grating when he saw her come in through the front gate. Ana raced along the dark corridor. The door to Isabel's cell was standing open. For once she wasn't sitting on the bunk, but lying down. Ana sat down on the stone floor next to the bunk. Blood was running from one of Isabel's cheeks and her mouth. It was obvious that she had been slashed with a knife.

Sullivan had followed her down to the cell.

"Maybe you should fetch that Indian doctor," he said.

Ana had the distinct impression that Sullivan knew Pandre was not at all what he had pretended to be, but just now was not the time to start wondering about what Sullivan knew or didn't know. He could think whatever he liked.

"He's already left," she said. "Why can't the fort summon a doctor?"

"He's on his way," said Sullivan. "But he had to deliver a baby first. Life always takes precedence over death."

"Not always," said Ana. "I think that life and death are equally important. Isabel might die if she doesn't get medical treatment."

The doctor who eventually arrived turned out to be an extremely deaf old Portuguese man who had lived in Africa for over fifty years. He surprised Ana by stitching up the gaping wound with admirable skill, and covering it with cotton wool.

"Will she survive?" Ana asked.

"Of course she'll survive," said the doctor. "She'll have a scar. But that's all."

"Did whoever attacked her want to kill her, or just to injure her?"

She had to shout loudly into the doctor's ear in order for him to understand.

"Both intentions are possible," he said, "but the probability is that he wasn't trying to kill her. To do that all he'd have needed to do was to slash her a bit lower down, over her throat, and a bit deeper. A sharp knife across a victim's throat can kill in less than a minute."

Ana stayed with Isabel. She couldn't be sure how much pain the patient was in. They shared the silence and listened to each other's breathing. Ana watched an insect creeping incredibly slowly over one of the cell walls.

"Who could have got access to her?" Ana asked.

"To be absolutely honest," said Sullivan, "I just don't know. But I can promise you that we shall get to the bottom of this. I don't want a prisoner for whom I'm responsible to be killed."

"Is that true?"

372

"Yes," said Sullivan. "It certainly is true. I don't care about her — I think she ought to be hanged or shot. But nobody is going to sneak into one of my cells and kill her, and get away with it."

That evening, when Ana returned to her house and was about to draw the curtains in her bedroom, she once again saw the black man in overalls standing in the street below.

Not long afterwards, she peered out through a gap in the curtains.

The man was still there.

He's waiting for me, she thought. There's something he wants from me.

She went down the stairs, carefully opened the front door and passed by the guards. She was possessed by an overwhelming desire to push them into the fire for falling asleep instead of standing guard over the entrance to her house, but instead she opened the gate leading into the street. The man was still there, on the other side. She was carrying a candle, and walked over to him.

"I'm Moses," he said. "Isabel's brother. I've come from the mines to set her free and take her away with me."

His eyes were completely calm. In some strange way he reminded her of her father.

CHAPTER
SIXTY-FIVE

Two fires were already burning where the guards were curled up asleep. But Moses lit a third one at the back of the house where Ana had arranged for a vegetable garden to be created, and planted some orange and lime trees. For the first time since she arrived in Lourenço Marques she found herself with an African who treated her as an equal. There was no trace in him of the false subservience the blacks felt obliged to assume. Moses looked her in the eye when he spoke to her. And this was the first time a black man had sat down on a chair in her presence. The norm was always for her to sit down while the black man she was speaking to remained standing. Ana Dolores had made that clear to her from the very start.

She put it to him straight out: why was he so different from all the others?

"Why shouldn't I look you in the eye?" Moses replied. "You can't hate or despise blacks or you wouldn't be trying to help my sister. And so you are an unusual person as far as I am concerned."

"What do you do down the mines? Do you dig for coal?"

"Diamonds. But of course, there is also coal there. It's the same stuff, after all."

Ana didn't know about the connection between diamonds and coal, and so she didn't understand his comment.

"You make fires with coal. You wear diamonds on your fingers. How can they be the same thing?"

"Really old coal develops into diamonds," said Moses. "One day perhaps I can explain it to you properly — all about the stuff we take out of the ground in the Rand."

Ana said that she knew who he was and where he worked — but wondered how he knew who she was. Has Isabel told him about her?

"I know what I know," was all he said in response. He gave her no further explanation, but instead embarked on a description of life in the mines, without her having asked about it.

"The whites who've landed on our coasts have always turned most of their attention to looking for what is hidden under the soil," said Moses. "That's why we Africans find it so hard to understand you. How can anybody travel so far and be prepared to risk dying of fever or snake bites, simply in order to look for things that are hidden under the ground? Of course, a lot of hunters come here as well. Others are running away from harassment they suffer in their homelands — what we don't understand is why they come here and choose to live a life harassing us. White people are basically incomprehensible — but for that reason we find it easy to understand them because we know what they are after. But they don't even do the digging themselves: they force us to do it. The whites have transformed us blacks into servants in the underworld. One day it will all come to an end, just as the sources of gold and diamonds will wither away."

"What will you do when your sister is free again?" Ana asked.

"I'm thinking of using those underground tunnels I know so well to protect my sister and her children. That's where I shall take them to once she has escaped. Moving into another country, passing over a border that the whites have established, that doesn't mean a thing. All the borders you have made are nothing more than lines in our red soil — they could have been drawn by children using sticks."

He stopped, and watched the fire dying out. It seemed to Ana that he had made a fire that would only burn for as long as he had something to say to her. Once the embers were no longer glowing, he stood up and left. His last words were that they would meet at the fort the following day.

Ana went back to her bedroom. Carlos woke up when she lay down in bed, and stretched his hand out towards her. But just now she didn't want an ape in bed beside her. Not just after having met and talked to the man known as Moses. She smacked Carlos — not hard, but enough to signal to him that he should move to the ceiling light. With a sigh and an irritated grunt, Carlos leapt up and lay down in the dish-shaped lampshade, one arm hanging down towards the bed.

She got up early next morning, sat for a long time in front of the mirror contemplating her face and thinking how she could barely contain herself until she met Moses again. To her surprise she found herself thinking an unheard-of thought: Moses was a man she could imagine herself becoming close to. She put her hand over her mouth, as if she had cried out in horror.

The person I can see in the mirror is somebody else, she thought. Or somebody I have become without realizing it.

A few hours later, when she had forced herself to go through Herr Eber's accounts in order to try and understand the claims about reduced income, Julietta announced that Father Leopoldo had come to visit her. Ana was immediately worried that something might have happened to Isabel. She ran down the stairs to meet him. But Father Leopoldo was able to calm her down. The old doctor had stitched up the wound very well, and the cotton wool was protecting her skin and preventing dirt from entering it.

"I've only come to say that I'm continuing with my attempts to talk to her," he said when they had sat down in the shade on the veranda and Julietta had served tea.

"But she's still silent, is she?"

"She doesn't say a word. But she listens."

"Can you be sure of that?"

"I can see that she's listening."

"I know it's none of my business, but what are you trying to talk to her about?"

"I'm trying to persuade her to confess to her terrible sin, and submit her soul to God. He will pass judgement on her, but His judgement will be mild if she confesses and submits to His will."

Ana looked at Father Leopoldo in surprise. He really believes what he says, she thought. For him, God is someone who hands out punishment — the same God that my grandmother in Funäsdalen used to talk about. He believes in the same hell that she did. He's not like me. I don't believe in hell, but I'm frightened of it all the same. If there is a hell, it is here on earth.

God is white, Ana thought. I suppose I've always thought that, but never so clearly as I do now.

She wanted to conclude the conversation.

"This is the first time you've been to visit me," she said. "I don't believe that you have only come to inform me that Isabel still isn't saying anything. I know that already, because I visit her every day."

"I've also come to tell you that the plaster and rendering in one corner of the cathedral is falling off and needs repairing."

"I'm not a plasterer."

"We are going to need voluntary donations so that we can carry out repairs as soon as possible, before the damage gets any worse. We can't wait for the Church authorities in Lisbon to pass resolutions to assist us."

Ana nodded. She promised to make a donation despite the fact that it felt humiliating to discover that this was the real reason for Father Leopoldo's visit. She no longer regarded him as a priest, but as a beggar pestering her.

He stood up, as if he were in a hurry to leave. Ana rang her bell and instructed Julietta to escort him out. She thought about her father's words, to the effect that priests should be kicked out into the snow in bare feet. He wouldn't have liked Father Leopoldo, she thought — but I would still have been a mucky little angel as far as he was concerned.

Ana avoided visiting the brothel that day. She sent Julietta there with a message to O'Neill saying that he would be responsible for what happened there until her next visit, but at the end she implied that she might well turn up before the end of the day despite everything. Senhor Vaz had taught her that everybody in the brothel needed to be kept on tenterhooks, suspecting that checks might be made at any time of day or night.

After the meeting with Father Leopoldo, Ana sacked one of the night security guards who had been asleep on duty. He pleaded in vain to keep his job. He had been ill, he said; he'd had a fever, his mother had had an accident, several of his children were in difficulties — that was why he had fallen asleep. Ana knew full well that nothing he said was true, it was a ritual from start to finish. But she allowed him to fetch his brother and appointed him as a night security guard instead, warning him that she would check up every night to make sure that he was awake.

After her afternoon siesta, when she had lain in bed unable to sleep, fanning herself, she was driven down to the fort. Carlos was sitting on the chimney when she left. She had realized that he was changing in some way, although it was not clear how. Perhaps I see Carlos as a reflection of myself, she thought. Something is happening, something with vital implications for my life. And hence also for Carlos's future.

CHAPTER
SIXTY-SIX

Moses was waiting in the shade of the wall surrounding the fort. Ana got out of the car and walked over to him. Moses selected a place where they could stand without being seen, and gave her a small leather pouch.

"What's this?"

"The crushed shell of a special snail that lives off the Inhambane coast. Plus dried blossom from a tree that only blossoms once every nineteen years."

"Surely there aren't any such trees?"

He looked offended, and she regretted what she had said.

"What do you want me to do with this?"

"Give it to Isabel. Say it's from me. She should eat it."

"Why should she eat flowers?"

"They'll give her wings, like a butterfly's. She'll then be able to fly out of the prison. I'll meet her and take her and her children to the tunnels in my mine. All that will be left in the cell is the leather pouch, and it will slowly rot away with a whispering noise."

"What? Can a leather pouch whisper?"

"This one can: it will tell the story of Isabel and her new life for anybody who wants to listen."

"It sounds like a fairy tale you tell to small children."

"But what I'm telling you is the truth."

Ana could see that Moses was serious. The person standing in front of her was no small child, and as far as he was concerned what he said was the truth, and nothing but the truth. Ana thought he looked very much like Isabel, you could see they were brother and sister, especially in his eyes and the high forehead.

"I'll give it to her," said Ana, putting the pouch into the basket with the food. "Does she know what to do with it?"

"Yes, she knows."

"And you really believe that she will grow wings?"

Moses took a step backwards, as if he no longer wanted to be too close to her. Then he turned on his heel without answering, and left. Ana remained where she was, hesitating. She put down the basket, took out the leather pouch and opened it. It was half full of a bluish-white powder that glittered when the sun's rays fell on it.

I'm taking part in a strange game, she thought. How can wings suddenly grow on a human being's back? If my father had given me these ground snail shells and flowers, would he then have been able to watch me flying off over the river and up into the mountains?

She tied the pouch again. There's a lot I don't understand, she thought. The wings are something that only Moses and Isabel can relate to. For me they are both laughable and deeply serious at one and the same time.

She went into the fort through the entrance doors. Sullivan was waiting for her on the steps as usual. Today, he was wearing his white dress uniform. He was holding his pipe in one hand. It had gone out. She asked if he had managed to throw any light on who was responsible for the attack on Isabel.

"No," he said. "But I can't believe that we won't be able to work out who did it."

"One of the soldiers?"

"Who would take the risk? I would send the guilty man back home, and doing one's military service in a penal settlement in Portugal is something every sensible soldier is scared stiff of."

"But who could get past the guards?"

"That's precisely what we are looking into. This is a small town. It will be difficult to hide away the truth about what happened."

I'll never get an answer, Ana thought. For all I know the man I'm talking to now could be the one who slashed her face.

She left the commanding officer and went down to the cells. She sat down beside Isabel. The basket from the previous day wasn't completely empty: she had eaten, but not very much.

"This pouch is from Moses," Ana said. "He wants you to swallow the contents so that you can escape."

For the first time Isabel took hold of Ana's hand. She squeezed the leather pouch hard, and for a brief moment leaned her head on Ana's shoulder.

"Go now," she said in a voice that was hoarse from lack of use. "I don't have much time left."

Ana left the darkness and came out again into the bright sunshine. Some black men were busy polishing the statue of a knight that had arrived on a ship from Lisbon, and would soon be put on display in one of the town's squares. The goats were standing motionless in a shady corner of the walled courtyard.

Ana was driven back home. She had hoped that Moses would be waiting for her outside the fort, but he wasn't there.

The next day, when she was woken up at dawn by Carlos kicking the quilt off the bed, she discovered that Moses was standing in the street below, staring up at her window. She hurried down the stairs and out into the street. The night guards had woken up, put out their fires and were getting washed at a pump at the rear of the house.

Moses was holding a spade in his hand.

"It didn't work," he said. "She's still locked up inside the fort."

"How do you know?"

"I know. She knows. There are too many white people around her, scaring away the spirits. And so I'm going to start digging today, so that I can get in under the wall. It will take longer than if she had been able to fly out, but we are patient."

"Where are you going to start digging? Do you really think it's possible?"

"It must be possible!"

"Can you really do it, all by yourself? Even if you are a miner and used to digging."

Moses didn't answer. He merely turned on his heel and began walking quickly down the hill towards the fort.

Ana stayed where she was, even though she was wearing nothing but a dressing gown. It was only when the night guards came out of the courtyard and set off for home that she went back indoors. No matter what Moses and Isabel believed about butterflies' wings, she was the only one who could help Isabel. She lay down on her bed again, and didn't get up until she had made up her mind what to do. She got dressed, and gathered together most of the money she had in Senhor Vaz's drawers and safes. She filled a large laundry basket with it, and was helped by Julietta to carry it down to the car when it was time for her to visit Isabel.

"Is she going to eat that much food?" asked Julietta inquisitively.

"You ask far too many questions," said Ana sternly. "I haven't the strength to answer them all. You must learn to keep quiet. Besides, this is a laundry basket, not something you carry food in."

The chauffeur helped her to carry the basket into the fort. Sullivan was waiting for her as usual, this time wearing his ordinary uniform.

"I want to talk to you in private," said Ana. "And I need help to carry in this basket."

Sullivan looked at her in surprise. Then he shouted for two soldiers who carried the basket into his office. Ana followed them, and closed the door when they had left. The basket with the money was covered by an

385

oriental quilt that Senhor Vaz had been given by a customer who didn't have enough cash.

Sullivan sat down at his dark brown desk and pointed at a visitor's chair.

"You want to speak to me?"

"I'll come straight to the point. Isabel won't survive if she stays here. So I'm prepared to give you this basket of money if you can arrange for her to be given the opportunity to escape."

She stood up and removed the quilt, exposing the money in bundles of notes that filled the whole basket. Sullivan contemplated the contents of the basket.

"It's all I have," said Ana. "And of course, I promise never to mention this money to anybody. I want only one thing, and that is for Isabel to be set free."

Sullivan sat down behind his desk again. His face was totally expressionless.

"Why does she mean so much to you?"

"I saw what happened. I know why she did it. I would have done the same thing. But I have never been locked up inside an underground hellhole. Because I am white."

Sullivan nodded without saying anything. The goats could be heard bleating in the courtyard. Ana waited.

There was a long pause before he spoke. In the end he turned to look at her. He smiled.

"It sounds like an excellent idea," he said. "I'm not impossible to do business with. But the money isn't enough."

"I don't have any more."

"It's not money I want."

386

Ana assumed Sullivan had the same desire as Pandre.

"You are of course welcome to visit my establishment whenever you like," she said. "Without needing to pay."

"You still don't know what I mean," said Sullivan. "You're absolutely right to think that I'm intending to visit your place and all the beautiful women who are so tempting to your customers. But I shall expect it to be you who accompanies me to a room and stays there with me all night. Nobody else will do. I want the woman no other customer could have."

Ana had no doubt that he meant what he said. Nor would he allow himself to be persuaded to accept any of the other women. He had made up his mind.

"The money can stay here until you have made your decision," he said. "I guarantee that nobody will steal anything. I'll give you until tomorrow to decide."

He stood up, bowed and opened the door for her. As he passed her he stroked his gloved hand gently over her cheek. She shuddered.

Ana's visit to Isabel that day was very short. Late that evening, when Carlos was already asleep, she made her decision. For once in her life, she would sell herself.

Once it was over she would be able to go away at last. To leave this hell on earth that her mother had never taught her anything about. She would vanish from this town where she had once gone ashore without knowing what she was letting herself in for when she walked down that confounded gangplank.

CHAPTER
SIXTY-SEVEN

In order to sleep she took a large dose of the chloral sleeping tablets Senhor Vaz used to use. She slept restlessly, but she did sleep.

All of a sudden, she was awake. She opened her eyes and found herself looking straight into O'Neill's unshaven and glistening face. His eyes were open wide, and bloodshot.

It was daybreak. Light crept in between the half-open curtains. O'Neill had a knife in one hand, and it was covered in blood. She thought at first that she had been the victim, but she could feel no pain. Confusion and terrified thoughts whirled around in her brain. Where was Carlos? Why hadn't he protected her? Then she saw that he was lying on the floor next to her bed, with blood on the part of his face that wasn't covered in hair. She couldn't make out if Carlos was dead or seriously injured. She now had a vague memory of hearing Carlos shout out while she was asleep — was that the sound that had lifted her into consciousness?

Once she had established that she wasn't injured, she realized that O'Neill was scared. Against whom had he used that knife? The sleeping night guards? Julietta? She tried to force herself to be calm, and slowly dragged herself up so that she was half sitting, leaning back on the pillows. O'Neill pulled open the curtains so that the last of the darkness disappeared. He seemed to be in a hurry. That increased her worries, as it could only mean that he had done something he needed to run away from, as fast as he possibly could.

"What do you want?" she asked, as calmly as she could manage.

"I've come to take your money," he said.

She could see that he was trembling.

"What have you done?"

Had he attacked one of the women in the brothel? Or perhaps several? Or even all of them? Was it the blood of Felicia and the others dripping from the blade of his knife?

"I have to know," she said. "What has happened? Who have you stabbed?"

O'Neill didn't answer. No more than an impatient groan passed over his lips. He pulled back the quilt and hissed at her that she should give him all the money she had in the house. She got out of bed, put on her dressing gown and thought about how remarkable it was that since yesterday most of her money was locked up inside the commanding officer's office, guarded by the town's Portuguese garrison.

"What has happened?" she asked again.

O'Neill was still holding the knife at the ready, as if he was afraid that she would jump at him. Carlos was lying unconscious, but Ana could see from the rising and falling of his chest that he was still alive. Whatever else O'Neill had done, she would never forgive him for attacking an innocent chimpanzee and almost killing him.

O'Neill suddenly answered her question. It was as if he were flinging the words out of himself.

"I went into her cell and finished off what I failed to do the last time. This time she really is dead."

Ana became stone cold. She groaned. O'Neill took a step towards her.

"I couldn't stand by and watch the women's earnings being squandered by you on a black woman who murdered her husband. Now I'm getting out of here. And I intend to take all your money with me. You won't even be able to afford a coffin for her funeral."

Ana sat down tentatively on the edge of the bed. It was as if O'Neill's knife had severed something inside her. She had only one desire just now, and that was to mourn the death of Isabel: but O'Neill was standing in her way. He wouldn't leave until he had received the money, and he wouldn't believe what she said about most of her wealth being in the commanding officer's office. Perhaps this was the end of the remarkable journey that had begun with a sleigh-ride in what seemed to be the far distant past. She would die here in this room, stabbed to death by a raving lunatic of a man she had made the mistake of employing. A man she personally had taken on for a trial period without knowing that in doing so, she had allowed a murderer into her house. She would die in this bedroom where she had spent her widowhood, and would die together with the remarkable chimpanzee who used to work as a servant in the brothel, dressed in a white suit.

But could what O'Neill had said happened possibly be true? She looked at him, and it struck her that this could be a trap she had fallen straight into. She had failed to notice the gap that had suddenly opened up in front of her, and was about to fall into it.

"Why did you kill her? And why should I believe you?"

"Because nobody else was able to do the only right thing — killing her — I took it upon myself."

"How could you get into her cell? Twice?"

"Somebody helped me, of course. Left doors open. But I'm not going to say who it was."

"Was it the commanding officer? Sullivan?"

O'Neill made an energetic gesture with the knife, and in doing so happened to tread on Carlos, who whimpered.

"No, it wasn't Sullivan. But I shan't answer any more of your questions."

He picked up a grey sack made of jute that was lying on the floor beside him.

"Fill this with your money!"

"I can't."

Something in her voice made him hesitate rather than repeating his demand immediately in an even more threatening tone.

"Why can't you?"

"Because nearly all my money is locked up in the commanding officer's office, in the fort."

She could see that he was nervously swaying between doubt and fury. The sack was hanging down in his hand.

"Why has he got your money? You didn't know that I was going to come here tonight."

"I gave the money to him as a bribe," said Ana. "So that he would secretly allow me to fetch Isabel and arrange for her to leave Lourenço Marques. Later this morning I was due to go to him with the rest."

"So there is more money here in the house?"

"Not more money, no. The rest of the bargain was to be paid in a different way."

"How? With what?"

"With me."

O'Neill didn't move. She could see that he was confused. He didn't understand what she meant. His uncertainty gave her the upper hand despite his knife.

"I promised to become his whore. Who would believe the immoral proprietess of a brothel if she tried to explain afterwards what had happened?"

At last the penny dropped for O'Neill. What Ana said couldn't be a lie, something she had simply made up. He picked her up from the bed, grabbed hold of her throat and shook the sack violently.

"Everything you've got," he said. "Absolutely everything. And you must never breathe a word to anybody that I was the one who came here."

"People will understand that even so."

"Not if you don't say anything."

He thrust her away so hard that she fell down on to the stone floor. She landed with her face right next to Carlos, who was still breathing awkwardly.

Just as she was about to get up, Carlos cautiously opened one eye and looked at her.

Ana stood up and began gathering together the money she still had in the house. She had filled two porcelain vases decorated with oriental nymphs with money she was going to use to compensate the women for their reduced earnings. She put it all into the sack while O'Neill urged her to hurry up. On the floor in the wardrobe she had two of Senhor Vaz's leather suitcases filled with money intended for her journey to wherever she eventually decided to go. The money she received for selling her house and the brothel would go to the people who worked there. She didn't intend to keep any of that herself.

When she had emptied the last of the suitcases, she saw that the sack was still less than half full. If the money in the CO's office had been available, O'Neill would have needed two, possibly three sacks.

"That's everything," she said. "If you want any more, you'll have to talk to Sullivan."

O'Neill punched her, hard, a blow loaded with his disappointment: he had expected so much more. In the midst of all the pain that the punch caused her, Ana managed to think about how brutal O'Neill was. How could she have failed to see that earlier? That she had appointed as a security guard a man who was worse than the worst of her clients?

"There must be more," he said, his face so threateningly close to hers that she could feel his stubble against her cheek.

"If you like I can swear on the Bible, or on my honour. There is no more."

She couldn't make up her mind if he believed her or not. But he pulled off the rings she had on her fingers and dropped them into the sack. Then he hit her so hard that everything went black.

CHAPTER
SIXTY-EIGHT

When she came round Carlos was sitting looking at her. He was swaying back and forth, as he always did when he was frightened or felt himself abandoned. O'Neill had left. Ana had the feeling that she hadn't been unconscious very long. The open window overlooking the upper veranda indicated the way O'Neill had chosen to leave, and perhaps also the way he had got in. She went outside and saw that the two guards were sitting by the spent remains of their fire, yawning as if they had just woken up. If she had had a gun, she would have shot them — or at least, the temptation to do so would have been very great. But even if she had aimed at them she would no doubt have pointed the pistol at the sky before pulling the trigger: she would never be able to kill anybody. She was a mucky angel, not a murdering monster.

She sat down on the bed and dabbed at Carlos's wounds with a damp sponge. Nobody would believe me if I told them about this, she thought. Me sitting on my bed after being attacked, tending the wounds on a chimpanzee's bleeding forehead. But I'm not going to tell a soul.

Quite early in the morning she left the house and was driven down to the fort. Julietta and Anaka had been horrified by the state of the bedroom — the torn sheets, the bloodstains and the broken mirror — but Ana had simply told them that Carlos had had nightmares. He had caused the wound on his own forehead. She didn't bother to comment on her swollen cheek.

As she arrived at the fort earlier than usual, Sullivan was not yet standing on the steps, pipe in hand. He hadn't even arrived at the fort from his lodgings in the upper part of the town, where the garrison's accommodation was situated. Ana took a deep breath and walked over to the entrance to the cells. The guard at the entrance was reluctant to let her in at first. He was worried because the lock on the grill had been forced during the night when another soldier had been on duty, but Ana yelled at him to get out of the way and pushed him aside.

Isabel was lying dead on the stone floor next to the bunk. Ana had the feeling that she had used up the last of her strength in an attempt to sit up, since that was how she wanted to be when she died, but she hadn't had the strength. One of her arms was resting on the bunk. O'Neill had turned her body into a bloody mess of skin, thoughts and memories, scars after the birth of her children, her love of Pedro — everything that had made her the person she was. O'Neill had not only stabbed and cut her with his sharp knife, he had disfigured her in such a way as to make her body almost unrecognizable. In her desperation Ana thought that O'Neill must harbour unlimited hatred for black people who refused to submit to the will of whites, even when they were locked up in prison.

With considerable difficulty Ana carefully lifted Isabel on to the bunk. She covered her with the blanket she had never used, even when the nights had been at their coldest. Every time she touched the corpse she seemed to be reminded of the cold that had always surrounded her when she was a child. Isabel's dead body transformed the underground cell into the countryside she had once lived in, always frozen, always longing for the heat of a fire, or from the sun that so seldom forced its way through the clouds drifting in from the mountains to the west. She looked at Isabel and was reminded of all these things that until a few minutes ago had seemed so far away but had now returned. Who is it I am saying goodbye to? she thought. Isabel or myself? Or both of us?

A soldier came into the cell and announced that the commanding officer was waiting for her. He was standing by his desk when she arrived. When he asked why she was making her visit so early, it dawned on Ana that he didn't know what had happened during the night. That gave her an unexpected advantage that she didn't hesitate to make use of.

"Come with me," she said. "I've something to show you."

"Perhaps we should first sort out the last part of our agreement?"

"There is no longer any agreement."

Ana turned on her heel and left the room. Sullivan hurried after her into the courtyard. Ana could see that the news had begun to spread among the soldiers. Sullivan entered the cell. Ana removed the blanket and revealed Isabel's mutilated body.

"I know who killed her," said Hanna. "I'll give you his name, but he's bound to be on his way to the interior of the country already, and he knows all the roads. Perhaps he has a horse to carry him? All I can do is to give you his name, then you can decide if you want to send your soldiers out after him."

She told him about O'Neill, about the attack in her house, and how he had admitted that he was the murderer. Sullivan listened with mounting anger. Ana didn't know if it was because he had been humiliated or because he would lose all that money in the laundry basket, and could no longer look forward to having sex with her. All she did know is that just now she had the upper hand.

"Her brother will come to collect the body," she said. "I shall take the money with me. We shall never meet again. But I want soldiers to continue keeping watch over her, even though she is now dead."

They returned to the courtyard. Two soldiers carried the laundry basket to the car and put it in the boot.

"We'll catch him," said Sullivan, who had accompanied her to the entrance door.

"No," said Ana. "He is a white man, and you'll let him escape. I don't believe a word you say. I had thought of agreeing to your request, but now I feel great relief at never needing to come anywhere near you again."

Before Sullivan had a chance to respond, Ana had turned away and got into the car. As they drove off Ana saw how the enormous statue of the knight was being dragged out into the street by several black men with ropes round their shoulders and waists. She closed her eyes. She now regretted not having agreed to Sullivan's request immediately. Perhaps that might have saved Isabel. During the night that turned out to be her last, Isabel might have been with Moses, on her way to freedom in the distant mine tunnels.

The rest of the day passed: Ana couldn't remember anything about it. Only a bright white light and a deafening roar in her ears. Nothing else.

Moses turned up outside her house as dusk fell. She had been standing by the window, waiting for him. He knew already that Isabel was dead. Ana never bothered to ask him how he knew about what had happened. He stood there, grubby and dirty after the digging he had just embarked upon.

He was digging to make a tunnel, she thought. An opening through which a person would be able to escape into freedom. Instead, what he is doing now is the beginning of a grave.

"You can collect her body tomorrow," she said. "It won't have started smelling by then. If you want me to help you, I will. Nobody will mistreat you at the fort. Soldiers are standing guard over her body."

"I'll collect her myself," said Moses. "I want to make the last journey with her by myself."

"What will happen now to her children?"

Moses didn't answer. He merely shook his head, muttered something inaudible, and left.

At that moment she was on the point of running after him, following him to wherever he was going — back to the mines in the Rand or Kimberley or anywhere else in the world that extended for ever out there, beyond the mountains and the vast plains.

But she remained where she was. Ana Branca and Hanna Lundmark didn't know which world they belonged to.

When she returned to the house, she saw that Carlos had returned to his place on the chimney. All that could be seen in the last light of the setting sun was his silhouette. Carlos looked like an old man, she thought. An ape, or a hunchbacked man weighed down by an enormous burden he was unable to free himself from.

That evening she made a note in her diary. She wrote: "Isabel, her wings, a blue butterfly, fluttering away into a world where I can no longer reach her. Moses left. I love him. Impossible, in vain, desperate."

She closed the book, knotted a red linen ribbon around the covers, and put it into the desk drawer.

She didn't touch the laundry basket full of money that evening.

CHAPTER
SIXTY-NINE

She stood on the veranda as the sun began to rise over the sea, but Moses wasn't around. Disappointed, she went back into the house, emptied the laundry basket of all the money and packed the bundles of notes into the safe and cupboards and drawers. She had great difficulty in making enough room for it all. When she had finished, she washed her hands thoroughly — but even so there was an unpleasant, lingering smell.

When Julietta came with her breakfast tray, Ana instructed her to go immediately to the fort and find out about arrangements for Isabel's burial. To Ana's surprise, Julietta didn't react to what ought to have been the news that Isabel was dead: she obviously knew about it already. There must be a secret way, she thought, for black people to send out invisible messengers to one another with important news.

"Be as quick as you can," said Ana. "Don't pause to look in shop windows, or to talk to any boys or girls you meet. If you are really fast and get back here so soon that I'm surprised, you'll get a reward."

Julietta hurried out of the room. Ana could hear her footsteps racing down the stairs.

Julietta arrived back less than an hour later, panting after all that running up the steep hills. Ana was forced to tell her to sit down and get her breath back, as to begin with she couldn't understand what Julietta was trying to say.

"The body has gone already," said Julietta in the end. Ana stared at her.

"What do you mean by 'the body has gone'?"

"He fetched it as the sun rose."

"Who fetched it?"

"A black man. He carried her away without any assistance."

"Did you not see the young commanding officer?"

"One of the soldiers said he was still in bed in his lodgings, asleep. He'd been invited out yesterday evening."

"Invited by whom? Had he been drinking? Do I have to drag everything out of you?"

"That's what they said. Then they tried to lure me down into the dark underground prison where Isabel had died. I ran away."

"You did the right thing."

Ana had prepared a reward for Julietta. She gave her a pretty necklace and a shimmering silk blouse. Julietta curtseyed.

"You may go now," said Ana. "Tell the chauffeur I'll be down shortly."

Julietta remained standing where she was. Ana realized immediately what she wanted.

"No," she said. "You're never going to be allowed to work in the brothel with the other women. Go now, before I take back what I've just given you!"

402

Julietta left. Ana put on her black clothes, the same ones as she had worn at Senhor Vaz's funeral. Once again she was going to accompany a person to her grave, someone who had died quite unexpectedly. Unlike Senhor Vaz's funeral, Ana would be the only white person among the mourners. And any whites who saw her would become even more antagonistic towards her, more adamant in what in many cases had already become their hatred of her. She was not only concerned about the welfare of blacks who were alive, but she also accompanied a convicted murderess to her grave.

She was unsure about black people's burial rituals, but she picked a few red flowers from her garden and sat down in the car. The chauffeur gave a start when he heard that he was being asked to drive her to the cemetery. He knows, she thought. He knows it's now time for Isabel to be buried.

A new wall was being built at the entrance to the cemetery. When Ana got out of the car the black workers paused and stared at her with bricks and trowels in their hands. She stood in the shade of a tree and told the chauffeur to ask when Moses and the rest of the family were due to arrive with Isabel's body. She watched him asking one of the bricklayers, and could see that the reply he received surprised him. He hurried back to her.

"They have already arrived," he said. "They are waiting inside the cemetery."

"Waiting for whom?"

"Waiting for you, Senhora."

Moses, she thought as she hurried into the cemetery, the red flowers in her hand. He knew that I wouldn't allow Isabel to be buried without my being present at the ceremony.

The chauffeur pointed out a part of the cemetery separate from the graves of white people, where a group of blacks were waiting. As she hurried along past the crumbling gravestones she detected a sort of sweetish smell of dead bodies rising up from the earth. She held her hand over her mouth, and was afraid that she would feel so sick that she would throw up.

The coffin was brown, made of rough planks. It had already been lowered into the grave. Standing round it were Moses in his overalls, Isabel's children and several black women Ana had never seen before. She assumed they were Isabel's sisters who were now looking after the orphaned children. There was no priest from the cathedral present. When she reached the grave, Moses led the mourners in the singing of a hymn. Everybody joined in, singing in harmony. Afterwards Moses mumbled a few words that Ana couldn't understand, then looked at Ana.

"Would you like to say something?"

"No."

Moses nodded, then began shovelling soil down over the coffin. All the others joined in to help. They dug with their hands, or with sticks and flat stones. Ana had the impression that they were in a great hurry. The coffin should be covered over as quickly as possible. She remembered something Senhor Vaz had said, about black people always wanting to get away from burials as quickly as possible because they were afraid that evil spirits would escape from the coffin and chase after them. Could it be that despite everything, Isabel was regarded above all as an evil, obsessed murderess, even by her own sisters? Ana placed her red flowers on the heap of earth on top of the grave. Then she saw that what she had heard was true: everyone apart from Moses scuttled away from the grave. Some of them jumped back and forth between the paths as if to confuse the evil spirits they were afraid might be following them. It looked so odd that she found it hard not to burst out laughing, despite her deep sorrow.

In the end there was only Moses and herself left.

"What happens now?" she asked.

"I go back to the mines."

"But surely you could stay here? I still have the money I'd saved to try to get Isabel set free."

Moses looked at her.

"I'm serious," she said. "You can build a house, and look after Isabel's children. You don't need to toil in the mines any more."

Did he believe her? She couldn't be sure. But in any case he said no.

"I can't take your money."

"Why not?"

"Isabel wouldn't have wanted me to. Her children are well looked after as it is."

"As I understand it you have been working for many years in the smoke and dust in the mines — it's not good to work for too long in those conditions."

"But that is where I'm at home."

She could sense that he was a little bit hesitant even so.

"I shall think about what you have said," he said. "I'll come to your house tomorrow, when I've finished thinking."

He turned on his heel and hurried off along the paths between all the unmarked graves. She watched him until he came to the white mausoleums, then vanished completely.

She was driven back to town and asked the chauffeur to stop at the brothel, but just before they got there she changed her mind and told him to drive her home. She still didn't know what she ought to say. Isabel's death and her meeting with Moses had increased her feeling of being totally absorbed by herself and her own thoughts.

After taking a bath, she lay down on her bed. Over and over again she relived the long journey that had eventually taken her to the room where she was now lying. But the images inside her head were jumbled up haphazardly. Now it was Senhor Vaz she had married in Algiers, and Lundmark she had met in the brothel. Moses was her bouncer, and O'Neill was dressed as Father Leopoldo in the shadowy cathedral.

The rest of the day and the evening was spent in the borderland between dreams and consciousness. She changed into a dressing gown when Julietta brought her a tray of food, but hardly touched the food on the plate. She occasionally opened her diary, and picked up her pen in order to make an entry: but in the end she wrote nothing at all. She merely drew a map of the river that was flowing inside her head, the mountains decked in white, and the house where her father seemed to spend all his time filling the gaps and cracks so that they could endure the never-ending cold of yet another winter.

After taking another large dose of sleeping tablets she managed to fall asleep. But all the time she dreamt that she was awake. Or at least that's how it felt when she eventually woke up.

CHAPTER
SEVENTY

She was already standing on the veranda when dawn broke. There was an expectation within her that she tried to dampen down, but without success. She had never felt as strongly as this when she had been waiting for Lundmark, or Senhor Vaz. But she certainly felt that way now.

Moses didn't show up. After having waited in vain all morning, she decided he must have already gone back to the mines. He hadn't meant what he said about coming back to her house. She didn't feel he had deceived her: he had been certain that she would understand his decision. He didn't want her money. All he wanted was to return to the mines, where he felt at home.

However, at around noon a little boy came to the front door of the house and handed in a sealed envelope with Ana's name on it. Julietta carried it up to her room. Ana asked her to leave before she opened the envelope. She didn't recognize the handwriting, but it was — as she had hoped — from Moses. He asked her to go to Beira and try to find his and Isabel's parents, and tell them that she was dead. It was a mission he wanted to entrust to her, and was sure that Isabel would have felt the same.

She put the letter in her desk drawer, and locked it. As usual, she hung the key round her neck.

The letter had made her both upset and disappointed. Why had Moses chosen to give her a task that he ought to have carried out himself? Had she misjudged him, just as she had misjudged O'Neill? Did Moses lack the courage his sister had possessed? She felt increasingly despondent, but at the same time wondered if she had misunderstood his motives for bestowing the honour of undertaking this journey upon her. She didn't even know who to talk to, in an attempt to understand better. Could Felicia be of help again? She was doubtful, and chose in the end to speak to Father Leopoldo, who had met Isabel after all, and might be able to explain Moses' behaviour.

She found him sitting on a chair in the cathedral, listening to the children's choir practising. Ana recalled her first visit, and tears came into her eyes. She wasn't sure if this was a result of the children's singing, or of the memory of that first time she had ever entered the cathedral.

Father Leopoldo noticed her, and took her into a room where the priests kept their vestments. The singing of the children's choir could be heard faintly through the thick walls. She told Father Leopoldo about Isabel's burial and Moses' letter.

"Why is he asking me to go and look for her parents?"

"Perhaps he wants to show them the greatest respect he can think of: sending a white woman to inform them about a death. How often does a white woman or man do something like that for a simple black miner?"

"But he was her brother, surely?"

"I think he wants to honour her memory by asking you to do it."

"Then why didn't he say so? Why did he promise he would come back, and then simply send me a letter?"

"In a way he did come back. He wrote down his plea to you."

Ana was still doubtful, despite the fact that there was something convincing about Father Leopoldo's voice. She thought that he might well have understood better than she had why Moses had done what he did. Then Father Leopoldo asked her cautiously how she had reacted to Isabel's death. She told him the truth: her sorrow still hadn't hit her with full force, and she was afraid of the moment when it eventually arrived.

"What are you going to do now, Senhora? You have frequently talked about leaving here."

"I don't know. But I do know that I must soon make up my mind."

The conversation was interrupted by Father Leopoldo being summoned to listen to a confession. Ana walked through the empty church. The choir had stopped singing and the children had left. Then she noticed somebody sitting in the darkness next to the big entrance door. It was Senhor Nunez. He was waiting for her. I'm being watched all the time, she

410

thought. There are so many who see me without my seeing them.

Nunez stood up and bowed. She raised her hand.

"Don't say anything! Give me a moment to think!"

Nunez nodded and sat down again. Ana flopped down on a chair after having turned her back on Nunez.

She stared out through the open door, straight into the bright sunlight. And she made up her mind almost immediately. She didn't need to hesitate any longer. She knew what she wanted to do.

She turned her chair to face Nunez.

"I'm going to sell my establishment," she said. "I want paying in English pounds, and I want the whole amount in one go. You must promise to observe the same rules and procedures as apply now. I don't care what you do after the women who are working there now have moved on. I don't believe in the children's home you spoke about."

"I shall respect your demands, of course. But I'm still thinking about that children's home."

Ana stood up.

"You don't need to lie to me. Come round to my house tomorrow afternoon, and bring the money with you."

"But we haven't agreed on a price yet."

"I'm not going to name a price — but I'll tell you if you come with too little money. In that case I'll sell to somebody else. A lawyer will have prepared a contract. I want the whole affair to be settled immediately."

She didn't wait for a response, simply stood up and left the cathedral. Now I'm the one who's leaving the underworld, she thought; but in contrast to Isabel, I'm still alive.

The following day Andrade drew up two contracts. One was for the sale of Ana's house, for which he was to pay £4,000, with all the furniture included in the deal. He also promised to keep all the staff on for at least a year, and after that to pay Anaka's and Rumigo's pensions.

The other contract concerned the sale of the brothel business to Senhor Nunez. To Andrade's surprise Ana requested him to leave a line blank for the selling price to be written in. Nor did the contract include any mention of the brothel being converted into a children's home.

At three o'clock in the afternoon Nunez arrived. He offered £4,000 for the establishment. Ana said that she wanted £5,000, as she was convinced that was the sum he had in his fat leather briefcase. Nunez smiled and agreed. All aspects of the sale were completed in less than an hour.

"Four days from now you can take over everything," she said. "Before then you are not allowed inside the premises. And you are not allowed to breathe a word about our deal until I've spoken to everybody who works here. Where have you got all your money from?"

Nunez smiled and shook his head.

"Revealing my source of income is not a part of our deal."

"Elephant tusks? Lionskins? Secret diamond mines that nobody knows about?"

"I've no intention of answering your question."

"As long as you are not a slave trader," said Ana.

"What will happen to the chimpanzee?" Nunez asked, pointing at Carlos who was sitting on top of the tall cupboard. "Is he a non-specified part of our agreement?"

"He's coming with me," said Ana. "His future is my responsibility, not yours. I hope you also noticed that I didn't require that the brothel should be converted into a children's home. Why should I demand something that you have no intention of doing? I want you to leave now. We've concluded our business, and don't need to talk to each other."

Nunez eyed her up and down. He suddenly appeared sorrowful.

"I don't understand why you distrust me," he said. "Just like you I am upset about the way in which we treat black people. Maybe I'm not good through and through, but I hate the contempt we show towards these people. It is lunacy to believe that such an attitude can continue for ever and a day — an illusion, and very stupid."

Nunez stood up.

"Perhaps you are not as lonely as you think," he said. "I share your disgust."

He bowed and left. She thought about what he had said. Perhaps she had been wrong about him after all.

When she was alone she looked at the contracts and the bundles of banknotes. She had arrived in Africa with nothing: now she was very rich.

All she knew about her future was that she would travel to Beira and look for Isabel's parents. What would happen after that she didn't know, and it was something that she was somewhat afraid of. But before leaving she would have to have a final discussion with the women in the brothel, and also sort out a future for Carlos.

That evening, for the second time in their shared lives, she and Carlos sat together and counted all the money that was piled up in enormous heaps on tables and chairs.

CHAPTER
SEVENTY-ONE

The next morning Ana carefully dug out the photograph of her and Lundmark from their wedding in Algiers. It was only eighteen months since that occasion, but even so it seemed like another world and another age, when everything had a context and she always looked forward to the next day. Now it seemed to her that darkness was closing in all around her. She had a long way to go, and she didn't know where the path would lead her. Moreover, she would have to do everything on her own. When she left the house by the river in the sleigh, she was not abandoning a large circle of friends, and although she was leaving behind her family, she had had Forsman's broad back in front of her. Now, though, she felt totally isolated. But she had no intention of giving up, the mucky angel still had its wings. She hated the gloom surrounding her on all sides, she missed all the happiness she had enjoyed. I'm a smiling angel, she thought. The life I'm leading at the moment will always be foreign to me.

As she looked at the photograph taken in the studio in Algiers, a thought struck her and she decided immediately to say a silent "yes" to it. She made up her mind to hold her final talk in the brothel during the quiet hours of the afternoon. That would give her an opportunity of paying another visit to the photographer Picard first.

But she also made up her mind to do something that had hitherto never been more than a passing thought. She now realized that the time had come to actually do it. She had nothing to lose by surprising the women in the brothel in a way that none of them would ever have been able to imagine.

The whites who lived in Lourenço Marques had themselves photographed by Picard when they got married, celebrated a birthday or some other anniversary, or lay dead, waiting to be buried or shipped back to Portugal in a well-sealed zinc coffin. He never took photographs of black people on principle, but Ana knew that the amount of money she intended to offer him would ensure that he made an exception. Picard was a skilful photographer, but he was also greedy.

He was in the process of photographing a newborn baby when Ana entered his studio. The baby was crying and Picard, who hated taking photographs of unruly children, had stuffed his ears with cotton wool. As a result he didn't hear Ana when she came into the room and sat down quietly on a chair. The mother holding the baby was very young. Ana thought it could well have been Berta sitting there with Forsman's child in her lap. Ana could see that the mother was looking at the child without a trace of pleasure in her eyes, and assumed she was one of those young white women who are forced to move to the African continent by their husbands, and soon become desperate and scared by what they regard as the realm of unbearable terror.

Picard disappeared under his black cloth and took a picture of the screeching baby. It was only after he had more or less shooed the woman and her child out of his studio that he noticed Ana. He took the cotton wool out of his ears, and bowed.

"Do you have an appointment?" he asked, looking worried. "If so my secretary hasn't been doing her job properly."

"No, I don't have an appointment," said Ana, "but I have come here to ask you to take a picture. At very short notice."

"What does that mean?"

"In a few hours from now."

"Here?"

"At the brothel."

Picard gave a start.

"I shall pay you more than you have ever received before," she said. "For a group photo. With me and all the prostitutes. None of them will be naked. Then I want as many copies as there are people in the picture. And the copies must be in my hands tomorrow morning before ten o'clock — but preferably this evening: if you can manage that I shall pay you extra, of course."

Before Picard had chance to reply or raise any objections, Ana had taken several English pound notes out of her handbag and placed them on the table in front of him.

"I want the picture taken at four o'clock this afternoon — three hours from now."

"I promise I'll be there."

"I know you will," said Ana. "You don't need to assure me of that."

After her visit to the photographer's Ana asked the chauffeur to drive her down to the promenade. She got out of the car and wandered slowly around in the shade of the palm trees, gazing out to sea. The small fishing boats with their triangular sails that she had become so fond of were on their way into port. She knew that this would be one of the images she would take away with her: fishing boats scudding along over the waves or swaying gently in the swell when the winds had dropped, just as she would remember the small black figures standing at the helm, or cleaning the nets and sorting out the catch.

I live in a black world in which the whites use up all their energy deceiving both themselves and the blacks, she thought. They believe that the people who live here wouldn't be able to survive without them, and that black people are inferior because they believe that rocks and trees have a soul. But the blacks in turn fail to understand how anybody could treat a son of God so badly that they nail Him on to a cross. They are amazed by the fact that whites come here and rush around all the time in such a hurry that their hearts soon give way, unable to cope with the never-ending hunt for wealth and power. Whites don't love life. They love time, which they always have far too little of.

What kills us off more than anything else is all the lies, Ana thought. I don't want to become like Ana Dolores who really is convinced that black people are inferior to whites. I don't want it to say on my gravestone that I was somebody who never appreciated the value of black people.

She sat down on a stone bench. The sea was glittering. The heat was bearable when cool breezes were blowing. She thought about what she was going to say in her speech to the women, then finally stood up and returned to the car.

She was driven back home to pick up Carlos. Needless to say, he was going to be in the picture that Picard would take.

When she arrived at the brothel she handed Carlos over to Judas, with whom he had always got on well. Carlos felt secure in his company. As Ana was early, the room with the red sofas was deserted. She went quietly up the stairs and into her old room. In the large wardrobes was a collection of clothes that could be worn if some customer had special desires about what his woman should be dressed in, or if for some reason or other one of the women was short of a garment.

She closed the door, undressed quickly and then opened the wardrobe doors. Several times towards the end of her stay in that room, when she was coming to the end of her long convalescence, she had taken out dresses and shoes, and even the tiaras and bracelets lying on the shelves. She had often been tempted to dress up in silk and adorn herself with rings and necklaces, but she had never done so.

Not until now. She slid her hand over the long row of silk skirts, dresses and suits. She settled on an oriental-style costume in green and red, with touches of golden embroidery. She put it on in front of the mirror. The blouse was low-cut and could be opened simply by unfastening a ribbon underneath the breast. She selected a circular tiara to match the clothes, and placed it on her hair. Then she slid a broad bracelet similar to the tiara on to her left arm.

Among the rings she also discovered brushes, powder and lipstick. She made up her eyes and painted her lips, put a pair of silk slippers on her feet, and was ready.

She looked at herself in the mirror and it struck her that the change in her appearance was much greater than she had expected. She was not Ana any longer, but a woman of oriental extraction. There was nothing left of Hanna Renström. Whoever she really was, she knew that she had transformed herself into a woman who would attract a lot of customers if she were to sit down on one of the red sofas and wait for a proposition.

She sat down on the bed. It would be some time yet before all the women had gathered.

The time eventually came. She went down the stairs and stopped by a half-open curtain that at night-time was closed in front of the opening to the inner courtyard.

The women were sitting around chatting as usual when she appeared from behind the curtain. Silence fell immediately. Ana could see that several of them didn't recognize her at first, and as she had expected, none of the women commented on the change in her appearance. Nobody laughed or admired her beautiful clothes. They daren't, Ana thought. Even if I have changed completely, I'm still first and foremost the white woman, nothing else.

She walked into the room.

Zé was sitting at the piano, tuning a single key deep down at the bass end of the keyboard. The guards had succeeded in not allowing any new customers in. A few sullen-looking and half-drunk sailors from a Norwegian whaling ship were staggering along towards one of the side streets where there was another establishment.

"Are there any customers left?" Ana asked Felicia.

"Just a couple, asleep. They won't wake up."

"Perhaps you've given them some of your magic medicine?"

Felicia smiled, but didn't reply.

Picard had arrived. He had set up his large camera, hung the black cloth over it, and rearranged the furniture so that there was room for everybody in the picture.

Ana decided to begin with the group photograph. With luck it would create an atmosphere in the room that would make it easier for her afterwards to say everything it was necessary for her to say.

"We're going to take a photograph," she said, clapping her hands. "Everybody's going to be on it, including Zé and the security guards. And not least Carlos, of course."

There was immediately an air of excitement as they all moved into the places where they were directed by Picard. The women giggled and tittered, exchanged combs and little mirrors, adjusted one another's clothes (which weren't covering all that much of their bodies anyway). Eventually everybody was ready, with Ana in the middle, sitting in an armchair. Carlos had jumped up on to a pedestal which normally held a potted plant.

"I want a serious picture," said Ana. "I want nobody to laugh, nobody to smile. Look serious, straight at the camera."

Picard made the final adjustments, moving somebody a bit closer, somebody else a bit further away. Then he prepared the flash by scattering some magnesium powder on to a metal tray. He ducked underneath the black cloth with a burning matchstick in his hand. The magnesium flared up and the picture was taken.

He prepared another flash, ducked under the cloth again and took a second picture.

Afterwards, when Picard had left and gone back to his studio to develop the photographs and choose the one from which he needed to make fourteen copies, Ana assembled the women under the jacaranda tree. Zé had returned to the piano where he was examining the keys before beginning to polish them. Carlos was sitting on one of the red sofas, smacking his lips noisily as he ate an orange.

It seemed to Ana at that moment as if everything surrounding her was a sort of artificial idyll.

A treacherous paradise.

CHAPTER
SEVENTY-TWO

Just as Ana was about to speak, Zé raised his hands and began playing. For the first time he had stopped merely tuning the strings. It took a few moments for what had happened to sink in. She watched Zé's hands in astonishment and listened to his playing. It was like a bolt from the blue in the brothel. After spending all that time tinkering with his piano, Zé now seemed to have reached the point when it was sufficiently in tune for him to play it. Everybody listened in silence. Ana felt the tears in her eyes. Zé knew exactly where each finger should be, and his wrists were moving smoothly despite the frayed cuffs of his shirt.

When he had finished the piece, he placed his hands on his knees and sat there in silence. Nobody spoke, nobody applauded. In the end Ana went up to him and put her hand on his shoulder.

"That was lovely," she said. "I didn't know you could play like that."

"It's an old piano," said Zé. "It's hard to tune it."

"How long have you spent tuning it?"

"Six years. And now I'll have to start all over again."

"I'll buy you a new piano," said Ana. "A good piano. You won't need to keep tuning it in order to play."

Zé shook his head.

"This the only piano I can play," he said quietly. "I'd get no pleasure out of a new instrument."

Ana nodded. She thought she understood, even though she had just witnessed something that could well have been a miracle.

"What was the piece you played?" she asked.

"It was written by a Polish man. His name is Frédéric."

"It was beautiful," said Ana.

Then she turned to face the others and started them off clapping. Zé stood up hesitantly and bowed, closed the lid, locked the piano, picked up his hat and left.

"Where does he go to?" Ana asked.

"Nobody knows," said Felicia. "But he always comes back. The last time he played for us was on New Year's Eve, 1899. As the century came to a close."

Ana could see that everybody was looking at her. She told them the facts: she was about to leave them. The new owner, Nunez, had promised not to change anything for as long as the women now working in the brothel stayed on.

"I came here by chance," she said in conclusion. "I was ill, and I thought in my innocence that this place was a hotel. And I was very well looked after. I might have been dead by now if it hadn't been for the care you gave me. But now it's time for me to move on. I shall leave here and go to Beira where I shall look for Isabel's parents and tell them that Isabel is dead. I don't know what will happen after that. All I do know is that I shan't be coming back here."

Ana then took the bundles of banknotes out of her handbag. Each of the women received the equivalent of five years' earnings. But to her great surprise, none of the women displayed the slightest sign of gratitude, despite the fact that they had never seen anywhere near as much money as that in their lives before.

"You don't need to stay on here now," she said. "Evening after evening, night after night. You can start living with your families again."

Ana had been standing up while she spoke. Now she sat down on the deep red plush chair they had placed for her under the jacaranda tree. Nobody spoke. Ana was used to this silence, and knew that in the end she would no doubt be forced to break it herself. She took one of the bundles of banknotes and tried to give it to Felicia — but Felicia declined to accept it and started talking again instead. She had obviously rehearsed her speech, as if everybody knew already what Ana was going to say.

"We shall go with you, Senhora," said Felicia. "No matter where you decide to open a new brothel, we shall go with you."

"But I have no intention ever again to run a brothel, not for as long as I live! I want to give you all money so that you can lead quite a different life. Besides, what would you do with your families if you were to accompany me?"

"We'll take them with us. We'll go with you, no matter where you end up. As long as it's not a country where there aren't any men."

"That's impossible. Don't you understand what I'm telling you?"

Nobody spoke. Ana realized that Felicia hadn't just been talking for herself: yet again she had been speaking on behalf of all the women assembled round the tree. The women really did believe that she was leaving in order to open up a new brothel somewhere else. And they wanted to go with her. She didn't know whether to be touched or angry at what seemed to be their incredible naivety.

She thought: they want me to lead a general exodus to an unknown destination. No matter where it is, they see me as what Forsman was for Elin — a guarantee of the possibility of a better life.

A Magrinha had suddenly stood up and left the garden: now she returned, carrying a large lizard. Ana knew that it was called a *halakavuma*.

"This lizard is very wise," said Felicia. "When people find a lizard like this one, they catch it and take it to their tribal chief. A *halakavuma* can always give the chieftain valuable advice. Senhora Ana has been listening for far too long to advice from unreliable people. That's why we have tracked down this lizard, so that it can advise Senhora Ana about what is best for her to do. This lizard is like a wise old lady."

The big, crocodile-like lizard was placed on Ana's knee. Sticky slime was dripping from its mouth, its cold skin was wet, its eyes staring, its tongue darting in and out of its mouth. Carlos had jumped up on to the piano, and was staring at the lizard in disgust.

426

I'm living in a crazy world, Ana thought. Am I really expected to listen to a lizard in order to find out what I ought to do with my life?

She put the lizard down on the ground. It disappeared slowly behind the tree, swaying from side to side on apparently unsteady legs.

"I shall listen to what it has to say," she said. "But not now. I'd rather hear from you than listen to a lizard."

She stood up again, uncertain of what to say as she thought she had already said it all. She could see that she was surrounded by disappointment and surprise. The money she had produced for the women had not had the effect she had expected. What was crucial as far as they were concerned was Felicia's words — that they wanted to accompany her to wherever she was going.

I don't understand this, she thought. I'll never understand it. But the time I've spent in this town has been characterized by my always being surrounded by white people claiming that it's impossible to understand the blacks. I no longer see whatever it is I'm looking at. My eyes are constantly enveloped by this white mist.

She left the garden and walked past the empty sofas. The only person in the room was a man trying to light a half-smoked cigar. For some reason his presence aroused her fury. She picked up a cushion and hit him in the face with it, sending the cigar stump flying.

She stared at him without saying anything, shouted for Carlos, and left. When she came out into the street she screamed loudly, as if for a moment she had been transformed into a peacock in distress. A street cleaner stopped what he was doing and looked hard at her. She got into the car, but her chauffeur made no comment of surprise or admiration when he saw what she was wearing. The street cleaner resumed his work, as if nothing had happened.

When Julietta opened the door and stared at her, Ana couldn't resist asking her what she thought of her get-up.

"I'd love to wear those clothes myself," said Julietta.

"You'll never be allowed to," said Ana.

She went upstairs to her bedroom. She threw the clothes she'd been wearing into a laundry basket. The masquerade was over.

Late that evening Picard came to hand over the prints of the photograph he'd taken. Long after he had left, she sat contemplating the picture he had chosen in the light of her paraffin lamp.

Everybody was wearing a serious expression and looking straight at the camera. Apart from Carlos, who was laughing — as if he were a human being.

The only person in the picture who seemed frightened was Ana herself.

CHAPTER
SEVENTY-THREE

The day after she had sat with the lizard on her knee, Ana was driven out to Pedro Pimenta's farm for what she had decided would be her last visit. On the way there it occurred to her that this place, among the cages with the white sheepdogs and the ponds with the crocodiles, was where her journey had reached its fateful end. She had come this far, and now she just needed to travel back. When Isabel had been let down by her husband, Ana had finally become aware of all the deceit that surrounded her on all sides. An environment that seemed to be comprised of nothing but hypocrisy and a repulsive contempt for the people whose home this country actually was. It was as if the guests had eaten their fill of the meal to which they hadn't even been invited. We are the uninvited guests, she thought. I no longer need to have any doubts about that, at least.

She had taken Carlos with her. It was for his sake that she returned to Pedro's farm. Carlos would be able to live there in freedom. There were trees and open spaces, and in addition he would be surrounded by both white and black people, which is what he was used to. Moreover, beyond the crocodile pools was the extensive countryside he had originally come from — the endless wilderness covered in bushes that he could go back to if he so wished.

Ana had realized that Carlos was just as far away from home as she was herself. Perhaps there was also a river with cold, brown water running through the forests where he had been born? Even if nothing else unites us, there is no doubt a longing to go home that we have both done all in our power to resist. I've done so in my way, but I'll never be able to understand how he's managed it.

When they reached the farm Ana shuddered at the memory of what had happened there. Carlos climbed on to the car roof and looked around curiously, as if he suspected that something important was about to happen.

Ana Dolores came out on to the steps. It was the first time Ana had seen her when she was not wearing her nurse's uniform, with the stiff nurse's hat on her head. She was surprised: hadn't Ana Dolores come here to nurse the sick Teresa?

The truth about the big changes that had taken place became immediately apparent. Ana Dolores bade her a low-key welcome, gave Carlos an odd look, then invited her guest to sit down on the veranda and have a cup of tea. When a maid came with a tea tray, it was obvious who ruled the roost in this household. Ana Dolores was not simply the nurse, she was also the mistress of the house. The black woman went down on one knee before Ana Dolores after having served the tea.

We have the same name, Ana thought. She is Ana Dolores and I am Ana Branca — but soon I shall return to the person I once was. When that happens, my name will revert to being Hanna. But perhaps other changes have taken place inside me. Things I can't see, only feel or perhaps suspect? I know that what happened to me after Isabel's death will be crucial for the rest of my life. Even if I don't yet know how.

She asked Ana Dolores about Teresa.

"She'll probably never become healthy again," said Ana Dolores. "But the chances of her throwing herself into one of the crocodile pools have decreased. Her sick mind hasn't completely eaten away what remains of her will to live."

"What does she say?"

"Not a lot. She mutters away about things that happened when she was a little girl. Her life before Pedro Pimenta entered it."

"What about her and Pedro's children? What will happen to them?"

"Just now they are on a ship to Portugal. Neither of them will ever come back here. The boy was given a crocodile skin to take back home with him, the girl a piece of cloth like those that women here wrap around themselves. All I hope is that their memories of Africa fade away and eventually disappear altogether."

"And what about you, Ana Dolores?"

"I live here."

"Looking after a woman who's never going to get better?"

"I also run the place. I sell dogs and harvest crocodile skins. I've grown tired of merely looking after people."

Ana said nothing more, but waited for Ana Dolores to ask a few questions about Isabel's death. Perhaps she might also be interested in knowing why Ana had made such a determined effort to help Isabel.

But Ana Dolores said nothing. She sat there with a smile on her face, gazing out over the farm she now ruled over. It occurred to Ana that this was the first time she had ever seen Ana Dolores smile.

A car approached in a cloud of dust, and pulled up outside the house.

"Please excuse me," said Ana Dolores, standing up. "I have a visitor, a man from Kimberley who's going to buy one of my dogs. It won't take long. Wait here for me. Just ring the bell if you want any more tea."

The man who stepped out of the car was wearing a pith helmet and seemed to be in a hurry. It seemed to Ana that he was one of those white men who had come to Africa to live a short life. He would die like a hunted animal — hunted down by himself.

She and Carlos went to look at the crocodiles. Carlos stayed a respectable distance away from the pools containing the biggest crocodiles, which were almost four metres long. There have never been any crocodiles in my river, Ana thought. But perhaps once upon a time Carlos lived by a river where crocodiles lurked just under the surface of the water. He knows about the threat they pose.

As she stood there watching the crocodiles, Ana suddenly noticed how things had changed since her last visit to the farm. She couldn't put her finger on it at first, but then it dawned on her that what she was looking at was becoming more and more decrepit: things had deteriorated markedly since Pedro's death. She noted the cracks in the concrete walls of the pools, the weeds growing up through the stone paths, the troughs of food beginning to rust, broken tools, rubbish that hadn't been collected and carried away for burning. Wherever she looked there were signs of decay. There was also a smell of death on all sides.

This was a change that had taken place in a very short time.

As she returned to the house she saw more and more signs of decay and decadence. The white sheepdogs in their kennels were not as well cared for as they had been in the past. Pedro Pimenta's farm was wasting away. When he and Isabel died, what they had built up together had immediately started to crumble away.

Ana Dolores had gone into the house with her customer. Ana sat down on the veranda and Carlos climbed up on to an abandoned dovecote. Ana suddenly had the feeling that she wasn't alone. When she turned to look she discovered Teresa standing at the point where the veranda branched off along the side of the house. She was very pale, and so thin that she was almost unrecognizable. At first Ana wasn't sure if it really was Teresa. She was uncertain what to do, but stood up and said hello. Teresa did not reply, but she hurried over and stood close by Ana. She smelled strongly of some oily perfume or other. Ana could see that the roots of her hair were caked in dirt and grease.

"Were you also married to my husband?" Teresa asked.

"No."

"I'm sure you were married to my husband. You used to have red hair, but then you had it dyed."

"I've never had red hair, and I've never been married to Pedro."

Teresa suddenly gave Ana a powerful slap in the face. It was so unexpected that the pain in her cheek and the surprise at being hit struck her dumb.

"As you know what my husband is called you must have been married to him."

Teresa turned round and hurried away. Then she suddenly turned round and started to come back. Ana braced herself for another smack, but Teresa turned yet again and disappeared behind the gable end of the house, and started shrieking.

Ana Dolores came running on to the veranda.

"Where is she?"

Ana pointed. Ana Dolores hurried along the veranda and followed it behind the gable end. When she came back she was holding Teresa by the arm. It was as if she were dragging along a rag doll. They both disappeared into the house.

The man in the pith helmet left with his newly purchased white sheepdog. He didn't even seem to have noticed Teresa's presence. Ana Dolores came back again. Ana wondered what she had done in order to calm Teresa down, but she didn't ask.

434

"I've come here because there's something I want you to do," said Ana.

She pointed at Carlos, who was sitting on the abandoned dovecote, scratching his fur absent-mindedly. He didn't seem to have noticed Teresa's outburst either, something that surprised Ana. Carlos always tried to protect her by screeching and kicking up a row. But not this time.

"I'm about to leave Lourenço Marques," she said, "and I can't take Carlos with me. I thought I would ask if he could stay here on the farm. As long as he gets food and is allowed to do what he wants to do, he's very calm and no trouble. One day he might well decide to go back to the forest again. He'd be able to do that from here."

"You mean that he would be free to wander around and sit wherever he likes, as he's doing now?"

"You could give him some rules if you liked. He's a quick learner."

"But you don't want me to build a cage for him?"

"Certainly not. Nor should you attach a chain to his neck. Obviously I'm prepared to pay you well for your trouble."

Ana Dolores looked at her, smiling.

"When you first came here you were in a pitiful state," she said. "But you've done well for yourself."

"I can at least pay you so that Carlos can lead the life he wants to have when I'm no longer here."

Ana Dolores stood up.

"Let me think it over," she said. "If I'm going to take on responsibility for an ape, I want to be sure that I really can and want to do that."

She stood underneath the dovecote, looking up at Carlos who was still picking away at his skin, searching for ticks. Ana watched them from her seat on the veranda. Ana Dolores left the dovecote and walked to the row of kennels and pens where the sheepdogs that were already trained were jumping up excitedly at the bars. She stopped at one of the pens and seemed to pat the dog through the bars. Then she returned to the veranda.

"Shout for the ape," she said. "Or at least get him to come down from the dovecote so that I can introduce myself to him."

"So Carlos can stay here?"

"As long as he doesn't bite."

Ana shouted for Carlos, who clambered slowly down from the dovecote. Looking back, it seemed to Ana that he had appeared to hesitate.

CHAPTER
SEVENTY-FOUR

What came next happened so quickly that afterwards Ana wasn't at all sure of the course of events. The sheepdog Ana Delores had just been stroking burst through the bars surrounding its pen and raced towards Carlos, who had just reached the ground. Ana shouted a warning, but it was too late. The dog leapt up and sunk its teeth into Carlos's throat before he had realized the danger. Ana ran down the steps and began hitting the dog with a sweeping brush that was leaning against the veranda rail, but it didn't release its grip on Carlos's throat. Ana screamed and hit out with the brush as hard as she could. Ana Dolores didn't move a muscle. Only when it was all over did she help to pull the dog away and drag it back to its pen.

Carlos lay motionless on the ground. His head was almost detached from his body. His eyes were open. He continued to look at Ana, even though he was dead.

Ana Dolores came back after locking up the sheepdog, which was still wild with fury.

"I don't understand how it could have happened," she said.

When Ana heard those words, she realized immediately what the facts were. At first she couldn't believe it, but there was no other possible explanation.

It had not been an accident.

Ana stood up and slowly brushed the dust off her dress.

"I don't know how you did it," she said. "I understand that you unfastened the gate to the dog's pen, but not how you then ordered it to attack. Perhaps the dog is trained to react not only to a spoken command, but also to a hand gesture or a movement of the head."

Ana Dolores tried to interrupt her.

"Let me finish," roared Ana. "If you interrupt me I shall beat you to death. You gave the dog a signal to attack Carlos. You wanted the ape to die. I don't know why you did it. Perhaps because you are so full of hatred towards anybody who doesn't look down on black people? Perhaps you are so full of hatred towards the ape who became my friend that it had to die? I have never met anybody as full of bitterness and hatred as you, Ana Dolores. One of these days the people in this country will have had more than enough of the likes of you."

Ana Dolores tried once again to say something, but Ana — who was so furious that she was shaking — merely raised her hand.

"Don't say a word," she said. "Not a single word. I don't want to hear a word from your mouth ever again. Just fetch me a sack so that I can take him away from here."

438

Ana Dolores turned on her heel and disappeared into the house. She never reappeared. Instead, a maid came out with an empty sack. She handed it over without even looking at the dead ape. Ana put Carlos's body into the sack, knowing that Ana Dolores was standing behind one of the windows in the house, watching her.

The chauffeur was waiting at the side of the car, and stepped forward to assist her. But she shook her head: she wanted to carry Carlos herself.

On the way back to town, she asked the chauffeur to stop on the bridge over the river. She got out of the car and stood by the rail. Some women were washing clothes in the river, not far from the bridge. They had hoisted up their skirts up over their thighs. They were chatting away as they did the washing, and Ana could hear them laughing merrily as they slapped and kneaded the piles of garments. She was very tempted to go down to the women, hoist up her own dress and help them with the washing. In those black women she could detect a trace of Elin, and perhaps also herself.

In the end she stepped back from the rail. By then she had decided where Carlos should be buried.

When she got back home, she found herself unable to cry over her dead chimpanzee, but she felt a boundless longing for Lundmark, to have him by her side to make the mourning for Carlos easier. He wouldn't have had much to say, as he was a man of few words: but he would have been able to console her, and assure her that she wasn't alone. She thought about the fact that in this continent she found so confusing and so full of contradictions, in the end the only thing she could rely on had been a chimpanzee.

She put the sack with Carlos's body in the icebox. She forbade Julietta and the other servants to go anywhere near it. She knew that they were very curious, so she had a large, heavy stone brought up from the garden and placed on the lid of the icebox, telling them all that white people also had their witchcraft, and that hers was now hidden away inside the stone. Anybody who touched the stone would find that his or her fingers were transformed into small, sharp pieces of granite and that nothing — no white or black medicine — would be able to restore them. She could see that they believed her, and couldn't help feeling a bitter-sweet pleasure in among all the misery she had experienced. Especially when Julietta turned pale and slunk away.

Once again, she slept that night with the aid of a strong dose of sleeping tablets. But she was up again as dawn broke. As the chauffeur had been instructed to be ready for an early departure, he had spent the night curled up on the back seat of the car. He helped Ana to carry the sack containing Carlos's body from the icebox, and also packed into the car a spade and a pickaxe that Ana had taken from the garden shed the previous evening.

All was quiet as they carried the sack into the brothel, past the sleeping guards, through the sofa room where a few men lay stretched out, snoring.

The chauffeur put the sack down where she indicated, next to the jacaranda tree. Then he went back to the car.

This was where she was going to bury Carlos. He would lie there under an array of blue blossom.

There was simply no other location worthy of being Carlos's last resting place.

CHAPTER
SEVENTY-FIVE

Ana raised the pickaxe. That very movement meant that she had reverted to being Hanna Renström. It was how she used to raise the pickaxe when she and Elin were preparing the potato patch in the spring, and again in the autumn when they needed to harvest the potatoes before the first frosts arrived, heralding the approach of the long winter.

The ground was hard on the surface, but softer underneath and easier to penetrate. She exchanged the pickaxe for a spade and began digging. She was in a hurry, but couldn't bring herself to work fast. Digging a grave was not something that could be rushed. A grave was not merely a hole in the ground: it was just as much a hole being made in her heart.

Once, when she was a child, she had buried a dead great northern diver that had been washed ashore by the river. It was the only grave she had ever dug in her life. But now she was about to commit a dead ape to its final resting place, and then leave it and the tree, never to return.

She rolled up the sleeves of her blouse and unbuttoned it at the neck — it was early in the morning, but already the temperature was rising. She could smell the scent of a little lemon tree that Senhor Vaz had planted in the garden.

The spade hit against something she thought at first was a stone, but when she bent down to pick it up she saw that it was a bone. A chicken bone, she thought. Somebody must have been sitting here, chewing the meat off it, and then thrown it away. She carried on digging. More bones appeared in the soil she shovelled to one side.

The spade hit against a biggish stone that sounded noticeably hollow. When she picked it up she saw that it was in fact a skull. A very small skull. She paused, wondering what it could be, and decided it must be from a dead monkey.

But then she realized that it was the remains of a human head. A child's skull. So small that it might well have been that of a newborn baby, or even a foetus.

She was beginning to feel very uneasy, but she continued digging. Wherever she dug she was coming across bones and skulls. These were not chicken bones at all, but the remains of human skeletons. She felt queasy, but she didn't stop digging. She wanted to bury Carlos that morning, and to have finished before the brothel came back to life.

It eventually dawned on her that she was exposing a mass grave, the remains of babies and foetuses that had been buried under this jacaranda tree to be hidden and forgotten about. She was faced with a children's cemetery, the results of unwanted pregnancies after all the thousands of nocturnal encounters that had taken place in this brothel. The bones were all white or grey, but all the foetuses and newborn babies that had been strangled or killed in some other way had been a mixture of white and black.

In the end she put down the spade and sat on the bench. She was in torment. The ground in front of her was covered in bones from dead children. It seemed as if this morning, once and for all, she had discovered what kind of a world she had been living in. Her queasiness had turned into a feeling of dismay, perhaps even horror.

Without Ana's noticing, Felicia had come out into the courtyard. She was wearing one of her many attractive silk dressing gowns. She looked at the dug-up soil and all the pieces of bone with a blank expression on her face.

"Why are you digging all this up?" she asked.

Instead of answering Ana opened the sack and showed her Carlos's stiff and shrivelled corpse.

"Didn't you know that this was a cemetery?" asked Felicia in surprise.

"No. I knew nothing about it. I just wanted Carlos to have a pretty resting place here under the jacaranda tree."

"Why have you killed Carlos?"

Ana was not surprised by Felicia's question. If she had learnt one thing during her time in this town, it was that black people thought whites were capable of all kinds of actions, even the most inexplicable or cruel.

"It wasn't me who killed him."

She explained what had happened at Pedro Pimenta's farm. When Ana mentioned Ana Dolores's name, she realized that Felicia understood that what she was saying was true.

"Ana Dolores is a dangerous person," said Felicia. "She is surrounded by all kinds of evil spirits that can kill. I have never understood how she could be a nurse."

It struck Ana that Felicia didn't seem in the least disturbed by all the bones that had been dug up. That only increased Ana's unease.

"Bury him here," said Felicia. "It's a good place for him to be."

Felicia turned to leave, but Ana stretched out her hand and took hold of her dressing gown.

"I must ask you a question," she said. "I realize that all these aborted foetuses or newborn babies that have been killed are the result of what happened here in the brothel. But there's something else I want to know, and I want you to give me an honest answer."

"I'm always honest," said Felicia.

Ana shook her head.

"Oh no you're not," she said. "Neither am I. I haven't met a single person in this town who tells the truth. But the truth is what I want from you now. Is my dead foetus buried here as well?"

"Yes. It was Laurinda who buried it. She dug a hole and emptied the bucket into it."

Ana nodded in silence. This seemed to be the moment when she discovered and understood everything about her time here in Lourenço Marques, from the moment she stepped ashore until now, as she sat here with all these human remains in front of her.

She stood up.

"That was all I wanted to know," she said. "Now I'll lay my ape to rest and replace all the soil as it was before. I understand that this is a cemetery. Right at the heart of the brothel is a secret burial place."

"And it tells a truth," said Felicia.

"Yes," said Ana. "The cemetery also tells a truth. One we'd rather not know about."

Felicia went back inside. But it dawned on Ana that she couldn't bury Carlos here as she had planned. She couldn't allow him to lie here among all these lost souls of foetuses and dead babies. She put Carlos back into the sack, and replaced the soil so that no bones could be seen. She went to fetch the chauffeur, who carried the sack back to the car. He didn't ask any questions. He's an old man who's seen and heard it all, she thought. Is there any basic difference between all the crazy things white people do, and me being driven back and forth with an ape in a sack?

She asked him to take her to the part of the harbour where small fishing boats were moored. It was next to the high wooden frames where the fishermen hung their nets and the baskets that were used to carry their catches up to the market stalls.

Ana got out of the car. Most of the fishing boats were already out at sea, and would return later in the day with their catches. But at one of the jetties there were a few boats still moored there, with their sails furled round the masts. She asked the chauffeur to accompany her there.

"I need to hire a boat," she said. "I want to take my ape out to sea and bury him there."

"I shall ask," said the chauffeur.

"Whoever takes me out to sea will be well paid, of course."

Two of the fishermen shook their heads, but a third one, an older man about the same age as the chauffeur, said he was willing. When Ana gathered the man was prepared to take her out in his boat, she went on to the jetty.

"I've assured him that you are not out of your mind," said the chauffeur. "He's willing to take you to sea, provided you go right away."

"I shall pay him well," said Ana. "I also need some heavy weights to put in the sack, to make sure that it really does sink."

The chauffeur explained that to the fisherman, and listened to his response.

"He has an old anchor that he can sacrifice as a sinker," he said. "He'll need to be paid extra for that, of course. He hopes you won't be afraid of getting your dress dirty, but he also has another important question."

"What does he want to know?"

"Can you swim?"

Ana thought about her father and his stubborn refusal to allow her to swim in the river. Should she tell the fisherman a white lie, or give him an honest answer? She felt that she couldn't cope with any more lies.

"No," she said. "I can't swim."

"Good," said the chauffeur. "He doesn't want to have people who can swim in his boat. They don't have sufficient respect for the sea."

They fetched the sack containing Carlos. Ana had the feeling that it was getting heavier and heavier.

"I'm ashamed to say that I've forgotten your name," said Ana.

"Why should you be ashamed of something you've forgotten? Does that mean you should also be ashamed of what you remember? My name's Vanji."

"I'd like you to stay here until we get back, please. Then I'll only need you and your car for a few more days."

Vanji was disappointed to hear that their time together would soon be over. Ana didn't have the strength to console him.

"What's the name of the man with the boat?" she asked.

"Columbus," said the chauffeur. "He never goes out fishing on a Tuesday. He's convinced he would never catch anything then. You are lucky that it's Tuesday today. It's unlikely that anybody else apart from Columbus would be prepared to go to sea with a dead ape in the boat, and, to cap it all, with a white woman as a passenger."

CHAPTER
SEVENTY-SIX

Ana sat down by the mast in the little boat. The sack and the rusty old anchor were lying at her feet. The boat smelled strongly of many years of catches. Columbus raised the sail with his sinewy arms and sat down by the rudder. When they came to the harbour entrance, the wind filled the sail and they started moving more quickly. Ana pointed out to sea, the wide strait between the mainland and the as yet invisible island known as Inhaca.

"Until we can hardly see land," she tried to explain, not knowing if the old fisherman could speak Portuguese or not.

He smiled by way of an answer. That smile calmed Ana down. The discovery of the child cemetery had been gripping her in a sort of stranglehold. Now that feeling was beginning to fade away. She let one hand trail in the water, which was both warm and cool at the same time. A few seabirds were circling overhead. They were like sparks coming out of the sun, white sparks that eventually formed a sort of halo over the fishing boat, which was painted red, blue and green. Columbus had lit an old pipe, and his gaze seemed to be permanently fixed on the horizon. Ana packed the anchor into the sack, letting Carlos embrace the rusty iron, then tied a knot just as she remembered it being done at Lundmark's burial. Perhaps the two bodies will meet? Could there be a sort of cemetery somewhere down at the bottom of the sea where all the corpses eventually gathered together? It was a childish thought, she knew that, but nobody could care less what she was thinking just now, least of all Columbus with his pipe in his mouth.

A school of playful dolphins attached itself to the boat. Carlos is not going to be buried in isolation, Ana thought. The dolphins dived, reappeared and swam along close to the boat, then vanished into the depths once again. She felt an almost irresistible desire to tell Berta about these dolphins and the remarkable funeral procession in which they were taking part. Once she'd located Isabel's parents, she would at last have a definite plan for the next stage of her life: I want to tell Berta about a dead chimpanzee, a school of playful dolphins, and me approaching the second seismic shift in my life.

They continued sailing towards the horizon. Lourenço Marques glided past in the mist. It seemed to Ana that they had now reached the point she had been looking for.

"Let's take down the sail," she said. "This is the right place."

Columbus tucked his pipe away somewhere behind his ragged shirt, took in the sail and secured it to the mast. The boat was stationary now, bobbing up and down in the swell. The dolphins were circling around them, at a distance. The seabirds above their heads were screeching like instruments out of tune. Columbus helped Ana to lift up the sack and drop it into the water with a gentle splash. She watched it sinking down into the depths. One of the dolphins swam up to it, nudged it with its nose, then swam away again, having said its final goodbye.

When Ana could no longer see the sack, she felt that her loneliness was now greater than ever before: but it no longer frightened her as much as it had done in the past. She was about to bid farewell to a world in which it had been impossible for her to have any friends. She had no feelings of community with the whites who lived in Lourenço Marques, and the blacks didn't trust her but merely saw her as a person in authority whom they must obey.

Senhor Vaz had given her a necklace when they got married: she suddenly wrenched it off and flung it into the water. A seabird dived after it, but not quickly enough to catch it before it sank.

They turned back to the harbour and berthed by the jetty. Ana paid Columbus and shook his hand. She wondered for how many years he would have to make his fishing trips in order to earn as much as she had just given him. But Columbus seemed unimpressed by the bundle of banknotes he had received. He continued to smile at her, but didn't even turn to watch her walking back to the car.

Ana stopped at the harbour office to ask about the next coaster heading for Beira. She was in luck. A ship would be leaving the day after next, at six in the morning. She booked a ticket and paid for the biggest cabin they had — and thought how easy everything had become. All she needed to do now was make sure that the photographs were taken to the brothel, say goodbye to her domestic staff, and hand over all her bunches of keys. Getting rid of those keys, which she had been obliged to carry around and take care of constantly, was something she longed to do.

She spent the last couple of days packing two light suitcases. She arranged with Andrade that all her and Senhor Vaz's clothes would be donated to those in need. All she kept were a few photographs, Lundmark's discharge book, and her diary. She disposed of everything else.

The last afternoon before her departure, Ana assembled all her domestic staff in order to say goodbye to them. As Andrade was about to move into the house he had bought from her, none of them needed to worry about their future.

She had prepared individual envelopes for each of them, so that nobody would know how much the others had received. She was quite sure, for instance, that Julietta would try to find out how she was valued in relation to Anaka.

Ana summoned them to her study. She recalled how Jonathan Forsman had done the same when he spoke to his staff. She told them the facts, that she was going first to Beira, and then to an as yet unknown destination. She thanked them for their services, and wished them all the best with their new employer, Andrade.

As usual, her words were greeted with silence. Nobody thanked her, nobody said anything at all. Ana sent them back to their duties, but asked Julietta to stay behind.

"You'll be okay with Andrade," she said, "as long as you behave yourself."

"I always behave myself," said Julietta.

"I'd like you to do something for me," Ana said. "Before it gets dark I'd like you to take this envelope down to Felicia and the other women. It contains photographs."

Julietta took the letter, then left the room. Ana heard the front door close with a bang.

Now that she was alone, she made a note in her diary. "I can't live in a world in which everybody always knows more than I do." Then she put the diary in one of the suitcases, still not entirely sure about why she was keeping it.

The next morning, when Ana got up very early to prepare for her journey down to the harbour, Julietta still hadn't returned.

She was worried — what could have happened to her? She sent for Anaka and asked her. Anaka didn't answer, but she didn't give the impression of being worried in the least.

Then the penny dropped. Julietta had stayed at the brothel. She had gone to Nunez, who had now taken over the premises, and told him she wanted to start working there. And, of course, he had taken her on. All that talk about a children's home had been a lot of hot air. Perhaps he had even taken her to one of the rooms to find out how good she was at satisfying a man.

Ana was highly annoyed when she realized that this was the most likely reason for Julietta's non-appearance.

But she banished the thought. She had no desire to leave this house weighed down with disappointment and unpleasant feelings. She'd had more than enough of her joyless existence. For the last time she spoke to Anaka, who accompanied her down to the front door.

"I'm leaving now," she said. "It's going to be a hot day — but it will be cooler at sea."

She thought she ought to say more than that — but what?

She had run out of words. She stroked Anaka gently over her cheek, then left her for the final time.

CHAPTER
SEVENTY-SEVEN

When Ana came out into the street, it was not only her car standing there waiting for her. Moses had also returned. So he hadn't returned to the mines in the Rand after all, but had stayed in town all the time. Perhaps he's been keeping an eye on me without my knowing it, Ana thought. Just like a leopard, who sees everything but is never seen.

Moses was wearing his usual overalls and a worn-out pair of sandals. His hands were dangling down by his sides, looking quite helpless.

"You're here," she said.

"Yes," said Moses. "I'm here. I wanted to say goodbye."

"How did you know I'd be leaving today?"

As soon as she'd said that, she knew it was a question to which she would never receive an answer. If Moses had said he'd discovered the date of her departure in the pattern of paving stones outside her house, she wouldn't have believed him: but he would have believed it himself. Anyway, here he was, just as she was about to step for the last time into the car that Vanji would return to its owner later in the day.

Moses looked at her and smiled, but he didn't answer.

It wasn't important, Ana thought. She was simply pleased that he'd come back.

She suddenly had the feeling that she didn't want to leave after all. She wanted to stay close to him, for as long as possible. But that wasn't on. She didn't have a house any longer, and had handed over all the keys. The only accommodation she had was a cabin on board a coaster that would take her to Beira.

Her feelings frightened her, but also filled her with happiness. She really loved this man standing in front of her. However, it was not possible for them to have a relationship, it would go against all the assumptions and conventions that held sway in this accursed town.

"Come with me to the harbour," was all she could say.

"Yes," said Moses, "I'll come with you."

But when she opened the car door for him, he shook his head, and instead started running with light, springy steps down the hills leading to the harbour.

Ana told Vanji to take a different route. She didn't want to pass by Moses as he was running.

She also handed Vanji two envelopes, one with the money she owed for renting the car, and the other with a payment to him.

Those were the last two envelopes she needed to give people: everybody had been paid. She didn't owe anybody anything now, and she had behaved in a way which all other white citizens would have condemned outright, if they'd known about it. They would have said she was spoiling the blacks, making them obstinate and lazy, and reducing their respect for their white superiors.

I'm in the middle of all that, with a foot in both camps, Ana thought. I don't belong anywhere. Not until now, that is. Now that Moses has returned, I belong with him. But that won't be possible.

He was standing waiting for her by the quay when she arrived. Despite the long run, he seemed totally unaffected by the strain. It struck Ana that she was treating him as she'd treated Lundmark. She only saw what she wanted to see. If she'd examined Moses closely she would no doubt have discovered that his hands were dirty and his overalls unwashed, and she might also have noticed that the run had indeed left its mark as his lungs must have been damaged after all those years down the mines.

She said farewell to Vanji, who stood up straight and saluted her awkwardly.

"We'll never see each other again," said Ana.

"Not in this life, at least," said Vanji, saluting her again.

When she turned round she saw that Moses had already picked up her suitcases. He went on board with her. The white officer by the gangplank saluted Ana and let them pass. A steward in a white jacket led the way to her cabin. Ana couldn't help but recall the first time she had seen Carlos, and chuckled sadly.

Nobody will understand this, she thought. I'm mourning the loss of a man I was barely married to. Another man I was married to died but I felt no sorrow.

But there is a black woman and a chimpanzee who will always be a part of me for as long as I live. And now there's a black man, by the name of Moses, who I want to be with.

The steward opened the cabin door, and waited in order to escort Moses back to the quay. But Ana closed the door, after explaining that Moses would unpack her suitcases before going back ashore.

For the first time, they were alone together in a room. Ana sat on the edge of the bed. Moses remained standing.

"I thought you had gone back to your mines," she said. "I was angry because you had left without saying anything."

Moses didn't respond. His usual calm smile seemed to have deserted him.

I must be bold, Ana thought. I've nothing to lose. If I've learnt anything from my time between the two gangplanks — the one I crossed when I first arrived here, and the one I've crossed now that I'm leaving — it's that I must dare to do what I want to do, and not allow myself to be held back by what others consider is permissible for a white woman like me.

To her surprise, everything seemed perfectly clear to her now, for the first time. Now, when she was about to place a full stop behind the confused months she had spent in the town by the lagoon. Meeting Isabel had awoken inside her an affection for a black woman whose fate had affected her so profoundly. But Isabel was dead. Just as Lars Johan Jakob Antonius

Lundmark, her first husband, was dead. And Senhor Vaz, who had made her rich, was also dead.

Then Moses had crossed her path. The affection she had felt for Isabel had turned into love for her brother. And he was alive, he hadn't left her.

Ana stood up and walked over to Moses. She leaned her face against his, and felt both gratitude and relief when he put his arms around her waist.

They made love in great haste, half-dressed, anxious but passionate — accompanied by the sound of footsteps on the deck over their heads and in the narrow corridor outside the cabin. She was possessed by the thought — and the desire — that this lovemaking would never end, that they would stay where they were until the ship filled up with water and sank. She appreciated Moses' sensual pleasure, his tenderness, and then when she heard him sob, Isabel and her children were with them in that cabin.

Afterwards everything was very still. They lay beside each other on the narrow bunk with its high sides of well-worn wood, designed to prevent passengers from falling out during a storm. Ana placed her hand on Moses' heart, and felt how his breathing slowly subsided from excited passion to deep calm.

Perhaps she thought about Lundmark at that moment, she couldn't be sure afterwards. But over and over again she thought about how so many aspects of her life kept repeating themselves. Making love in cramped bunks, sudden departures, burials at sea. She hadn't been prepared for any of this, not by her father or by Elin. In her life by the river, Ana had learnt how to handle a pickaxe, to look after children, to wade through deep snow and endure freezing temperatures and emerge smiling — and even to be afraid of a God who punished you for your sins, according to her grandmother's angst-filled convictions. Now she had done courageous things without being prepared in the least, and without anybody forcing her to do them.

Time was short. The ship would shortly be leaving.

"Come with me," she said. "I want you to come with me."

"I can't."

"Why not?"

"You know that, Senhora."

"Don't call me Senhora! Don't call me Ana either. Call me Hanna. That's my real name."

"I'll be killed, just like Isabel was."

"That will not happen as long as I'm around."

"You couldn't even protect Isabel."

"Are you accusing me?"

"No. I'm just stating the facts."

Moses sat up, then stood and put on his overalls again. Ana was still lying in bed, half-dressed, her clothes in disorder, her hair all over the place.

At that moment there was a sound of loud footsteps outside the cabin door. Somebody hammered hard on the door, which was then flung open. The officer who had been on duty by the gangplank — a first mate — stood in the doorway, accompanied by another man who Ana assumed was his colleague.

CHAPTER
SEVENTY-EIGHT

Ana thought the two men looked like rampant beasts of prey.

"Has he attacked you?" roared the mate, punching Moses in the face.

"He hasn't touched me," shrieked Ana, trying to put herself between them. But the mate had already managed to kick Moses on to the floor, and he sat on him with his hands round his throat.

"I'll kill the bastard," yelled the mate. "A porter who dares to attack one of my passengers in her cabin."

"He hasn't attacked me," shouted Ana in desperation, pulling at the mate's hands. "Let go of him!"

The raving officer stood up and dragged Moses to his feet. Blood was dripping from Moses' face.

"What did he do?" asked the man in the doorway, who hadn't spoken so far.

"He didn't do anything apart from what I asked him to do," said Ana. "And I'm disgusted by the way you have treated him."

"We're the ones who decide how to treat the niggers who come on board this ship," said the mate.

As if to emphasize what he'd said, he punched Moses again. Ana forced her way between them. She was only

461

half-dressed, and realized that her appearance might have led the mate to jump to conclusions. But she didn't bother about that now. At one of the happiest moments in her life, she had been more outraged than ever before.

"Let him go," she said. "And don't set hands on him again."

"No," said the mate. "He's off to jail. The fort can take care of him."

Ana was struck dumb by the thought of Moses ending up in the same miserable dump in which his sister Isabel had died.

"In that case you'll have to take me there as well," she said.

Something in her voice was so convincing that the two officers backed off. Ana took out a handkerchief and wiped Moses' face. The blood clinging to the handkerchief suddenly made her aware of a sticky feeling on the inside of her thigh. She knew what it was, and thought that just now, it was the biggest and most important secret of her whole life.

When they left the cabin, all the passengers and crew stared at the procession, wondering what had happened. Everybody on board knew that something out of the ordinary had taken place inside the ship's biggest cabin.

Moses walked along the gangplank, not having been able to say a proper goodbye to Ana. She watched him walking along the quay without so much as a backward glance. She continued watching until he was out of sight, then she went back to her cabin and lay down on

462

her bunk, completely exhausted, but also furious about what had happened. She lay there until she heard various commands being issued, felt the shaking as the pressure rose in the boilers, and listened to the rattling of chains as the moorings were shed.

Why hadn't she left the ship and gone with Moses? Why hadn't she dared to do that?

For one brief moment I saw everything clearly, she thought. But then I didn't dare to accept the consequences of what had happened.

After many hours, she went up on deck. She had combed her hair carefully and changed into a different dress. She stood by the rail. The other white passengers on board made room for her — not out of politeness, she felt, but as an indication of their disapproval.

At that last moment I was transformed into a whore in their eyes, she thought. I took a black man with me into my cabin, and performed the most outrageous act a person can imagine.

She contemplated the white town climbing along the hills in the far distance. She watched it fading away in the gathering heat haze. Their course was now almost due north, the sun was high in the heavens, and she was called to the first meal after embarkation. But she declined: she was quite hungry, but she didn't want to interrupt her leave-taking of the town she would never see again.

Suddenly a man was standing by her side. He was wearing a uniform, and she gathered he was the captain. She had a vague feeling that she recognized him, but couldn't quite place him. He saluted her, and held out his hand.

"Captain Fortuna," he said. "Welcome on board."

He smelled strongly of beer, and his breath was like a distant memory of Senhor Vaz. He was in his forties, suntanned and sinewy.

"Thank you," she said after shaking hands. "What's the weather going to be like on this voyage?"

"Calm and tranquil. No rough seas."

"Icebergs?"

Captain Fortuna looked at her in surprise, then burst out laughing, thinking she was joking.

"No ice apart from what we have in the iceboxes," he said. "There are no underwater reefs around here, nothing dangerous as long as one stays sufficiently far from land. I've been in command of this ship for nearly ten years. The most dramatic incident I've experienced was when we had a bull on board: it went mad and jumped over the rail. Unfortunately we couldn't rescue him. He swam at amazing speed towards India. It was night-time, and we couldn't locate him."

"I've never been to Beira," said Ana. "I know nothing about the town, but I know I shall need to book into a hotel."

"The Africa Hotel," said Captain Fortuna. "They've just finished building it. It's a splendid hotel. That's where you should stay."

"Is it a big town?"

"Not as big as Lourenço Marques. It's not far at all to the hotel."

464

Captain Fortuna saluted her again, then walked over to the rope ladder leading up to the bridge.

It dawned on Ana where she had seen him before. On one occasion, perhaps more, Captain Fortuna had visited her brothel. He hadn't been wearing his uniform, so that is why she hadn't recognized him at first.

I'm surrounded by my old customers, she thought. And he knows who I am.

She returned to her cabin and lay down on her bunk again. She ran her hand over her pelvis, and decided that if in fact she had conceived, she would allow the baby to live. No matter where she went after doing what she had to do in Beira, she would avoid going anywhere near a cemetery for foetuses and unwanted babies.

That's a promise, she thought. I'm swearing an oath that only I know about. So what is its significance?

She took dinner in her cabin, so as not to come into contact with curious and gossiping people.

In the evening, after darkness had fallen, she went out on deck again to breathe in the cooling air. The starry sky was completely clear. She could feel the proximity of Moses. And of Lundmark as well, and perhaps even Senhor Vaz. A coil of rope by her feet could easily be Carlos, curled up and asleep.

In the distance: lanterns, shooting stars, the beam from a lighthouse pulsating into the horizon.

Captain Fortuna suddenly emerged from the shadows. He no longer smelled of beer, now he smelled of wine.

465

"Senhora Vaz, I don't interfere in other people's lives," he said, "but please allow me to express my admiration for what you did to try to rescue that black woman they locked up in prison. Pedro Pimenta was a nice man, but he was a scoundrel. He let down all the women he ever came across."

"I didn't do enough," said Ana. "Isabel died."

"People from our part of the world change into insufferable creatures when they come to Africa," he said sorrowfully. "Here on board this ship I don't come into close contact with all the suffering and misery that exists on land. But there is no doubt that we treat the blacks in a way that will come back to haunt and punish us, there's no doubt about that."

Perhaps Captain Fortuna expected her to respond, but she said nothing for a while, then began to talk about something quite different.

"Let's be honest," she said. "I know you visited the brothel I inherited when my husband died. You paid up as required, and you treated the women well. But there's one thing I wonder about. Which of the women did you visit?"

"Belinda Bonita. Never anybody else. If it had been possible, I'd have married her."

"That black porter who came on board with me," said Ana. "I love him. I hope I'm carrying his child."

Captain Fortuna eyed her in the flickering light of the lantern he was holding in his hand.

He smiled. A friendly smile.

"I understand," he said. "I understand exactly what you mean."

That night Ana slept long and deep. It seemed to her that the sea was like a rocking chair in which she was swaying gently back and forth as the night passed, and another life slowly became possible.

EPILOGUE

Africa Hotel, Beira, 1905

For the second time in her life Hanna Lundmark walked along a gangplank and left a ship that she would never board again. During the voyage she had abandoned for ever her other names: Ana Branca and Hanna Vaz. She had even considered dropping Lundmark's name and reverting to what she was at the very beginning: Hanna Renström. She had stood leaning on the rail of the little coaster, occasionally watching dolphins playing in the ship's wake, and once, just off Xai-Xai, she had even seen a pod of whales spouting in the distance. But mainly she had just stood there with her various names in her hand, dropping them into the water one after another.

She had chosen to stand in the stern of the ship because that's where the galley was — just as it had been on the *Lovisa*. Working inside the cramped kitchen, oozing with smoke and cooking smells, were an incredibly fat black woman, and two men who might well have been chosen because they were so thin. Otherwise there would never have been room for them as well as the wood-burning stove and all the pots and pans and chipped crockery.

468

There were not many passengers on board. Hanna had the best cabin, but every evening she had to wage war on masses of cockroaches, which she crushed with a shoe. Over her head she could hear the coughing and scraping noises made by the deck passengers as they wrapped themselves up in their sleeping bags to sleep.

She occasionally spoke to Captain Fortuna. Hanna gathered his origins could be traced back to practically everywhere in the world. On her second day on board he had asked her where she came from.

"Sweden," she had said. "A country up in the far north. Where the Northern Lights illuminate the night sky."

She had not been totally convinced that he knew where her homeland was, but she politely asked where he came from.

"My mother was Greek," he said. "My mother's father came from Persia and his mother was born in India, but she had her roots in one of the South Sea Islands. My father was a Turk, but his ancestry was in fact a mixture of Jewish, Moroccan and a drop of blood from distant Japan. I regard myself as an Arabian African, or an African Arab. The ocean belongs to everybody."

Hanna took her meals in her cabin, served by one of the thin men she had seen in the galley. She ate very little, spent most of the time resting on her bunk or standing in the stern, tracing the contours of the dark continent through the heat haze.

At one point the steam engine broke down. They drifted for almost a full day before the mechanic managed to trace and repair the fault so that they could continue their voyage to Beira.

It was dusk when she walked along the gangplank and set foot in the unknown town. She was followed by two crew members who had been ordered by Captain Fortuna to carry her luggage and accompany her to the Africa Hotel. That was where she would stay while she was searching for Isabel's parents.

As she entered through the illuminated doors, she was astonished by the splendour surrounding her on all sides. She had thought the hotel Pandre stayed in was the most palatial she had ever seen in her life, but the Africa Hotel in Beira exceeded anything she could possibly have dreamt of. She moved into the second-largest suite in the hotel as the marriage suite was already booked. That first evening she was served a meal in her room, and drank champagne for only the second time in her life: the first time was the evening when she and Senhor Vaz had married.

The following day she started looking for Isabel's parents. She had been assisted by the hotel to recruit two African men who could show her around the slum districts where she assumed Isabel's parents would live. With the aid of the two men she spent over a week combing all the outlying settlements around Beira. As she had never visited any of the African districts in Lourenço Marques, it came as a shock for her to discover the conditions in which black people lived. She discovered squalor and suffering way beyond her imagination. Every evening she would sit in her lovely rooms in a state of petrified horror. She almost stopped eating altogether while the search was taking place. At night she had a succession of nightmares, nearly all of which transported her back to the river and the mountains where she failed to find the home she had left so long ago.

But after a few days she noticed something else when she made her repeated visits to the black settlements. She discovered an unexpected lust for life among the poorest of the poor. The slightest reason for feeling joy was not tossed disdainfully aside, but seized with both hands. People supported one another, even though they had virtually nothing that they could share.

One evening she tried to note down in her diary what it was she thought she had discovered, once she had managed to dig down deeper under the surface of all the poverty and squalor.

She wrote: "Amidst this incomprehensible poverty I can see islands of wealth. Happiness that ought not to exist, warmth that should never really have survived. This discovery enables me to see in the white people who live here a different kind of poverty among all their riches and well-being."

She read through what she had written. She thought she hadn't quite managed to work out exactly what she had experienced; but nevertheless she felt that for the first time she had seen the reality of the black people and their lives. Until now, her perspective had been twisted.

Perhaps, coming from the most poverty-stricken level of society in Sweden, she had more in common with blacks than she had previously realized.

The next day she continued her search for Isabel's parents. Every step she took, every person she saw, convinced her that what she had written the previous night had been correct.

For the first time she was struck by a totally unexpected thought: perhaps I might be able to feel at home here after all. She realized that she was not just searching for Isabel's parents: she was also searching for an entirely new way of looking at herself.

During the days she was looking for Isabel's parents, the hotel was making preparations for a major wedding celebration. A Portuguese prince was going to marry an English duchess. At anchor in the roadstead were several large yachts that had made the journey from Europe. Hanna was the only person staying at the hotel who was not one of the wedding guests. Needless to say, she received an invitation even so, seeing as she was on the spot. She accepted, and despite everything had to acknowledge that she felt safe and secure to be surrounded by white people after all the misery and squalor she had encountered in the African settlements.

She was on the point of giving up: she didn't think she would ever be able to find Isabel's parents and tell them that Isabel was dead. She paid her two guides, and watched them stare at the many banknotes she handed over with amazement, almost fear.

The wedding was due to take place that same evening. Hanna spent the afternoon in the shady part of the hotel grounds, so as not to disturb the intensive preparations.

472

She suddenly found an elderly man standing in front of her, a white man wearing a dark suit. He must have been about sixty. Hanna wanted to be left in peace, and at first found his presence importunate: but she noticed that his friendliness seemed to be genuine, and that he was simply looking for somebody to talk to.

They watched the colourful birds with long beaks flying around the bushes and flowers.

"I'm on my way," said the man suddenly.

"Aren't we all?" Hanna responded.

"My name's Harold ffendon," said the man. "I used to be called something completely different — I can no longer recall what. But my father was called Wilson, John Wilson, and was never known as anything but Jack. Now I'm on my way to what in his time was known as Van Diemen's Land."

"Where's that?"

"It's called Tasmania nowadays. But when my father lived there it was a notorious penal colony — England sent many of its worst criminals there either to die, or simply to disappear from the city streets in their homeland. My father had stolen a pair of shoes in the city of Bristol and for that he was exiled for fifteen years. When he'd served his sentence he chose to stay on there. He became a sheep farmer, but he also learnt the art of building organs. He's dead now, but I intend to go out there and live close to where he did."

"How come you have ended up here?"

"It's a long way to Australia."

Yes, Hanna thought: it's a very long way to Australia. I never got there. I also ended up here.

"You can see icebergs on the way there," she said.

"I know," said ffendon. "Many of the ships taking criminals to Australia and Van Dieman's Land never got there. Some of them were sunk by icebergs."

The conversation died away, just as quickly as it had begun. Ffendon suddenly stood up, bowed and held out his hand.

"I need help to complete my journey," he said. "I'm ashamed to admit it, but I'm asking for help even so."

Hanna went up to her room, fetched fifty English pounds and returned to the garden.

"How did you know that I had a bit of money to spare?" she asked.

"You give the impression of not being worried about anything," said ffendon. "A person like that either believes in God, or has plenty of money. You didn't seem to be a believer, so as far as I was concerned there was only one other possibility left."

"Good luck with your journey," she said, handing over the money.

She watched him leave. If he really would go to Tasmania or if he'd gamble away the money, she had no idea. She didn't really care.

Hanna attended the wedding ceremony itself, saw the handsome young couple and recalled the simplicity of the occasion when she and Lundmark had married in Algiers. But at the reception afterwards, her chair at one of the round tables was empty. She had gone back to her room in order to work out where she would go next. Where was the Tasmania that she could head for? What choices did she have? Did she have any choice in

474

fact? Or should she simply stay on at the Africa Hotel until her money ran out?

Late that night she made up her mind to go to Phalaborwa, the place the missionary Agnes had talked about on board the *Lovisa* the day after Hanna had arrived in Africa. She could go there and maybe find inspiration for what to do with her life. At the missionary station she would be able to discard the final remains of what she had become during her time in Africa.

She slept for a few hours before getting up as dawn broke. The wedding party was still in full swing. She looked out of the window and gave a start: Moses was standing there under a tree. He was staring up at her window. She shouted out, knowing that she wasn't mistaken. Beside herself with happiness, she got dressed and hurried down into the garden. Moses was no longer there under the tree — but she knew what he was thinking. It was not appropriate for a black man to meet a white woman in the grounds of a hotel. And so he had withdrawn to somewhere discreet. She looked around and saw a dense clump of bushes next to the stone wall surrounding the hotel.

He was standing there, waiting for her. He wasn't wearing his usual overalls, but was dressed in a shabby black suit. She was surprised that he had been allowed in: the blacks who worked in the hotel or in the park-like grounds all wore uniforms.

"I climbed over the wall," he said. "They'd never have allowed me in. In the mines we learn how to climb over and past piles of fallen stone. There's no wall a miner can't climb over."

475

She barely listened to what he was saying. Instead she stood close to him and felt how he put his arms round her.

"How did you get here?" she asked.

"On another ship."

"When did you arrive?"

"Yesterday."

"No doubt you know that I haven't found your parents."

"I know."

She looked at him.

"Why did you come here?"

He took a step backwards and produced a little pouch from out of his pocket. Hanna recognized it immediately. He had once given a similar pouch to Isabel.

"I wanted to give you this."

"Is it the same as you gave Isabel?"

"Yes."

"You said then that it didn't work on her because she was surrounded by too many white people who took away all its strength. Why are you giving it to me, then?"

"Because you are not like the others. I know you are called Ana Branca. But that's wrong. For me you are Ana Negra."

Black Ana, she thought. Is that my real name?

"Your last task in the life of the white woman you were born as is to find my parents," said Moses. "Once you've done that, you are one of us, Ana Negra."

"What will happen if I grow wings?"

"You'll fly to wherever I am."

476

Without another word he handed over the pouch, climbed up the wall and disappeared over the other side. It all happened so quickly that she had no time to react.

She continued searching but didn't find the parents. Nobody seemed to recognize their names. Every evening she went back to the hotel and contemplated the pouch lying on her table. And every morning she stood by the window, but Moses never reappeared.

In the end she gave up. Isabel's and Moses' parents had been swallowed up by the mass of black people: she would never be able to find them. What she wanted more than anything else — to see Moses standing down below in the hotel grounds once again, and then to run off with him over the high stone wall — would never become reality.

That evening she started packing her belongings. The pouch remained where it had been all the time, untouched. She had not changed her resolve to go to the missionary station.

In the end only her diary was left. She was determined to be rid of the notebook that she had tied a red ribbon around. She considered burning it, but changed her mind without really knowing why.

By chance she noticed that although the hotel was newly built, the parquet floor in her room was already cracking. When she poked a finger into one of those cracks, a piece of parquet came loose. She knelt down and pushed the diary into the gap, as far as it would go: then she replaced the loose piece.

She later summoned one of the hotel's black caretakers who made sure that the crack was repaired.

She stayed for one more day and one more night at the Africa Hotel. All the wedding guests had left by now. The white yachts in the roadstead had weighed anchor and departed. The hotel seemed deserted.

That last evening she sat by the open window where the curtain was swaying slowly in the evening breeze. She emptied the contents of the leather pouch into her hand and swallowed them, washed down with a glass of water.

Nobody saw her leave, and afterwards nobody was able to confirm if she had rented a carriage or left Beira in a boat or on horseback.

When the hotel staff let themselves into her room the following day, her payment was lying in an envelope on the table.

Her suitcases were no longer there.

Nobody ever saw her again.

AFTERWORD

As a general rule, everything I write is based on truth — it might be a big or a small truth, it can be crystal clear or extremely fragmentary; but nevertheless, there is always something based on real events that leads to the fiction in all my novels.

As in this particular case. It was Tor Sällström, author and Africa enthusiast, who mentioned in a conversation, almost in passing, some remarkable documents he had come across in old colonial archives in Maputo, the capital of Mozambique. According to what he read, at the end of the nineteenth century and perhaps also the beginning of the twentieth century, a Swedish woman had been the owner of one of the biggest brothels in the town, which in those days was called Lourenço Marques. She was mentioned because she had been a significant taxpayer.

After a few years, she is no longer mentioned in the documents. She apparently came from nowhere, and vanished just as mysteriously as she had appeared.

Who was she? Where did she come from? I did more research, but it seems her origins really were unknown, as was her fate. All conclusions had to be theories, more or less probable.

But we do know that Swedish ships berthed in Lourenço Marques, often carrying cargoes of timber to Australia. And most probably there were women crew members now and then, mainly cooks.

In other words, everything beyond those basic facts is speculation. Apart from the bureaucratic evidence in an old ledger. When it came to taxes gathered, colonial civil servants were scrupulous with the facts. Every year it was necessary to convince the government in Lisbon that the colony really was a profit-making venture.

So, she really did exist and lived in Lourenço Marques, because the archives do not lie. She paid impressive amounts of tax.

My story is therefore based on the little we know, and all that we don't know.

Henning Mankell
Gothenburg, June 2011

GLOSSARY

Tontonto	Nickname of a home-brewed spirit with a high alcohol content
O Paraiso	Paradise
Shangana	A language spoken in southern parts of Mozambique
Capulana	Piece of batik cloth used by women as a loincloth in Mozambique
Pau preto	Very hard, black type of wood found in Africa
A Magrinha	The thin one
Feticheiro/a	Male or female witchdoctor
Xhipamanhine	One of the oldest black settlements in Maputo, Mozambique. Maputo used to be called Lourenço Marques
Bombeiros	Firemen
Ana Branca	White Ana
Ana Negra	Black Ana
Belinda Bonita	The beautiful Belinda
Halakavuma	The name in Shangana of a large lizard that is considered to possess magical wisdom
Fortuna	The fortunate one

The Shadow Girls

Henning Mankell

Tea-Bag, a young African girl, has fled a refugee camp in Spain for the promise of a new life in Sweden. Tania has made a long and dangerous journey to escape the horrors of humna trafficking. Leyla has come with her family from Iran. All of them are facing challenges in their new home.

Meanwhile, celebrated poet Jesper Humlin is looking for inspiration. Harried by his mother and girlfriend, misunderstood by his publisher and tormented by his stockbroker, Jesper needs a new perspective on life. A chance encounter with Tea-Bag leads him into the shadow world of the immigrant experience in Sweden. Initially he sees the girls purely as material for his next work, but soon discovers they have very different ideas.

ISBN 978-0-7531-9206-1 (hb)
ISBN 978-0-7531-9207-8 (pb)

The Pyramid

Henning Mankell

A damned good crime writer **The Times**

Mankell's lugubrious Swedish detective, Inspector Kurt Wallander, is one of the most impressive creations in crime fiction today **Guardian**

When Kurt Wallander first appeared, he was a senior police officer, just turned 40, with his life in a mess. His wife had left him, his father barely acknowledged him; he ate badly and drank alone at night.

The Pyramid chronicles the events that led him to such a place. We see him in the early years, doing hours on the beat; witness the beginnings of his fragile relationship with Mona; and learn the reason behind his difficulties with his father. These thrilling tales provide a fascinating insight into Wallander's character. From the stabbing of a neighbour in 1969 to a light aircraft accident in 1989, every story is a vital piece of the Wallander series, showing Mankell at the top of his game.

ISBN 978-0-7531-8384-7 (hb)
ISBN 978-0-7531-8385-4 (pb)

The Man Who Smiled

Henning Mankell

Staying alive becomes a precarious task for Inspector Kurt Wallander as he plays both hunter and hunted in a terrifying game of money and power.

Spiralling into an alcohol-fuelled depression after killing a man in the line of duty, Wallander has made up his mind to quit the force for good.

When an old acquaintance, a solicitor, seeks his help to investigate his father's death, Wallander doesn't want to know. But when the solicitor also turns up dead, Wallander returns to work to head what may now have become a double murder case. A rookie female detective has joined the force in his absence and he adopts the role of her mentor as they fight to unravel the mystery.

An enigmatic business tycoon seems to be the link between the two deaths. But while Wallander is on the trail of the killer, someone is on his trail, and closing in fast.

ISBN 978-0-7531-7626-9 (hb)
ISBN 978-0-7531-7627-6 (pb)

The Bat

Jo Nesbø

Detective Harry Hole is meant to keep out of trouble. A young Norwegian girl taking a gap year in Sydney has been murdered, and Harry has been sent to Australia to assist in any way he can.

He's not supposed to get too involved. When the team unearths a string of unsolved murders and disappearances, nothing will stop Harry from finding out the truth. The hunt for a serial killer is on, but the murderer will talk only to Harry. He might just be the next victim . . .

ISBN 978-0-7531-9166-8 (hb)
ISBN 978-0-7531-9167-5 (pb)

Blessed Are Those Who Thirst

Anne Holt

It is only the beginning of May but the unseasonable heat already feels tropical. Criminal investigating officer Hanne Wilhelmsen is sent to a macabre crime scene on the outskirts of Oslo: an abandoned shed that is covered in blood. On one wall is an eight-digit number written in blood. There is no sign of a victim — is it just a kid's prank, or foul play? Is it even human blood? Hanne has a bad feeling about the numbers, but without further evidence, she can do nothing. As more bloody numbers are found throughout Oslo, Hanne's colleague Håkon Sand discovers that the eight-digit number corresponds to the filing number of foreign immigrants waiting to be granted Norwegian citizenship — all female, all missing. When a dead body is finally unearthed, Hanne and Håkon fear they have a serial killer on their hands.

ISBN 978-0-7531-9116-3 (hb)
ISBN 978-0-7531-9117-0 (pb)

ISIS publish a wide range of books in large print, from fiction to biography. Any suggestions for books you would like to see in large print or audio are always welcome. Please send to the Editorial Department at:

ISIS Publishing Limited
7 Centremead
Osney Mead
Oxford OX2 0ES

A full list of titles is available free of charge from:

Ulverscroft Large Print Books Limited

(UK)
The Green
Bradgate Road, Anstey
Leicester LE7 7FU
Tel: (0116) 236 4325

(Australia)
P.O. Box 314
St Leonards
NSW 1590
Tel: (02) 9436 2622

(USA)
P.O. Box 1230
West Seneca
N.Y. 14224-1230
Tel: (716) 674 4270

(Canada)
P.O. Box 80038
Burlington
Ontario L7L 6B1
Tel: (905) 637 8734

(New Zealand)
P.O. Box 456
Feilding
Tel: (06) 323 6828

Details of **ISIS** complete and unabridged audio books are also available from these offices. Alternatively, contact your local library for details of their collection of **ISIS** large print and unabridged audio books.